Praise

"You can always count on Emma St. Clair for sweet romance packed full of sizzling chemistry, page-turning storytelling, and actual, legitimate laugh-out-loud moments. *If All Else Sails* is Emma at her finest, from hilarious opening line to pitch-perfect HEA (and through all the heart, humor, and hijinks that fill the pages between). Long-time fans and new readers alike are going to love this one!"
—Bethany Turner, award-winning author of *Brynn and Sebastian Hate Each Other: A Love Story*

"Sassy, swoony, sweet, and sea-splashed—*If All Else Sails* is a total delight! I was laughing at page one."
—Melissa Ferguson, bestselling author of *The Perfect Rom-Com*

"When I want a swoony love story that's certain to give me all the feels, I know I can always count on Emma St. Clair to deliver. Her trademark wit and humor are alive and well in this sweet romance that readers are certain to add to their list of favorites!"
—Courtney Walsh, *New York Times* bestselling author

"I'm not usually a fan of the enemies-to-lovers trope, but in the skillful hands of author Emma St. Clair, the trope not only works but sizzles for all the right reasons. And who doesn't love a wounded, tough-yet-tender hero and a strong, sassy-yet-compassionate heroine? Add some humor and a deeper storyline of healing and you have a book that's worth every page. Highly recommend."
—Pepper Basham, author of *Some Like It Scot*

If All
Else Sails

If All Else Sails

A NOVEL

EMMA ST. CLAIR

THOMAS NELSON

Since 1798

If All Else Sails

Published in Nashville, Tennessee, by Thomas Nelson. Thomas Nelson is a registered trademark of HarperCollins Christian Publishing, Inc.

Thomas Nelson titles may be purchased in bulk for educational, business, fundraising, or sales promotional use. For information, please email SpecialMarkets@ThomasNelson.com.

Publisher's Note: This novel is a work of fiction. Names, characters, places, and incidents are either products of the author's imagination or used fictitiously. All characters are fictional, and any similarity to people living or dead is purely coincidental.

Library of Congress Cataloging-in-Publication Data

Names: St. Clair, Emma author
Title: If all else sails : a novel / Emma St. Clair.
Description: Nashville, Tennessee : Thomas Nelson, 2025. | Summary: "In this enemies-to-lovers romance, school nurse Josie and her brother's best friend—hockey player Wyatt Jacobs—are tricked into spending a summer together that's anything but smooth sailing"—Provided by publisher.
Identifiers: LCCN 2025003560 (print) | LCCN 2025003561 (ebook) | ISBN 9781400346943 trade paperback | ISBN 9781400346950 epub | ISBN 9781400346967
Subjects: LCGFT: Romance fiction | Christian fiction | Novels
Classification: LCC PS3619.T2324 I3 2025 (print) | LCC PS3619.T2324 (ebook) | DDC 813/.6—dc23/eng/20250404
LC record available at https://lccn.loc.gov/2025003560
LC ebook record available at https://lccn.loc.gov/2025003561

Printed in the United States of America

25 26 27 28 29 LBC 5 4 3 2 1

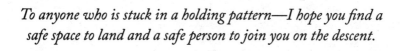

To anyone who is stuck in a holding pattern—I hope you find a safe space to land and a safe person to join you on the descent.

And always, especially, forever to Rob. Eye heart sheep.

Content Warning

Attempted sexual assault (past—brief recounting)
Loss of a family member (past)
Neglectful parents
Oversize attack pigs
Improper storage of ashes
A small dog in a scandalous bikini

1

A Quaint Little
Murder Cottage

Josie

I am standing outside of what could best be described as a quaint little murder cottage, wondering if, instead of going on vacation with my brother, I'm about to die.

Jacob's cheerful recorded voice comes over the phone I'm pressing to my ear. Again. This time, I do what I almost never do because I'm not a heathen. Or a boomer.

I leave a voicemail.

"Jacob, hi. It's Josie—the sister you seem to be pranking right now. Why am I here? Where *is* here? I double-checked the address, but this cannot be the site of any kind of vacation. I did not pack to defend myself against a serial killer. Where are you? Call me back. You've got my number. Use it. Preferably now."

I immediately follow up with a text, which reads CALL ME NOW in all caps with no punctuation. My brother will know the lack of a period or a neat row of exclamation points means either I've been kidnapped or I'm really and truly angry.

The message doesn't show a read receipt. It just sits there. Delivered.

Concern fissures through me. Maybe Jacob was in a wreck. Maybe he fell asleep at the wheel and drove right off one of the bridges on the way here. Maybe he's dead somewhere and my last message to him was full of snark and anger.

Or . . . maybe my mind sometime jumps too quickly to the worst possible scenario.

A less morbid and much more likely explanation is that Jacob got caught up working. Like always. He could have gotten a last-minute meeting with a big client. Or a potential client. An up-and-coming college football star poised for NFL greatness. Or a basketball player having a great year with endorsement offers coming in hot. He could have left the office late and gotten stuck in DC commuter traffic.

Or maybe he met a woman. Difficult, considering it's not quite noon, but I've found that, with Jacob's charm, anything is possible.

I know what my best friend would say. Toni would tell me I shouldn't have driven two hours to an unfamiliar address just because my brother held out promises of a fun trip together.

Never leave the house without your underwear or your boundaries, I can practically hear her saying.

But when it comes to my brother, I understand the concept of boundaries; I just can't seem to apply them.

I scan his text from yesterday, searching for any clues I might have missed.

The Super Summer Sibling Extravaganza is upon us! Pack a bag for warm weather and maybe swimming. Comfy clothes. Maybe one or two nice things, but this will be casual. Address in the next text. Don't look it up on Google Street View! TOMORROW AT 4 PM.

Yes—that's all the information he gave me.

And yes, after packing this morning, I adjusted the GPS to take me on the most scenic route from Fredericksburg to Kilmarnock, a small town on what's known as the Northern Neck. I even resisted the urge to look at the Google Street View, a decision I now regret. Because I definitely would have asked questions.

What if . . . he isn't coming?

"You're being ridiculous. He'll be here," I say out loud, like voicing it into the world will make my brother appear. He doesn't.

That doesn't mean he *won't*. But my worry expands, braiding with the excitement and nervousness of being in a new situation. While packing, I shoved down my anxious thoughts, stuffing them away like I stuffed half my closet into my suitcases—just in case.

Adventures are fun! I told myself while carefully rolling my shirts and lining them up in neat rows at the bottom of my roller bag. *So are surprises! You are a woman who lives for excitement!*

I didn't come close to convincing myself. But I packed. I came.

And now, as I stand on a driveway made of crushed oyster shells, baking in this sweltering oven of a June day, I wish I were back in my comfy but cramped apartment, working my way through my summer reading list. This year I've decided it will be composed entirely of books written by women—from the Brontës and Jane Austen to Toni Morrison and Madeleine L'Engle, whose young adult books I've always loved.

But no—I chose to leave the cocoon of home to find out what's behind Door Number Three. Which is apparently the sad little cottage in front of me, desperately in need of an extreme home makeover. Or a bulldozer. The siding, which may have been cream once upon a time, is now the color of a load of whites thrown in the washer too many times. Most of the wood trim is rotten. I'm no roof expert, but this one looks like it's one heavy rain away from collapsing.

If I squint, it's almost cute. More like it *had* been cute and is now disappointed by its owner's lack of upkeep. The front looks like a face—the windows its sad eyes above the half circle of frowning glass inlaid in the door.

The property, however, is gorgeous, with a swath of lush green grass fringed by pines on either side. The real star of the show is the glittering water behind the house, complete with a dock and a sailboat, which looks to be in much better shape than the house.

Parked near a structure that's somewhere between a standalone garage and a metal shed is an old Bronco. Definitely not Jacob's. He prefers his cars new and sleek and shiny. Lots of dollar signs and detailing involved. This SUV looks as though it's been restored, but that's not Jacob's thing either. I briefly wonder if the car's owner is inside the house watching me, but I see no sign of movement. The place has the abandoned vibe going on.

Abandoned but also the perfect hideout for a serial killer.

I give the sad little house a wide berth, walking toward the water as I swat away birdlike mosquitoes and wipe the sweatstache off my upper lip. By the time I get there, my shirt clings damply to every part of me. The dock is sturdy, if a little splintered, the deep navy gleam of water almost inviting. Almost. A small dinghy motors past, driven by an older man with two little girls in pink life jackets. They all wave.

I wave back, like this is my dock. My sailboat. My little murder cottage.

The name painted in neat script on the side of the sailboat reads *QUINTessential*. The *quint* in all caps is likely some inside joke, because I don't get it. Frankly, it's a disappointing boat name. Aren't boats supposed to have clever names—like *Nauti & Nice* or *Little Boat Peep* or *Signed, Sailed, Delivered?*

I pull out my phone—still nothing from my brother—and take a few pictures of the water and then the boat. I stop just shy of climbing aboard. I've never been on a boat this size and I'm itching to explore. It's a little longer than the dock, just tall enough that I can't see much of the deck. I'm curious but not one for trespassing, so I turn and snap pictures of the back side of the cottage, which really should have more windows considering the view.

When I walk back across the lawn, three birds rocket away from a hidden nest under the cottage's sagging eaves. I come to an abrupt stop when a lacy curtain flutters in one of the windows. My heart leaps into my throat.

Is someone in there watching me?

I mean, it *could* be Jacob. He did send me the address. But he wouldn't be hiding in there. He would have run out and given me a bone-crushing hug—his specialty.

I also can't actually picture my brother stepping on the porch of this place, much less spying on me from inside.

As a cloud passes in front of the sun, I take another picture of the little house. You know—just in case it's evidence in the event of my disappearance or death.

The phone vibrates in my hand, and I don't bother with greetings when I see Jacob is calling.

"Tell me you're the one watching me from inside the creepy murder cottage."

He sputters a laugh. "The what?"

"You know—the sad little white house that's falling apart and might be haunted or home to a serial killer. The one whose address you sent me last night. The one I'm standing outside of, hoping it doesn't collapse when the wind blows."

"It's that bad, huh?" His voice sounds strained.

I close my eyes. Breathe in and out slowly for a few counts. Reopen my eyes just in time to see the curtains flutter again. "If you don't know the condition, that means you aren't here."

It also means he isn't the person inside watching me. I scan my surroundings as I take a step back toward my car.

"I . . . am not there."

Disappointment curdles all the happy hope I've been holding on to since his text last night. So much for the Super Summer Sibling Extravaganza. And any trust I had in my brother.

When I speak, my voice holds the icy depth of a walk-in freezer. "Jacob, whose house is this? And where are you?"

"It's kind of a long story."

"I've got the whole drive back home to hear it," I say, striding toward my car.

"Don't go yet," he says quickly.

"Give me a reason not to. A *good* one."

"The thing is," he continues, ignoring my questions, "I need to call in a favor."

I squeeze my eyes closed. "A favor."

By my secret count—*secret* because you're not supposed to keep records of wrongs by people you love—the favors are already stacked high on my side and somewhat lacking on Jacob's part. We are as unbalanced as a single person on a seesaw. If anyone should be calling in favors, it's me.

Jacob is the gas giant at the center of our family's solar system. My parents and I don't even wait for him to ask us to jump or say how high. We just stay ready, knees bent and muscles flexed.

Is it a bit of a trauma response to Jacob coming *this close* to dying when he was twelve? Probably.

But even before that, he was the golden boy of the family. Almost losing him simply elevated his status. It also brought us all closer. And if we're a little lopsided in terms of who runs the show, there are way more toxic family issues we could struggle with. My parents have escaped his orbit the last few years after buying an RV, trading in my childhood home for something a little more manageable, and spending most of the year motoring around the country. I think they're in South Dakota right now. Or was it South Carolina? Possibly just the South. They're hard to keep up with these days.

Which might be the point.

In my older brother's defense, though he's a wee bit self-focused, Jacob is a decent guy. He's generous. Goofy. Bighearted. Able to make friends anywhere. Loyal.

Usually loyal.

"You see—"

Jacob's explanation is interrupted by sirens. I registered them a few minutes ago, soft whines in the distance. But now they are loud, pealing cries. Two cop cars turn and speed down the driveway, kicking up clouds of dust behind them as they head straight for me.

"Any idea why the police are here?" I ask.

He groans. "Oh no. He didn't. He wouldn't."

"He *who* wouldn't *what?*"

I've never been arrested, never considered running from the police, but find myself slowly backing away as the cruisers pull to a stop.

A swarm—okay, it's just two—of cops throw open the doors, leaping out like I am the fugitive they've been chasing for days. Not a confused elementary school nurse who might be trespassing as some kind of favor to the man formerly known as her brother.

One cop looks barely old enough to be out of high school, and the other has eyebrows so bushy they deserve their own zip code. They're thicker than his mustache, which is saying something.

"That," Jacob says, as the cops point what looks to be one gun and one taser at me, "is probably because of Wyatt."

Ah, I think, as the cops order me to drop my weapon—a.k.a. my phone—and put my hands up. *Wyatt.*

It all makes sense now.

2

The Fine Line Between Detained and Arrested

Wyatt

"Would you mind signing this too?" one of the cops says. He's young enough to still have a gleam in his eye and pink in his cheeks, then he adds, "For my wife."

I take the proffered index card he pulled from his uniform. Then he hands me a permanent marker from a different pocket. While I'm scrawling my signature, I wonder what he'll pull out next. Maybe a protractor or a little clutch of paper clips, like he's some kind of human clown car stuffed with office accessories.

The worst part of my job as a professional athlete has always been signing autographs. Actually, any kind of interaction with fans leaves my mouth tasting like I've just downed day-old burned gas station coffee. All I want is to play hockey and be left alone. But apparently that's too much to ask.

It usually takes me about four hours to come down from the

anxiety high I experience after any public event I'm forced to attend. Especially after a game, though it's worse when I run into fans unexpectedly.

At restaurants. In parking garages. Wandering the grocery store.

It's gotten so bad that one whiff of a permanent marker is enough to trigger a mild PTSD response and a three-day migraine. I think I feel one coming on now.

I play hockey well and love everything about the game, but it's a job. One I happen to excel at.

Or . . . did before my injury.

Regardless, no one is going around asking dentists to sign their bras because they do the best fillings. So, the fame that comes standard with my job has never quite made sense to me.

I briefly consider asking the cops to sign my T-shirt just to see how *they'd* react.

But I have no desire to prolong this encounter. (Also, I can't remember how many days it's been since I showered, and I doubt my shirt smells fresh.) I just want the police to go and take the trespassing paparazzi with them.

I've been standing for too long without my crutches. More slumped against the doorframe than standing, sweating profusely. Something must be wrong with the air conditioner or the thermostat. I've been sweating through my clothes all day, then the air kicks on and I'm freezing. Until I start sweating again.

I hand back the marker and everything I've signed. The young cop stares at the note card, shaking his head. "Thanks, man. This is . . . this is awesome."

It's a four-by-six index card with the illegibly scrawled name of a person who happens to play hockey. *Not* awesome. But I keep my disagreement silent.

"You'll be back next season, right?" This question is from the older cop, the one with a mustache and thick, bristly eyebrows reminiscent of Bert from *Sesame Street*.

He glances down at my splinted foot, the one hovering just off the ground.

"I don't know."

Both men look as though a second head has just sprouted from my neck. I shouldn't have answered at all because this only invites more questions. The arch of my foot gives a hearty throb.

"At least it was just your foot and not your knee," the younger cop says, suddenly an expert in sports medicine. "When I tore my ACL in the championship football game—"

He's winding up to tell me about a game that probably happened in high school, but thankfully, my phone buzzes in the pocket of my baggy athletic shorts. It's been buzzing, but I ignored it, choosing the autographs as the lesser of two evils. Also, I'm on day six of avoiding my mother's calls. I am simply not in the frame of mind for her kindness and her . . . mothering.

Now, I slip the phone out of my pocket and hold it up, not even looking to see who it is. "I need to take this."

I try to force the words *It's been a pleasure* out of my mouth, but they're logjammed inside me, never to emerge because they aren't true.

"Thanks again," the older cop says, hesitating as he backs down the front steps. Like he's hoping I'll change my mind and invite them in for coffee. I wave and let the cheap screen door slam as I reach for my crutches, hobbling over to slump on the couch with my foot up on the wobbly coffee table.

I frown down at the phone screen. It's not my mother. But it's another person I've been avoiding. He's called three times in the last ten minutes. With a sigh, I answer.

"Jacob," I say dryly. "Color me surprised to hear from you."

My agent and best friend skips the pleasantries. "Color me surprised to hear your voice. I wasn't sure you still knew how to operate a phone."

"Muscle memory."

He chuckles—not a real laugh because I know those. This is a Professional Jacob laugh. I almost cave and tell him right then that I miss Friend Jacob. His job has fully polluted his personality, like he stepped into a sports agent skin a few years ago and now it's fused to him.

"Look, I know you're not thrilled with me. I get that you're tired of my calls. Even if I care and just want what's best for you," he says.

"Debatable," I mutter.

"But you don't have to take it out on Josie."

The mention of his younger sister throws me. My brain shifts into spin cycle as I try to make sense of the context. But it's a spin cycle with a down comforter and two towels, making my thoughts off-balance and wonky.

"I— What?"

"A few minutes ago Josie and I were on the phone, and she said the police pulled up. I assume you called them."

My eyes flick to the front window where the cops are just now climbing into their cruisers. "Are you saying *Josie* was the one creeping around my yard taking photos?"

"I seriously doubt she was 'creeping around' your yard. You didn't recognize my sister, man?"

No.

I didn't. And it floors me.

I remember the last time I saw Josie—of course I do—two years ago at dinner with Jacob's family when I was fresh off the worst personal and best professional year of my life. Josie's hair was the shortest I'd ever seen it, the brown waves just barely dusting the tops of her freckled shoulders. Her eyes barely skimmed over me when she said hello. And I stared too long and too hard, hoping she might notice me.

She said two words to me that night: *That's good.* It was after Jacob spent far too long bragging about me moving from the Appies, a beloved AHL team in North Carolina, to the even more beloved and higher-paying NHL team in Boston.

Josie's tone was polite but cool, tempered with years' worth of mistrust and dislike. Same as always.

And I remember every word she's ever spoken to me. Just like I remember every one I've said to her, all of which somehow came out of my mouth wrong.

I'm aware people call me a grump—both the ones who know me personally and the ones who interact with me professionally. I guess the description fits, though I'd say it's more that I'm a very reserved guy in a very public profession. I just want to skate. But you can't play hockey at the highest level without dealing with the press and fans and people.

So. Many. People.

I think back to the woman I watched wandering my property earlier, the one I assumed was another reporter looking for a story. Long brown hair tucked through a baseball cap. Baggy, nondescript khaki shorts. A T-shirt and flip-flops. Sunglasses. She had her phone out, taking pictures of the dock and the back of my house.

I assumed she was an overeager reporter who'd figured out where I was hiding and showed up to hound me about my injury and plans to come back to Boston.

That was Josie?

Which means . . .

"You'll have to hang on," I tell Jacob, heaving myself to my feet and grabbing my crutches.

"Dude," he says, voice pitching higher as I secure the phone between my ear and my shoulder. "You didn't let them *arrest her*, did you?"

"Detain," I mutter, heading for the door. "They said they were just going to *detain* her."

But *detain* sure looks a whole lot like *arrest*. I can barely make out Josie's head in the back of one of the cop cars.

I hang up on Jacob's string of expletives because I can't operate crutches on stairs with the phone.

Moving as fast as I can in my current state, I fly outside, knocking the screen door right off its hinges. It lands in the yard. But I don't care. My only focus is on flagging down the police cruisers carrying the last person on the planet I'd want arrested—or detained—because of me.

3

It's the Honey

Josie

Despite my vehement protests of innocence, I am—for the first and hopefully last time *ever*—wearing a pair of handcuffs in the back of a police cruiser, sweating profusely.

To be clear, I'm not talking metaphoric sweat. Jail time is not a legitimate concern of mine.

I don't *think*.

No, I am sweating literally and to an embarrassing degree because Officer Eyebrows left the car engine off with only the front windows down while they were getting Wyatt's autograph.

At least, that's what it *looks* like they're doing. I'm only able to twist so far with my hands cuffed behind my back. My line of sight can just barely make out Wyatt with a permanent marker in hand and a permanent scowl on his face while the officers stand on the porch with goofy smiles.

It's so very Wyatt. Just like this whole experience.

At first, when the two cops jumped out of their vehicles and ordered me to drop my weapon and put my hands up, I chalked their overzealous response up to boredom. I drove through the postage-stamp town of Kilmarnock, made up of about four blocks of adorable storefronts, boasting antiques, restaurants, and things branded with the word *rivah*. A trespassing call is probably the most exciting event the cops have had in months.

I figured Wyatt would clear this up a little more quickly. We've known each other for years through Jacob. Disliked each other for just as long. But this is taking it a bit too far. A prank gone wrong sounds even less likely than a misunderstanding. Wyatt is not known for his sense of humor. And the handcuffs digging into my wrists don't feel like a joke.

What I know for sure is that when my brother gets here, he'll kill Wyatt, and I will kill my brother.

Killing isn't really my style, though, so maybe instead I'll find one of those zoos where you can pay to name a cockroach after your ex before it's fed to a monitor lizard or something.

I'll submit both Wyatt's and Jacob's names.

When Officer Eyebrows passes my door and climbs into the front seat, reality sinks in.

I'm so confused I barely register the relief of the air-conditioning blasting as he turns on the car. "Wait—you're actually arresting me? He didn't, I don't know, decide to drop the bogus charges?"

"Sorry, hon," Officer Eyebrows says, putting the cruiser in Drive.

"I *know* him," I say. "My brother is his agent."

"I'm sure he is. Make sure you hold on back there. Might be a little bumpy."

A lovely suggestion when my hands are cuffed behind my back.

I'm honestly stunned. Wyatt saw me walking around this—his?—yard. Called the police on me. And is letting them drive me away.

I know the man never liked me, but *this?*

There's always been something hostile between us, ever since the very first time Jacob brought Wyatt home from college for the weekend. If it were a one-time incident, maybe I could write it off. Consistently, though, Wyatt finds a way to ruin things: my self-esteem, my birthday dinner, my college graduation. You know—little things like that.

Still, Wyatt and I are not quite Taylor Swift "Bad Blood"–level enemies, so I don't understand this sudden escalation to having me *arrested.*

Before now, our interactions have been snarky, though minimal. We give each other a wide berth, even if I'm always half aware of his gray eyes piercing into me, like he's watching for me to make a mistake.

Jacob has always defended Wyatt, a fact that chaps my hide. Where's the sibling loyalty? *You just don't understand him,* my brother has said more than once.

What's not to understand? The man is some kind of egotistical sports player who has the attitude of a honey badger with a hangover. And for whatever reason, he seems bound and determined to make me suffer every chance he gets.

"Do you mind not kicking my seat?" the cop asks.

This only makes me want to kick it harder.

Look—I'm not normally the kind of person who enjoys bucking authority. In our family, that's always been Jacob's role, where I'm more of a rule follower. Not quite a people pleaser, but maybe with people-pleasing tendencies. I've always been polite to police officers in the brief interactions I've had with them. Which is probably why, even though I've gotten pulled over twice for speeding, I've only ever driven away with warnings.

But after spending at least ten minutes in a hot car, I am plumb out of politeness.

"Oh, sorry." I don't even attempt to sound sorry or soften the bite in my tone. "I'm just trying to avoid smashing my head into the window. But if you don't mind the legal ramifications of me getting a concussion while in custody, that's cool."

He slows down. He also glares at me in the rearview mirror. Then his eyes suddenly widen, those massive eyebrows shooting upward. Without warning, he hits the brakes. Hard enough that I actually do hit my head—my face, really—on the wire mesh separating the front and back seats.

"Was that really necessary?" I ask, but he's out of the car, leaving the door wide open as his boots crunch on the driveway.

And of course, he turned off the car, which means the air flow stops. Again.

I wiggle to look out the back window, wondering if I have an imprint of the partition on my cheek.

"Oh, *now* you want to come outside," I grumble when I see Wyatt standing in the middle of the driveway, talking animatedly to both cops.

I'm shocked to see Wyatt leaning on crutches. Did he get injured? I didn't hear about it, but I also don't follow hockey. Jacob knows I've never been the least bit interested in updates on his clients. Especially Wyatt. I think it kills Jacob a little bit that I don't get starstruck.

He doesn't understand or know *why* I have an aversion to athletes. No one does. And I'm not about to start explaining.

Still, considering his friendship with Wyatt, an injury seems like something Jacob might have mentioned.

All three men look toward the cruiser I'm in, and when their gazes fall on me, I tilt my chin up in the universal dudebro signal for *What's up*. Best I can do in handcuffs.

"Come on, Wyatt," I mutter. "Before I melt into a puddle, tell the nice officers of the law this is all just a misunderstanding so I can get out of here."

And that's exactly what I'll be doing the moment I'm freed: getting out of here.

I also plan to have a strongly worded conversation with Jacob because *what was his endgame here?* Why am I here at Wyatt's murder cottage while my brother is nowhere to be found? You can't have a Super Summer Sibling Extravaganza without both siblings.

Wyatt is still having what looks like a heated discussion with the cops. Speaking of heated . . . A bead of sweat rolls down the center of my spine. People are always going on about why you shouldn't leave pets in hot cars—not even for five minutes.

But what about innocently accused trespassers? Don't I have at least as many rights as a dog?!

Maybe I can sue Wyatt for emotional damage. If the officers leave me here much longer, I'll tack heatstroke onto the list. I may not have known about the crutches, but Jacob did brag to me about Wyatt's latest contract with Boston. He is *perfect* lawsuit material. And my school nurse salary could do with a little boost.

The two officers suddenly turn and walk toward the cruiser I'm in. Wyatt does not move but continues standing in the driveway, leaning on his crutches, staring at me. Even from here, I can see the hard clench of his jaw.

Like *he* has any reason to be frustrated.

Then again, he always looks caught in a state of frustration. Or constipation? Maybe for all these years, I've misread Wyatt's expression as open disdain when really, he just has a wicked case of IBS.

If so, serves him right.

Officer Eyebrows scuttles over to open my door. You know it's bad when hot summer air entering a car brings relief. I sag toward the doorway and don't even fight Officer Eyebrows when he takes my elbow and helps maneuver me out of the cruiser. A lot more gently than when he put me in.

"So sorry about this," he mumbles.

"Which part are you sorry about—leaving a human being in a hot car on a summer day? Or putting me in handcuffs when I haven't done anything? Maybe both?"

I shake off his hand and close my eyes, leaning against the car.

I don't think I really understood the extent of *how* hot it was—or the impact of those minutes in the back seat—until this moment. My stomach roils, and I hope I don't throw up.

But if I do, I'm aiming for Officer Eyebrows's shoes.

"I'll remove the cuffs if you could just turn around."

I crack open my eyes as the younger cop steps forward, looking slightly panicked. Moving makes me feel a little woozy, so I stay leaning against the car, turning to give him my back. My cheek presses against the warm metal as my stomach dips and clenches.

"All good," he says as he slips off the cuffs.

Are we? I almost ask. *Are we* really *all good?*

I pull my arms forward, rubbing my wrists. I need water. And maybe an ice bath. Somehow I doubt Wyatt's little murder cottage has this amenity.

"He decided not to press charges after all," Officer Eyebrows says, and I shoot a glare Wyatt's way.

He's standing about twenty feet behind the second cop car, leaning on his crutches and still looking disgruntled. Not apologetic, the way a normal human would. But almost angry, like this whole thing is my fault.

"Can *I*?" I ask.

The officers stare at me blankly for a minute. "Can you what?" the younger one asks.

"Can I press charges?"

"Press charges for what?"

"I don't know. Maybe for being left in the back of a hot car while you collected autographs?"

Busted. They exchange a glance. Then they laugh, as though they think I'm joking. I am not.

"What do you want us to do, honey?" Officer Eyebrows asks. "It was a misunderstanding, and now it's all cleared up."

It's the *honey* that does it.

"I *do* want to press charges," I say, hopefully loudly enough for Wyatt to hear me. "For attempted negligent vehicular homicide. And false imprisonment."

The string of words pulled straight from a patchwork collection of *Law & Order* jargon sound halfway legitimate. Again, the cops exchange glances, the corners of their lips turned upward.

Apparently, I've got a future in stand-up comedy.

A fat bumblebee buzzes past my ear, and a laughing gull careens in slow circles overhead.

I am suddenly reminded of precisely how thirsty I am. And how dizzy. I slump back against the cruiser and wipe sweat from my face.

"Do you need to sit down?" the young guy says, and when I shake my head, black dots crowd my vision. "You don't look so good."

I don't *feel* so good. My stomach churns again, and a spike of pain drives through my head. I don't need my nursing degree to tell me what this is: dehydration mixed with overheating. Standard summer fare when you're left in the back of a closed vehicle for ten minutes and it's nearing one hundred degrees out.

But knowing what it is doesn't slow the effects, and my vision goes hazy. Turns out, knowing is not half the battle. Or if it is, it's not the important half.

My mouth feels dry, my tongue thick as I try to speak. "I think I . . ."

My words slur, then trail off altogether as I slump, the black dots returning like an angry swarm of bats.

I'm going to pass out, I realize, half a second before the bats fully block out the sun. The last thing I'm aware of is Wyatt's voice, closer than it should be, as strong hands grab my shoulders to break my fall.

4

Vengeance upon Your Children's Children

Josie

When I come back to the world again, I'm staring at the slow-moving blades of a ceiling fan so out of date it's probably about to come back in style. Too bad it looks like it might fall out of the ceiling first.

I blink a few times, taking stock. Of my surroundings. Of myself.

I don't immediately know where I am.

I feel . . . not great. Nauseated, a headache forming at the top of my skull, and hot.

Hot. This sensation brings the afternoon's events back in a jumbled mess of memories.

Handcuffs in the back of a cop car.

The oystershell driveway crunching under my flip-flops.

A gorgeous white sailboat at the end of a splintery dock.

Jacob's text and the drive to Kilmarnock and—

Wyatt.

The man responsible for me being in handcuffs. The one who called the cops on me, then let me sit in a hot car while he signed autographs before finally changing his mind and deciding *not* to press charges for trespassing.

And now it appears that I'm inside his tiny murder cottage underneath his wobbly murder-cottage fan.

And if I'm inside, someone carried me. The cops, I assume, since Wyatt was on crutches. The idea of being touched like that by men I barely know, especially while I'm unconscious, makes my stomach riot.

It was just to bring you inside, I tell myself, but squirming, dark feelings have my heart racing. I draw in a slow breath.

"You're awake," a voice says.

Even without seeing his face, I know the voice belongs to Wyatt. I'm not sure why I recognize it at all, but it is lodged inside me like a piece of shrapnel. The timbre of it is deep and throaty with the slightest bit of roughness. The kind of voice I'd love to hear narrating audiobooks—if it weren't actually *Wyatt* reading them.

He actually sounds relieved. Surprising.

I don't turn my head. I need to collect myself a little more before facing the beast. "Sorry to say, your plan to kill me failed."

"I wasn't trying to kill you." I can hear the frown in his voice.

"Right—you just wanted me arrested and left in the back of a hot car. The cops are gone?"

"Yes. How do you feel?"

"Somewhere between flame broiled and blackened," I say.

Which is true. But I'm also very happy to know Officer Eyebrows and his Boy Wonder sidekick are gone. I wouldn't want to look at them after knowing one or both of them carried my limp body inside.

Slowly and carefully, I sit up. Thankfully, the dizziness is mild, and there are no more black spots threatening to steal my vision. But my head pounds like there's a second heart in there, beating angrily.

I'm still not ready to look at Wyatt, so instead, I glance around the room. Despite the run-down exterior, the inside of the cottage is clean, though small and woefully in need of some TLC. We're in a living room. The front door is just to the left of the couch where I'm seated. The hardwood floors are narrow planked and slightly warped, with water stains here and there, and the wood is darker in some places where furniture might have sat for years. It has the musty scent of an older home, but a faint, rotting smell lingers underneath.

The walls are a dingy white. No pictures or paintings, just a few nails or holes where they apparently used to hang. The windows have ratty curtains that resemble oversize doilies, a perfect companion for the faded floral furniture. The newest thing in the room is a large flat-screen television sitting on an old dresser that's missing a few knobs.

My gaze finally lands on Wyatt. More specifically, the black boot encasing one of his feet. He's leaning against the wall across the room, crutches propped up next to him. When I look up and meet his eyes, his gray irises are like harbingers of a storm.

It's the same expression he always wears when he looks at me. As though I've somehow committed a personal affront just by my mere existence.

He looks *terrible*. Still unfairly handsome but really not good.

His normally dirty-blond hair just looks dirty. It either darkened since the last time I saw him, or it's in serious need of a good wash. His olive complexion looks sallow and waxy, like he has been living in an underground bunker for six months without seeing sunlight.

Which makes no sense considering the waterfront location with a gorgeous sailboat ready and waiting to be, you know— sailed. Though his crutches probably have something to do with how he looks.

Why is he on crutches? A sprain? Fracture? Something else?

I suddenly notice what I should have seen right away. Wyatt has stubble. His cheeks and jaw are covered with what falls some- where between a five-o'clock shadow and a short beard.

This is more out of place than the walking boot and crutches.

I've never seen Wyatt anything other than clean-shaven. To the point I once asked my brother if Wyatt keeps a travel razor in his car in case of a stubble emergency. Jacob laughed, but he didn't give me a straight answer, so I've held it as canon ever since.

The scruff doesn't look bad—shockingly good, actually—but it does make me concerned.

Not an emotion I usually—okay, ever—have when it comes to Wyatt.

His expression is tight, his grumpiness amplified into some- thing almost threatening. His jaw is clenched so hard I bet he could turn coal into shiny diamonds right between his molars.

I clear my throat and ask, "Are you okay?"

Of *course* Wyatt's okay.

And remember—you don't care, I tell myself. Though I shouldn't need the reminder.

It's the nurse in me. I've taken an oath to help people—even surly ones who just had me put in handcuffs. Not that nurses sign the Hippocratic oath, but it's generally understood that our job is to help rather than harm.

And Wyatt appears to be in need of great help.

"I'm fine," he finally grits out, and I swear I can hear his teeth grinding as he clamps his mouth shut again.

Typical Wyatt-speak. Possibly IBS induced. Or maybe it's not an irritable bowel thing but just an irritable personality one. Not IBS but IPS—irritable personality syndrome.

"Great," I say with a little more sarcasm than I'd typically use. Not sure whether to blame the man or the heat exhaustion. "I'm a little *less* fine, what with the unlawful arrest—"

"They just detained you," he says.

"Semantics. Whatever they technically want to call it, all I know is that I was put in the back of a cop car in handcuffs."

I wait for an apology that I know will never come.

It doesn't. Wyatt simply stands there, looking sweaty and miserable and like someone poured expired milk in his cereal.

I remind myself that this is *Wyatt*. The grouchiest of grouches himself. On the ice, this really works for him—from what I've heard. According to my brother, Wyatt channels all his surliness onto the ice. He even picked up a new nickname in Boston: Oscar.

As in: the Grouch.

Despite my lack of interest in sports, I do use social media, and I once ran across a video of fans wearing shirts that featured Oscar the Grouch peeking out from his trash can with a hockey stick and a Boston jersey with Wyatt's number. I'm not sure whether those shirts were aboveboard from a licensing perspective, but who cares? I immediately bought one. Even if I've only ever worn it to sleep in, lest anyone find out that I own it.

Because the cringe part of the new name is that his ladyfans now refer to themselves as Grouchies. As in, groupies for the Grouch. I'm definitely no Grouchie, but I do love the shirt. It's just so . . . fitting.

The shirt is packed in my bag, I remember with no small amount of discomfort. As though somehow Wyatt will sense its existence.

It's at this moment I realize Wyatt and I are—perhaps for the first time ever—alone in a room together.

My mouth goes dry, and I don't think it's just the heat this time. It's a strange surge of nerves, exacerbated by his cool gray gaze and permafrown.

"We skipped right over the pleasantries," I say. "Hello, Wyatt."

He gives me the smallest of nods. "Josie."

The way he says my name makes my stomach twist uncomfortably. Or maybe that's just a remnant of the heat exhaustion. I can't read his tone, but it's definitely not neutral.

"I'd say it's good to see you again," I tell him, "but . . ." I shrug.

"But it isn't," he finishes for me. Or is he agreeing with me? Probably both.

"You didn't have to roll out the red carpet of the law to welcome me. Answering the door would have been just fine."

"You didn't knock," he says, like this is the most logical explanation for calling the cops. "You were wandering around the yard, taking pictures."

"Ah. Criminal activity for sure."

"I thought you were a reporter."

"A reporter?" I snort. "You're not *that* important."

He says nothing to this, probably because he vehemently disagrees with my assessment.

And he'd be right.

I *know* Wyatt is a big deal. Though this place is too far out of the way to be crawling with paparazzi, it wouldn't shock me if some enterprising sports reporter drove out here hoping for a story. Or something else. I can imagine Grouchies lined up outside the door or peeking in the windows.

Hockey fans aren't unlike the fans of any major sport—they can be obsessive to a degree that frightens me, and there is a distinct percentage of fans who would cross a lot of moral and ethical lines to get close.

Or to brag about spending time—or the night—with a player.

But wait—Wyatt thought *I* was a reporter?

As in, he really didn't recognize me?

I hadn't considered the extent of how insulting this is until now.

Wyatt and I have spent enough time together for him to recognize me, for heaven's sake. It's not like I've gone through a magical transformation or extreme makeover since I last saw him. My hair is longer than it's ever been, and I've taken to letting the natural waves do their thing rather than straightening it the way I used to. I've been the same height since my fifteen-year-old growth spurt, when I shot up to a respectably average five six. I've gained a little weight, but not enough to make me unrecognizable.

Here I thought Wyatt and I had a shared rivalry. A bond of equal dislike. But instead, maybe Wyatt hasn't ever cared enough about me to pay attention. The disdain I saw was perhaps more disinterest. Could he even pick me out of a crowd? A lineup?

Guess not. He can't even pick me out of his own yard. By myself.

It shouldn't sting. Wyatt is Jacob's friend—or client slash friend. Not mine.

But it bothers me. Deeply.

My phone, sitting face down on the coffee table, starts to buzz.

"That will be your brother," Wyatt states.

"What are you, an oracle?"

"He hasn't stopped calling me for the last ten minutes. Except to call you. While you were . . . unconscious."

"Which is because you called the cops on me and then let them leave me in a hot car."

Wyatt has the decency to wince.

I lean forward and grab my phone off the coffee table, which has seen better days. Wyatt watches me as I answer, and I force myself to look away. The intensity of his expression is familiar, but there's something new and different about how it's hitting me today.

Maybe it's just the heat.

"Give me a good reason not to write you out of my will," I tell my brother in lieu of hello.

"For the last time, I don't want your old collection of One Direction posters." He pauses. "Are you okay?"

"I've been better."

"This is *not* how I saw today going," Jacob says, which I think counts as an apology in some other dimension. He and Wyatt have the same severe allergy to apologies.

"I sure hope not," I say. "Because if this was your plan, I *will* seek revenge. Tenfold, brother. Upon your children's children's children's pets."

"Please—not my great-grandchildren's puppies!"

"Fine. I'll let the puppies live. But no promises with regards to your progeny."

Wyatt makes a noise that sounds suspiciously like a chuckle, but when I glance up, he's coughing behind his hand.

I turn my full attention and anger on Jacob. "Now, do you mind telling me why you sent me this address when you are *not* here, and Wyatt, who *is* here, didn't know I was coming?"

"Uh" is his not-so-promising start.

"Hang on. I'm putting you on speakerphone so you can share with the class." I adjust the volume and set the phone back on the coffee table. "Okay," I say loudly. "Go ahead and fill us in on your little plan."

"Wyatt?" Jacob says.

"Present," Wyatt says, like he's answering a roll call.

I almost smile.

There's a long pause. "So, here's the situation," my brother says. "Neither of you is going to like it."

"I'm not sure I can like it any less than what's happened so far," I say. "Which has consisted of a drive to a mystery location for a surprise trip with my brother that's clearly not happening, being arrested—"

"Detained," Wyatt corrects.

"Semantics." I glare but Wyatt glares right back. "Where was I? Oh, right—sitting handcuffed in the back of a hot cop car—to be clear, the car was hot, not the cops—while Mr. Big Deal over here signed autographs. Then I passed out from heat exhaustion, and now I'm inside Wyatt's murder cottage, feeling like utter and total garbage."

There is silence.

I would feel bad except . . . I don't. Nothing I said was exaggerated, except maybe the murder cottage part. Jury's still out on that one. Some of the stains on the hardwoods could conceivably be blood.

Finally, Jacob speaks, his voice guitar-string tight. "You let them leave my sister in the back of a cop car? In the heat?"

Wyatt looks away, his gaze dropping to a stained plank of wood near his boot. "I didn't know the car wasn't running," he says quietly.

Pressing a hand to my throbbing skull, I hunch over the phone. "All of this is your fault, Jacob. So, tell me—why am I here?"

I'm glaring at the phone so hard that I don't notice Wyatt trying to hand me a water bottle until he thrusts it in my face. He's leaning on his crutches, cheeks flushed, mouth downturned.

How little attention was I paying that I didn't hear him crutching his way over to give this to me?

"Thanks," I mumble, taking the water.

Don't be too thankful, I remind myself. *It's honestly the* least *he can do.*

Wyatt only nods, then hauls himself back across the room, leaning the crutches against the wall again. The tense look on his face is even tenser. His cheeks are flushed. Embarrassment or . . .

Pain, I realize. And I should have recognized the signs earlier.

But I was a little preoccupied—what with the whole police situation.

"What's wrong with you, by the way?" I ask, unable to stop myself. "You broke your foot?"

Wyatt's grimace of pain deepens into a frown. "It's not broken," he mutters. "I'm fine."

"He's not fine," Jacob says, as clear as if he were in the room. "He has an injury—ironically from playing disc golf, not from hockey—"

"That's not irony," Wyatt says.

What I really want to know is, how does one get injured playing *disc golf*? So many questions.

Jacob snorts.

"It's a little ironic," I say, earning me a dark look from Wyatt. "Getting injured in a noncontact, non-sport when you play hockey with body checking and fistfights and blades strapped to your feet."

"Disc golf is a sport," Wyatt says.

"It's the equivalent of, like, cornhole. Or pickleball."

"Both of which are also sports."

"Just because something has a ball—"

"Or a bean bag," Wyatt interrupts.

I roll my eyes. "—does not make it a sport."

"ESPN televises pickleball tournaments and cornhole. There are professionals who play in the ACL—the American Cornhole League."

"Next you're going to tell me there's a professional league for disc golf," I say with a laugh.

"The PDGA," Wyatt says with a smug little smile.

"Anyway," Jacob says, raising his voice, reminding us that he is still on the phone. "If you're all done with this delightful little argument, that's why you're there, Josie."

"To help Wyatt understand what is and is not an actual sport?"

"No." Jacob sounds exasperated, which makes me happier than it probably should. "Wyatt's not taking care of himself," he continues. "Blowing off doctor's follow-up visits and not going to his PT appointments."

Okay. Well, none of those behaviors sounds good. Especially for a pro athlete. But I'm not sure what they have to do with *me*.

Unless . . . he's not planning to go back?

Surely a *disc golf injury* wouldn't kill his hockey career. I can't see a professional athlete ever living that down.

Wyatt's cheeks are still red, and he's slumped a little more against the wall now. He looks worse than a few minutes ago.

Which is saying something. The man normally looks like someone waved a magic wand and made a model step right out of a *Men's Fitness* ad selling underwear or abs or smoldering gazes. As much as I dislike the man, I can't deny his pure physical appeal.

Right now, though, the only kind of feature Wyatt could secure in a magazine would be as the before picture for a transformation piece.

"He needs someone to get him back on track," Jacob says.

I don't realize at first that Jacob means me. He sent *me* here to help Wyatt get back on track.

I am the *someone*.

I snatch the phone off the table and storm outside, ignoring my body's protests at the quick movements and at returning to the oppressive heat. I find a shady spot under an overgrown shrub that's nearly as tall as the house.

"Please explain why you think I would ever agree to this," I hiss.

"Wyatt's having a rough time. Physically and mentally. He needs help."

"So, hire someone," I tell him, staring at the screen door lying in the grass.

Wasn't that attached to the house earlier? I can't remember. My brain feels like a bell jar dropped over it, my thoughts soft and fuzzy. I massage my temple with one hand, wishing I'd grabbed my water bottle on the way out.

"I tried," Jacob says. "Two different people. Wyatt chased them off."

This does not shock me. "With a pitchfork or just his personality?"

Jacob ignores this. "He needs more of a . . . personal touch."

I laugh. Loudly. "There will be zero personal touching. I mean, not that I'm staying at all. But I don't see how you thought I would be a good option."

"You're qualified. Because you're a medical professional," Jacob continues as though reading a list of why he thinks this is a good idea.

To be clear, it's not.

"I'm an *elementary school nurse*." Usually I'm making the opposite argument, reminding people that yes, I do have an actual degree in nursing, and yes, I *am* a medical professional. "Also, you know Wyatt hates me," I point out.

I don't say that the feeling is mutual. I don't need to. It's a truth universally acknowledged that Wyatt and I do not get along. My brother doesn't even try to argue this point. He only sighs.

"I'll pay you."

"It's not about money."

I *want* to mean the words. I really want to. But I'm already feeling my resolve crumble.

It's a Pavlovian response for anyone working in education. Money is always an issue, and most of my teacher friends work other part-time jobs or, at the very least, work over the summer.

If Jacob is offering compensation, he'll pay far more than what I'd make at school. Plus, trying to engage students over video chat while they're actually playing *Minecraft* or texting isn't my idea of a summer vacation.

Working for Jacob would mean less tutoring. Or *no* tutoring. But more of Wyatt.

The thing is, I've wanted to get out of my apartment for years. Plenty of people live in apartments. But at almost twenty-seven, I want my own place. I don't feel like a real adult when I share walls with college students who play YUNGBLUD until three o'clock in the morning.

Those neighbors are the only reason I know who YUNGBLUD even *is*. Same with Dua Lipa and Jelly Roll.

Sleepless nights and musical introductions aside, I want out of my apartment. It's a small goal. But where most people think of life like a ladder—full of rungs to climb, steps upward leading to more successes in some distant future—all I want is to have a little space that's my own.

I don't need a big house or a big life. Just something small and mine. A small life with small goals isn't a bad thing—this is what I keep explaining to Toni when she tells me to *Live a little* and *Dream big* and *Come out, it's a Friday night!*

On an elementary school nurse's salary, a house is dreaming big—financially speaking.

I've obsessively scoured real estate websites for years, making note of areas with cute homes that are also close to my school but not *completely* out of the realm of financial possibility.

Jacob paying me could be my big break. I happen to know how much Jacob's athletes make. And I know how much of a percentage he gets. He can't skimp on paying me the big bucks.

I could ask for an amount that would make a significant dent in my down payment fund. I'd feel icky about it, but it is what it is.

"He needs you," Jacob says. His thinnest and least persuasive argument by far.

"He needs *something*. Not me specifically."

"You," he repeats. "Listen—though I really do want him back on the ice, I'm seriously concerned about him. When pro athletes deal with injuries, a great deal of the recovery work is mental. And since Wyatt has holed up in this house I didn't even know he owned and hasn't been showing up to his physical therapy appointments or answering his phone, it's fair to say he could use a friend."

I'm not his friend. The man didn't even recognize me in his yard. Still. Jacob's concern gives me pause.

"So, why aren't *you* here? If your bestie needs a friend."

"I've just signed two new clients and . . ."

He drones on about sports things. Negotiations. Contracts. Draft picks. I wipe sweat from my forehead while my eyes glaze over. I should get out of the heat. Even in the shade, the temps have to be cresting ninety degrees. My head throbs again.

"I can't get away or I would have been there already," Jacob concludes.

I believe him. But I also believe he didn't try as hard as he could have, probably assuming I would, per the usual, spring into action the moment he asked.

"Think about it. He's lost the most important thing in his life. At least temporarily."

This strikes me as desperately sad. If hockey is the most important thing in Wyatt's life, I get why he's burrowing into his own pit of despair in this little murder cottage.

Which, honestly, is the perfect setting for a pit of despair.

"The man is in a dark place," Jacob says. "Being around you is like taking hits of pure sunshine."

That's actually . . . really nice. So nice that I might be softening a little to his ridiculous plan.

Until the sun pokes out from behind a cloud and I remember being stuck in the back of a cop car.

"I'd appreciate the compliment more if you hadn't tricked me into coming here and now weren't trying to manipulate me into an inconvenient favor." A very profitable inconvenient favor.

This last point is another inconsequential argument for me to stay. Jacob doesn't seem to have realized, but I am not sunshine for Wyatt. Based on the way he treats me, Wyatt views me more as a tiny dark cloud raining on only his head.

Over the years, anytime I wasn't avoiding him and we were forced to interact, I was snippy. Snappy. Sarcastic.

In return, he has been surly and sardonic. I suspect he spends time quietly noting all the ways I'm lacking. He probably has a notebook somewhere with a long list.

"Please, Josie. He's struggling and needs someone." Jacob pauses. "It's not just about his career but his life."

"Well . . . that sucks for him," I say finally.

It's the nicest platitude I can offer, though it comes with a pang of guilt. Because I know I'm being too harsh. Except this is about Wyatt. The man who, as I'm reminded by the bead of sweat trickling down my neck and throb of my head, is responsible for the time I spent in the back of a cop car in cuffs.

But aside from the man in question, I also resent the fact that Jacob is asking this of me. Because while I hate to think this of my own brother, I know his motives aren't simply altruistic or about his friendship with Wyatt.

"He won't want me to stay," I say.

"No, he won't," Jacob agrees. "But he doesn't have a choice. He knows I'll keep sending people. And now I've brought out the big guns."

"I'm the big guns, huh?"

He chuckles. "You're like a battleship cannon."

"Um, thanks?"

"Look," Jacob says with a sigh. "I know this situation sucks. I should have been honest with you both, and that's on me. I am sorry about how today went. But I really think the guy needs help, and I think you're the only person who can get through to him."

"I think you're confused. Wyatt hates me," I say again.

"He doesn't hate you, Josie. Hardly." He gives a little chuckle, like this is funny.

"Are we talking about the same person? The one who has despised me from the first moment we met?"

"I'm not sure you're remembering correctly," Jacobs says.

The thing is: I *am* remembering correctly.

And even if I could somehow forget the night Jacob first brought Wyatt home, I have now acquired years' worth of Wyatt's dark looks, single-syllable answers, and surly comments like souvenirs. A neat row of evidence behind glass, showcasing Wyatt's disdain aimed right at me.

"Doesn't he have family who could be doing this instead of me?"

"No." Jacob doesn't say more, but he manages to make that one word sound both weighted with subtext and also final.

I'm dying to know what this means. Does Wyatt not have family? Or does he not have family willing or able to help?

I switch gears since I'm not going to convince Jacob. "What about the Super Summer Sibling Extravaganza?"

I have a feeling I already know the answer. Even though I desperately want to hear a different one. Maybe one where Jacob says he'll be meeting me here later today or tomorrow so we can take our mystery trip. The two of us. Without a grumpy disc-golf-injured hockey star.

Jacob and I have been taking—or *trying* to take—an annual Super Summer Sibling Extravaganza for the past five years. But at this point, it's less annual and more occasional.

The first time we made it happen, I was finishing up my LPN certification, just before I landed my current job as an elementary school nurse in Fredericksburg. Jacob was in his third year as a sports agent and was a whole lot less busy than he is now.

We prematurely declared it an annual event and then struggled to hit even two more times in those five years. Mostly due to his job or a new girlfriend.

Since I'm the flexible one with most of the summer off, the issue has never been my schedule or my significant other. A boyfriend would have to exist in order to impact my life and plans. So far, I haven't found a guy I feel comfortable enough with to let my guard down, much less plan trips around.

Anyway. I had really been looking forward to this year's trip—even if Jacob kept the details totally secret. Apparently in order to lure me here for this nefarious purpose.

"I plan to make it down there to see you," Jacob hedges. "In a few weeks. Maybe a month."

"Wait—you expect me to stay here for weeks? A *month*?"

"Again, I'll pay you," Jacob says. "Loads more than you'd make tutoring or whatever."

"No," I say. But my brain is screaming, *Say yes! Say yes! Say yes!*

"Double what you would normally make in a summer."

"Not enough." But getting closer. I can literally feel my resolve crumbling, coming down like a building blasted with dollar signs rather than dynamite.

A house, I think. *A down payment.*

But . . . *Wyatt.*

"Fine. Triple what you normally make tutoring for a whole summer."

"Quadruple."

I think I've pushed too far when he's quiet for a long moment. Then he groans. "Fine."

The air shimmers, and I sway a little. I need to get out of the heat. I need more water.

I need a minute to think about what I've just agreed to.

"Do we have a deal?" Jacob asks.

I glance out over the water, watching a gull circling lazily overhead as the sun starts to dip low in the sky near the trees. "We have a *maybe*."

5

Nothing Easy About You

Wyatt

If there weren't already bad blood between my possibly soon-to-be former best friend and probably soon-to-be former agent and me, it would be poisoned now. Because Jacob sent Josie here to do a welfare check and make sure I'm alive (I am) and well (I'm well enough) and get me back on track. Whatever that means to him.

Probably in physical therapy so I can be back in Boston and on the ice as soon as possible.

Which is something I'm not even sure I want anymore.

Regardless, Jacob sent Josie *here* to see me like *this*—with multiple days' worth of scruff on my face, as many or more days' of unshoweredness, and a week's worth of trash piling up in the kitchen. I'm essentially living in my own filth—not unlike the pigs that belong to my neighbor up the road. He owns a whole herd, which I know because I came face-to-face with them by my mailbox the first day I came here. I can smell them when the wind blows from the east.

That's me: piglike and wholly unprepared to see Josie.

If Jacob had warned me she was coming, we might have avoided the little snafu with the police.

Which I'm pretty sure Josie doesn't see as *little*.

To be honest, I don't either. It's huge and it's horrible. I'm not sure how to come back from having Josie detained—which, in practical terms, seems exactly synonymous with *arrested*—and stuck in the back of a hot cop car for close to ten minutes while I begrudgingly signed autographs. Guilt clings to me like the stink of smoke.

In my defense, I had no way of knowing they left her there without the car running. Without the air-conditioning. Honestly—someone should lose their badge over this. People aren't supposed to leave dogs in hot cars. Much less a whole *person*!

I plan to file a complaint with the department later. I've had little else to occupy my time lately, so I've been going down a list writing letters of complaint for days now. Technically, emails of complaint, but that doesn't have the same ring to it.

So far I've written to the Department of Parks about the hole on their disc golf course that resulted in my injury, the city of Kilmarnock about their lack of a public trash service, and DoorDash about the one driver I had to practically chase off with my crutches when she recognized me and got *ideas*. Plus a few other emails I've now forgotten.

The response rate is low, but typing out my every frustration and annoyance is surprisingly cathartic. I'm not sure how much it will help in this situation though.

Just when I thought I couldn't sink any lower in Josie's eyes, I took the already low bar she set for me and buried it in a shallow grave.

My new catchphrase should be "You can *always* go lower."

I use my crutches to hobble closer to the window, watching as Josie argues with Jacob on the phone. She stands in the shade of the overgrown azalea, swaying slightly. It makes me wish my stupid foot wasn't injured so I could go outside and steady her.

I hated not being able to carry her earlier. Instead, I watched helplessly while the two officers struggled to move her from the driveway to my couch. The urge to yank her out of their arms was almost primal.

I frown. Josie really shouldn't be out there in the heat again. What she needs is more water and a cold shower with a fresh change of clothes. I could offer her my bathroom but . . . well. The cottage has only one bathroom and it's in terrible shape. It's been thoroughly scrubbed by the service I hired, but cleaning only goes so far when it comes to a house this old.

I don't want Josie to even *see* the bathroom.

Uncle Tom, who left me this house, became something of a hoarder in his last few years. When I was too busy with my career to visit—something I'll never stop regretting. I hired a company to go through his things while I was still in Boston. Most was thrown away, and I had them sell the remaining salvageable items and furniture. Anything sentimental went into a small storage unit nearby, leaving only the bare minimum here.

I imagined this summer as a time of peaceful relaxation *alone*, happily living as a hermit while deciding what my plans are for this cottage. And, of course, my sailing trip.

The last is the one I'm bitterest about. Now, I can't manage the boat on my own.

Teaching me how to sail was the biggest legacy Tom left me. The summers my mom dropped me with my uncle could have been dark core memories for me—one more reminder I wasn't enough. I wasn't wanted. At least by one of my parents.

Tom taught me to sail. The only thing in the world I like as much as hockey. I never feel as peaceful and like myself as I do with sun on my face, salt air in my lungs, and the movement of a boat beneath my feet.

Now I'll spend the next few months staring at a boat I can't sail.

I realize Josie is off the phone and marching back toward the house—where I'm watching her from the window like some kind of creeper.

But as I try to step away, I forget my foot injury, like I do multiple times every day. I stumble as pain shoots through my arch. Grabbing the wall next to the front door for support, I take several hissing breaths through gritted teeth.

I managed to knock over my crutches in the process, so I can't even grab them to make a quick escape.

There are three sharp knocks on the door, and I do my best to force my expression into some semblance of normalcy before I open the door.

"You didn't need to knock," I say.

Josie shrugs, squinting in the bright afternoon sun. "You called the cops when I set foot on your property. Who knows what you'd do if I walked inside without knocking?" she says airily.

There's an awkward moment where we both try to close the front door while I'm essentially in the way. Since I've dropped my crutches, my movements are limited to hopping.

"Wyatt, just move and let me close the door," Josie insists, and though everything about this feels like embarrassment upon embarrassment, I hop a little.

The room is sweltering again, probably from having the door open. Even just a few moments and I can feel sweat trickling down my spine.

I think I can smell myself. Or maybe that's the trash in the kitchen.

Possibly a combination of both.

"Why are your crutches on the floor?"

"I dropped them," I say and bend, reaching for them, almost falling over in the process. Josie lurches forward and grabs my arm, steadying me. Her fingers are a brand, and heat licks along my skin all the way up to my scalp.

Josie's brown eyes snap to mine.

She looks surprised by—I'm not sure what, actually. But the surprise quickly shifts to something more apologetic. Something bordering on pity.

How humiliating.

This whole thing—from the very start of my injury until this new low point—has been nothing but a heaping slice of humble pie topped with disappointment and a weird sense of shame.

I hate the taste.

"Wyatt?" she says, and I realize I'm frozen here, Josie's fingertips still curled around my bicep.

I jerk my arm away, more forcefully than I mean to, needing space, needing to breathe again, needing to separate myself from her touch before I go and do something stupid like get used to it.

But she clearly misreads the way I pull back because her expression closes down. Once again I've made her feel bad. Josie turns away, bending to pick up my crutches.

She holds them out to me. "Here."

I take them.

"How's Jacob?" I ask, though her brother is the last person whose well-being I care about right now.

Josie sinks down on the couch and brings the water bottle to her lips. I force my eyes away from her throat as she swallows.

"You know—same old same old. Scheming and plotting with the quick and brutal efficiency of a bulldozer while assuming the whole world revolves around him." Setting the empty bottle down on the table, she rolls her eyes.

"So typical Jacob, then."

"Yep."

This may be the first time ever that Josie and I have agreed on anything. She seems to realize it the same time I do.

Blinking rapidly, she gives her head a little shake, then clears her throat. "This is a nice property."

"I believe you called it a murder cottage earlier." An accurate description. I might have laughed if circumstances were different.

"I said it's a nice *property*. This house needs some work. Murder cottage fits."

She glances around the room, but I know she doesn't see what I do. She can't.

The couch where Josie sits is where I used to watch old westerns with Uncle Tom. A bird feeder once hung outside the window behind Josie. Whenever cowbirds showed up to feed, my uncle would run outside and chase them off with a broom.

Cowbirds are obligate brood parasites, he would say, and I can almost hear his voice now. I didn't ask what the words meant, just nodded along like I understood.

After a few years I asked my science teacher, though I mispronounced *obligate*. Mrs. Sorenson explained that these kinds of birds lay their eggs in the nests of other birds, often outcompeting the host babies for food.

"So, they're like baby bird assassins," I said, and I couldn't understand why Mrs. Sorenson laughed until tears leaked out of her eyes, then later sneaked a red Jolly Rancher out of her prize drawer for me.

Josie can't see any of that when she looks around the room.

I'm sure what's visible to her is the lack of repair, resulting from so many years of deferred maintenance. Uncle Tom took excellent care of the boat, while the house was more of an afterthought.

A hot defensiveness rises in my chest. Or maybe that's just the busted air conditioner. I woke up sweating, and I'm not sure I've stopped. Even when I turned the thermostat down to the high sixties. It says it's working. It's wrong.

I need to get an HVAC guy out here ASAP.

Is Josie too warm? Has she noticed the cottage isn't much cooler than outside?

By the looks of it, yes. Her cheeks are flushed, a deep pink rising from the collar of her shirt as she takes a sip of water.

Josie is still scanning the room, and I have a sudden urge to tell her about my plans for this place. How I hired an architect to draft two sets of plans. One set expands the existing cottage, flipping the footprint so all the living areas have the water view and adding another bathroom and a few bedrooms. The other set is for a brand-new build, one that would take the place of the cottage.

But Josie wouldn't want to hear about my plans. Or this place. I'm honestly surprised she's still here.

Which reminds me: I need to get her out of here now. Before she realizes how bad things are. Or how bad I smell.

Actually, considering the way she helped prop me up just now, she probably knows about the latter.

"Don't feel obligated to make small talk," I tell her. "Now that you've completed your brother-ordered welfare check, will you be on your way?"

"About that."

Uh-oh.

She picks up the empty water bottle and turns it over and over in her hands. No nail polish. When did she stop wearing it? I've long used the different colors she chose as a way of navigating my memories of her.

The unfortunate first time we met, Josie's fingernails were bright purple. I remember fixating on them, both because something about the color intrigued me and because it kept me from staring too long at her big brown eyes.

When I made the mistake of going with Jacob to her graduation dinner, her nails were a deep navy. Chipped. I remember noticing the color when she covered her mouth, laughing at something Jacob said.

Over the years, there's been a whole rainbow of nail colors: hunter green, pale blue, silver. Almost like a mood ring, though Josie is always smiling.

Except when it comes to me. I seem to have the effect of throwing a blanket over her fire.

The last time I saw Josie, her nails were a pale pink—the color of her lips if she wasn't wearing makeup. The color looked good on her, but it made me a little sad because I always liked the bright, fun colors. They seemed like her, while the pink seemed almost like a giving up. Or a growing up maybe. Like she was putting the bright side of herself on mute.

The last thing Josie needs is to be muted.

"Here's the thing," she says now, pulling my gaze away from her unpainted nails to her face. Her expression is guarded and carefully blank. Instantly, I'm on high alert. "Jacob wants me to stay."

"I don't want you to stay." Only when this comes out of my mouth do I realize how rude it sounds. I couldn't be a worse communicator with Josie if I tried.

"Of course you don't," she says, toying with the water bottle and looking suddenly exhausted. "And *I* don't want to stay."

I already knew as much, so I don't let the words hurt.

"But Jacob made some compelling arguments."

"Like?"

The arch of my foot gives a deep throb, a tiny punch of pain, and I lean more of my weight against the wall, hoping Josie's sharp brown eyes don't notice. I should probably be sitting, but it's hard to get up sometimes. And I'm not about to have Josie witness me trying to heave myself off the couch.

I wait. She doesn't say anything, twisting the bottle in her hands, strangling the plastic with a loud *crunch*, then tugging at a loose string on her shorts. When she pulls, the hem starts to unravel.

"He says he's worried about your health."

"It's fine."

"And your mental health."

"It's even better."

"You're not going to your appointments."

I sigh. "I hate doctors."

"I'll choose not to be offended."

"You're not a doctor," I snap, immediately wishing I could suck the words right back into my mouth.

This is the story of me around Josie. I say the wrong words in the wrong tone every single time. Things like *You're not a doctor*, which managed to make it sound like I was belittling her career as a nurse. That's not what I meant, but if I try to explain, I know I'll somehow make it worse.

"I'm a nurse," she says. Slowly. Patiently. But still with irritation bubbling under the surface.

"I know," I say.

I know she's been an elementary school nurse in Fredericksburg and loves her job. I know this because I keep up with her through Jacob. Culling information from him while trying not to look desperate for every scrap about her life is a skill I've honed.

But the way I say *I know* sounds like I'm doubling down on my not-a-doctor insult.

Josie ignores this and continues. "He wants me to stay for a few weeks. Or . . . a month."

I blink.

Jacob wants her to—*no.*

No, I will not have Jacob send his sister as a replacement for the two people I already sent away. I don't want to see anyone right now. I don't want help of any kind. I don't want to hear platitudes and false encouragement that sounds like it's been pulled straight off a motivational poster.

I don't want to appear broken.

Especially not in front of Josie.

"What's your medical experience level?" I ask. This time I intend to sound rude. I *need* to be rude if I want her to get offended and leave. "Are you equipped to handle postsurgical care?"

She holds my gaze, though the pink in her cheeks burns a brighter red. "I deal mostly in skinned knees, upset tummies, and hurt feelings. Oh, and lice."

"I don't have lice."

She holds up a finger. "Yet. I've learned that with lice, it's best to say you don't have lice *yet.*"

A bead of sweat rolls down my temple, getting lost in the scruff on my jaw.

The other people Jacob sent were easier to scare off. They actually seemed afraid of me, whereas Josie is used to my abruptness. My sharp words, which pain me to say on purpose to her, are not having any effect that I can see.

Guess I need to push harder.

"Do you give sponge baths?" I ask.

It's hard for me to voice a question like this, even in a sardonic tone that's not in any way flirtatious. I obviously don't mean it. Nor do I need sponge baths. I'm capable of showering. I've just chosen not to for the last few days. Week. Whatever.

But I hope the mere suggestion will send her running.

Josie rarely touches me. Which is maybe why I responded so strongly to her hand on my arm moments ago.

If anything will get her back in the car, heading home, joking about giving me a sponge bath should do it.

But her expression doesn't change. She doesn't blink. We are at the poker table, and she's tossing her chips to the center, calling my bluff.

"A sponge bath? No. But a garden hose would work. Really gets a good deep clean. You do have a hose outside somewhere, yeah?"

She leans back on the couch, spreading her arms like she's getting comfortable, and I realize she's going to be harder to dislodge than a tick.

Which seems incongruous for her. Usually I'm saying something accidental to send her running away from me. Why is it that now, when I'm trying to send her away, she's settling in?

"But I don't think you need the hose," she says. "I bet you can shower fine with the boot. You're just choosing not to do it, so far as I can tell."

When she looks me up and down, I want to shrivel under her gaze. I know how I must look.

Abruptly, she asks, "What's the injury?"

"It's a Lisfranc," I mutter.

"Liz Frank? Never heard of her."

"It's not a woman."

"A band?"

"Not a band."

She waits. "Are you going to make me google it?"

"That's up to you. But you don't need to know." I pause. "Because you're not staying."

"Jacob hired me."

This makes more sense. She's being stubborn about staying because Jacob is paying her. She's determined to stay not for me but for the money.

There's no reason this should hurt my feelings. None at all. Still—it does.

"Then you're fired."

She smiles. "The thing is, *you're* not paying me. Jacob is. Which means you can't fire me," she says, then stands, brushing her hands off on her shorts with their now-loose hem. "And you're not going to scare me off with threats of sponge baths or your surly attitude. I'll go get my bags from the car."

"I'll pay you double what he's paying," I tell her, and she pauses with her hand on the doorknob. "To leave."

"You don't even know what we agreed on," she says, glancing at me.

"Don't care. I'll pay more."

Josie goes quiet, and a riot of emotions passes over her face. When she speaks again, her voice is soft. "You really hate me that much—enough so you'd pay me to leave?"

The question is a sledgehammer. One edged with tiny blades. It hits me with force, but also cutting precision. Deeply.

"I don't hate you," I tell her, but my tone is off. Probably because my feelings are somewhere in the opposite realm from hate, and I don't want her to hear it in my voice.

I doubt she'd believe me anyway.

She *definitely* doesn't believe me now.

"I haven't decided if I'm staying long term," she says. "But I will stay tonight. Be right back with my suitcase." With that, she storms outside, slamming the door behind her.

Panic squeezes around my ribs. Along with a confusing swell of relief.

I don't want Josie to stay. I also don't want her to go.

While she's outside, I hobble to the thermostat. It says the temperature is seventy-four, but it feels like ninety-four. I nudge the lever down to seventy, hoping it might help.

Josie reappears a minute or two later with a backpack and a rolling suitcase that's bright purple with stickers all over it.

She waits for a moment, then says, "Well—are you going to give me a grand tour?"

"There's not much to see."

"You'd never make it as a real estate agent," she says. "You know, if the hockey thing doesn't work out."

Her words strike too close to home, and I find myself tightening up. She must notice.

"Not that you're thinking about changing careers," she adds quickly. "I have no idea what your plans are after your recovery."

"You and Jacob didn't discuss my contract and my return to play?" I sound bitter, and once again I'm not keeping my emotions in check.

Usually this is not a problem for me. But whether it's the heat, the events of the day knocking me off-balance, or just Josie, I'm cracked wide open.

"He seemed more concerned about you," she says softly. "Not your contract. And normally, no—we don't discuss you. I make it my business to know as little about Jacob's clients as possible."

I almost ask, *What about his friends?* but manage to keep at least this question locked up tight.

"You want a grand tour?"

"Actually," she says, a yawn mangling the word. "I think I need water and a quick nap. Tour later." She yawns again.

"A nap? It's almost dinnertime."

"Are you going to tell me when I can and cannot nap?" she asks.

"Follow me. If you're serious about staying even when I'm telling you to leave, this will be your room."

The hallway leading to the cottage's two bedrooms is tiny with both of us crammed in here. I step back, gesturing toward the open guest room door with one of my crutches.

The guest bedroom is sparsely furnished with a brass bed, dresser, and a bedside table. I wish I'd done something to update the room, but at least I know the housekeepers washed the sheets recently.

Josie wheels her suitcase next to the dresser and then picks up a book I hadn't noticed. Her lips curve into a smile as she holds it up to me. A shirtless man and a woman with a very low-cut dress are locked in a passionate embrace, their hair blowing in a fictional wind. I can't picture Uncle Tom reading this, and I have no idea where it came from.

"Not mine," I say quickly.

"Of course not," she says. "I'm sure paranormal romance is more your speed. Wolf shifters, dragons, and all that. You just left this here because you want to share your love of steamy Regency romances with guests, right?"

I frown. "I don't know what paranormal romance is. I certainly don't read it. And I don't have guests."

"With your attitude I'm sure you don't."

"I don't have an attitude."

"Okay," she says cheerfully.

"I *don't*."

Josie turns the book toward me, cover facing out. "Will you require a bedtime story as part of my services?"

"*No.*"

The idea of Josie, curled up next to me, reading, almost makes my heart explode.

"But this looks like the perfect book to inspire good dreams and good sleep," she teases.

I am not someone who blushes, but I feel heat creeping up my neck. "My sleep is fine." Needing to change the subject, I say, "The sheets are clean."

She sets the book down and wanders to the window. This room has the best view in the house, facing the water. It's the room and the bed I grew up sleeping in, long summers spent waking to diamonds of light on the water. When I moved in last month, I chose the other room. It felt a little strange sleeping in Tom's room. But it would have felt even stranger to sleep where I always did. I was afraid one morning I'd wake with hope, forgetting he wasn't in the other room.

I'm glad Josie will get to wake up with the water view.

She glances around the room once more. "None of this decor looks like you. Did you buy the house fully furnished or something? Is it a rental?"

"No." I clear my throat, ready to tell her it was my uncle's house. But then I don't. "What kind of decor would you expect me to have?" I ask, curious.

Josie tilts her head. "I guess I don't know. But not this."

I only realize I'm sagging against the doorframe when Josie's gaze narrows in on me. First she scans my face, then darts a look down at my boot. She doesn't miss much.

I wish she did.

"Stop," I say, the word coming out harsher than I mean it to. I sweep a hand across my forehead, wiping away the sweat.

Her eyes snap up to meet mine. "Stop what?"

"Looking at me like I'm something broken you need to fix."

She holds up both hands. "Not trying to fix you. Pretty sure that's way beyond my skill set."

I snort. Even though she's making light of things, it's the truth.

"But at some point, if I'm going to stay," she continues, "I *will* need the details on your injury and will need to talk to your doctor about—"

"You're not staying."

She sighs, then places her fists on her hips, drawing up her shoulders and a serious expression to match. She's clearly so exhausted that the look is almost comical. "Look. I don't want to be here. You obviously don't want me here."

I say nothing.

"But my idiot brother seems to think you *do* need me here. You look terrible."

"Thanks."

"It's not an insult; it's a fact."

"Thanks again."

"Based on the little I've seen, you need support right now. Maybe not a live-in nurse who specializes in strep throat and skinned knees. But *someone*. You have to know isolating your-self like this is counterproductive to recovery. You do want to recover, yeah?"

"Yes," I say.

The word leaves my mouth, sounding and feeling strange. Not just because I'm not sure it's true, but because I'm suddenly lightheaded.

What was the question?

I really need to sit. Or lie down. Heat pulses through me. Sweat drips steadily down my spine. I've *got* to get the air-conditioning looked at.

If not for me then for Josie.

I squint at the thermostat, but the numbers swim. Definitely broken.

"Then stop making this harder on yourself," Josie says, but I'm no longer certain what we're talking about. I nod anyway, my head suddenly an anvil atop my noodle neck.

"What's the bathroom situation?"

I blink away the sweat dripping into my eyes. *Focus, Wyatt. Bathrooms . . . bathrooms . . .*

"There's only one," I manage, my voice thick and my mouth dry.

"Wonderful," Josie mutters, looking back toward the window and the water beyond.

My vision has gone hazy. Swaying, I almost lose my balance and just keep myself from collapsing in a boneless heap. The heat is suddenly unbearable.

My body is lava. No—magma.

I'm beyond grateful when Josie yawns again and starts to slump. "Okay. Well, we'll revisit this thrilling conversation when I wake up."

I barely manage to scurry back when she steps forward to grab the doorknob. Her eyes are half lidded as she says, "Good-night, Wyatt."

"It's still afternoon," I say, and as she closes the door in my face, I can hear her laughter just beyond.

It's the last thing I hear from her as I shuffle toward my room, where I plan to collapse into bed.

But the floor feels wiggly. So do my legs. Like I'm walking on the deck of a boat.

Something is wrong. Am I feverish? I almost call out to Josie, but I tell myself it's just the air-conditioning. When did I last eat? I haven't been sleeping well. It's probably just exhaustion. And an HVAC problem. I'm fine.

I'm not fine. I need to stop and rest. When did this hallway get so long? I'm trapped in a funhouse mirror. Sweat rolls down my back.

Unable to take another step, I slump against the wall and puddle onto the floor.

Just a tiny nap.

No—not here. I'll crawl to my room if I have to. I try to drag myself there.

My fingers brush the doorframe, but I'm not going to make it.

Even my eyeballs feel hot as they fall closed, and my last thought is that I need to wake up before Josie sees me like this.

⚓

"Wyatt?" Josie's voice is suddenly very close.

I open my eyes. When did I shut them?

I'm lying on the floor in the hallway and it's dark. Is it night?

"M'okay," I mumble.

Something cool touches my face. A hand. Josie's hand.

Josie is touching me.

I shiver.

"Wyatt, you're burning up."

"'S broken."

"What's broken?"

"The AC."

"No," her sweet, soft voice says. "It's not. You've got a fever."

"Broken," I insist.

"Stubborn," she murmurs. "Why didn't you call for help? You're barely two feet outside my door."

Her hand starts to move away from my cheek. I gather the strength to lift my own heavy hand, covering and holding hers there.

"You're cool," I say. "Feels good."

She sighs. "We need to get you to the hospital."

"You're a nurse. You can fix me. You handle lice." She laughs at this. I squeeze her fingers, still pressed to my cheek. "No hospital."

A pause, and my eyes flutter shut. Even my eyeballs are hot.

"No promises. Did you have surgery? I'm concerned this could be some kind of infection."

"It's not an infection." *Probably.* "No hospital. Sick of that place."

A long pause. "I could try to get your fever down first," she says, and I can hear the reluctance in her voice. "But I'm taking you in the morning if I don't see improvement."

"I'll be good. I'm easy."

A soft chuckle, and I lean my face into her hand shamelessly. Nuzzling into her cool palm.

"There's nothing easy about you, Wyatt. Not a single thing."

6

Snuggling a Pizza Oven

Josie

Ever tried to hoist a feverish, six-foot-four-ish, two-hundred-something-pound man into bed?

Would not recommend. Negative stars. Scathing Yelp review to follow.

"Can you"—I grunt, shoving at Wyatt's torso—"just get up there?"

The man draped over me only groans. His eyes are closed. A little drool escapes the corner of his mouth.

I really hope this is the right call—putting him in bed rather than going straight to the ER. When I awoke in total darkness, my bladder was about to explode. There were a few moments of heart-pounding panic where I had to remind myself where I was and realized my nap had stretched well beyond the hour or two I'd expected.

Then I almost tripped over Wyatt's big body in the hallway

just outside my door. Where he'd apparently collapsed right after I did. The difference being, of course, that I was in a bed and he was on the floor, burning up with fever.

I don't have a great feeling about putting him in bed rather than in the car, but I also want to respect Wyatt's desire to stay home. If we don't *need* to go to the hospital, I don't want to. Maybe he's just got a virus. Which I will undoubtedly catch after being practically plastered to him like this.

An even worse possibility is that it's some kind of infection. If Wyatt had surgery—and I don't know if he did or didn't—the incision site could be infected. The lack of information I'm working with here kills me.

It's the opposite of my normal job, where six-year-old Daisy Whittaker came in with a skinned knee from the playground and proceeded to tell me about her mother's facelift recovery protocol. Elementary school kids will spill all the beans.

After I get Wyatt in bed, I'll call Jacob and ask. He has to have some information since he knows Wyatt hasn't been going to his scheduled appointments.

What I won't do is panic and assume the worst.

After my brother's actual brush with death, I had years of medical-related PTSD. Which is understandable given that Jacob almost died due to a simple mosquito bite.

The mosquito bite turned into something much worse when Jacob scratched the heck out of it and then spent hours in hockey gear. You don't want to know what kind of bacteria can exist inside stinky hockey gear. And then, of course, Jacob was a preteen boy who didn't think to mention the redness and swelling until he became septic.

In his defense, who thinks of mosquito bites as life-threatening?

Turns out, when it comes to bacteria and infection, almost

anything can be. One of Jacob's nurses told me she had a patient almost die from a zit, which got infected and created an abscess on the brain.

Obviously, Jacob didn't die, though he did stop playing hockey after that and has a very mild limp most people wouldn't notice.

Me? I ended up in therapy a few years later because a simple well-visit to the doctor made me hyperventilate and I was convinced even a paper cut might kill me.

Almost losing your big brother to something as simple as a mosquito bite will do that to a person.

Therapy worked *so* well, I ended up interested in nursing. Though I never wanted to work inside a hospital. And I still sometimes, like right now, for example, have to battle invasive thoughts about the worst-case scenario in any given situation.

Wyatt doesn't have sepsis, I tell myself. *If the fever doesn't go down with meds or if he gets worse, we'll go in. Everything is* fine.

What's not going to be fine is my back if I can't heft his bulk into bed and stop wearing him like a scarf.

"Come on," I grunt, forcing a cheer I don't feel. My legs are shaking.

"Tired," he mumbles, not opening his eyes.

"Then let's get you in bed."

Instead of complying, he leans harder into me.

I'm grateful his bedroom is only about ten steps from where we stand in the hallway. Otherwise I couldn't play the part of his half crutch, half wheelbarrow. I'm sweating profusely, clothes sweat-damp and stuck to my slick skin. And I'm still not nearly as hot as Wyatt with his fever. Holding him up is like snuggling a pizza oven.

I've always been a little awed and intimidated by Wyatt's

size. He's tall and broad. Well muscled. Thighs thicker than a normal person's torso.

But there's a difference between acknowledging his size from a distance and wearing all that bulk like a very heavy, very hot scarf draped over my shoulders. This close he is practically bigfoot-ish compared to me. And he feels like he outweighs a hippo.

Surprisingly I don't feel any of my normal discomfort from being so physically close to a man this size. Just the physical discomfort from hoisting his giant body.

With a groan he snuggle-slumps into me, and my arms tighten around his waist to keep him from tilting over. I definitely don't think I could get him off the ground if he falls. Not unless I'm endowed with the kind of adrenaline that helps mothers lift cars off their infants.

Is that even a real thing? I wonder as Wyatt's scruff bristles against my neck.

A little shiver moves through me at the gentle scratch on my sensitive skin. It's been a long time since a man has been this close to me. Since I've *wanted* a man this close to me.

Not that I want Wyatt nuzzled into my neck. I don't. It's *Wyatt*. With his personality pricklier than his uncharacteristic stubble.

But there's a surprising sense of emotional warmth—not to be confused with the feverishly warm physical sensation of Wyatt—spreading through my chest. Probably because I like taking care of people.

He is, if nothing else, a person.

A person who is starting to drift into feverish sleep, his breath hot like a desert wind on my throat.

Which is, apparently, the theme right now. Hot, hot, hot.

"Here we go, buddy. One, two, three!"

Using what feels like the last of my energy, I bend my knees and try to launch Wyatt up onto the queen-size bed. Thankfully, the frame is low, and I manage to get his torso firmly on the mattress. Which leaves my face pressed to his abs.

I jerk away. He moans, smacking his lips. I'd laugh if I were less exhausted. And if I didn't still have to get his tree trunk thighs up into the bed.

As I'm working to lift and move them up with almost no help from him—all while trying not to jostle his injured foot—I chastise myself. I should have seen this earlier. The flush in his cheeks. The sweating. The constant clench in his jaw.

I can blame my own heat exhaustion for this or maybe the fact that I don't often allow myself to really *look* at Wyatt.

I'm looking now.

And I feel like I've failed him. It makes me doubly irritated because since when did it become my job to oversee Wyatt?

Since today, when I decided to consider taking a paycheck I *do* want for a job that I really, really *don't*. Technically, I guess it was yesterday. The quick glance at my phone before I left my room told me it's five in the morning.

Once Wyatt's in bed and my muscles feel like they're going on strike, I grab ibuprofen from my bag and the rest of my bottled water from the living room. I *still* need to pee, but right now, Wyatt takes precedence over my bladder.

"I've got your medicine," I say. "Up we go."

Wyatt groans as I lift his hot, heavy head enough that he can take the pills with a swallow of water.

I watch the way his throat moves as he drinks, wishing my observations felt more clinical and less . . . personal. Somewhere in the last half hour, I became emotionally invested. *Fabulous.*

When he pulls back slightly, I move the bottle from his lips and guide his head down to the pillow.

"I don't like this," I whisper, unsure if he's already asleep. "I'm concerned."

He opens one eye. His mouth lifts in the smallest of smiles. "You're concerned. About me."

"Only because my brother will take a massive pay cut if you die," I tell him, though it isn't true. I mean, yes—the pay cut part is true. But it's not why I'm concerned.

He releases a soft breath, almost a chuckle, and his eyes flutter closed again. Just when I'm about to slide my hand out from under his head, he cracks his eyes open again.

"So pretty," he whispers.

I freeze, my mouth dropping open as his eyes drop closed. His head lolls, and I slide my hand from under it, telling myself he doesn't know what he's saying. And he certainly won't remember saying it.

But for just for the tiniest moment, I allow Wyatt's words to curl around me, to mean something. Even if they don't.

7

Rabies on My Mind

Josie

"He's that bad, huh?"

My brother sounds wide awake and like he's running on four shots of espresso when I call him. Despite it being just shy of six in the morning.

After leaving Wyatt snoring softly, I finally went to the bathroom and am now multitasking, trying to make a dent in the mountain of dirty dishes in the sink while calling Jacob for advice.

"He's bad," I tell him, using the rough side of the sponge to scrape at some unidentifiable food particle at the bottom of a bowl. "And so is the house."

Wyatt's murder cottage is thirteen- or maybe fifteen-hundred square feet of *needs work*. Mostly in terms of updating, as the bedrooms and living room are tidy and I detect a faint scent of lemony cleaning spray that suggests a professional might have been here.

But it has signs of aging no amount of cleaning can wipe away. I swear there's a bit of a slant to the floors. If I dropped a marble, I bet it would roll all the way to the left side of the house, coming to rest against the chipped baseboards.

A strong breeze or a wolf huffing and puffing just might blow the whole thing down.

The bathroom is where things start to go downhill. It's an homage to mint green and mildew. The classic tiles have come back into fashion—a mix of subway and tiny square floor tiles—but the white porcelain sink has orange water stains, and the faucet is practically crusted over with calcium deposits. There's a dark ring in the toilet bowl I'm sure bleach can't even touch. When I sit down to use it, the seat wobbles, almost sending me to the floor.

But the kitchen, a narrow room tacked onto the back of the house like an afterthought, is the first double punch of disrepair *plus* filth. It surprises me, given that Wyatt never gave off the messy, uncaring-frat-boy vibe, not even when he was in college. I'm going to give him a pass and chalk the mess up to his injury.

I don't love cleaning, but I do love mindless tasks as a way to distract myself. And while the other rooms in Wyatt's house are neat, the kitchen is an epicenter of disaster. There are bags of trash, dirty dishes everywhere, and a table covered in takeout containers and what look to be rolled-up blueprints of some kind.

There's a pile of laundry in front of the ancient washing machine at the back of the room. I should probably have started a load, but I couldn't bear the idea of potentially touching Wyatt's underwear.

"I'm questioning whether I made the right choice in not taking him to the hospital," I tell Jacob. "Or calling an ambulance, since in his current state, I'm not sure I can lift him into a car. How's his insurance?"

"Not an issue. Look—he had surgery, but it's been a month. Long enough that I'm sure it's not an infection at the incision site." He pauses. "Probably."

"*Jacob*."

"No, really. I think waiting to see if the fever goes down is a good idea. I can give you his doctor's number if you want."

"Yes. Absolutely. Why do you even have his doctor's number?"

A brief pause. "Wyatt put me down as his emergency contact. They called me when he stopped going to his appointments or answering his phone."

I turn off the water, letting my hands drip-dry in the sink as I mull this over. I'm not sure why it shocks me. Jacob and Wyatt are good friends. But again—where is Wyatt's family? Does he seriously have no friends besides my brother—who loves Wyatt, yes, but also has a vested financial interest in his recovery? I assume he doesn't have a girlfriend or I wouldn't be here.

Is Wyatt's circle of support really so small?

The thought makes me want to march right in where he's sleeping and give him a hug. Almost.

"You still there?" Jacob asks.

"Yeah. Just thinking."

"Thinking you might stay for sure?" He sounds so hopeful.

The thing is—I do want to stay. Or, rather, I feel like I *need* to stay. Not just for the money, though I absolutely plan on price gouging my brother. I don't like the idea of Wyatt out here with no one. Not when he seems so unwell. And possibly self-destructive.

It has nothing to do with him saying I'm so pretty in his feverish state, something I wish I could forget.

He might have been talking about something else anyway— not me. He didn't say *You're so pretty, Josie*. Just . . . *So pretty*.

Maybe he meant the curtains behind me. Maybe the fever made him hallucinate something—or *someone*—pretty.

In any case, those two words aren't factoring in to my desire to stay, though they do keep whispering through me like a faint heartbeat.

"I'm still a maybe." I quickly add, "Though I don't know how long I'll stay. If I do. Maybe just until this fever is under control. Absolutely not weeks or a month like you mentioned before. I don't like being away from home that long."

"It's not like you've got pets or anything to get back to," Jacob says. "Do you even have any plants?"

"Yes," I say defensively.

Though they're fake. I don't have the best track record with living plants. I seem to personally offend them somehow, and every one I've ever bought has shriveled up and died with prolonged exposure to me. The succulents too.

It's almost a talent. Too bad I can't monetize it.

I refuse to tell Jacob this, however, because he's making my life seem insignificant—which is completely unfair. I know for a fact he also has zero pets and zero plants. He does occasionally have girlfriends, even if they never seem to last long. They've got a shorter lifespan than my doomed houseplants. Still, it's better than my sad love life. More like my sad *lack* of a love life.

Toni has been trying to convince me to get out there for years now. She insists that if I do, I will find good men out there, ones who will treat me like a queen.

To which I typically reply: *Does such a mythical creature exist?*

In an attempt to prove that it does, Toni has introduced me to a number of "nice" guys in group settings. I've been on a handful of awkward first and second dates. They were fine. Like a meal you enjoyed but never thought about repeating. There was never a pull or a sense that I wanted to see any of them again.

The very last date I went on was when Toni strong-armed me into going out with an art teacher from her middle school. It took her an entire school semester to wear me down before I finally agreed. Five minutes later I regretted saying yes.

And ten minutes into the date with him, I got back in my car and left.

Joe—who had gold hoops in his ears like a pirate, a detail Toni left out—told me we were going to do something creative but wouldn't say more than that.

"Should I dress up or dress comfortably?" I asked, already feeling the pinch of panic that comes from new situations.

When he laughed and said, "It doesn't matter," the red flag unfurled and slowly started to wave.

I went into the date feeling more nervous and anxious than I'd normally be, which is saying something. As it turned out, I had cause.

Creative according to pirate-hoop Joe meant going to a place with giant canvases rolled out on the floor for us to paint—by getting naked, covering ourselves in paint, and then rolling around.

Which, obviously, I was not interested in doing on a first—or *any*—date.

Toni is still making it up to me by bringing over dinner from our favorite Italian place once a month.

If anything, I'm far less likely to dive back into the dating pool now. Not after that belly flop.

In any case, not having a boyfriend, pet, or plant doesn't mean it's an easy decision to stay and take care of Wyatt. I have a life. A good friend. Plans to read my way through the women of literature.

"That was out of line," Jacob says, his version of an apology.

"It was. Even if you're right—I don't have any plants." He chuckles, which I ignore and continue on. "And I guess I'll stay. Not indefinitely. Just until he's . . . better."

"I know it's a sacrifice no matter what," Jacob says, though I'm not sure my wonderful but also very selfish brother understands the word. "Thank you, Josie. For real."

"Don't thank me yet. I haven't told you how much it's going to cost you."

⚓

I'm just shoving laundry into the machine, underwear included—and no, I don't want to talk about it—when a voice in the doorway startles me.

"You don't have to do that."

I scream and bang my elbow into the washing machine. Wyatt stands in the doorway, leaning on his crutches and looking . . . well, at least upright, which is an improvement from an hour ago when I last checked on him.

I tiptoed in after my call with Jacob and found Wyatt in the same position he'd been in when I left him. According to the digital thermometer I always travel with, his fever was down a little, though 102 is still higher than I'd like. I figured I should give the ibuprofen a little more time to kick in before insisting on the hospital.

And if I allowed myself a minute to examine and appreciate Wyatt's sleeping form—the thick golden stubble I really think he should keep; the full lips, slightly parted; the thick lashes brushing his cheekbones—well. No one can prove a thing.

Now, remembering the way I stared at him makes me blush.

It also makes me irrationally angry. With myself, with Wyatt, with Jacob. With the world, really.

I yank the earbud out of my right ear, which stops the true crime podcast that's been playing. "You scared me," I say, as though it's not obvious. "I was listening to a podcast."

"About what?" he asks.

I blink. Because Wyatt is asking me a question. Has he ever asked me a question about me or my life?

I don't trust it. "About stuff," I say vaguely. "How are you feeling?"

Wyatt doesn't smile with his mouth, but I swear, his eyes are laughing. I'm not sure I've seen Wyatt *happy* before. It's unnerving.

"It's a true crime podcast, isn't it?" He ignores my question. "That's why you got scared. You're obsessed with me and my murder cottage."

If possible, my blush reaches higher. I swear, I feel it singeing the roots of my hair.

"It's a podcast about a court case," I say, knowing full well I sound defensive. I'm not lying. It *is* about a court case. An ongoing one that just so happens to be for a murderer. "Why are you out of bed? You look . . ."

He looks less feverish, his eyes more focused. But he also doesn't quite seem like himself. I can't pinpoint exactly why that is. Maybe it's the light in his eyes, the trace of amusement that's so un-Wyatt. I catch myself staring and look down, only to realize I'm still clutching a pile of his laundry to my chest. Including his underwear.

I shove it into the washer and slam the door.

When I turn back, there is the barest hint of a smile on his face. Even sick and unwashed, the man could be the face of just about any brand campaign. In fact, I think he had this exact expression on the boxer briefs ad he did a few years ago. I remember tossing the magazine across the room, feeling like I'd actually walked in on him like that.

There's something completely disconcerting about seeing the face of a person you actually know in an advertisement. Especially when they're wearing a lot of body oil but not a lot of clothing.

Even so, that wasn't as uncomfortable as the time I went to Atlanta for a school nurse conference and saw Wyatt's face was on a larger-than-life-size advertisement on the MARTA platform. Some fellow nurses and I were waiting for the train to take us from our hotel area to a shopping mall after the day's sessions. I happened to casually turn around . . . and then screamed.

Because Wyatt's giant, attractive, familiar face—and not so familiar but just as giant and attractive bare chest—were *right there* in black and white.

It was an ad for a watch, and he wore *only* a watch, the photo stopping near his hips. He stared out with the kind of eyes that follow you, his hand with the watch casually resting on his opposite shoulder. My fellow teachers all laughed and catcalled once they realized I hadn't screamed because I was in danger.

Then they made me take pictures of them leaning up against the ad. One of the youngest, who I think had been hitting the minibar hard beforehand, pretended to lick his abs, which made me distinctly uncomfortable for a lot of reasons.

I refused to be in a picture.

I also refused to tell them I knew the man in the image, that he'd given me that same glower in person, and it was every bit as potent. Even with a shirt on.

Even if I've never admitted out loud—and rarely admit to

myself—that the man I share a mutual dislike with is also a man I find highly attractive.

It's not attrac*tion*. Wyatt simply is attractive.

At least, until you get to know his personality.

But I'm not sure any of the other women I was at the MARTA station with would give a hoot about his personality.

"I feel better," he says.

"Good." I grab the first of several full trash bags sitting on the floor. There's a puddle of goo oozing out from the bottom. I try not to think about what said goo consists of. "Where does the trash go? I didn't see trash cans outside anywhere."

"You don't need to—"

"Wyatt. Don't make me keep standing here while this leaks more toxic waste onto the floor. Tell me where the trash cans are."

With a heaving, dramatic sigh, his tiny smile totally gone, Wyatt points one crutch toward the back door. "In the garage," he says, and I take this to mean the building I saw earlier next to where the Bronco was parked. "But . . ." He trails off and doesn't finish.

I pause with the back door open, holding the gross, goopy bag over the back steps leading out of the kitchen. "But what?"

"There's no trash service here."

I blink at him. "What does *that* mean?"

"It has to be driven to the dump," he says. "Eventually."

Wonderful. One more delightful thing I can add to my ever-growing résumé: trash woman.

As I walk to the garage, I imagine emailing an itemized list of charges for my brother. I could have it notarized. I picture him pulling out a paper that unfurls and stretches halfway across the room. That would be highly satisfying.

The garage's two large doors swing open with loud groans. The gray paint on the wood siding is chipping away.

Inside, it's dark, musty, and oppressively hot. I ignore the sound of something scurrying away. Yikes.

"Hello," I call loudly. "Warning! Scary human approaching. Please disperse!"

More shuffling noises at the back of the building, behind what looks like a car with a big tarp over it.

I quickly locate two metal cans and deposit the bag inside one, making a final trip to the kitchen for the last two bags, which thankfully are not leaking toxic ooze. Wyatt tries to argue me out of it. This time I don't even answer him.

The garage is silent the second time I enter it. Hopefully, whatever was here will not return.

Wyatt is still standing in the doorway when I get back to the kitchen. I grab a handful of paper towels to clean the sludge from the floor. "I think you have a creature living in your garage. Know anything about that?"

"No," he says. "What kind of creature?"

"I didn't see it, just heard it scurrying around."

"Probably a rat," he says. "Maybe a raccoon, though if it's out in the day, it could have rabies."

Fabulous. Rabies is just the thing I want on my mind.

"Don't worry, though. I won't let it hurt you." The small smile is back on his face, and I have to turn away because it's glorious and does weird things to my insides.

I focus on breathing through my mouth as I clean the floor. Once that's done, I move to the table. I already bagged the empty takeout containers, but that still leaves the table full of papers and rolled-up blueprints. All the while I ignore Wyatt, who hovers in the doorway, watching me. At least he's stopped trying to tell me not to do things, though I'm a little surprised he doesn't also tell me how I'm doing things wrong.

"What should I do with these?" I ask. "Are they blueprints?"

"Leave them," he says.

"You don't want to use the table for, oh, I don't know—eating?"

"No."

Okay, then. I almost ask about the plans, but I've already been intrusive enough. I realize I never started the washer, so I locate detergent and dump in a capful. The washing machine sounds like a car with a bad engine, but at least it's running.

"You should get back in bed," I tell Wyatt, who hasn't moved. I don't look directly at him, like this will somehow encourage him to leave. "I'll come take your temperature again in a minute. Do you want some water?"

I peer into the fridge, which resembles a ghost town. The only thing missing is a tumbleweed blowing by the half-empty (and likely expired) ketchup, some water bottles, and a container of Cool Whip, which I think should be kept in the freezer. It has a piece of duct tape on the front that reads DO NOT THROW AWAY.

I'm all set to ask about it when Wyatt says, "This was my uncle's house."

Turning slowly, I meet his gaze. "Yeah?"

The small smile from a few moments ago is gone, replaced by a frown. Not the normal grumpy one. This one is more somber, and it shoots a bolt of concern straight through my chest.

"He died." Wyatt sniffs.

Oh my gosh—is he about to cry?

I find myself frozen, one hand wrapped around the fridge handle like it's my only lifeline.

"Wyatt, I'm so sorry."

He only nods. But a moment later, his expression shifts once again, like a curtain has been lifted.

"It's okay, JoJo," Wyatt says with a smile. "Now *you're* here."

I frown. Because no one calls me JoJo. Definitely not Wyatt. We're not exactly nickname people with each other.

Not only that, but his voice is lighter, with a musical lilt.

It sounds almost . . . *flirty*.

Didn't he just seem like he was about to cry over his uncle dying? It has to be the fever. Maybe he's not doing better but is actually just fever high. It would explain the mood swings. Or, you know, Wyatt having moods other than surly.

I take a step toward him, noting the way color has risen in his cheeks. "Wyatt?"

Then he smiles—a real, full smile like I've never seen. And I know something's very wrong.

But it's when he tries to use his crutch to—I think—boop me on the nose while slurring, "I like you, JoJo," that I know.

It's time to get him to the hospital.

Free-Range Zombie Pigs

Josie

Getting Wyatt's big injured body down the sagging front steps and to his car isn't quite as hard as it was getting him in bed earlier. That's not to say it's *easy*.

"You've got to keep moving," I grunt as Wyatt's nose finds my hair.

"You smell like pie. Coconut cream—no! Buttermilk."

I would laugh. I *want* to. Because this is ridiculous.

Also, buttermilk and coconut pie both sound delicious right now. My stomach rumbles and I tell it to settle in—I have a feeling it's going to be a while.

Wyatt tossed one of his crutches in a bush outside the house, muttering something about liking me better. Now I'm his human crutch as we hobble awkwardly to his Bronco—which he insisted in his sloppy, feverish state that I drive.

I am limping along, all sweat and screaming muscles, as Wyatt nuzzles my hair. Apparently, feverish Wyatt sheds the

Grouch for a full-on snuggler. It would be endearing if I weren't about to collapse.

We finally reach the old Bronco, and I lean against it, breathing heavily as he slumps his full weight onto me. I need a moment to recover. Even my bones hurt.

But then his nose moves from my hair to my neck, and I freeze.

"Mmm," he says, inhaling audibly. "Pie."

I don't know how I smell like anything but sweat and possibly dish soap at this point, but I'm not going to argue with the man. Especially not as his nose traces along my throat, sending waves of goose bumps over my skin. My nerve endings electrify and the temperature goes up at least ten degrees instantaneously.

This is . . . weird. And kind of delightful. Which makes it very, very dangerous.

"Wyatt." I shake him a little with my hands on his lower back, like he's falling asleep and I'm trying to wake him. He might as well be.

Underneath his sweaty shirt, he's a solid mass of muscle. I can feel him flexing as he shifts, mumbling something.

I need to get him in the Bronco and off me. But now that we're leaning against it, I still don't know if I can get him in there unless he can actively help.

"I think we should take my car," I say again. It's low. I can open the door and pretty much shove him inside. This would involve less touching, which is a very good idea right now.

"Too small," Wyatt slurs. "Like you—tiny."

"You're just a Sasquatch. I'm an average height," I say, not sure why I'm defensive.

He lifts his head slightly, and his scruff brushes my cheek. We are way too close. I try to lean away, but that only makes him lean harder into me. He drops the other crutch.

"Nothing about you is average," he murmurs, his breath on my jaw.

I have no response to this. There's no reason to respond. He doesn't know what he's saying. And it's probably not meant as a compliment anyway, even if that's how it sounds. Then again—he did call me pretty. And say I smell like pie.

It's irrelevant, I tell myself. *He won't remember this. He doesn't mean this.*

But every touch, every kind word, every little moment with this foreign version of Wyatt is setting itself up as a core memory. I can almost feel the tectonic shift happening as my brain adjusts to thinking of him in a new way. A softer and kinder way.

Maybe also a semi-romantic way.

That realization is enough to get me moving again. Because under no circumstances am I allowed to have any kind of feelings for Wyatt.

Wiggling out from under him, I manage to maneuver him off the passenger-side door. He's as floppy and unruly as an overcooked noodle. And still much warmer than I want him to be, especially after the ibuprofen.

I press him against the car as I open the door, and his head lolls forward. Even with his eyes closed, he's smiling. It makes me feel a bit better. But only the tiniest bit. Instead of putting him in bed with ibuprofen, I should have gotten him to the hospital.

Still, I refuse to devolve into panic about infection. Or sepsis. He's going to be fine. I'm both sad and relieved thinking about him returning to the grump I know. The grump is safer than this version of him.

Holding him in place with a hand on his chest, I give his cheek a little slap. When he doesn't react, I take a breath and slap him a little harder.

His eyes blink open, unfocused at first. Then his gaze locks with mine. He smiles again. "Hi."

"Wyatt, you've got to get in the car. I can't lift you."

"M'kay. Keys are in my pocket." Heavy breaths punctuate each word. "Here."

He thrusts his hand into his pocket, nearly taking down his shorts, then tries to pass me the keys. But my hands are full of unwieldy man, and the keys fall to the driveway.

He frowns, looking like he's about to grab for them.

"Leave them," I say firmly. "I'll get them in a sec. You—get in the car."

Speaking firmly seems to be the most effective way to get him moving, and though it's awkward and he almost slides right back out, he mostly makes it into the passenger seat.

I think of all the ways I'm going to kill my brother. And also how much these tasks will be worth on my itemized list.

Half carrying Wyatt to the car: a hundred dollars. No—five hundred. Hoisting him into the seat is another two-fifty.

Listening to his feverish rambling and having my face pressed into his cheek will earn me overtime.

"Can you lift your leg in there so I can shut the door?"

"Too tired," he says, lips barely moving.

With a sigh, I put both hands behind his knee and gingerly lift, being careful with the boot. I haven't had a chance yet to look up the injury he mentioned, the one that sounds like a woman's name.

While we're at the hospital, I can get caught up on exactly what I'm dealing with. I couldn't connect to Wi-Fi at Wyatt's house, and the internet on my phone is too slow without it. Maybe I'll even get to talk to his doctor and get the number for his PT.

The moment I've got his leg and foot safely inside, his eyes open. There's that unfamiliar smile again, this time a little mischievous.

"I was faking," he whispers dramatically.

"What?" I'm tempted to smack him again, but for wholly different reasons this time. Also, there's no way he's faking the fever and this whole mood shift.

"About my leg. I just wanted you to touch me." He wiggles his leg as though to prove his point, still grinning before his smile fades and his eyes close again. "I like it when you touch me, and you never do."

I stare for a moment at the stranger in front of me, then slam the car door on him because *what is happening?*

Wyatt is fever-flirting with me. *That's* what's happening. He's making it sound like I'm not in the running for his least favorite person on the planet.

And it's breaking my brain.

Though I need to get my purse and his crutches, I pick up the keys and walk around to the driver's side first to turn on the AC. I'm not about to leave Wyatt in a hot car. Even if it would be an exact sort of revenge.

A minute later, I've shoved the crutches into the back next to a bunch of hockey gear and am reaching for the driver's side door. It opens with a creak, a sound that reminds me of my childhood. Newer cars don't make these sorts of sounds; they probably aren't even made of the same material. This door feels weighty in my hand, the whole car like a tank, really. I like it.

Unlike the house, which is in a sad state of disrepair, it's obvious that painstaking care has gone into restoring the vehicle. I find myself wondering whether Wyatt worked on it or just bought it like this.

I adjust the seat and mirrors, then catch Wyatt watching me.

No smile right now, but his gaze is softer, not the usual flinty gray.

"You like vintage cars, huh?" I ask.

Wyatt makes a choking sound that turns into a laugh. "Vintage? I'm older than this car."

"Oh."

I attempt some math in my head. Fail. Try to think what year this car might be. Fail. How can I not know how old my brother's best friend is? I always associate the two of them together, often forgetting Wyatt graduated from college before Jacob. Which would make Wyatt five years older than me? Six?

"How old are you, anyway?"

"Vintage."

Normally, if Wyatt said something like this, it would come out snappish. But he's looking at me with that goofy grin on his face again.

When he smiles . . . saying he's attractive is not an objective observation anymore. I'm not acknowledging it. I'm *feeling* it.

This reminds me of my favorite episode of *The Office*, where Pam and Dwight bond only because he has a concussion. If Wyatt kept a spray bottle in the car like the one Jim uses while driving Dwight to the hospital, I'd totally spray Wyatt right now.

Not because he's doing something wrong. But because I don't like the way his smile makes my stomach twist.

I need him to snap out of it. I don't want to get used to this version of him or how it's affecting me. Because it's not who he is. He'll go right back to being a grump in no time.

The Bronco bumps along the oystershell drive, which has Wyatt adjusting and hissing in pain a few times. I slow down, but he waves me on.

As I watch the cottage in the rearview, I remember what

Wyatt said in the kitchen. Putting the pieces together, I'd guess Wyatt's uncle left him the property when he died. I wonder if this has anything to do with his current situation and the lack of care about his own health and recovery. Jacob never mentioned it, which makes me wonder if he even knew.

I reach the end of the drive, turn onto the gravel road, and am forced to stop both thinking and driving.

By a herd of pigs.

Not small, pink piglets either. There is not a Wilbur in the bunch. These are gigantic exhibits of porcine mass. Dark gray, almost black, and with so many fat rolls on their heads that I can't see their eyes. Which I assume are beady.

"What *is* this?" I ask. "Because it looks like the start of a horror film."

Wyatt groans. "Neighbor pigs," he mumbles. "His fence is always broken, so they're somewhat free range."

"Free-range pigs aren't a thing, Wyatt."

Or are they? Perhaps I spoke with too much confidence. I don't know much about *free-range* anything, aside from the fact that free-range eggs are just slightly out of my price range.

"Are they mutant pigs?" I ask. "They're massive. And I thought pigs came in pink. Not black."

"X-pigs," he says with a giggle. "Like X-Men . . . but pigs."

Conversations with fever-high Wyatt are turning out to be quite fun. Too bad this is the exception to his personality. I wonder if he'll remember any of this?

"Or zombie pigs," I suggest. "They look like they could be hungry for brains."

"Pigs are highly intelligent," Wyatt says, his tone suddenly quite reasonable.

There is nothing reasonable or acceptable about this entire situation.

"You're delusional. On several counts." I roll down my window. "Shoo, piggies! Go sooey somewhere else!"

Testing the waters, I inch the car forward and give the horn a light tap. No sound comes out, so I press a little harder. An excessively loud sound blares, possibly rupturing one or both of my eardrums.

I gasp, jamming my foot on the brake pedal.

The pigs are undeterred, barely flinching, and Wyatt glares.

"What's your problem?" he demands.

"What's your *horn's* problem?" I snap back. "Is it trying to compensate for something? Tiny tires? A V4 engine? Being an SUV without four-wheel drive?"

"I didn't know it would be so loud."

"Maybe it's compensating for your negative attitude," I grumble. "It didn't scare the pigs, so any other ideas?"

"Just pull forward slowly. They'll move." He sounds confident, as though pig traffic is a common occurrence. Maybe it is.

I do as Wyatt suggests.

The pigs, however, do not move.

They simply stand there. Stare. Make me wonder if we actually *are* in some kind of horror movie.

"Will your neighbor be upset if I run them over? Or would that mean we get fresh bacon?"

"I'm more concerned about the car and the damage they might do to the undercarriage."

Wyatt is throwing me with his slips in and out of lucidity. He's way chattier than normal, shifting between giggly goofiness and spouting random facts. In any case, I have at no point in my life given thought to the undercarriage of a car. In fact, this is basically a new vocab word for me. *Undercarriage.* For reasons I cannot explain, it seems like the most ridiculous thing to be discussing right now, and I hide a sharp bark of laughter with pretend coughing.

I continue to inch the Bronco forward, but the pigs remain in a formidable and bristly wall. The closer we get, the more disturbing this whole thing becomes.

"Do we wait them out? Lead them into the woods with a trail of fresh slop?"

Wyatt snorts at this. "I'm all out of fresh slop. You?"

"None on me." I pause. "I don't want to continue this battle of the wills with the oversize Wilburs forever. Or damage your precious *undercarriage*. Can I go the other way on this road?"

Wyatt shakes his head. "It dead-ends at my neighbor's house."

"Of course it does."

"I do have my practice gear in the back," he says, as though this is some kind of answer to the pig problem.

"That's . . . cool. I have a Target gift card I bought for a friend three years ago in my purse, but it won't help us with the pigs."

Wyatt gives me a long look. One that is trying to convey something he clearly seems to think I should have picked up on.

Finally, it clicks. "Oh. Like you've got the stick?"

He stares at me like I've sprouted another head. "Yes. I have *the stick*. Which is an integral part of my hockey gear."

"And you want me to . . . use it to scare the pigs?"

Wyatt raises a brow. Slowly. With attitude. "It's strange Jacob always talked about your quick wit."

"My *wit* is just fine. If I'm not in top form, I'm going to blame the leftover heat exhaustion. You know, from being handcuffed in the back of a hot cop car."

"Are you going to bring that up forever?"

"Until the day I die," I say solemnly.

Wyatt leans toward me and, without thinking about it, I

shrink back against my door. The look he gives me would be enough to wither an entire farm's crops. Especially since he's been so goofy and sweet. Now I'm getting whiplash from the various versions of him.

With a grunt, he twists, rummaging around behind our seats. His shoulder brushes mine, even as I try to lean away. The heat from the open windows is suddenly oppressive, though not as intense as the heat of *him* being this close.

But then, Wyatt pulls a hockey stick from the back of the car, practically taking off half my face.

"Hey," I protest. "That's cross-checking."

His expression remains unamused.

"High-sticking?" I am trying to dredge up hockey terms I learned from having to attend Jacob's high school games. But he played lots of sports, not just hockey, and I think I know more about football.

"Roughing the driver?"

He shakes his head and shoves the stick my way, the end of it going right out my open window. "Here."

My hands automatically close around the taped-up end. It's a little sticky. "You really want me to go chase the pigs with this?"

"I would, but I'm currently not a good candidate for pig management." He gestures to his boot.

I don't think I've *ever* been or will be a good candidate for pig management. Unless we're talking about how many slices of bacon I can eat in one sitting.

I try to hand back the stick. Wyatt doesn't take it. "I don't think this falls under the purview of nurse and driver."

"Then I guess we can wait them out while I die from scarlet fever." He closes his eyes and slumps back against the seat.

"You don't have scarlet fever," I scoff, but I study him.

The coherence of the last few minutes appears to have exhausted him. He's slumping again, chin to chest. Cheeks red. Sweat trickling down the side of his face. Even with his body relaxed, his expression is pained.

Wyatt probably has a high pain tolerance, given his sport of choice, which means he could be in worse shape than he's letting on.

I glance out at the pigs.

Do pigs bite?

Not willing to take the chance, I twist around, locate a helmet in the back with Wyatt's gear, and pull it over my head. The visor part over my eyes is a little smudged, but it's good enough.

"I don't think the helmet is necessary," Wyatt says.

His comment only makes me want to wear it more. It's a little big and has a smell that isn't altogether pleasant, but I'm committed now.

"Safety first," I tell Wyatt, adjusting the helmet but not cinching the strap.

Before he has a chance to respond or I have a chance to chicken out, I put the Bronco in Park and open the door. I almost hit Wyatt in the jaw with the end of the stick and bump my head on the way out, making me glad I've got the helmet, but I eventually manage to extract myself.

And now, I'm standing on the road, facing down the pigs.

An erratic giggle escapes me. This whole day has been a study in the ridiculous. From start to now. And we've barely passed lunchtime. Wait—have we passed lunchtime? I honestly don't know what time it is, but I'm suddenly starving and can only think about bacon.

"Are you just going to stand there?" Wyatt calls. "You shouldn't be scared. You've got a helmet."

"Are you teasing me?"

"I would never."

Gripping the hockey stick like a baseball bat, I advance toward the front of the vehicle. The pigs are unperturbed. If I couldn't see them breathing and occasionally flicking their tails to dissuade flies, I might wonder if they were dead where they stood.

"Okay, piggies," I say, lifting the stick to my shoulder like I'm ready to swing. "I'd really rather not have to use this stick. Mostly because I don't know how to use this. But also because I love animals. I also *eat* animals—"

There's a snort behind me, and I turn, realizing that Wyatt is leaning out of his window, watching with an amused expression. Though his eyes are half lidded, like it's too much work to keep them open.

"Stop threatening and start swinging," he advises. "And if you don't want to be stampeded, maybe don't talk about your love of bacon."

"Who knew you had any sense of humor buried under your grumpy exterior?"

He mutters something that sounds like "You don't know a lot of things about me" and then ducks back inside the car. Immediately, I feel more alone.

Just me and the pigs.

Sweat trickles down my back, and the stick feels heavy in my hands. I give it a test swing, nowhere near hitting the pigs but in their general direction.

Finally, some movement. The pigs go from silent, slothful statues to tense and jumpy in an instant. They still don't get off the road, but now they're stamping their feet and bumping into each other. Snorting ensues.

Progress!

Emboldened, I take a step forward, swinging the stick in

a wide arc the other way, narrowly missing Wyatt's headlight. *Oops.*

"Go on, now! Shoo!"

I take a bigger step closer this time and lift the stick above my head to avoid hitting the car or the pigs, who are now nearer than I really want them to be, considering their size. Each of these pigs probably weighs at least what Wyatt does. Maybe even double his weight. In my best nonprofessional pig-judging estimation.

And suddenly, my proximity to the oversize beasts doesn't seem like such a good idea. If they stampede, I'll be trampled.

One of the smaller pigs toward the back squeals and tears off into the woods beside the road.

"There we go! The little squealer has the right idea," I say, lifting the stick for another swing. "Now, if all of you would kindly just—"

Three things happen at once. So quickly my brain seems to slide through molasses to process each one.

First, Wyatt shouts, "Josie! *Move!*"

Second, the pigs stampede. Not toward the woods like the first one. Toward *me*.

And third, I fling the hockey stick and leap onto the hood of the Bronco.

It's all over in seconds that somehow feel like they've taken years off my life. The sounds of squealing and a running herd of pigs fade. Leaving me curled in the fetal position on the hot hood of the car, listening to the sound of my panting breaths.

"You okay there, pig wrangler?"

The concern Wyatt had while shouting his warning has shifted into barely contained amusement.

I lift my head and glare through the windshield. Wyatt's

smiling again. He really needs to stop doing that. Especially when it's at my expense.

"I'm just fine and dandy," I mutter, peeling myself off the hood. Which is considerably more difficult and painful than jumping on. I am oddly exhausted. My muscles aren't used to fast-twitch responses or having to hurl my body weight up on a vehicle.

I'm also pretty certain some of my skin is burned onto the hot metal of the hood permanently.

"'Fine and dandy'? Where did you learn to talk?" he asks. "A 1950s time capsule?"

I'd like to tell Wyatt exactly where he can put a 1950s time capsule, but apparently his hockey stick is too expensive to leave in the woods where I flung it. So instead, I spend the next five minutes looking for it in the surprisingly dense undergrowth.

Which is how, when we arrive at the hospital, we are *both* admitted; Wyatt for his fever, and me for a particularly alarming case of poison oak that made my whole body swell up.

9

The Human Equivalent of a Stress Ball

Josie

"So, you've never had a reaction like this before?" the doctor asks, lifting my arm by the wrist and shaking it.

"Take a picture; it'll last longer," I mutter through swollen lips.

Given the way Dr. Charlie's eyes light up, he must not realize I'm joking. I'm pretty sure if it didn't violate a million HIPAA laws, he would have already taken a video.

And I get it.

The way my arm—now filled with a layer of fluid—jiggles long after he stops shaking it is an awesome sight. Not awesome in the popular usage of the word but the biblical sense.

Awesome like a plague of locusts.

Not exactly eager to become a viral video or, worse, a meme

that might have a longer shelf life, I hold up a swollen hand. "Kidding. No flash photography, please."

Dr. Charlie's face falls, and he gives my arm another small shake, like he can't help himself. Truly, my body's reaction to poison oak is one of the most disgusting, and therefore fascinating, things I've seen. You'd think an ER doctor would have examined much worse, but Dr. Charlie has spent far longer than necessary with me. I should consider charging him for admission at this point.

When I asked if this reaction was typical, he gave me an emphatic and way too excited no. Good to know I'm a complete freak of nature.

"To answer your question, I've never had a run-in with poison oak before," I tell him.

My words are understandable but muffled, what with the swelling in my lips, tongue, and throat. It's gone down significantly since they gave me a shot of corticosteroids a few hours ago. But I still look completely freakish.

My throat closing up was actually frightening. The strange tingling sensation in my hands and mouth that I noticed on the drive turned into massive swelling. To the point where I was struggling to breathe and starting to panic by the time I pulled up in front of the ER.

Should I still have been operating a motor vehicle? Probably not. But swollen beggars can't be choosers, and thankfully, the hospital was only about fifteen minutes away.

Wyatt was so concerned—probably that Jacob would blame him for my untimely demise—that he yanked his crutches from the back and hobbled inside the hospital shouting before I could even get out of the car.

And then he passed out on the floor.

The two of us make quite a pair.

I don't know who parked Wyatt's car. I don't know where Wyatt went after we were separated in triage or what's wrong with him.

I only know that it's been a few hours, and I'm able to breathe normally again. The swelling in my lips is starting to go down, at least according to the selfies I took before and after the steroids kicked in. I currently look more like someone who's had a normal amount of lip filler versus one of those plastic-surgery-gone-wrong people. Or a monster in a horror flick.

Now, if only the fluid in my arms and legs would dissipate.

I wonder where Wyatt is now. *How* he is now. If his fever is some kind of virus or somehow related to his injury. The worry I feel is a lot gentler than it was before—the kind you have for a friend or someone you actually like. Probably a remnant of his fever-sweet moments with me in the car. When he was in his Dwight concussion era.

"I've heard of reactions like this, but I've never seen anything close," Dr. Charlie says. I think it's about the fourth time he's said something similar. "You have no allergies to any other foods? Nothing?"

"Nope. Not to pets or peanut butter or even poison ivy."

My mom had me run through a series of allergy tests after one of my classmates had a severe reaction to the eggs in another student's birthday cupcakes. I think we were all traumatized seeing an ambulance driving Matthew away from the school.

The rest of the year, birthdays were celebrated without food.

But I guess the doctor glossed right over the poison oak allergy test. Or maybe it's a new allergy? I've heard of them developing or worsening over time.

"Is there anyone you need to call?" Dr. Charlie asks. He's no longer touching me, but I swear, he's looking at my arm like he's tempted to shake it again. "Anyone who can drive you home?"

I decide not to explain the Wyatt situation. "Um, no. But I should be fine to drive. I'm uncomfortable, but I can move."

I lift my arms to demonstrate, but that makes the fluid jiggle again. Dr. Charlie's expression is almost hungry. I briefly consider pressing the call button. But I'm not sure what I'd say to a nurse who came—*Help, I'm afraid the doctor might kidnap me and lock me in his basement so he can study me like some kind of experiment?*

Nope. I'll just get through this, find Wyatt, and get us out of here.

"Let me check one more thing," the doctor mutters distractedly, lifting my arm by the wrist.

Maybe I *should* have pushed the call button.

Dr. Charlie jiggles me again. I can almost hear his interior monologue, which I imagine like a narrator from one of those *National Geographic* shows. In my mind the narrator is also British, though Dr. Charlie has a light Southern lilt.

Fascinating! my inner doctor monologue opines. *Despite the steroids, the patient retains so much subcutaneous fluid she appears to be filled with Jell-O. When fingertips press into the dermis, for a few seconds the indentation will remain and—*

"Would you mind *not* poking me?" I ask. I've finally met my limit of prodding. Jiggling. Being stared at like a freak of nature.

Though physical touch is my love language in theory, actual touch is also . . . complicated. Because I don't always feel comfortable being touched. Especially not by people I barely know, doctors included. But this also *hurts*, what with my skin stretched and taut to accommodate all the fluid.

Dr. Charlie drops his hand but doesn't move away.

"I'm starting to feel like the human equivalent of a stress ball," I tell him. Not that I owe him an explanation.

His eyes light up. "Yes! That's exactly the description I was looking for."

Maybe my made-up monologue for him wasn't so far off.

I do agree it's strangely satisfying to watch my skin slowly get its shape back where Dr. Charlie has been poking me. But his fascination seems a little over the top. Maybe unprofessional is the vibe here.

Dr. Charlie still hovers by my paper-covered bed. I stand up, but the doctor has me hemmed in. There's no chance of running either, because even the bottoms of my feet are swollen.

"So, am I free to go?" I ask. "I'll just pick up the prescription and drink lots of water."

"And stay out of the bushes and away from poison oak," Dr. Charlie adds, shaking his finger and smiling, like this is an actual joke and not a new life rule I'll never forget.

He told me earlier that future reactions could be *more* severe, and I don't want to find out how much extra fluid it would take for me to burst like an overfull water balloon.

"No worries. I have no plans to go anywhere near nature for a long time." I wave my hand, flinching at how tight my skin feels. Each of my fingers is like a small, overstuffed sausage. I'm not sure I could even hold a pen at this point. Can I even hold the steering wheel to drive? I guess we'll see.

First order of business will be finding Wyatt.

He appears in the doorway like some kind of specter I've summoned with my thoughts. A specter who looks decidedly less feverish, crutches under his arms and leaning against the doorframe. I'm relieved but also distinctly uncomfortable as Wyatt's gaze falls on me. And then on Dr. Charlie, who is still standing closer than I'd like. The heat in Wyatt's eyes could incinerate whole villages. Or, at the least, incinerate doctors with a bad bedside manner.

"Are you ready to go?" Wyatt's voice slices through the moment like a scalpel.

I *want* to be irritated by his intrusion. He could be interrupting a real love connection, hospital-style. For all he knows, Dr. Charlie caught feelings while examining my throat with the tongue depressor my students use for crafts. Uvulas are an underrated feature, and maybe mine is dead sexy. Dr. Charlie took one look, and he was a goner.

But that's not the case, and I'm beyond grateful for the interruption.

Wyatt crosses the small room to stand beside me. Even injured and leaning on crutches, he exudes a pure masculinity that practically cloaks the room in a testosterone fog. It's a fog I'd happily get lost in right now.

Especially paired with his dark, threatening stare, aimed at Dr. Charlie, who edges toward the door. "I'll send a nurse back with your prescription," the doctor says. And with one last longing glance at my swollen arms, he's gone.

I expect Wyatt to step back now that the doctor is gone, but he doesn't.

"What's your diagnosis? Or . . . prognosis?" I ask Wyatt.

"I'm a little closer to death every day," he deadpans. "How about you? You look"—he scans me quickly, frowning as he does—"better?"

"Thanks." I laugh and shake my head. "I told Dr. Charlie I look like a human stress ball." Wyatt's frown deepens, so I quickly continue. "But really—what did the doctor say? Unlike me, you do actually look better."

"Would you believe an ear infection?"

I stare at him. I'm relieved it doesn't have to do with his

injury and isn't something contagious. But . . . really? "An ear infection? What are you—five?"

He ignores this.

"They gave me some ibuprofen and a prescription. I'm as good as new. Now, let's get out of here."

"Can I talk to your doctor first? Or your physical therapist? Both, preferably. Do they work out of this hospital?"

"No" is all he gives me.

A nurse pokes her head in the door, sees Wyatt, and walks right in. She's pretty and young and smiling up at him. I'm not sure she even sees me.

"You ran off without your discharge papers," she says, a note of playful scolding in her voice. I can almost hear how much she wants to add, *And without my number.*

I reach around Wyatt to snatch the papers from her hand. "Thank you."

Startled, she glances at me. Then does a double take, her jaw popping open before she snaps it closed.

Right—because I look like someone injected me with gelatin.

"Do you need anything else?" I ask, meeting her gaze head-on until she starts to back away. With one last glance at Wyatt, who's watching me, she slinks back through the doorway.

"What was *that*?" he asks, an amused expression on his face.

"I was just trying to scare her off before you called the cops on her for trespassing," I tell him, and his eyes narrow. "Since you seem to be in the habit of doing that to women who come near you."

I start to scan Wyatt's discharge papers, and he tries to snatch them from me. "Hey! Let me do my job."

"It's not your job."

"It is since I agreed to let Jacob hire me as your . . ." I search for the right word. *Nurse* sounds somehow like an innuendo.

Babysitter would just be rude, though not so far off. "As your wrangler. Officially."

Wyatt manages—even with crutches—to corner me between the hospital bed and the wall. His fever may be down, but I feel the heat of his body pressing against me like a brand. I yank the papers behind my back as he reaches for them.

"Josie," he growls. "You know you're breaking privacy laws right now. Give me my papers."

I try to sidestep and he sticks one crutch out, blocking me, swaying a little as he readjusts his weight.

"Your agent has authorized me to help with your recovery," I tell him, shifting the other way. But he steps even closer, until I'm arching backward over the hospital bed as he leans forward.

All this movement is reminding me of my current condition. My feet throb, and it hurts to hold my arm behind my back. Bending with my skin so tight and my body so filled with fluid is not ideal. Even my hand aches from clutching the paper.

But I am not about to give in.

"Josie," Wyatt says again, a note of warning in his voice. His gray eyes narrow, the pupils darkening as he leans closer. "Give me the papers."

"No." It takes all my effort not to say, *Make me.*

But I'm not twelve, playing keep-away.

I'm an adult woman. Trying to help a very stubborn adult man.

We both just happen to be acting like children.

Dropping one crutch, Wyatt leans on the other and reaches around me with his other arm. We're so close it's almost like we're embracing in an uncomfortable contortionist's hug. Wyatt's hand brushes mine, and he pries the paper from my sausage fingers.

"Oh," a voice calls from the doorway. From around Wyatt's shoulder I see Dr. Charlie, papers in hand, gaze sweeping over us, eyes narrowed in disapproval.

His presence in the room sends a shockwave of embarrassment through me because what are we doing? Wyatt and I never behave like this. With all the touching and the . . . wait—are we *flirting?*

Wyatt takes advantage of my momentary paralysis and grabs his papers. Then he takes mine from Dr. Charlie. I'll say this— when he's not feverish, Wyatt sure knows how to get around on his crutches.

Dr. Charlie hesitates in the doorway. "Would you mind if I check on the swelling one last time?"

Before I can politely decline, Wyatt maneuvers in front of me again and uses his crutch and his stormy glare as a blockade. "Yes," he says. "We do mind."

10

Grocery Store Girls

Josie

With the shared stress of the day, my lingering exhaustion from overheating, and the various drugs we've taken, Wyatt and I retire to our separate bedrooms when we get back to the cottage. We stopped for our prescriptions and fast food on the way, riding and eating in almost total silence as the sun set. I can't believe I've been here an entire day already. The whole thing feels like a hazy dream.

I'm out almost immediately after climbing in bed, after only a few seconds of anxious thoughts about the fact that I am *sharing a house with Wyatt*.

I wake up with the sun the next morning, starving and sleep sated. From my bed, I can hear Wyatt's steady breathing, which is heavy but not quite snoring. The weird intimacy of it sends a burst of restlessness through me. With my swelling almost completely resolved, getting out of the house and moving sounds great. It also will put some needed physical distance between me and Wyatt.

The temperature is just warming up and so are the cicadas, who drone on and off sleepily rather than maintaining the consistent buzz that comes in late summer afternoons. I walk to the end of the driveway and, upon seeing zero zombie pigs lying in wait, head to the stop sign and back. I steer *very* clear of the sides of the road and any plants.

When I get back, feeling endorphin happy and summer sweaty, I bypass the cottage and wander down to the dock, where I sit on a wooden bench built right near the end. Even with the heat increasing exponentially by the second, it's peaceful. Something about the light on the waves and the gentle slap of water against the boat calms the skittering nerves that have plagued me almost since I got here.

I could live here. The stray thought slams into me and makes me jump to my feet and head inside.

Because no—I *cannot* live here. At least not more than however long it takes to get Wyatt back on his feet, crutch-free. And if I have my way, it will be as few days as possible.

First step: Get Wyatt to his follow-up appointments.

Which sounds deceptively simple and turns out to be stupid hard.

"No," Wyatt says simply when I ask to speak to his doctor.

"What do you mean, no?"

"I mean," he says, slowly, like spacing out the syllables will help me understand, "no."

We're having this argument, which sounds very much like the kind I'd have with one of the students at my school, in the kitchen. After my walk and a quick shower, I sat down and shoved the blueprints out of the way to write a grocery list. A dire necessity considering the barren state of the kitchen and of my stomach.

Wyatt crutched in a few minutes later, looking disheveled in the way only very good-looking people can. Meanwhile, I've got wet hair starting to frizz and clothes wrinkled from being stuffed in a suitcase. I'm assuming there's no iron in the house.

"Wyatt, that's why my brother has me staying here. My job is to make sure you see the doctor and—"

"No."

"Fine," I tell him. "I won't talk to your doctor. *You* talk to him. Make an appointment, and I'll drive you."

"No," he repeats.

"I don't accept your no," I tell him loftily in a case-closed kind of tone. Even though I'm positive he can out-stubborn me. "We'll circle back to this conversation later."

Because it's too early for this, especially since the only caffeine I've had since I arrived in Kilmarnock was a disgusting cup of hospital coffee I practically had to bribe a nurse to bring me.

"But for now, I'm going to the store." I set down my pencil and fold my grocery list.

And then I almost fall out of my chair when Wyatt says, "I'll come with you."

⚓

At Wyatt's insistence, we end up at the Rivah Maht. I find myself muttering the name over and over in a very bad Boston accent as I walk inside, Wyatt crutching along behind me.

Because this is a thing I do now—I share a house and grocery shop with Wyatt Jacobs.

The teen girl behind the nearest register looks up from a

magazine. She has platinum hair and three eyebrow rings. On a scale of enthusiasm, her expression is about a one-point-five out of ten.

"Welcome to River Mart." She pronounces both words in the proper way, not how the name is spelled, vindictively saying the r's. Picking up a paper, she holds it out to me. "Map?"

"A map? Of . . . Kilmarnock?" I ask.

The main part of the town is like six blocks, if I'm being generous. Maybe more like three.

"A map of the store," she clarifies. "Take it. Trust me."

Before I can explain that I have, in fact, been inside a grocery store in my life, Wyatt appears next to me. The girl's expression shifts to recognition. "Oh," she says, and snatches the map out of reach. "Guess you don't need this."

I don't think I needed it anyway, considering I'm not some grocery store novice. But now I kind of *want* the map. Too bad the employee has disappeared behind one of several empty registers and is flipping through a tabloid magazine.

"Do you come here often?" I ask Wyatt as we move past the register, then huff out a breath when he arches an eyebrow. "I mean literally. Not like a pickup line."

"Yes" is his enlightening answer.

The man has mastered single syllables. He should sell an online training course.

Briefly, I wish for his antibiotic to fail. I vastly prefer feverish Wyatt to this closed-off version. Which is, I guess, his default setting.

For years Jacob has tried to brush off my assessment of Wyatt as a series of misunderstandings. Just like he did the other day with Wyatt calling the cops on me.

But at a certain point, patterns speak to character. You can only chalk up so many incidents as misunderstandings.

It wasn't an accident when Wyatt tagged along with Jacob for my nineteenth birthday, which resulted in two of my friends getting into a fight over him that permanently tore apart my friend group. Or when Wyatt also felt the need to come to my graduation celebration, then got a call about some issue with a sponsor that required him to leave in the middle of dinner, taking Jacob with him as well. No biggie. I didn't need my own brother at my graduation dinner.

And both situations are made worse in the context of the night Wyatt and I met.

During the spring of my freshman year of college, I came home for a long weekend. At the very last minute, my brother decided to come home too. I was thrilled. When Jacob left for college I missed him a ridiculous amount, but inexplicably I missed him even more when I started school.

I got home first, and our house shifted into the usual frenzy of excitement whenever Jacob is involved. My parents and I rolled out all the metaphorical red carpets for my brother. Mom baked his favorite cake—tres leches, which to me is not a cake but a sponge soaked in dairy. The pantry and fridge were stocked with his favorite foods, and I even scrubbed the toilet in our Jack and Jill bathroom, my least favorite chore.

We fell just short of hanging a banner on the front porch. And I think if Jacob had given more than twelve hours' notice, Dad would have made one at the print shop he owns. As it was, he was too backed up with orders for birthday yard signs and a set of car magnets for a steamy romance author featuring a man's glistening and overly muscled torso. (I only know because Dad sent me a selfie with the car magnet, his face next to the abs looking appropriately frightened.)

When Jacob's car pulled into the driveway, however, he

wasn't alone. Mom gasped at the sight of another figure, probably thinking it might be a woman—which would have been a first.

But it was a man who stepped out of the car. Not just technically a man in that he was over eighteen. Where my brother still hadn't outgrown his boyish qualities, Wyatt already looked like a *man*. Both in his build—tall and broad—and the way he carried himself. There was something firmer and steadier about him, something more serious about his eyes. And he had the kind of handsome features normally reserved for A-list actors.

All of which made me suddenly feel very young and very self-conscious.

"This is Wyatt," Jacob said after his required extensive hugging of Mom and Dad. "He plays hockey."

I stiffened at this, but no one noticed. Maybe no one except Wyatt, whose slate-gray eyes stayed pinned on me even as he shook Mom's and Dad's hands.

When Jacob noticed me slipping behind our parents, he yanked me past them and toward Wyatt. "Don't be shy," he said. "Come meet the man who's going to make me rich one day."

Before even finishing high school, my brother decided he was going to be an agent. Once he had this plan, he never wavered. Clearly, Wyatt was aware, as he didn't protest or even react to that introduction.

But when Wyatt held out his hand, I had a reaction. It wasn't about him specifically. More about his size. Who—and what—he reminded me of as he stepped closer, towering over me.

I flinched, taking a big step back, almost behind my brother, like he was going to be a human shield between me and his new best friend.

My reaction, one I hadn't planned but couldn't take back or

explain, seemed to mortally offend him. Though I felt bad, I had no intention of explaining to him or my brother.

I scurried into the house and attempted to avoid Wyatt. The same way I'd avoided all Jacob's jock friends since my junior year of high school. I couldn't skip dinner together, during which I felt Wyatt's heavy stare—*glare?*—on me all the way up until I helped clear the table and retreated back into the safety of my room and its locked door.

When the guys went out for snacks—because the fully stocked kitchen wasn't fully stocked enough—I headed down to the kitchen for hot cocoa. I intended to be back upstairs by the time they returned, but instead was standing there in slippers, fuzzy pajama pants, and a tank top when Jacob stumbled through the back door, shushing a giggling blond I'd never seen before.

"My parents are asleep," Jacob stage-whispered to her, putting his finger on her lips before kissing her quiet.

Leave it to my brother to pick up a woman in a grocery store.

Wyatt stalked in behind them, a tall, disapproving shadow carrying Kroger bags. To my utter shock, our gazes locked, and he gave me a little eye roll, like he and I were suddenly in on a private joke. The butt of which was, of course, my brother the lothario.

That one tiny gesture changed things. And though we didn't talk much after Jacob convinced me to watch a movie with them, it felt for a moment like Wyatt and I had bridged some gap or joined the same team. He didn't sit too close to me on the couch, but he wasn't all the way on the other end either. A good distance.

When I was licking salt off my fingers, Wyatt handed me a napkin. I didn't even mind the feel of his fingertips brushing mine. It actually felt, for the first time in a long time, okay to be touched.

Meanwhile, Grocery Store Girl sat in Jacob's lap, and they made out like we were not in the room. Or in the house at all. For a little while, Wyatt and I pretended like it wasn't happening and just watched the movie, ignoring them and the awkward tension completely. Then Wyatt shocked me for a second time that night by throwing a piece of popcorn at them.

It landed in the back of Jacob's hair, which he was wearing a bit shaggy at the time, and almost stuck. When I giggled, they didn't even stop sucking face. And for the next few minutes, Wyatt and I alternated throwing popcorn at them and pretending to watch the movie. He never smiled, but his eyes seemed to. There was a connection there—at least I thought there was.

When our popcorn bowls were empty and we were halfway through the forgettable action movie with explosions and a beautiful female assassin whose eyeliner never smudged, Wyatt and I stood at the same time, made awkward eye contact, and then left Jacob with his mouth fused to Grocery Store Girl's.

Wyatt lingered in the kitchen, looking at me intently but not saying anything. And I, a person who could usually make small talk with a baked potato, got nervous because he was so cute and so tall and broad. And because I didn't hang out with guys like him anymore. Athletes. With the kind of body shape and size that made me feel powerless all over again.

So, I bolted upstairs.

A few minutes later, I pretended not to hear him on the other side of the Jack and Jill bathroom door, but it was hard to sleep knowing a guy I barely knew was over there—even with my favorite calming music on and my desk chair jimmied under the bathroom doorknob the way I always kept it at night.

Just in case.

Jacob might have trusted Wyatt enough to bring him home, but it wouldn't have been the first time his trust proved misplaced.

I woke up disoriented and very thirsty somewhere around two a.m. and tiptoed down to the kitchen where I ran into something in the darkness.

Not something. Someone. *Two* someones actually—Wyatt and Grocery Store Girl.

For a few seconds, she and I formed a Wyatt sandwich. Me smushed up against his broad back, my nose full of what had to be an expensive cologne, and GSG plastered to his front. Which I'm sure was equally broad and smelled just as expensive.

My sleep-addled brain fired off quick warning signals like *This is a person, not a piece of furniture* along with a few *Does not compute* messages, but for a few seconds, I stayed frozen against Wyatt's spine, trying to make sleepy sense of it.

The situation, not his spine.

I was already in the process of stepping back when Jacob turned on the kitchen lights, leaving me blinking in confusion at Wyatt and his—or rather, *Jacob's*—lady friend. My stomach felt less like a pit and more like an open wound.

I couldn't even look at the man I had felt a sense of camaraderie with and maybe even a spark of attraction toward earlier. He showed me how broken my radar was.

What can only be described as a mild ruckus ensued. Jacob said, "Nadia?" followed by, "Dude. Seriously?"

At which point Grocery Store Girl—Nadia, I guess—slipped out the back door, and I hoped to escape through a hole in the floor, which unfortunately did not materialize.

Dad appeared in the doorway with a baseball bat and no shirt, subjecting us all to the shag carpet on his chest and belly. Mom was behind him, squinting without her glasses and yelling at Dad to put on a shirt before he scared the children.

The only thing Wyatt could say for himself was "She came on to me."

Considering that I was the only *she* in the room at the moment, both my parents' heads swiveled in my direction, multiplying the awkwardness by an infinitesimal amount.

I really, *deeply* wished for that hole in the floor right then. Except, instead of using it for my own desperate escape, now I wanted to push Wyatt into it.

I didn't think the situation could get any more embarrassing. But I realized you should never, ever think to yourself: *It can't get worse than this.*

Because right then Wyatt took a huge step away from me and said, "Not your *sister*."

Maybe he meant to provide clarity. But the horrified look on his face combined with his word choice and the particular emphasis on *your sister* plummeted me to new depths of humiliation. Especially considering how I had sort of thought we were—well, I don't know what I thought we were doing when he shared looks with me, handed me a napkin, and threw popcorn with me. When I thought about all those things, listed out that way, they all seemed so stupid.

I seemed stupid.

So, I did what anyone else in my situation would have done. I said, "I would *never*," and then ran for my room.

Jacob forgave Wyatt. Or he at least made peace with the whole *stealing the woman Jacob plucked from the supermarket like a head of lettuce* thing.

Me? I made zero peace with the way my brother's friend could hook up with the same girl the same night. Or the way Wyatt could build rapport with me, then so quickly and thoroughly dismiss me. From what felt like the start of a friendship maybe, but also from the realm of any eventual romantic possibility.

Not that I wanted romantic possibilities—with him or anyone else. Especially not *that* year.

But did Wyatt have to sound so disgusted by the idea of me?

I returned to college early the next day rather than staying for the whole weekend as planned.

The next year, Wyatt went on to play for the team that had drafted him while he was still in college. Minnesota or Wisconsin or somewhere—I don't remember. Just that it felt far, and I was glad to have half the country between us. Jacob graduated and started working his way up the steep ladder at a killer agency, using his relationship with Wyatt to skip ahead a few rungs.

After that, whenever I was forced to see Wyatt, I kept my distance. Just like I always did with athletes.

And yet . . . Wyatt keeps popping into my life like some kind of recurring rash. Never pleasant. Always leaving me with a lingering itch.

But as I trail behind him now into the first aisle of the Rivah Maht, I have to admit I've maybe softened just a little bit toward him. I definitely feel more comfortable around him.

"You coming?" he demands, turning and giving me a look that would kill a fake plant.

Maybe I haven't softened *that* much.

Very quickly, I realize that the map was, in fact, necessary. Rivah Maht appears to have been organized by someone who had a distinct vision. An artistic vision. One that does not align with practicality or any other grocery store in existence.

It reminds me of how Toni arranges her bookcase: first by author, then by color and height. It's very aesthetically pleasing but not so easy to understand if you're trying to find a specific title. Unless you're Toni.

Normally, I'm good with patterns, but if there's an order to this madness, I can't pinpoint it. Some aisles seemed to be arranged by color. A few times I thought I found a pattern of reverse alphabetization. I was wrong.

"Why would someone do this?" I ask. "I mean, it makes no sense."

"Not to you," Wyatt says, tossing a bag of frozen chicken thighs into the cart.

"And it does to you?" I add a box of mint ice cream sandwiches from the freezer across the aisle. Because ice cream and chicken thighs makes sense. Wyatt wrinkles his nose.

He moves a little ahead of me, leading the way through this madness. He doesn't answer, not that I expected one from Mr. Monosyllabic. I grab a box of cookies. Is it because I think it will bother Wyatt? Maybe.

A few minutes later, while examining the label on a loaf of bread, Wyatt surprises me by saying, "I grew up shopping here with my uncle."

I process this. "And he left you the cottage?" I ask, hoping I'm not prodding too fresh a wound.

"And the boat. We used to sail."

Wyatt is saying so little, but I'm snatching up each breadcrumb of information like a squirrel hoarding for winter. The fact that Wyatt is voicing any of this speaks to the significance of the relationship with his uncle.

"Do you still sail?"

He uses his crutch to point at the boot on his foot. "Not at the moment."

I don't know the first thing about sailing, but I imagine mobility is kind of important. I'd like to ask more questions, but the subject of sailing dropped a dark cloud over Wyatt.

"Is all this really necessary?" Wyatt asks, frowning down at the cart.

"I'm not sure we need ten whole pounds of ground beef, but I don't know how much a guy like you can put away."

"I meant Willy Wonka's chocolate factory." He nods toward the collection of desserts I've accumulated.

"Do you have a problem with sugar?"

Before he can expound on his clearly incorrect judgment of sweets, Wyatt's phone rings. He glances at the screen and heaves a sigh.

"I need to take this. Here."

He readjusts on his crutches to pull out his wallet, but I wave him off. "I'll send Jacob the bill."

With a quick nod, he heads through the automatic doors in the front, sending a wave of heat blasting inside. As I start placing items on the belt, I wonder whose calls Wyatt Jacobs actually takes.

When I'm done checking out, I find Wyatt in the parking lot, pacing in his boot and crutches, a clunky gait. One that seems punctuated with some kind of tense emotion. It's less like he's walking with crutches and more like he's trying to aerate the sidewalk, stabbing it forcefully with each step.

"What's wrong?" I ask as I reach him, readjusting the grocery bags in my arms.

He stops, dragging a hand through his hair and frowning. "My mother is coming."

11

High Society Steamroller

Josie

I do not even consider telling Wyatt *why* his mother is coming, which I suspect is my brother's doing. I texted Jacob right before we left for the store, telling him this job might be short-lived since my patient refused to go to the doctor.

I have a plan, Jacob texted back cryptically. You'll see.

I'm guessing Wyatt's mother is that plan. Kind of a low blow, going directly to someone's mom. Very Jacob.

Also—Wyatt has a mother? I've been wondering about his family this whole time, and some part of me thought Wyatt sprang fully formed from the head of some hockey titan or something.

Not really, but I just can't picture him with a mom and dad. Or siblings. Does he have siblings? Now that I'm thinking about it, I can't wait to meet the woman who gave birth to this enigma of a man.

"I have so many questions for your mom," I tell him as I grab the first load of groceries from the back of the Bronco.

"You will not talk to my mother," Wyatt says forcefully, and hurt pricks me deeper than it has any right to.

My cheeks burn, but I start up the cottage steps, keeping my face turned carefully away from him. The words he just hurled my way land in the center of my chest like a boulder. So—he doesn't want me to meet his mom. Why should he? We're not close.

We're not *anything*.

But it hurts my feelings. For no justifiable reason.

"Right. You don't want me to meet her. That's fine. I can drive into town later. I've been meaning to check out the library. Or stop by the coffee shop. I'll just—"

"No, Josie," Wyatt interrupts.

He crutches up the steps behind me, and I close the door behind us both. "You don't need to explain."

"It's not that," Wyatt says.

We stand there in the living room, just a few feet between us. It's too close, especially considering how much physical space Wyatt takes up. He's not a bull in a china shop, but more like a water buffalo stuffed into a coat closet.

"I know it's weird having me here. Being your nurse or your handler or whatever you want to call it. You don't even have to tell your mom about me. I'm just here because Jacob hired me."

"You don't understand," he says. But that's all he says.

I wait a few more long seconds, eyebrows raised, inviting him to help me understand. When he doesn't, I brush past him to get more groceries. He's standing in the same place when I return with the last of the bags.

"Things are complicated with my family," Wyatt grits out

finally. "It's not that I'm embarrassed about you. It's more that my mother is . . ."

"Awful?" I suggest. "Judgmental? Grumpy?"

Wyatt frowns, though I can't be sure if he suspects I'm listing qualities in him that might be shared with his mother.

"She's *a lot*," he says.

"Does she bite?"

He breathes out a laugh. "Not literally."

"Will she get the wrong idea about me being here?"

I don't elaborate, but I think Wyatt gets my unspoken question: *Will she think we're dating? Or get hopeful and try to play matchmaker?*

It's a common parental tactic. My own parents have tried it several times with a number of men. Obviously, my single status is living proof they've had zero success.

"Maybe. But that's not why I'm concerned. She's kind of like . . ." He shifts, briefly putting weight on his booted foot before readjusting. "Kind of like a high-society steamroller."

I snort. "That is a very specific description."

"Yeah, well, it's apt."

"I'm not worried about being steamrolled. When will she be here?"

"Probably in the next two hours."

"That's fast. Where does she live?"

He pauses, then glances out the front window. "My family lives in Richmond."

This feels like fake news. Like a statement that needs rigorous fact-checking and would come up short.

I've known Wyatt for *years* without knowing this fact. *My* family is from Richmond. Whenever Wyatt stayed overnight at our house, I got the distinct impression it was because he was visiting from out of town. But he had his own family some-where nearby? This does not compute.

I swear neither Wyatt nor Jacob ever mentioned this.

"Why didn't you ever tell me?"

"I assumed Jacob did," he says. "Does it matter?"

It doesn't, but it's weird to learn we are from the same place but never discussed it. I also feel more than a little guilty that I never asked him something so simple as where he's from.

"Where did you go to high school?" I say now, like this ques-tion will make up for all the ones I never thought to ask.

"Collegiate," he says, naming one of the elite private schools.

Immediately, I can picture it: a younger version of Wyatt in pressed khakis and worn leather Top-Siders like he's wearing now. Even his current hair, barely curling over the collar of his shirt, has the private school vibe. Collegiate had a code for hair length, and every guy I met who went there kept theirs as long as possible, a tiny act of rich-boy rebellion.

"Where do your parents live?" I ask.

He pauses. "Windsor Farms."

One of the oldest of old money neighborhoods. Closer to the city and snootier than even the West End of Richmond, where Collegiate is located. Windsor Farms has huge homes. *Historic* homes. Some even with the white historical marker. It's the epitome of Richmond old money.

"And you're still willing to associate with Jacob and me? Tell me the truth—is the real reason you don't want me to meet your mom because she'll flip if she finds out you're hanging out with someone from the Southside?"

Wyatt rolls his eyes. "She knows where you're from. It's fine." He pauses. "She'll probably want to go to lunch at the yacht club."

"There's a yacht club here? And *you're* a member?"

"Our whole family is. My parents have a place in Irvington."

"Another little murder cottage?"

He snorts. "Hardly. More like a giant murder mansion. Without the murder."

"Fancy."

Not meeting my eyes, he says, "My family owns the Jacobs Restaurant Group."

I blink at this. Everyone from Richmond knows the Jacobs Restaurant Group. They own a huge number of—*duh*—restaurants around the city. Many of them the finer dining establishments in trendy, historic places like Carytown and Shockoe Bottom. They've even expanded, adding a handful of restaurants to the booming Short Pump area, where everything is shiny and new.

If I thought the information about Wyatt living in Richmond was a lot, trying to absorb this new tidbit is like attempting to swallow a watermelon whole.

"*You're* Jacobs Restaurant Group?" I ask.

He makes a face. "My dad and brother run it. Not me."

I stare openly at him, trying to reconcile this information with the man beside me. Who is, I'm coming to understand, way more of a mystery than I ever thought.

Not that I've spent much time pondering Wyatt's existence. Other than the times I had to see him when he was hanging out with Jacob, Wyatt didn't occupy much of my headspace. When we were around each other, I was mostly playing the avoidance game, not trying to figure out the grumpy enigma that is Wyatt.

Now I know he grew up with a sterling silver spoon for a pacifier and family money before he had hockey money. And when I ate at any of the popular restaurants in town, I was doing my part to fund Wyatt's private school education.

"Okay, so don't mention my Southside roots and put on my good pearl earrings—check and check. But if me being here makes things more complicated for whatever reason, I'm happy to leave."

"I don't want you to leave."

"Okay," I say slowly, feeling far too happy at his words.

He's not exactly saying he wants me to stay, I remind myself.

Also, I don't need to be scrambling for Wyatt's scraps. It's stupid. And I never felt this way before, so I'm not sure why I suddenly *almost* care what he thinks about me and whether his mom will like me.

⚓

It takes all of five minutes for me to understand Wyatt calling his mother a high-society steamroller. She sweeps into the cottage in a cloud of expensive-smelling perfume, perfectly coiffed blond hair, and rib-fracturing hugs for us both.

I wasn't expecting the embrace but especially not the force of it, which squeezes an awkward squeak out of me. She doesn't fully release me but holds me at arm's length, her eyes warm as she studies me as though we're long-lost friends.

"I'm so thrilled to *finally* meet you," she says, clearly laying the Southern charm on thick to match her accent.

People who haven't spent much time in the various regions may not realize how many Southern accents there are—from twangy to lilting to the crisp and sophisticated Southern belonging to Mrs. Jacobs. It's what I think of as the aristocratic Southern accent, which is both melodic and posh. Like her words have been coated in a very rare and very expensive warm honey.

I'm not sure how Wyatt escaped without it when his mother's

is so strong. I don't have much of an accent, but then, neither do my parents.

"It's lovely to meet you too, Mrs. Jacobs." I don't clarify her use of the word *finally*, though I'm sure she didn't know I existed until whatever Wyatt told her on the phone this morning.

"Oh, you must call me Susan," she says, waving a hand and nearly blinding me with not one but several diamonds. "I am so grateful you're here taking care of my Wyatt. Heaven knows he won't take care of himself."

She's got that right. But I don't agree out loud. It feels oddly disloyal. Wyatt's usually hard-to-read expression is pure gratefulness when I meet his gaze.

I also suspect from her cavalier comment that Mrs. Jacobs has no idea how bad things were just yesterday. I try to imagine her reaction to the overflowing garbage bags I took out yesterday morning or Wyatt's feverish state. And let's not forget my fluid-filled body. I'm intensely grateful all of that has subsided.

"Your brother is simply wonderful," Mrs. Jacobs—*Susan*—says. "I offered to adopt him, but he said he couldn't go by the name Jacob Jacobs."

That—and he's not exactly an orphan. More like the king of our family. But it's on brand that Jacob would have other families clamoring to draw him in. The man could charm a snake charmer.

I'm about to say something regarding my brother when I notice Susan has gone quiet. Her mouth is a tightly closed line as her eyes scan the room. It's then that I think about the significance of this house to her.

Though Wyatt didn't say which side of the family his uncle was from, based on her reaction to being here, I'm guessing Tom was Susan's brother. It's hard to reconcile the idea of someone so polished being close with someone who called the murder cottage home. But as I know from personal experience, siblings can be completely different but still be close.

"Mom," Wyatt says quietly, and he manages to balance on one crutch while putting an arm around her waist.

The tightness eases from her face, softening as she looks up at him, nodding once, then a few more times until the gesture seems to move from *I'm okay* to *No, really—I've got this.*

It's far too intimate a moment for me to be witnessing, and I must shift as I consider sneaking out of the room because the floor betrays me, giving a loud groan. *Tattletale.*

Wyatt's eyes meet mine as his mother slips from his embrace.

"You simply *have to* join us for lunch at the yacht club," Susan says, her exuberance returning full force.

Wyatt's face behind her shoulders is clearly communicating what looks like a *no, you simply do* not *have to join us* vibe.

Which only makes me more amenable to the idea. Something about giving Wyatt a hard time gives me a wicked dopamine high.

Also, his mom is kind of awesome. Her attention might be intense, but it makes me feel special. I find myself surprisingly eager to be steamrolled.

"I'd love to," I tell her, ignoring Wyatt's deep sigh.

I'm grateful I had time to shower and change before she arrived, though I'm not sure my black pants and top are yacht club material. Susan clearly thinks I look just fine. While I was putting away groceries, Wyatt changed from athletic shorts into khaki pants, a belt, and a button-down shirt. All of which emphasize his athlete's build. Normal thighs don't stretch the bounds of common decency in a pair of khakis.

"You made your mom sound scary," I whisper to Wyatt as I lock up the cottage. His mother is already in her Jaguar, checking her perfect makeup in the visor mirror. "I like her."

Wyatt only snorts a response as he folds himself into the back seat.

Susan Jacobs is a *terrible* driver. The kind where I can't decide if it's better to look at the road to be prepared for imminent death or close my eyes and hope for the best. Thankfully, there are no pigs in our path when she peels out of Wyatt's driveway in a spray of oyster shells. She would have mowed them down without a thought to her undercarriage or anything else.

I spend most of the ten minutes it takes to reach Kilmarnock proper trying to discreetly hold on for dear life as she disregards speed limits completely and uses the brakes as though they're optional tools only for sissies. Turn signals absolutely don't exist, and she seems to consider other cars like they're gnats— annoying and inconsequential. She passes more than one slow driver, even over double yellow lines, while I clutch at the car door.

I'm grateful when we reach Kilmarnock's North Main Street, which necessitates a substantial slowing down. It's impossible to speed through with the pedestrians and a tiny traffic jam of cars.

"You know what," Susan says, suddenly jerking the car into a space reserved for accessible parking. The front right tires bump the curb while the back end of the car is very much still out in traffic. "I love this little shop. And we've got some time before our reservation!"

"Mom," Wyatt warns.

"They've always got the cutest earrings, and I need some for a charity auction this weekend," she continues, completely ignoring her son. "Josie, come in with me! You'll love it."

Somehow, I doubt that I'll love it. Any store that carries the perfect earrings for a charity auction is probably not going to be a mainstay for me.

"You can't park here, Mom," Wyatt says.

She lowers her sunglasses, turning to give his boot a pointed look. "We may not have a permit, but I'd like to see any cop who'd argue we can't use this space with your injury."

I briefly consider telling her the police will let Wyatt do just about anything he wants because they're total fanboys. Considering the way she acted like she'd been dying to meet me, Wyatt obviously told her about me. But there's no way he included a description of me being shoved into a cop car. Or our joint hospital visit, which I'm also happy to keep under wraps.

"Not sure it counts if I'm not getting out of the car," Wyatt says. "And having crutches isn't the same as having a permit."

She waves him off.

"I can just wait here with Wyatt," I say, but she's already slammed her door and hustled around the front of the car in her navy dress, which probably came straight from Saks.

"Have fun shopping," Wyatt says, a note of something in his voice—warning? Amusement?—as Susan flings open my door and tugs me from the car with the strength of a much younger woman. Or an older woman who plays tennis five times a week. "Come, come. Just us girls! We'll be quick."

Before we enter the store, I turn and mouth *Help* at Wyatt. He lifts his hand like Katniss Everdeen, and I swear I see the smallest smile on his face.

Then Susan and I are inside the boutique, which at first glance is clearly out of my price range. More like out of my price galaxy. She must see my look of horror when I glimpse a price tag because she takes my hand and drags me farther into the store.

"Oh, don't pay attention to the numbers," she says, her laughter like a little bell. I don't have time to argue as Susan greets the younger woman who walks out from behind the counter with a smile. "Anna! So lovely to see you again! We'll need a dressing room."

"For earrings?" I ask.

The first thread of unease weaves through my belly. The two of them ignore me.

"I'll get one started for you," Anna says. "And what can I help you find today?"

Susan turns her attention toward me, and both women look me over. My unease deepens. I'm wearing black slacks and an emerald-green top that's not a name brand but looks expensive (according to my mother). It's the nicest outfit I packed, aside from a sundress, which felt a little too skimpy around the shoulders for brunch at the yacht club. Suddenly, I feel like I got dressed in the dark with clothing found in a donation bin.

"Let's see," Susan says. "You're a size six?"

My cheeks are hot. "What? I mean, yes, but—"

"Size six," she tells Anna. "Color, prints—nothing muted. That emerald with your hair! Gorgeous."

Anna is already moving through the store, collecting items on velvet-padded hangers. Dresses, blouses, skirts, pants all stack up on her arm.

"Wait," I say.

But Susan takes my hand, shaking her head with a sad *tsk*. "I have two boys, neither of whom have settled down. Which means no women to shop with—can you imagine! This is so fun for me. Thank you for being willing."

She's thanking *me?*

"Please," she says, squeezing my hand. "Do this for me?"

I feel a sudden thickness in my throat and nod quickly, ducking into the dressing room. Am I about to cry because Wyatt's mother has essentially taken me hostage for a ridiculously expensive shopping spree that she's somehow twisted into a giant favor *I'm* doing for *her*?

Yes. Yes, I am.

It is at this point I realize I have been one hundred percent steamrolled.

I also realize that I've unknowingly harbored a secret hunger for a mother-daughter shopping spree. My mother's wardrobe is ninety-nine percent from catalogs like Talbots or Coldwater Creek. Back-to-school—or any other—shopping consisted of her giving me a credit card and a firm limit while she read a book in the mall food court while I shopped alone. No one to zip me up or help me out of a too-tight dress or tell me which pants were more flattering.

It's not like my mom—or dad—neglected me. I mean, sure, Jacob sucks up ninety percent of the attention in any room and consistently did so with our family, but my parents are great. Fantastic. Slightly distracted and physically distant with all their RV-ing and before that, their other hobbies, but still wonderful. Maybe it feels a little like once my brother and I were out of the nest, they set the nest on fire and moved on to another tree, but it's not like there's bad blood or trauma I can complain about. Sometimes I just miss my mom.

Which leaves me here, emotion climbing its way up my throat while trying on a dress I definitely can't afford.

I just can't remember a time I ever had either of my parents' complete focus like this. Or the level of delight Susan seems to take in something so small and simple. Especially considering I've known her for all of twenty minutes.

I guess this is a dream unrealized for me too—even if it is Wyatt's mother.

He must take after his dad.

"You okay in there?" she calls as I work up the side zipper.

"I've just got the first dress on. Do you . . . want to see it?"

"Of course I want to see it," she says, and I can hear the smile in her voice. "What fun is it if you don't model for us? Don't be shy."

Drawing in a breath and making sure my tears are tucked away, I do.

Susan wasn't kidding about this being a quick stop. She shops like it's a sprint—on which the fate of the world hangs. Twenty minutes later, I've tried on half the store and am leaving with several bags and wearing a new dress, new shoes, and a new necklace.

None of which I paid for.

I couldn't have stopped her if I tried. And her absolute joy over the whirlwind shopping spree made me not want to.

Wyatt's smirk tells me he knew exactly how this would go. Like he was well aware that his mother's master plan was not to find auction earrings after all but rather to force an almost complete makeover on me. My hair is even twisted up into a fancy knot with a new clip. If the store had sold cosmetics, I'm sure I'd have a whole new line of that as well.

I climb into the car first while his mother puts the bags in the trunk. "Don't say a word," I tell Wyatt in a quiet voice.

"Wasn't going to."

I raise an eyebrow and twist to peer back at him. "You weren't going to say *I told you so*?"

"Do I even *need* to say it?"

"Say what?" Susan asks, climbing behind the wheel again. She touches up her lipstick, a coral color that looks great against the olive skin tone she and Wyatt share. "How beautiful Josie looks? She's stunning, Wyatt. Don't you agree?"

Wyatt makes a noncommittal noise from the back. I want the leather seat to open up and swallow me whole.

"Thank you," I say again. To Susan, not Wyatt, since not even his mother can drag a compliment for me out of him. Best to pretend she never asked him. "I really—"

"Nonsense," Susan says, waving me off without hearing the rest of what I was going to say. Then she swivels in the seat, her eyes fiery as she glares at Wyatt. "Wyatt."

"Mother."

"*Wyatt Hamilton Jacobs.*"

I bite back a smile. Even if I don't like her forcing him to say I'm pretty when he clearly doesn't think so, I'm her new favorite person while Wyatt's getting called by his full name.

But the tension in the car stretches to awkward levels, and I wonder if I should get out and let Wyatt and his mom continue their silent standoff alone.

I've just grasped the door handle when Wyatt leans forward, catching my eye. Despite all the eye contact we've made in the last few days, only now do I realize his irises aren't a solid gray. They're mostly gray, but with navy and brown flecks, like a gray hazel. *Grayzel.*

They are hypnotic.

"Josie," he says, voice low and firm.

My *yes* is an unsteady wobble.

"You look beautiful," Wyatt says.

He holds my gaze for another moment before sitting back. I can't tell if he's being sincere or sarcastic. His voice and his expression are too even to know. But my cheeks heat and my stomach dips like I've just gone over the crest of a roller coaster's biggest hill.

It's Wyatt, I try to remind my overloaded nervous system. *Just Wyatt.*

But I think the fact that it's Wyatt makes the compliment mean *more*.

"There." Susan throws the car into Reverse and slams on the gas without looking, to a chorus of honks and screeching brakes. "Was that so hard?"

Yes, I almost tell her. It was probably the hardest thing he's done this week, aside from accepting my help. Still, I find myself turning my head so he won't be able to see my smile.

"Did you get the earrings you needed?" Wyatt asks his mother, his tone indicating he already knows the answer.

"Oh, shoot," Susan says. "Guess I'll have to look when I get back to Richmond."

Or—she doesn't need earrings at all and the whole thing was a ruse. An excuse to take me shopping.

Wyatt whispers, leaning so close to my seat that his breath is a caress on my neck, "Told you—high-society steamroller."

12

Just a Little Girl Talk

Josie

We pull up to the yacht club, and I'm not sure if the man Susan hands the keys to is an actual valet or just an unfortunate yacht club patron who happened to be standing out front. Either way, he is now parking her car. Or stealing it. Guess we'll see after lunch.

Susan links her arm through mine, marching us inside. Wyatt follows, the sound of his crutches on the hardwoods a persistent thump echoing through the tastefully decorated building, which looks more like a grand old mansion than a country club.

Or maybe this is how all yacht clubs are? I wouldn't know.

We get a table upgrade when the view wasn't to Susan's liking and fresh glasses when she sees a smudge on one. Despite what otherwise might be diva-like behavior, Susan charms the staff the same way she charmed me. She's polite and cheerful and firm, giving compliments that feel genuine to every person from our waitress to the older couple a few tables away.

When she turns the full weight of her attention on a person, her gray eyes so similar to Wyatt's but infused with warmth, it seems impossible not to be hungry for more. It's an absolute art she's perfected.

As we settle in with a basket of warm bread and pats of butter shaped like roses, I listen to Susan fuss over Wyatt and wonder why he described his relationship with his parents as *complicated*. Because Susan manages to drag a few small smiles out of Wyatt. Genuine ones.

Maybe Wyatt's father is the complicated part? Or the combination of both parents along with the brother I've never heard of?

"So, Josie," Susan says when she's done fussing over Wyatt and pressing him for details on his recovery, which he only gave in vague terms. She leans forward, resting her chin on her hand and directing the full force of her weighty attention on me. "Wyatt tells me your parents are on an RV adventure and that you and your brother take trips together too—a traveling family! I'd love to know more."

When, exactly, did Wyatt tell her all this? He was only on the phone for like five minutes at the store. I glance at him, but his expression gives nothing away.

I explain a little about my parents retiring, downsizing, and then spending most of the year traveling to places all over the United States in an RV. Talking about them has me missing them with a fierce yank of longing that surprises me. Maybe a little leftover emotion from shopping with Susan.

"And what about your trips with your brother?"

"It's supposed to be an annual sibling trip." I leave out the name we call it, which feels silly to say in a yacht club.

Her eyes sparkle. "Wyatt, did you hear that? I wish you and Peter would consider something like this!"

The quick frown Wyatt tries to hide tells me he has no desire to consider a trip with his brother. More complicated family dynamics, I wonder?

"He's probably too busy with work," Wyatt says, and there's a layer of bitterness edging his voice. Susan doesn't seem to notice. But I file it away under Mysteries to Unravel.

"What would be your dream trip?" she asks me.

"Probably something near the beach. I love being near the water. The ocean, preferably, but I'd take a lake or river."

My ideal vacation would include lazy naps in the sun with a book in hand and a cold drink within reach. The refreshing feel of rinsing salt and sunscreen off at the end of the day, cold water a shock on my warm skin.

"Wyatt has always loved the ocean," Susan says, her expression turning mischievous. "You two have that in common."

"Mom," Wyatt groans.

"Which reminds me," Susan goes on, releasing my hand as she turns to Wyatt. "Have you worked out a solution for *your* trip?"

Wyatt's planning a trip?

His gaze is fixed firmly on the tablecloth as he drains half his water glass.

So it's a trip he doesn't want to talk about, then. At least not with me around.

We're momentarily interrupted as the waitress brings our food, and I can tell Wyatt is hoping this distraction will be enough to make his mother forget her question. She doesn't.

"Well?" she asks the moment our waitress is out of earshot.

Wyatt sets down his fork, still chewing an enormous bite of pasta he put in his mouth, I think in hopes it would keep him from having to answer. Wiping his mouth, he slides a quick glance my way before focusing on his mother. "It's not happening. Obviously."

Susan tilts her head, eyes and voice soft. "Are you sure? I know there are some people you could hire to—"

Wyatt shakes his head. "Maybe next year."

"What trip?" I ask, knowing full well I'm butting into a conversation Wyatt doesn't want to have in front of me. Or *with* me. But having his mom as a buffer doses me with a little more confidence.

His frown deepens, and he takes another bite of pasta rather than answering.

But the benefit of asking with Susan around is that if Wyatt won't answer, his mom will.

"Wyatt was going to sail down the Intracoastal this summer. All the way to Georgia."

I don't really know what the Intracoastal is, though it sounds vaguely familiar. Like something I maybe *should* know but can't remember.

"Did you even tell Josie that you sail?" Susan asks.

Wyatt shrugs. It's the shrug of someone who not only knows how to do something but can do it expertly. "I told her."

"Oh, don't be modest." Susan turns to me with a laugh. "He's been sailing since he was knee-high. My brother taught him. Wyatt won several youth sailing championships. Then hockey became his full-time focus and sailing became just a hobby."

Wyatt only grunts at this, his attention fixed on what must be the most interesting plate of pasta in the world.

I guess I shouldn't be surprised that he's some champion sailor. I know very little about him personally—his likes or dislikes, hobbies, dating life. What I *do* know is that my brother once called Wyatt a driven machine and said that anything he did, he did expertly. Whatever it took. He'd put in more hours and push himself harder than anyone else.

It's one reason I think my brother attached himself to Wyatt early on. They were friends, yes, but my brother always had his own master plan in mind.

Because Jacob calling Wyatt *driven* was a classic pot-and-kettle situation.

"Do you sail?" I ask Susan.

She laughs. "Not even a little. I don't know a flying jib from a flying monkey."

I don't even know what a jib is, so she's ahead of me there.

"Yachting is more her speed," Wyatt says with a small smile, and Susan shushes him like he just announced that she's a frequent rewards member at Red Lobster.

"Hush, now. I may not sail, but your uncle and I spent our weekends and summers paddling a canoe up through the creeks and marshes around Fort Eustis," Susan says, straightening her shoulders.

Fort Eustis . . . Was theirs a military family? I wonder. I can picture it suddenly—the vivacious woman in front of me as a girl. Her hair a lighter blond, sun-bronzed skin, a baseball cap on her head and an oar in her hand. Maybe a row of string friendship bracelets up her arm instead of pearls on her neck.

The mental image makes me ache. It also makes me like Susan all the more.

"We'd fish and bring home dinner for a week," she adds.

Wyatt's mouth tips up. "Who cleaned the fish, Mom?"

She points her fork at him. "Your uncle mostly. But I *could* have. I just didn't like it, and he was faster with a knife."

Her voice breaks a little at the end, and suddenly the man they both lost is as present at the table as any of us. I want to say something, but no version of *I'm sorry for your loss* seems like enough.

Plus, I suspect neither Wyatt nor his mother want to address it. They wear matching expressions—lips firmly pressed together, jaws tight, eyes focused on their food and only their food. I don't know where to look, but I have a hard time keeping my gaze from Wyatt.

His mother recovers first. "Well," she says brightly, as though hopping back in time before the last few minutes. "Surely, you'll be back on your feet—no pun intended—before the summer ends and can make a trip. Even if it's shorter and—"

"It's fine," Wyatt grumbles. "Excuse me." Tossing his napkin into his chair, he grabs his crutches and makes a slow beeline to the bathrooms. Presumably.

I turn to Susan the moment he's out of sight. I don't even need to ask my questions. They're clearly written all over my face.

Susan leans close and whispers conspiratorially as she grips my hand. "He won't be gone long, so I'll give you the abridged version."

I don't have time to ask, *The abridged version of what?* before she barrels on, still squeezing my hand like it's the life raft keeping her afloat.

"Wyatt was very close with my brother. Big heart, bit of a hermit. You have to understand, Wyatt spent summers here, learning to sail. Doing . . . whatever my brother was into. Tinkering with cars, fishing, sailing. A lot like our summers growing up, I'd imagine."

Again, I see past Susan's designer clothes, diamond earrings, and manicured nails to a woman who grew up on an army base, catching dinner out of a creek.

All this raises more questions, though. Ones I don't feel right asking. Questions about Wyatt's mother and her transition from the girl she was to the wealth she wears now. Questions about why Wyatt spent his whole summers with his uncle, who, in her own words, was something of a hermit.

And a whole company of questions regarding the rest of Wyatt's family: the brother and father who haven't been mentioned. Not once. Silence in this case says more than words would.

I file my questions and concerns away to ponder later as Susan continues. Her eyes flick toward the doorway where Wyatt disappeared a few moments ago. The good thing about his crutches and boot is that he's much easier to spot. And his size already makes him stand out in any room.

"Tom died a little less than a year ago. Left everything to Wyatt." She pauses, her grip growing tighter. There is the slightest bit of moisture in her eyes before she blinks it away. "They had planned to sail down to Georgia together this summer. It's a trip they do—or did—most summers."

"Oh," I say, a flood of emotions rising in my chest. I want to say more. *I'm so sorry* or *That's so sad*, but all the phrases within easy access are too easy. Too trite. So I simply squeeze Susan's hand.

"Wyatt decided to go by himself. And then . . ."

"He got injured," I finished.

She nods and purses her lips. I'm filled with a bone-deep sympathy for her, but even more for Wyatt, whose curmudgeonliness now seems to have a very relatable reason.

He lost someone close to him. Wyatt made special plans to honor him—and it hits me right in the feels to think of Wyatt alone taking the trip he and his uncle should have taken together—then got injured, which ruined everything.

No wonder he was wallowing and not taking care of himself when I got here.

"Which is why I'm so glad you're here," Susan says. "I can already see the difference you've made in his attitude."

I don't bother arguing that the only difference I've really made is forcing him to the hospital and to take his antibiotics. Barely.

She gives a little gasp and then says, "He's coming. This conversation never happened."

Faking a laugh, she presses a hand to her chest and looks believably normal, like she wasn't just whispering secrets to me. Wyatt reaches our table, balancing his crutches carefully on the empty chair and scanning my face as though for clues.

Based on the look he gives me, he found some.

"What were the two of you talking about?" he asks, eyes narrowing.

Susan winks at me. "Just a little girl talk. Isn't that right, Josie?"

"Right," I say, despite not knowing what girl talk with someone like Susan could possibly entail. Maybe why diamonds are a girl's best friend and the long-term benefits of facials.

What I do know is for every question I get answered about Wyatt, five more spring up in their place, leaving me with a ravenous curiosity I wish I could satisfy without becoming more invested. But I suspect I'm already far more invested than I should be.

Especially when I find myself wondering whether Wyatt could take his sailing trip if someone went with him. Someone who was willing but maybe didn't have much boat experience.

Someone like . . . me.

13

Cat-Cow in the Dark

Wyatt

People talk about sleeping like it's something passive—you *fall* asleep or *slip into* sleep. Even saying people *go* to sleep makes it sound like a simple travel destination.

Just follow the road map and go to sleep! Hop on that train! One ticket to sleep, coming right up.

But for me, every night is like waging war. My mind against my body. Or me against my mind—I'm not sure.

All I know is that when my head hits the pillow, my brain decides it's time to wake up. My thoughts won't quiet, and my limbs hum with restless energy. During the season, it's not so bad. My physical exhaustion overrides the thoughts.

Now . . . I can't run. I can't even walk without stupid crutches. And knowing my outlet is gone makes me worry more about sleep, which adds fuel to the dumpster bonfire happening in my head every night.

With Josie sleeping in the bedroom just a few steps away, that challenge is multiplied by infinity.

I knew tonight would be worse after Mom's visit. From the moment I watched her hug Josie practically to death while winking at me over her shoulder, I knew it. The hopefulness in Mom's beaming smile hit me with crushing force.

I caught a glimpse of what could be. More like . . . a glimpse of what I *want* to be.

A giant tease—that's what it was.

Then there's the fact that seeing Mom is always bittersweet. It's impossible to see her without being reminded of my dad and brother.

So it's no shocker that I'm lying in bed with my brain lit up like Times Square and my limbs twitching with the need to *move*.

I'm not the only one struggling to fall asleep tonight. At least based on the sounds I can hear through the completely non-soundproof walls.

There's the frequent squeak of the mattress and now the creak of the floorboards as Josie gets up to go to the bathroom. I'm grateful for the exhaust fan, which is on its last legs and sounds more like an airplane engine. The only thing that could make this whole living situation more awkward would be the inability to mask bathroom sounds.

The exhaust fan turns off, and I listen as the door opens, sounding like something ripped straight from a spooky Halloween soundtrack. Maybe Josie wasn't so far off calling this place a murder cottage.

I can tell she's trying to pad quietly to her room, but it's like trying to walk silently across a marble floor wearing tap shoes. Impossible. Every floorboard seems committed to announcing her next step.

Her bed groans and squeaks again as she settles in, and I press the heels of my hands over my eyes. Trying to force them shut. Trying to force myself not to think about my injury. Or my future.

Or Josie.

Squeak. Squeeaaak.

It sounds like she's violently flailing around in there. And now I'm picturing Josie in bed. I press my hands harder into my eyes until I see stars behind my eyelids.

Squeak. Squeak. Squeak.

"Do you mind keeping it down?" I finally shout, my voice edged with frustration. "Some of us are trying to sleep."

I hear her quiet laugh. "Yes, some of us *are* trying to sleep. But it's impossible to keep it down or sleep in this bed. This mattress is like a giant dog toy."

Her voice is almost as loud and clear as if we're in the same room. Note to self: Whether I renovate this house or build a new one in its place, there *will* be soundproofing. Lots of it.

Squeak.

And better furniture.

I sit up, punching down my pillow. Not because it's un-comfortable, but because I want to punch something. "A dog toy?"

"Yeah. You know, the ones shaped like a hamburger or a bumblebee or something, and they squeak."

As though to demonstrate, it sounds like she's using the bed as a trampoline. *Squeak, squeak, squeak, squeak.* I half expect to hear the crash of the bed breaking apart and hitting the floor. It holds.

But it *does* sound like a dog toy.

I want to laugh. But I don't. Because now, I'm *never* going to sleep. Not when I know how easy it is to have a conversation with Josie from bed, our voices carrying intimately through the darkness.

"Maybe if you stopped flopping around and tried going to sleep, the squeaking wouldn't be an issue," I call.

"Gee, and here I was going to suggest you invest in some new furniture," she says. "But I'll go with your suggestion and just try harder to sleep. How's that working for you, by the way?"

"Every time I drift off, you wake me up with your squeaking."

"Which is the fault of your mattress," she says. "Not me."

"Just *try* being still."

There are approximately five seconds of silence. Interrupted by a *squeeeeeak* and a giggle. "Sorry," she says. "I tried."

I groan and swing my legs over the side of my bed.

And not for the first time since my injury, I stand, forgetting about my jacked-up foot.

Pain shoots through my arch, and I quickly lift my foot, then lose my balance in the process, tumbling to the floor.

I've barely landed on my knees and palms when Josie bursts through my door. Her hands find my back.

"What's wrong? Are you okay? What happened?"

I try to shake her off, but she's as stubborn as a burr, her palms flattening, a warm and comforting press. "Nothing happened. I'm fine."

And I am. Mostly. The pain in my foot subsided as soon as the weight came off it, but my knees ache from taking the brunt of my fall. And I think I have splinters from the roughed-up hardwood floors.

"Something happened or you wouldn't be doing cat-cow in the dark," Josie says.

"Doing what?"

"It's a stretch. Never mind. Did you fall out of bed?" Josie asks.

"No."

"But you're on the floor."

"Gee, I hadn't noticed."

"Save your sarcasm for someone who isn't trying to help you."

"I don't need help."

"Of course not. You're doing just fine," she says.

"I am."

"Obviously."

"Who's being sarcastic now?" I challenge.

"I've earned the right to be sarcastic."

"And I haven't?"

"No," Josie practically growls, tucking her hands under my arms like she thinks she can hoist me up that way. When I don't budge, she leans farther down, her chest against my back as she wraps her arms around my torso and tugs.

And she calls *me* stubborn.

"Just go," I tell her. "I can get up by myself."

"Then why aren't you? Admit it—you're just trying to be difficult."

I don't admit it. Though it may be true.

She grunts, tugging at me again. "I want to help you get up without injuring yourself even more."

"You're more likely to injure yourself trying to help me."

"Says the man still on his hands and knees on the floor."

I'm torn between irritation, amusement, and a pull toward Josie I have no business feeling. But it's hard to suppress any-time she's close. This feels a thousand times more intimate than when she helped me get into bed or to the car when I was feverish. Maybe because now I'm fully cognizant.

I flush with embarrassment thinking of that day. My memories are hazy, like some kind of drug-induced waking dream.

Thankfully, my fever has stayed down since the hospital. Probably because Josie has alarms set on her phone for when I need antibiotics and ibuprofen.

The first time she gave me the meds, she asked me to show her my empty mouth. She's probably been watching too many movies. I glared and refused until she laughed and walked away.

Now I feel bad. About all of it.

She's stuck here with me, and I'm being ridiculously, stupidly stubborn. About everything. I can't even explain why. Am I so desperate for her attention that I'll even take it in the negative form?

Maybe.

And maybe it's time I tried something like kindness and reasonableness instead.

Josie's hands shift on my torso, and I tense. Her fingers have drifted closer than I'd like to the one ticklish spot on my body.

"Stop that," I growl, already forgetting my resolve to be kinder. The threat of tickling will do that to a person.

She tugs again. "*You* stop that."

"Stop what?"

"Stop being a stubborn oaf!"

"An *oaf*?"

"How about you stop fighting and *let me help you!*"

She gives me another tug, this one more forceful. Her hands move even closer to the spot on my upper ribs.

"Josie," I grumble, trying to wiggle away while keeping my torso flexed and mentally willing myself *not* to be ticklish. Mind over matter.

"Wyatt," she snaps back, her fingers shifting and squeezing. "This is ridiculous. Please just—"

It happens. Her fingers hit the exact spot I hoped they wouldn't and a giggle bursts out of me. Not a laugh, but a giggle.

I suck in a breath and clench my teeth.

"Did you just—"

"No."

"But was that—"

"It wasn't."

"A *giggle*. It totally was. You *giggled*, tough guy." Josie laughs, and I feel the vibration of it move through me where she's pressed against my back.

I sit up, taking Josie with me since she's still latched onto me. "I did not giggle."

Her fingers flex, and it happens again. Why am I not laughing like a normal person? Have I ever giggled in my life? I feel certain I have not. And now I can't stop.

The giggles turn into laughter as Josie's fingers move and dance over my T-shirt. Normally, I sleep bare chested, but it felt weird to do so with Josie in the house. Now I'm very grateful for even this thin barrier.

Although I have to wonder if she would have come this close or touched me at all if I didn't have a shirt on. I have a feeling she'd have taken one look at my bare torso and gone running.

That's the thing about Josie—she's bold about so many things. Until she isn't.

Her hands find another spot, then another, moving faster than I can swat them away. I swear she's all arms. Like an octopus. A relentless one.

"Stop," I wheeze through a laugh, twisting to catch one of her wrists in my hand.

"Can't," she pants, doubling down with her free hand. "Too fun."

I'll show her *fun.*

I've been holding back. I mean, the reality is that I've got inches and pounds on Josie. Muscles I've trained and honed for years in the gym and on the ice. Even with my foot injury, someone like Josie is no match for me.

And I don't need my foot for this.

Before she can react, I've spun us, flipping her onto her back. I cup my hand behind her head so it doesn't hit the hardwood. Which means my knuckles take the brunt of the impact. And maybe pick up a few more splinters.

Josie makes an *oomph*, all traces of laughter disappearing as she blinks up at me.

I freeze, hovering over her, one hand under her head and my other circling her wrist. "Are you hurt?"

"Don't think so," she whispers.

We're both breathing hard, like I've pinned her after an hour-long wrestling match, not flipped her like a pancake after a tickle attack.

It's silly. Yet I can't catch my breath. Pressed into the floor under the weight of her head, my knuckles throb. My other hand is still curled around her wrist.

When Josie came in, her hair was in a ponytail, but it's loose now. A pink rubber band sits next to my thumb on the floor. Her hair is everywhere, wild and unfettered in a sweep of caramel. The urge to run my fingers through it hits me with a blast of heat.

Is my fever returning?

Nope. Not a fever.

I'm staring, pinning Josie in place as much with my gaze as with my hold on her. This is as close as we've ever been, and the weight of the moment hangs between us.

Even though Josie is very affectionate with her family, I've noticed her flinch or pull away from the touch of strangers or people she doesn't know very well. Especially men. It's one of the reasons I've rarely touched her over the years, keeping my distance, trying to respect her space.

That distance has been obliterated in the last few days.

But *this* . . . it reminds me of our fight over the doctor's notes. It's playful, with a current of attraction running between us that's different. New.

At least on her side.

Me? It's been my best-kept secret for years.

Too late, I realize Josie still has one free hand. Her fingertips find my ticklish spot again, and I tense. But with a tiny smirk, she ghosts her fingers over my ribs. A threat. Or a tease.

"I wouldn't do that," I warn.

"Oh yeah? Or what?"

Or I just might kiss you.

The desire to do just that crashes over me in a wave. And before I lose the control I've built up with years of practice, I release Josie and push myself back into a seated position. Giving her—and myself—some much-needed space.

She sits up too, scooting back until we're both seated on the floor, facing each other. The dim moonlight casts her skin in silver and shadow.

Beautiful.

"How are you feeling?" she asks in an even tone. Like I imagined the intensity of that moment. "Your fever didn't come back, did it?"

"Do I feel feverish to you?"

She was just plastered to my body, but she reaches out, gently touching the back of her hand to my forehead before pulling away. "Nope. But I wasn't asking because you felt hot. I was asking because you were . . . different. Like you were the other day. A little less . . ."

"Stubborn?"

She gives a little snort. "No. I was going to say less *grumpy.*"

"I'm not grumpy; I'm *reserved.*"

"Is that what we're calling it these days?" She doesn't give me time to answer. "Are you going to let me help you up now, or do I need to tickle you again?"

In answer, I stand in one swift motion, using only my uninjured leg to push myself up. Then I hold out a hand to Josie.

Am I showing off? Maybe a little.

Do I regret it? Nope.

Josie's eyes widen slightly before she frowns at my outstretched hand. "Seriously?"

"You think I'm not able to help you up?"

"But your foot . . ." She trails off as I wiggle the appendage in question, which is hovering an inch above the hardwoods.

"I can stand on one foot and still help you up."

To prove my point, I grasp her hand, wincing slightly as the splinters remind me of their presence in my palm. I tug her up, keeping my weight fully on the one leg, trying to ignore the pinpricks of pain in my hand.

Josie makes no move to step back, and without my crutches, I can't.

I'm not sure I would move anyway.

"What's wrong?" Josie asks, frowning.

"Nothing."

"You winced."

I drop her hand. I didn't realize I was still holding it. The movement jostles however many little pieces of wood are jammed into my palm and a hiss escapes me.

"There!" Josie points at my face. "Is it your foot? Do you need more ibuprofen? Did you hurt your knees falling out of bed?"

"I didn't fall out of bed. That's not what happened."

"Then what *did* happen? Wyatt, you have to talk to me or this isn't going to work," Josie says. "I'm supposed to be helping you."

She *is* helping. She may not know it, and it may not be the kind of help she wants to provide, but Josie is helping.

For the first time since I got to my uncle's empty cottage a month ago, seeing it filled with memories and emptied of most of his things, I'm not waking up with dread cloaking me like a thick fog. I still haven't said yes to the doctor, but today I did do the exercises and stretches he recommended. Just not where Josie could see.

And I *thought* about saying yes. I even pulled out the blueprints while Josie was walking this morning and thought about house plans and what I'll do with this place.

Having Josie here has given me purpose, though I'm still unsure what my purpose *is* or what I want my next steps to be. It's something to be thinking of next steps at *all*.

It's a testament to who Josie is that she's had such an impact on me just from existing in my space. Talking to me. Heckling and arguing with me.

Jacob was a genius for sending her.

An evil genius, but still.

I sigh, putting a slight amount of weight on my other heel so I can sit down on the edge of my bed. The pain shooting through the arch of my foot hurts, and I wonder if I'll ever be able to walk without crutches. Without pain.

I wonder if I'll ever get back on the ice.

"Tell me what hurts," Josie demands, crossing her arms.

For the first time, I take in what she's wearing—a matching T-shirt and sleep shorts in some kind of soft fabric. Blue with fluffy clouds and sunshine. A few dark storm clouds are mixed in, lightning bolts shooting out of them and crisscrossing the backdrop of blue.

So very Josie. Sweetness and light but with a fighting edge.

I jerk my eyes back up to hers, which are narrowed in on me. Like she's trying to figure me out.

Can't have that.

"My foot is fine. I actually fell trying *not* to put weight on it, so it's okay," I say finally. Then I clear my throat and hold out my hands. "But how much experience do you have with splinters?"

Josie grins, and I feel that smile reach all the way through me. "Splinters just so happen to be one of my strengths."

14

Good Patients
Get Lollipops

Josie

"May I ask why you travel with a headlamp?" Wyatt says.

"You may."

I don't look up at him, keeping my focus on the tiny sliver of wood I'm trying to grip with my eyebrow tweezers. I might need to invest in a new pair after this. I'm sitting on the edge of the coffee table and he's on the couch, his forearms braced on his thighs. When he's not jerking his hands away from me, that is.

After a moment, he sighs. "Why do you travel with a headlamp, Josie?"

Almost on instinct, I adjust the headlamp in question, which I happened to throw into my bag at the last minute. When Jacob is planning a trip, you just never know. I didn't expect it would help me extract splinters from a hockey player's hand, but here we are.

There are splinters of varying sizes in both of Wyatt's palms. I have three more to go before switching hands. Though with the way Wyatt keeps twitching and jerking away from me, we'll be here all night.

"Hold still," I order when he flinches. I tighten my grip on his hand. The man might get bodychecked for a living, but he's not so good with splinters. "Jacob didn't exactly tell me what we'd be doing for the trip I *thought* I was going on with him. He likes to surprise me. I packed accordingly."

"You packed like you thought your brother might want to go spelunking?" Amusement colors Wyatt's voice, and when I glance up to try to catch a smile, the headlamp shines right in his face. He puts a hand in front of his eyes.

"Sorry." I tilt the lamp down slightly and shift my focus back to his hand. "Good point. I can't see Jacob purposefully entering a cave. Maybe if he fell in one?"

"Or was being chased by a bear. They probably don't make designer spelunking suits," Wyatt muses.

I tilt my head a little more, hiding my smile. "Then Jacob definitely wouldn't go. In any case, I'm glad I packed the headlamp. Even if I didn't expect to use it for this."

I go quiet, needing complete focus as I try to grip the smallest of the splinters on Wyatt's palm, right near what I think is his life line. Or is it a love line? I don't know much about reading palms.

Or about Wyatt's life. Or love life. I've never seen so much as a tabloid picture of him with a woman—not that I went looking—but I assume he must have had girlfriends over the years.

What I do know is that he has really nice hands. Big. Strong.

Long fingers with calluses on the tips. I've become very ac-quainted with them in the last half hour, and I approve.

"So what *have* you done on your trips with Jacob? You didn't say over lunch. Not caving, obviously."

It seems weird to me that Jacob wouldn't have told Wyatt something about our trips. But then, I wonder how much of their relationship is still based on friendship now rather than work.

"They've mostly been disasters. We did Miami first, which was great for Jacob since he loves nightlife and clubs. Fine for me because I like the beach."

"But you don't like clubs."

My skin prickles at his confidence. It's a statement, not a question. I've always assumed Wyatt ignored me the same way I tried to ignore him. Instead, I'm starting to get the feeling he was paying a lot more attention than I realized. Like he *knows* me. At the same time, I think this is the first conversation where he's asked any questions about my life.

Actually, this feels like our first real grown-up conversation. And it's kind of . . . nice. I swallow and try to keep my focus from drifting to his impossible-not-to-find-handsome face.

"Not clubs," I agree. "Though I do make an excellent desig-nated driver and semi-decent wingwoman."

"Not an *excellent* wingwoman?"

"No." I smile at the memory. "People kept assuming we were a couple. I thought it was funny. Gross—but funny. Jacob did *not* find it amusing at all."

"I'll bet."

I suddenly wonder if Wyatt has ever been Jacob's wingman or vice versa. If the two of them ever went out together, looking to meet women. I drop the tweezers.

Leaning over to pick them up, I clear my throat and continue.

"For the next trip we went to the resort in Virginia where they filmed *Dirty Dancing*—"

"Jacob picked *Kellerman's*?"

I pause and look up at him. "You're a *Dirty Dancing* fan?"

Wyatt crosses his arms. "I've seen it."

"Enough times to know the name of the resort. Interesting. *Very* interesting. Do you happen to know any of the dance numbers? Or the songs? It's got a killer soundtrack."

Wyatt mumbles something under his breath while giving me a cool stare. I laugh and go back to his splinters.

"Anyway, I'm pretty sure Jacob didn't realize until we got there. He found a good deal, which we discovered was because it was mostly under construction. There was nothing to do—well, except family games and crafts. Which I enjoyed but . . ." I shrug.

"Jacob did not. I'm sensing a theme—you and Jacob don't have a lot in common."

"Not particularly. It's kind of funny how he plans the trips—usually based on what *he* likes—but then ends up unhappy. The last one was a cruise where we got norovirus. We both came back paler and five pounds lighter. And then there's this trip. Which is . . ."

I trail off, unsure what words to use. Not a sibling trip at all. But . . . surprisingly fine? Norovirus-free? Enjoyable despite me not wanting it to be?

"I'm sorry," Wyatt says.

"This isn't your fault. I don't think Jacob had any intention of taking a trip this summer. He just used it as an excuse to get me to do what he wanted."

I can't quite keep the bitterness from my voice. Or the little tremble at the end.

Because yeah—I'm going to get a down payment for a house

out of it. I should focus on that. Not the fact that my brother basically tricked then ghosted me.

But I got excited about taking a trip with him. Nervous too, as I always feel when I travel or dip a toe into the water outside my comfort zone. I miss my brother. And it feels a little like I got stood up. I should be mad, but instead I'm just a little sad about it.

That's the thing with family—they're like a bunch of stubborn splinters. Really difficult to remove, even if you sometimes want to.

"Josie." Wyatt's voice is soft. Briefly, he shifts his hand, brushing his fingertips over my knuckles and letting them rest there. "I really am sorry you're stuck with me."

Hearing him say it—even if I've *thought* it—makes me feel protective of him. And angry all over again with my brother.

"I'm not stuck with you. Even if Jacob got me here using false pretenses, I'm *choosing* to stay."

"For money," he clarifies.

I hesitate. "In part."

The reality is . . . I'm staying for more than the money. Maybe I didn't realize it until he said it, but I'm here for Wyatt now. I'm unexpectedly invested in his recovery. And if someone had told me I'd feel this way three days ago, I'd have laughed while calling them a liar.

Honestly, I've barely thought about the money. As excited as I was at the idea of a down payment, I haven't looked once at the real estate sites bookmarked on my laptop and phone. Sure, I haven't had much time, but I've had *enough*. At home I sometimes scroll the sites a few times a day just to see new listings or what's gone under contract.

Looking for a house just hasn't been on my mind. Or . . . something.

Taking Wyatt's hand again, I start back in on the splinters.

"Jacob aside, do you usually travel or take trips with friends during the summer?"

Friend, my brain silently corrects. Sad as it is, Toni is my only real friend. I have lots of acquaintances, but my friendship standards are high, I guess. Plus, no one tells you how hard it is to make friends once you're out of college and in the real world, the working world.

"No."

"Really? All summer off and no vacation? Nothing for *you*?"

It does sound sad when he puts it like that. But I wouldn't expect a man with a multimillion-dollar hockey contract to get it.

"I usually tutor during the summers." I can hear the defensiveness in my voice. "Just to pick up a little extra income."

"You don't usually— Ow!"

Wyatt yanks his hand to the side because maybe I wasn't as gentle as I should have been just now. The splinter breaks into two tiny pieces. An almost microscopic bit remains between the points of my tweezers, but most is still lodged in his hand, which he's now clutching to his chest like an injured paw.

"Maybe we should leave them. They'll eventually absorb into me, right?"

"That's not a thing. They'll drive you nuts until I remove them," I tell him. "Hand?"

I hold out my own, palm up, trying to meet his gaze without blinding him with the headlamp again. With a sigh, he drops his big hand onto my smaller one. But he continues flinching every time I come at him with the tweezers. I wish I had a roll of duct tape or a horse tranquilizer.

"You are a terrible patient," I tell Wyatt as he tries to jerk his hand away from me. Again. "And that's saying something considering my usual patients are under ten years old. Be *good*."

"If I'm good, will I get a trophy?" he asks.

"No."

"A medal?"

"Nope."

"A ribbon?" he asks. "You do this for elementary school kids. Surely you've got a stash of rewards for them."

"My good patients get lollipops."

"I'll take a lollipop."

I smile at the mental image of Wyatt with a lollipop in his mouth. "Sadly, I did not pack lollipops. Even if I did, you wouldn't deserve one with all your arguing and the way you keep jerking your hand away." He pouts. "If you're lucky, your reward will be a splinter-free hand. But to get that, you'll have to *stop moving*."

I'm still trying to wrap my head around this—the fact that Wyatt has a whole other personality hiding beneath his perpetually grumpy exterior. There's even *humor* under there. I wonder what else I'll find if I keep excavating. I doubt I'll see the uninhibited, goofy version of him brought out by his fever again.

And that may not have really been *him*. I mean, calling me pretty? Pretending he couldn't lift his leg so I'd have to touch him? None of that seems like the Wyatt I've known for years. The phrase is *in vino veritas*, not *in* fever *veritas*. It felt more like a glitch in the Matrix than the truth seeping out.

All that aside, Wyatt is a *little* softer now. And I'll take it. Anything to make this unplanned and definitely unwanted wrench in my summer more tolerable. Maybe even enjoyable.

The whole idea of enjoying time with Wyatt sends a skittering sort of worry up my spine.

I may enjoy the banter we've had going, but it's best to keep Wyatt in the neat box I've assigned him to. He's my brother's best friend and client. A surly grump who doesn't like me.

And, finally, an athlete, which, for me, comes with its own box wrapped in caution tape and barbed wire with a neon-yellow Danger sign.

If I'm being honest, already the few days I've spent with Wyatt have dismantled all those things. Snipping through the barbed wire, pulling off the caution tape, unplugging the sign. There's a crowbar on the edge of the box, working it open.

No one is more shocked by this than me.

Wyatt hisses as I dig the tweezers in and come out with an intact splinter. The last few kept breaking, which meant it took longer and I had to root around more. I know that didn't feel good. Amazing how something as tiny as a sliver of wood can cause so much discomfort.

"Check this one out," I tell him, holding the tweezers closer to him. "All in one piece. See what happens when you stay still?"

He only grunts.

I drop the piece into a cracked white coffee mug I found in the kitchen. Once I finish his hands, I should probably check his knees. He didn't mention anything about them, but if he landed on hands and knees when he fell, there might be splinters there too.

Apparently, these floors aren't to be messed with. I've been walking around barefoot but probably need to use my flip-flops. Or buy some slippers. I try to grasp the end of the next one, and Wyatt's fingers close around my hand holding the tweezers.

"That's good enough."

I level him with a look, and he sighs, releasing me and opening his hand again. "You know what you remind me of?" I ask.

"No, but I'm sure you'll tell me."

"The crocodile who had a toothache."

He furrows his brow. "What?"

"It's a children's book about a big, powerful, scary crocodile who is totally debilitated by one tiny tooth. Or, I guess, one *big* tooth. But still."

Wyatt's hand is heavy in mine. Warm. His skin is smooth, other than the calluses. I've stopped myself more than once from tracing over them, my curiosity urging me to map them out. Or to ask about them. I'm sure they come from handling a hockey stick for years.

"What happens to the crocodile in the story?" Wyatt asks.

I drop Wyatt's hand for a moment, stretching out my fingers before letting my hands flop into my lap. Suddenly, I'm aware of how close we are. I was in professional mode, focused only on the splinters.

Now . . . our closeness feels far too intimate. Especially with his heavy-lidded, sleepy but interested eyes and mussed hair. The fact that we're both dressed in pajamas only adds to the effect. I tug my shorts down my legs.

But I can't back up now without drawing attention. It's no closer than we were in his bedroom when he flipped me on my back and hovered over me in a way that sent a tidal wave of fluttery feelings through me. As though my whole body became a sanctuary for butterflies who were performing some kind of synchronized flight. It was both pleasant and mildly nauseating.

While I was rooting around in my bag for my headlamp and tweezers, I shut down the butterfly sanctuary, mentally hanging a Closed sign on the door. Of all the men in the world, Wyatt isn't one I can feel that way around.

This moment in the living room is thankfully missing the tension I'm sure was one-sided in Wyatt's room. But there's a different kind of intimacy in our closeness and conversation as I tell Wyatt children's stories and answer his questions about me. Mentally, I add this to the charges I plan to send my brother.

Thinking better of it, I erase it from the list. This isn't for Jacob or his money.

"Well," I say slowly, tugging on the hem of my shorts again, "the crocodile roars from the pain, which scares all the other animals, who think the crocodile is angry. They won't come near him. Except for one tiny little mouse."

I pause, searching Wyatt's expression for any sign he's bored. Or just making fun of me. But he seems oddly invested, his gray eyes unwavering on mine.

"So, what happens?"

"The mouse scampers right up to the crocodile, climbs into his mouth, and pulls out the tooth. Instantly, the crocodile's pain is gone."

"Let me guess," Wyatt says. "Then the crocodile eats the mouse?"

I laugh. "Um, no. Clearly you haven't read enough children's books."

Something flashes across his face, there and then gone. Too quick for me to pinpoint. Especially when trying to read him is like staring at a book written in some foreign language.

But my teasing struck some kind of nerve. I'm not sure how or what, but I file this away to think about later. When it's not almost midnight and I'm not playing actual nurse.

"The crocodile thanks the mouse and they throw a party." I make a face. "I think it's based on the fable of the lion with the thorn in its paw. That story ends with a lesson about . . . something. Kindness, maybe? But I'm really tired of the trend where every children's book must be didactic."

"Didactic?"

I blush a little, realizing I'm totally going off about my pet peeves regarding children's literature to Wyatt. But he *did* ask, and I don't see anything but sincerity in his expression.

"Didactic means having some kind of moral or lesson to teach. It's fine for some books to have a takeaway. Fables, for example. But I think a lot of children's books have gotten preachy. Do kids need to be kind? Yes. But can a crocodile simply host a party with his new mouse bestie for fun? Also yes."

"You have given this some serious thought," Wyatt says.

"I considered becoming a librarian," I confess. "I like books."

"Why did you choose nursing?"

"Believe it or not, more schooling was required for library stuff than nursing. Lots of job competition. I also worried all of it might take away my love for books. Like if they became my job, I wouldn't get to just enjoy them anymore. You know?" I'm quiet for a moment. "Also, after everything that happened with Jacob, I had anxiety about medical stuff, then confronted that anxiety by getting interested in it."

"What medical stuff did Jacob have?"

I stop and look at him. "Wait—you don't know?"

Wyatt slowly shakes his head. I find myself shaking mine too. It's unbelievable how something so pivotal in my brother's life isn't something he talks about freely.

Is it because it doesn't matter? Or because it matters *so* much?

Knowing my brother's uncanny ability to bounce back like he's made of rubber, my guess is the former. But it's strange how something so impactful to me that I needed therapy and chose my career based on it was some kind of blip to my brother. For my parents, too, this was a huge, life-altering moment.

I must be hesitating too long, because Wyatt shifts the hand I'm working on and brushes the smallest circle on my palm. "You can tell me," he says, "but you don't have to."

I'm suddenly self-conscious under Wyatt's attention. The man is *intense*. And now all that intensity is directed my way.

I am *not* used to someone so focused.

It makes my stomach clench, which is the last thing I want it doing as a reaction to Wyatt. Stupid stomach better get the memo.

I'm probably just reacting this way because I can't remember the last time a man was this attentive to me. Which is sad considering Wyatt's not looking at me like *that*. He's probably just trying to distract himself while I pull splinters from his palms.

"I'll give you the short version," I say, and he nods. I go back to his splinters. "Jacob got a staph infection from a mosquito bite under his hockey pads when he was twelve. It moved into his bloodstream, he got sepsis, and he almost died. That's why he's super into sports but didn't really play after high school. The infection left his knee a little janky."

Wyatt is quiet for a long moment. "He never said anything," he says finally.

"Which is very on brand for my brother," I say.

I suddenly find myself thinking about Wyatt's family, about his brother. Peter, I think his mom said? And the barely mentioned Mr. Jacobs of Jacobs Restaurant Group. There has to be some kind of bad blood there. I can't think of any situation in which you see one of your parents and don't ask or even mention the rest of the family. Unless you're not on good terms.

I almost work up the courage to ask, but I can't bring myself to do it. I do, however, manage to free the final splinter from his first hand.

"Ooh—all done with this one. Time for your other hand. Gimme. We'll be done soon as long as you don't make it more difficult."

With a sigh, he offers me his other hand. "I'm not *that* difficult."

"Says you."

I pick up his right hand and examine it. To my relief, only three splinters are visible when I brush away a few specks of dirt.

"Maybe you should have chosen the librarian path."

I get started on the first splinter, which immediately breaks apart as I try to tug it out. "Maybe. But this is pretty satisfying."

"Says you."

There are a few moments of quiet where neither of us speaks and Wyatt doesn't grumble as I manage to pull a whole splinter from his palm.

"I have a question," Wyatt says.

"You've had a lot of those tonight."

There's a pause. "Not just tonight. I simply asked them tonight," he says, and I have no idea what to do with this statement.

So, I do nothing. I focus on my task. I remove the second-to-last splinter.

"My mom brought up the trip I planned," he says.

"I remember you didn't seem to want to talk about it."

He's quiet. Then he says, "It was supposed to be a solo trip like I used to take with my uncle in the summers. Obviously, I can't do it alone. Even once I'm off crutches it would be iffy. I think it would be feasible if I had another person with me."

Even if he were in full physical health, the thought of Wyatt taking the trip alone that he used to take with his uncle makes me ache.

He clears his throat. "I don't know if you'd consider it," he says, and it takes me a solid ten seconds to realize Wyatt is asking me to come on a sailing trip with him.

I drop the tweezers. Again.

He's asking *me*. To go with *him*. On a *sailing trip*.

Me. Him. Sailing trip.

At least, I *think* that's what he meant.

"What are you asking?" I force myself to look Wyatt right in the eyes as I ask this.

The expression on his face falls somewhere between severely constipated and waiting to get four fillings done at the dentist.

"I'm asking if you'd want to go with me. Sailing."

"To where?"

"Georgia."

"Sailing to Georgia," I repeat, like saying the words aloud will help all of this make sense in my brain. It doesn't. Or maybe I'm still reprogramming my brain from thinking Wyatt can't stand me to . . . I don't know what.

So pretty, I hear him saying again while in his fevered state.

My cheeks flush as I fumble for words and come up empty.

"You could bring your headlamp," Wyatt says, and I can tell he's trying to make light of this. Trying to make a joke.

He's so *very* bad at it.

"Are you saying . . . you *want* me to go with you?"

He nods, but that's not enough.

"Me?"

"I can't go alone," he says.

Ah. So it's not about me. It's about having another person to help considering his injury. This makes more sense, but it stings. More than it should.

"Have you ever been sailing?" he asks.

I shake my head. "I wouldn't be much help."

"I'd teach you."

Wyatt—teaching me to sail. The idea is a bowling ball, rolling around my brain and knocking over every thought that tries to form. My pulse is racing and my cheeks and the back of my neck both feel hot.

There's an uncomfortable prickle of *something* at the idea of taking a sailing trip with Wyatt.

Dread? Desire? I'm honestly not sure.

"How long would it take?" I ask.

"A few weeks," he says. "Weather determines a lot in terms of how far we get each day."

I want to say yes. I want to get in my car and drive home.

I want to push past the anxious thoughts and do something I've never done. Something I realize I *want* to do. Which is more terrifying than the idea of being alone with Wyatt on a boat doing all new things.

"I have conditions. *A* condition," I find myself saying.

Meanwhile, a terrified voice in my head screams, *Abort! Abort! Abort! Mayday!*

"Which is?"

"You start physical therapy. See your doctor for whatever follow-ups you're supposed to do. If you work toward recovery and get clearance from your doctor to sail with another person there to help, I'll go."

He says nothing for another long moment, and I pull the last splinter from his palm. Finally.

"You're all done," I tell him, setting down the tweezers and stretching my neck. Telling myself not to think about the fact that Wyatt hasn't given me an answer.

I click off the headlamp, and the single remaining lamplight bathes the room in a soft glow.

Guess this answers that. If Wyatt is so set on sabotaging his recovery, it saves me from taking the trip. I stand up, ready to head back to bed—like I can sleep *now*—when Wyatt lightly traps my hand, tugging me to a stop.

"I'll do it," he says.

"It's that easy?"

He swallows hard, like this decision is anything but easy, and it makes me wonder why he seems so set on not doing what's best for him.

"Yes," he says simply.

"Okay." I slip my hand from his because the contact and the late night and the whole conversation and the idea of being alone with him on a boat is too much.

But before I even take a step, Wyatt says, "Also . . . I think I have a few splinters in my knees."

With a sigh, I sit back down.

15

This Is Called a Hug

Josie

I'm not sure what to expect the next morning when I see Wyatt in the light of day. The vulnerability of our middle-of-the-night conversation, plus all the physical touching, has me feeling jittery with nerves. I'm staring into the refrigerator, wondering what I should make for breakfast, when Wyatt crutches into the kitchen and says, "I made an appointment."

I look over at him and freeze. Even when cold air gusts over my bare feet, I can't move.

Because Wyatt shaved.

The dark blond stubble I've just gotten used to seeing is gone in favor of a cleanly shaven sharp jawline. His dark blond hair is damp, and the scent of his body wash wafts through the room. I can almost picture it like a cartoon with its tendrils snaking across the room and wrapping around me like some kind of spell.

"What?" I work to rearrange my face so I'm not staring at Wyatt's jaw.

"For physical therapy," he says. "I called my doctor."

"You did?"

"Yep. How was your morning walk? Did you bring home any fresh bacon?" he asks like this whole moment isn't revolutionary. Like he wasn't just telling me no the day before in this very same room. And like me being here and taking morning walks is a given.

A shaved face and calling the doctor *and* he's teasing me? I wonder if the fever's back. But Wyatt looks totally healthy. No sign of pain or fever. Just a smooth, sharp jawline that's somehow throwing me for a loop.

"No pigs were harmed, but only because I haven't taken my walk yet. I slept in. *Someone* kept me up last night with his splinters."

"Only because you kept me up with your bed squeaking."

"Only because your stupid bed squeaks. So, when is the appointment?"

"This afternoon."

"Can I come?" I should have thought before asking, but Wyatt's whole thing this morning is throwing me off. It's possible I might need to up my coffee intake to three cups, not just two.

He hesitates but then shocks me even more by saying, "Yes."

"Cool. I was going to go to the library later this morning if you want to come with me. No pressure. Oh, and what do you want for dinner?"

"Surprise me," Wyatt says, then nods toward the still-open fridge. I have officially cooled the room at least a few degrees by forgetting to close this door. "Don't throw that away, okay?"

I follow his gaze. "Do you mean the Cool Whip that says DO NOT THROW AWAY? I don't know—notes like that make me want to do the exact opposite."

His expression shifts. "It's not Cool Whip."

I wait for him to say more, and when he doesn't, I sigh heavily.

"Are you going to tell me what *is* in the Cool Whip container that I shouldn't throw away?"

There is a long pause before Wyatt finally says, "My uncle."

⚓

"Who keeps their dead uncle's ashes in a Cool Whip container?" I ask Toni when I'm taking my walk after the whole kitchen insanity of the morning. "Serial killers. Murderers. *Hockey players*, that's who."

"I doubt that's a general statement you can make about hockey players," Toni says. "A better question is: Who agrees to go on a sailing trip with a hockey player who keeps his uncle in a Cool Whip container? Also, why Cool Whip?"

"He says that's what he had on hand."

She stifles a snort, and I can tell she's trying not to laugh. Toni spends her summers proctoring SATs and ACTs. She's not supposed to be on her phone, but this never stops her from using it anyway. We have our best summer talks in the mornings while she's at work. Normally, I'd be calling her from my couch at home, not while walking along a poorly paved road in a small town a few hours away.

I groan. "Agreeing to this was a bad idea, wasn't it?"

"Actually," Toni says, "I think it's one of your best ideas. That man is husband material on a stick."

"Wyatt? No. Absolutely not."

Toni is under the mistaken impression that my first meeting with Wyatt was the meet-cute we'll one day laugh about while telling our children how we fell in love.

Did I mention my best friend is romantic to the point of delusion?

There was nothing meet-cute-worthy about the first time Wyatt and I met. I'd call it more of a meet-ugly.

"I can't wait to tell you *I told you so* when you fall totally and irreversibly—"

"Don't say it," I beg.

"—in love with him," she finishes, then cackles. As much as one can cackle when they're trying to proctor a standardized test. It sounds more like she's choking. Which is what she deserves for suggesting such a thing.

I step out of the way as a large delivery truck rumbles down the street. "Have fun turning that truck around," I mutter as the tires kick up gravel.

"What?" Toni says.

"Nothing. Let's go back to the ashes. Is this a thing— people keeping their loved ones' ashes in old food containers in the fridge? Do ashes expire?"

"We keep my granny on the mantel in a vase so she's always there. Give the man a break. Grief doesn't exist in a straight line. So, things must be going well, huh? Honestly, I'm shocked you haven't beaten Wyatt to death with his crutches."

"You just mentioned me falling in love with him. Now you're saying you're surprised I haven't murdered him?"

"The line between love and hate is paper thin, baby."

"Please. I fundamentally disagree with that statement." I pause. "Plus, the last kind of person I want to date, much less marry, is an athlete. And it's Wyatt's *life*."

"You and your aversion to athletes," Toni says. "Such a shame considering your brother's connections."

I swallow, coming this close to telling Toni about where my aversion to athletes came from. But I hate even *thinking* about the guy who poisoned me on athletes. And, honestly, guys in general. But especially athletes.

Their size, their ego, their inability to understand the word *no*.

I'm not *completely* unreasonable; I wouldn't write off a guy just because his career happens to be in sports. Probably. But he'd have to have a whole lot of other things going for him to make me get over that very high hurdle.

And Wyatt . . . well. I would have said that he didn't have anything else going for him.

But that was before the last few days.

"For real, though," Toni says, her voice quieter and more serious. "I think this trip will be good for you. Get you out of your little comfort zone."

"I like my comfort zone," I grumble. "It's . . . comfortable. Don't knock it."

"Speaking of comfort zones—how's the house hunt coming? Have you found anything you like now that you'll be rolling in your brother's money?"

"Nothing yet," I say, hoping she doesn't press me on it. I don't want to admit I haven't looked. Toni will latch onto that and grill me about why. I'm not even sure I'd have an answer for her. I don't fully understand it myself.

I'm saved from having to think about it when I come around the bend, catch sight of Wyatt's house, and scream, dropping the phone.

Admittedly, this is an overreaction.

Or maybe not. Because the big truck that passed me on the road is now in Wyatt's driveway. And two men are carrying a new mattress through the front door, directed by a man on crutches—a man I'm realizing I barely even know.

⚓

The furniture delivery is almost as shocking as Wyatt deciding to come with me to the library. He said it makes more sense to go together and then straight to the physical therapist's—ever the practical man.

I said yes, of course, though I am, for once, struggling to find words on the drive into Kilmarnock.

"You're quiet," he says as I pull into the parking lot.

"I must be if *you're* talking," I say, and then my mouth clamps shut again.

Because who came and body-snatched Wyatt? Someone clearly did. Starting with the shaved face, then the setting up of the doctor's appointment, the ordering of furniture for his house, and now . . . coming with me to the library?

It's too much.

I can almost hear Toni cackling, asking again why I'm not falling for this man.

I don't have words for that either.

As I park the Bronco, which Wyatt still insists I drive everywhere, I clench my hands around the wheel and stare at my fingers.

"Thank you," I say finally, feeling something ease in my chest. I tilt my head, giving him a sideways glance. Full on seems like too much. "You didn't need to buy new furniture."

I almost add *for me*, but I don't know that he did it for me necessarily. I mean, I asked why he hadn't and complained about the squeaky bed, which now makes me feel horrible, but never did I imagine him buying two whole new bedroom sets. And a new couch. Rugs, a new kitchen table, and a bookshelf.

The house needed it, so maybe he ordered it like a month ago?

Somehow, though, I think not.

Especially when he caught me staring at the bookshelf and told me it's for my books.

I had to shut myself in my room and sit on the new, non-squeaky bed so I wouldn't start crying in front of him.

So, I guess at least *that* piece of furniture was for me.

"It's nothing," Wyatt says, like it isn't.

I clear my throat. "It's *not*, though. And I need you to know I appreciate it."

"Can we go into the library now?" he asks like a man totally not in touch with his feelings.

"Yep," I say, but then I quickly walk around to his side of the car as he pulls out his crutches and stands. "But first, I need to do this."

Without waiting for a response, I wrap my arms around his waist and hug him.

I've missed hugs. While Toni says she runs purely on coffee and a steady stream of Twizzlers, I run on hugs. Physical touch from people I love, really, but hugs are the best. And as my cheek presses into the hard yet snuggly planes of Wyatt's chest, I can't stop the deep sigh from leaving my chest.

Wyatt's frozen at first, but then he shifts on his crutches, one hand landing between my shoulder blades and the other arm fully circling me, pulling me in tight.

My breath catches in my throat, and it takes a few moments for me to swallow down the swell of emotion.

"This is called a hug," I say. "People do this for many reasons, but often as a thank-you or a show of comfort or affection."

"Huh," Wyatt says. "I had no idea."

"Well, you're doing great. Totally a natural at this."

It's starting to go on too long. I know this, but it's still hard to peel myself away from him. I can't meet his eyes when I do.

Giving him a pat on his arm like he's a really good puppy, I start toward the library. He follows, catching up quickly. I swing open the door, sensing his gaze on me. But I'm still feeling a little too emotionally raw to meet his eyes.

"Do you like to read?" I ask. Seems like a low-risk question. I only half expect him to answer.

Wyatt shrugs. "Not really. Sometimes biographies or history books."

"I thought you said you were into wolf-shifter romances," I tease.

"Only during Halloween."

"And then you switch to Hallmark-style Christmas romances in December?"

"Nah. I prefer abominable snowman rom-coms during winter."

I'm still laughing over this minutes later. Who knew Wyatt had wit buried under thick layers of grump? I've seen the occasional signs of life from him this week, though most don't count since they came from Fever Wyatt. Still. My strongly held assumptions about who he is are crumbling like dust. Or—melting like romantic abominable snowmen.

It's like the bargain I struck with him helped him find his will to live.

Whatever the reason, I'm glad.

I head to the desk to return my books, and I lose him in the stacks. We're not likely to cross paths if he's looking for biographies or books on history. To appease Toni, I do pick up a few romance novels to go along with my all-female author list and a women's fiction beach read about sailing.

I'm passing the children's area when I hear a deep, familiar voice. Wyatt is standing at the help desk, talking to a woman wearing a red hat with a colorful feather sticking out of the top. Based on her clothing and the children gathered around the rug, she's probably about to start story time.

"I don't know the name," Wyatt is saying, "but it's about a crocodile with a toothache."

16

Sayonara, Dr. Dimples

Wyatt

"When Wyatt mentioned his injury, I thought he was talking about a person." Josie grins from her perch on a stool near where my physical therapist stretches my bare foot. "And I wondered, *Who is this Liz Frank, and why is she so mean?*"

Dr. Parminder laughs, louder than he needs to, in my opinion. Not that Josie isn't funny. Or charming. She's both.

And yeah, I get it. I have the stupidest injury known to man with the absolute dumbest name.

But the PT is overdoing it, and it's no secret why. He almost did a double take when I walked in today with Josie, and he hasn't stopped smiling at her since. With dimples. Because, of course, my physical therapist has dimples.

He also insists we call him doctor, though I'm pretty sure even if he has a doctorate, you don't usually refer to physical therapists as *doctor*. Unless they insist, like Dr. Dimples did.

I'm also pretty sure Josie knows this too. Because when he

introduced himself, smiling with those stupid dimples as he said, "You can call me *Dr.* Parminder," her eyes flew to mine.

I swear, I could see the knowledge on her face. Like, *Do you believe this guy?*

If it bothers her, though, she's not showing it now.

I can't tell whether Josie is into his flirtations or just being friendly, but they've been chatting almost nonstop. It's been thirty minutes, though it feels like a whole month of my life has been drained away in this room.

That's what happens when you become the third wheel at your own physical therapy appointment, all while having your foot and ankle manipulated into strange and mostly uncomfortable positions.

I grunt, and Dr. Parminder's eyes snap up to mine. "Too much?" he asks.

"It's fine."

I hate physical limitations of any kind. It makes me furious each morning when I slide the boot on my foot. Every step with crutches makes me want to set something on fire.

It's a total cliché, but my injury really did make me realize how much I took for granted, how much I wasn't grateful for simple things. Like walking unassisted. Like not seeing pity in people's eyes or having to answer the question "So, when do you think you'll return to hockey?"

My slide into wallowing at the cottage—because I can call a spade a spade and I was totally wallowing—had very little to do with not wanting to get better and everything to do with other issues I'm still not ready to confront.

It's like this injury shut down my trajectory and opened the floodgates of all the worries and concerns and wounds I've stuffed down over the years.

I didn't intentionally set out to sabotage my recovery. Not at first. It started with the issue of getting around. Rideshare apps and taxis aren't common in Kilmarnock, and trying to figure out transportation felt like too much. Then everything started feeling like too much.

Not physically. But more like I settled in under a weighted blanket of negativity I couldn't—or no longer wanted to—shake.

By the time Jacob realized I wasn't only avoiding his calls but not going to appointments, I was pretty set on staying put. I didn't let myself play out the long-term effects of this behavior. It was easier just to get up each day and continue on as is. Alone. In pain. Completely miserable. Jacob sending people to "help" only made me angrier—at him, at myself.

Then he sent Josie. Probably the one person who could have pulled me out of this cyclone of self-destruction.

"Lisfranc isn't super common," Dr. Parminder tells Josie with another flash of dimples. "But we're seeing it more and more. Not usually with hockey players, though. It's not very likely to happen on the ice, so it makes sense Wyatt did this during another activity."

I wait for Josie to make a crack about disc golf again, but this time she doesn't.

"What kind of injury is a Lisfranc exactly?" she asks.

"Mr. Talkative here hasn't explained it?" Dr. Parminder teases, and I briefly consider kicking him with my good foot.

Let's see how his attitude is when *he's* recovering from an injury.

"Believe it or not, no," Josie says, taking a sip of coffee. "He won't talk about his injury, but he won't shut up about the new season of *The Real Housewives of Orange County*. Go figure."

She grins at my scowl. And as our eyes meet, a little zing moves from my toes up my legs to my spine, lodging somewhere in my chest.

Dr. Parminder's laugh breaks through the moment. "First, you're not too far off," he says. "Lisfranc is the name of the French doctor who first diagnosed injuries to this ligament. Jacques Lisfranc de St. Martin."

I want to roll my eyes at Dr. Parminder's terrible attempt at a French accent, but it makes Josie laugh. He offers her another unnecessary flash of dimples and runs a hand through his thick, dark hair.

I really hope we're almost done with my treatment. I'm not sure how much more of this I can take.

The stretches aren't much fun either. Before this, he had me do seated leg raises with a resistance belt and practice pushing down on an exercise ball with my injured foot. All I could think about was how much I miss gliding on ice, the cut of my blades as I deke an opponent, the satisfying exhaustion after a game.

This all feels so . . . silly. Especially with Josie watching.

"There's a specific ligament and a joint called the Lisfranc. Right here between the medial cuneiform and the second metatarsal." Dr. Parminder taps the spot on the bottom of my foot. "The injury can be a tearing of the Lisfranc ligament or include other secondary ligaments. It can even encompass breaks in bones."

"So, which kind of injury does Wyatt have?"

"Just tears," I say, wincing as Dr. Parminder bends my foot.

"Two tears," he amends. "Significant but not full tears. Thankfully. Ready to try some walking in the pool?"

I can think of a hundred things I'd rather do than walk in a pool, but Josie looks at me expectantly. "Sure."

Grabbing my gym bag, I head to the small changing room just off the main physical therapy space. And if I almost fall over changing into my bathing suit, it's because I'm in a hurry to finish this appointment.

Not because I don't like leaving Josie alone with Dr. Dimples.

Though when I come out, he's standing very close to Josie, his whole body turned toward hers like he's some kind of satellite. As I crutch my way across the room, her eyes meet mine. She stumbles over her words, and a flare of pride goes up at the way her eyes widen, taking in my bare chest. Dr. Dimples steps back from Josie, his smile faltering a little when he sees me.

Maybe I don't mind walking in the pool after all. And maybe he's rethinking this particular exercise.

I'm not particularly modest—years spent in a locker room full of hockey players rid me of that quickly—but neither am I particularly prideful about my appearance. Part of it is genetic, with my height and build coming from my dad. The rest is a result of my body being my job and, as I've come to realize since my injury, my whole world. This is the weakest and most out of shape I've been in years, but I'm aware my body still doesn't show it—yet.

I definitely feel it as Dr. Dimples starts me on a ten-minute walk in the pool with full weight—buoyed by the water—on my foot. I hate how challenging something so small is. I've been stupid, sitting in the cottage feeling sorry for myself. It shouldn't have taken Josie coming and offering me a bargain to get me here.

But now I'm determined to give this everything I have. For me. Not for hockey or the team or Jacob. Not even for Josie.

Though, I'll admit, it feels good to climb out of the pool and have her waiting for me, grinning like I just won gold, not like I just walked a few slow laps in a pool.

She hands me a towel, and I catch her eyes dipping to my chest as I dry off. Why does this make me want to flex every muscle I have? When her eyes snap back to mine and she knows I caught her looking, her cheeks flush.

"You did so good!" she says. "How did it feel?"

I shrug. "Like I shouldn't have avoided this for so long."

Her smirk says, *I told you so*, but she doesn't actually say it.

Dr. Parminder is also smiling, though still directing it too much at Josie. "The good news is, you won't be needing your crutches anymore. Despite your best efforts to avoid me, you're recovering well. No more crutches, and we'll see how you do with just the walking boot."

"That's great," Josie says. "What does that mean as far as activity?"

"If it doesn't hurt, don't hold back," the doctor says, shifting to stand a little too close to Josie. He waggles his eyebrows as he says, "Do what feels good."

What would feel good is grabbing him by the shirt collar, dragging him away from Josie, and throwing him into the pool.

Josie takes a step back from him and asks, "Is there anything I can help him do at home? Or any exercises he should be doing?"

"Sure." Dr. Parminder reaches for a folder on the table and flips through pages until he finds one to hand to Josie. "Here's a list of some exercises he can do. Foot massages are also helpful, and there are a few resources to help with that."

I almost fall over from shock when we leave without Dr. Dimples asking Josie for her number. Unless he did it when I was changing, and I'm not about to ask her what they talked about without me.

As Josie and I ride the elevator downstairs, I fidget, trying to figure out where my hands should go. In just those few weeks, I got used to the crutches. Now everything feels awkward. Or maybe it's how close to me Josie's standing, with the elevator almost at capacity. I can smell her sweet scent as she shifts beside me, humming under her breath.

Now that we're sharing a shower, I know it's her shampoo and conditioner. But she must have been using them for years, because I remember it from the very first time we met—a night I wish I could erase and redo.

On the way to Jacob's house, which was only about twenty minutes from my parents' house, a fact he didn't yet know, he did the stereotypical brother thing and warned me about his sister.

"Don't even think about my sister. Not that you'd be into her. I mean, she's awesome, but she's my *sister*," he said, making a face like the thought of her dating at all was nauseating.

"Cool," I said, completely unworried about the idea of being attracted to his sister. I had only recently shifted into what I called total hockey focus mode, and despite what everyone thinks about athletes and women, I had no desire to date—casually or otherwise. Least of all my best friend's sister.

"But I mean, if you did like her, like *for real* like her, that's cool," Jacob amended. "I'd just need a heads-up. And a few days to, like, deal with the idea. Though she really doesn't date."

"Like . . . at all?"

"Not in, like, the last few years." He must have seen the question on my face, because he added, "I'm not sure if she's just picky or has something against dating or what."

I knew a guy in college who both smelled like funky cheese and was obsessed with magic—like the card-and-coin-trick kind of magic. Sometimes I saw him walking across campus in a cape and top hat. And that guy went on dates.

So I figured there must be something about Josie that was more offensive than stinky cheese and magic. That or she had some kind of personal reason for not dating, which Jacob didn't know about.

"Anyway, it's a moot point," Jacob continued. "She won't be

into you because you're a jock, and if there's one thing Josie hates, it's jocks."

Jock.

It struck me that I'd worked so hard to avoid one set of labels in my life that I'd accidentally traded it for another.

I needed an escape from the life my father carved out for me. The one he continually tried to force me into—even when it became clear that I had no interest in being primed to work with Jacobs Restaurant Group from the time I was eight. The moment I picked up a hockey stick, my dad basically shut me out. No more prepping me to take over. No more business lessons or spreadsheets.

But also . . . no more *anything*. My dad stopped talking to me or even looking at me.

Instead, his full focus went to Peter.

My brother fell into line as though he wanted it. Probably he did. Maybe? I don't know because my brother and I, much like my dad and I, barely speak.

So, in Jacob's car that day, driving to my hometown to stay with his family, hearing him call me a jock hit me in a new way.

I was still mulling over this idea of label switching, in the quiet obsessive way my mother says I obsess over everything, when we arrived and I actually saw Jacob's sister.

She definitely didn't have any stinky cheese or magic issues.

At some point during his warning, Jacob had told me his sister was pretty. But calling Josie pretty is like saying a sunset is cute or the Grand Canyon is big.

Pretty was not nearly a grand enough word to encompass the reality of the situation. Stepping out of the car, I felt like someone had whacked me in the head with one of those oversize fairground hammers used to test your strength.

Awkwardness, in a heavier dose than the usual amount I experience when meeting new people, struck me mute as I reached out to shake Josie's hand. I felt uncomfortable and idiotic, and it was made even worse by the way she flinched, like she had some reason to be afraid of me.

Guess Jacob was right about his sister hating jocks. Or . . . something. There was definitely something there.

But if her brother had no clue, it wasn't like I was going to figure it out when we'd barely met. Still, I wondered.

Things went downhill from there. From the flinch to the KITCHEN INCIDENT, which is still how I think of it—in all caps. Thanks to Jacob's ridiculous grocery store hookup, every person in the Rowland household got the wrong impression of me. One I managed to correct—with everyone but Josie.

The truth, which I never did get to fully explain to Josie, was that the woman from the grocery store recognized me at the jump. I wasn't well known then—not unless you followed college hockey or NHL draft news. But Grocery Store Girl, as Jacob referred to her, did both. She was fully aware I'd signed my first contract to play for Edmonton, which meant she was aware of the dollar signs on my contract. And the signing bonus.

I ignored her when she approached us in the frozen dessert aisle, but Jacob did the opposite and decided to bring her home. Looking back on it, I suspect she figured she'd use him to get to me. Which she attempted to do when I came down to the kitchen and she tried to make a move. Only seconds before Josie also walked in.

I realize in hindsight what came out of my mouth—*She came on to me* followed by *Not your* sister—was very easily misconstrued.

But there was no misunderstanding Josie's words: *I would never.*

For years those words have bounced around in my head.

They've finally lost most of their sharp edges, like stones in a tumbler, worn smooth over time and with force.

But I still feel them—even now as I remember that night. And Josie's face when she said them—the embarrassment, the disgust, the vehemence.

She went back to college the next day before I could work up the courage or find the right words to explain what I'd said. And the next time I saw Josie, she was closed off. Detached and cool. Barely made eye contact. Said little more than hello. I couldn't find a good way to work an explanation into a conversation when there was no conversation.

And so on it went. For years.

Now, that night seems like stagnant water under the bridge. I'd still like to address it.

But I don't know how without revealing how much it's bothered me ever since.

Or revealing why what Josie thinks about me matters so much.

She glances up now, catching me watching her. I look away.

The elevator doors slide open, and I see Dr. Parminder standing just across from the elevator, a little out of breath, like he ran down the stairs.

"Did we forget something?" Josie asks.

He readies his dimples, aims, and fires. "My phone number."

Bold move, Doctor. Bold move.

At least he did ask when we came in today if Josie was my girlfriend. When she laughed and said no, I guess he took that to mean she's fair game.

What he didn't ask was whether I'm interested. Which I guess would have been a little outside of his professional scope, but then—so is this. I hope he can feel my stare burning into him. But he doesn't seem to.

"Oh?" Josie takes a step back. Actually, not back. A step closer to me. Her gaze flicks my way, and I swear, she looks almost like she's asking for help.

Or . . . is she asking my permission?

I'm not entirely sure, so I say nothing. But I do shift closer to her.

"I guess it would be good to call you if I have any questions about Wyatt's recovery," Josie says.

"That and so I can take you to dinner sometime," Dr. Dimples says easily. "Give me your phone, and I'll shoot a text to myself." He holds out his hand, still grinning.

"You know what?" Josie says. "I think it's actually best if we keep things strictly professional. I'll be coming in with Wyatt for his sessions and—"

Dr. Parminder leans closer to Josie. "I can be professional in this context and still take you on a date. Like the separation of church and state."

His grin takes on a flirty edge I'd like to remove with my elbow. If we were on the ice, I'd check him the first chance I got. Right into the boards. Hard.

Now, I stand here, trying to cool my rage into a tight ball, as he waggles his dark eyebrows and says, "I can be as *un*professional as you'd like when we're not in this setting."

Forget a clean check. The gloves would come off for this guy.

Josie and I exchange a glance. I don't miss the way her lip curls slightly. Neither does my physical therapist, whose smile falters for the first time all day.

Sayonara, Dr. Dimples.

He drops his hand and takes a small step back. I take one forward, though I'm not sure Josie notices.

"I'd better not," she says. "But thank you for the offer. Have a good day!"

She says this last part too brightly, her voice bordering on manic as she waves once, then speed-walks right out the front doors of the building, not looking back once.

Dr. Dimples wears the expression of a man who doesn't hear the word *no* very often.

I can't stop myself from shooting him a smug little smirk as I follow Josie out, more relieved than I want to admit.

17

You Don't Drive Boats

Josie

Wyatt and I fall into a new daily routine over the next few weeks. One that includes my morning walks and nightly bingeing of a drama about first responders. Plus twice-weekly PT visits where I wait in the car to avoid Dr. Parminder. Every spare moment I get, I'm cramming sailing information like I'm studying for the most important exam of my life. I'm still waiting to actually get on the boat though.

Sometimes I wake up with boat terminology on my lips: aft, windward, keel, starboard, tacking, lines.

Of all the vocabulary words I've learned, my favorite is baggywrinkle. Which sounds like a hobbit name but is actually a protective cover to prevent rope chafing and looks a little like a Muppet.

Wyatt just rolls his eyes when I ask about his baggywrinkles and tells me to stop studying things I don't need to know. To which I challenge him to actually take me on his boat.

But the morning Wyatt promised we could finally get on the boat, I catch something in the garage trap.

A small creature is huddled toward the back of the wire trip, and it takes me walking right up and squinting at the mess of matted grayish-brown fur to realize it's a dog. It cowers, but when I carefully open the trap and reach in, the little dog lets me pull him or her out. It can't weigh more than ten pounds.

"Wow," I say, holding it firmly but away from my body. "You smell terrible."

It starts to shake.

"But that's okay!" I amend. "We can handle smelly. Have you been living out here all this time, you poor thing?"

Obviously, I don't expect the dog to answer, and I have no idea what, exactly, I'm going to do now that I've caught him. Her? I can only hope Wyatt doesn't freak out. Because by the time I've carried it to the house, I'm already feeling protective over this stinky little pup.

"What is that?" he asks, wrinkling his nose. Probably at the smell. But maybe also at what looks like a shaking ball of matted fur with buggy eyes.

"I told you something was living in your garage! This is the something," I tell him in my most told-you-so voice. Because Wyatt absolutely didn't believe me when I told him there was a creature out there. Now I'm holding the stinky proof. "It's a dog."

"Looks like trash."

I gasp, pulling the dog closer to my chest before the smell makes me hold it out again. "Don't call him or her trash! Do you have an old towel? I'm taking it to the vet."

Wyatt gets to his feet with a frown and a heavy sigh. "I'm going with you."

Turns out the garage dog is a girl. And underneath the fur

the vet shaved completely off, she's a little bigger than a Chihuahua with a broader snout and eyes that bug out a like a pug or Boston terrier. Thankfully without the snorty breathing noises, which might have brought back too many pig memories.

Despite needing a flea dip (shudder) and a full round of vaccinations, the vet says she's in pretty good shape. And that based on the scarring on her belly, she thinks the dog has likely been spayed but never microchipped.

"Do you want to take her to the shelter or are you planning to adopt her?" Dr. Stephens asks.

"Adopt," I say, just as Wyatt says, "Shelter."

We glare at each other.

"It's a high-kill shelter," Dr. Stephens says, looking between us. "And in summer, they usually get pretty full."

I give Wyatt my best pleading eyes, the dog curled against my chest. I'm not sure whether she looks better or worse bald. She definitely is not going to win any doggy beauty pageants. She looks at Wyatt, too, then starts to shake again.

"Fine. But we'll have to figure out what to do with her while we're on the trip. A dog is not going with us," he says.

We'll see, I think.

By the time we get home after we've stopped for pet supplies, I've picked a name that makes Wyatt roll his eyes. Which tells me it's perfect.

"I've decided on her name. Meet Jib-Jabberwocky—*Princess* Jib-Jabberwocky."

"It's too long," Wyatt complains. "You must have been reading too many *Alice in Wonderland* retellings along with your sailing books."

"It's her name. It can't be changed."

"You just decided this, what—five minutes ago?"

"Ten."

"Fine. But we'll call her Jib for short," Wyatt says when I reject his suggestions of Spot (she has no spots), Belle (ironic, he says, because she's so ugly—which makes me smack his arm), and Garbage (since I found her when taking out the trash).

And though he acts like the little dog is ridiculous and keeps grumbling about it, when I leave Jib alone with him so I can make dinner, I come back to find her curled up in his lap with one of his big hands lightly stroking her back, the tiniest of smiles on his face.

⚓

Because of Jib, we don't get on the boat for the first time until the next morning. And despite what Wyatt said about her not coming with us, the little dog is apparently used to boats because she hops right up with no hesitation, sniffing everything before she scampers below deck like she owns the place.

"Looks like I'm the only real newbie here," I say.

"Not for long. Also, I prefer the term *rookie*."

Wyatt turns out to be an excellent tour guide. I mean, I wouldn't tell him to quit his day job for the pay, but even with the boot, he moves effortlessly around the deck, pointing out various boat things I've only read about or seen in videos so far.

When I interrupt with questions, which mostly consist of me pointing to things and saying, "What's that?" he is shockingly patient.

"There are so many ropes," I say.

Wyatt coughs behind his hand. I'm pretty sure to hide a laugh. "Yes, Josie. Ropes—*rigging*—are a really important part of most boats. Especially sailboats."

"Thanks, smart guy. When do we go inside?"

"Right now," he says. Then, faster than seems wise given his boot, he disappears through the opening leading down below. I don't hear a crash or grunt, only a dull thud.

Still, I lean down quickly. "Are you okay?"

It takes me a moment to adjust to the dim light down there, but Wyatt's face is shockingly close to mine. The smile he's wearing is even more shocking. Apparently, all I needed to make him smile was get the man on a boat.

"I'm fine. Now, get down here, Rookie."

Did Wyatt just give me a nickname?

I like it. Maybe too much.

I'm much slower than he was descending what I'd describe as a stair-ladder, but a moment later, I'm inside. Wyatt is still smiling, casually leaning against a counter.

"This is the saloon," he says, spreading his arms wide. "A.k.a. the living room, dining room, and galley."

I'm already moving around the galley, peering inside the tiny oven and running my fingers over the miniature burners.

"Good thing those weren't hot," Wyatt says.

"Why would they be hot right now?"

"Maybe I was making soup while waiting for you to climb down."

"I wasn't that slow," I say. "Is soup something you eat a lot of on the boat?"

Wyatt leans over, opening one cabinet, then another. He makes a face as he pulls out a can, frowning at the labels. "One of the things. But we'll need to restock. I think they stopped selling this brand in the nineties."

"I can make up a menu," I say, opening another cabinet. This one contains only spiderwebs. I close it quickly. "And if something isn't as easy to make with this setup, you can tell me."

"Sounds like a plan. We'll also stop at various marinas with restaurants. There are some great ones along the way."

Probably ones Wyatt ate at with his uncle. He sets the can back on the shelf and closes the cabinet door slowly, resting his palm flat against the wood for just a moment. Both corners of his mouth are turned down. A few weeks ago, I might have just thought this was his normal grumpy—or IBS—face, but now it seems like something else.

"Where's the bedroom?" I ask. "I mean, the cabin?"

I hadn't thought about the sleeping arrangements before now and am relieved when Wyatt says, "There are two. The first is right through here. After you."

The first cabin we see is right off the saloon. There are two berths, or beds, a dressing table or desk between them. The walls are lined with little built-in shelves and cabinets, and there are narrow windows all along the top.

"Cozy," I say.

"This is where I slept," Wyatt says. "And where I'll sleep. Unless you decide you'd rather have this cabin. Lady's choice."

"Can you fit?" I ask. It's not exactly cramped, but Wyatt is large and has to duck through the doorways.

"Well enough."

The other cabin is at the front, and we stop to look at the engine and the head, or bathroom, on the way. Everything feels so small, especially with Wyatt's big body putting off heat like an engine. He's everywhere, and with every step and movement, our arms brush or our hands touch or our hips slide against each other.

You're going to have to survive three, maybe four weeks of this, I realize.

It will be the most delicious—and dangerous—kind of torture.

"This little hallway is known as the captain's quarters," Wyatt says, stopping just outside the second cabin's open door. "Some people hire a captain to sail the boat. I'd never do it, but if I did, they would sleep here."

He pats a flat, shelflike area, which I suppose could be a bed if there were a tiny mattress.

"It would have to be a short captain," I say.

"Perfect for you if you don't like this cabin."

"As I keep trying to tell you, I'm not short."

Wyatt stretches to his full height, which means his head touches the ceiling. Looking down his nose at me, he says, "Okay. You're not short."

"Shut up, Sasquatch."

I walk ahead of him into the second cabin, which has barely a shoebox to stand in because the whole thing is *bed*. Probably a double? Like the other cabin, there are small windows along the top of the walls and various storage cubbies.

Wyatt is suddenly behind me, and the small room seems even smaller. And hotter. Literally and figuratively. There's no escape either, with him blocking the whole doorway and his Wyatt-ness suffocating me.

Just like there will be no escape for the weeks you're on this boat with him.

"How comfortable are these beds?" I ask. "I mean berths."

"Either one is fine. Try it out."

I do, if only to get some space from Wyatt. But lying in a bed while looking at him standing just a foot away does nothing to help.

"Not bad," I say. Sweat beads on my forehead. "Is there AC on this thing?"

"There is, but we won't run it much. It uses up a lot of power, so we'll run it for a few hours later in the day, then turn it off at night. Some of the windows open, but they'll just let humidity in. And mosquitoes."

"Wow. You're really selling me on this."

Wyatt stretches his arms up, grasping the doorway as he leans forward, grinning. His biceps strain against his sleeves, and I wish I could slap him with some kind of fine whenever he does something like this.

"Too bad you already entered into an agreement," he says. "There's no getting out now, even if you wanted to. You're stuck with me."

The thing that bothers me most about this is that I think I want to be.

"When can we actually go out?" I ask when we're back on deck and I can breathe again. Even if it's humid summer Virginia air.

"We could motor out anytime. But I wouldn't feel comfortable actually sailing until I've got this thing off." Wyatt nods down at his boot.

"Like now?" I ask, and Wyatt surprises me with another full smile. They're going to lose value if he keeps giving them out at this rate.

"If you want."

"I want!"

My squeal and hand clapping wake up Jib, who barks once like she's telling me to keep it down and then promptly goes back to sleep. That is, until Wyatt starts the motor. Then she bolts awake and stands at the very front like she's recreating her own *Titanic* moment as we cast off and pull away from the dock.

"I'll never let go," I say in a falsely high voice.

Wyatt snorts. "Are you going to quote bad movies about boats or the ocean the whole time?"

"Like maybe 'We're going to need a bigger boat'? Or 'The sea was angry that day, my friend'?"

"Yes, like that. But what's the second one from?"

"*Seinfeld.* My parents' favorite, and they indoctrinated me early. Ever watch it?" He shakes his head, and I *tsk.* "You're missing out on a big piece of nineties pop culture. That quote is from a classic episode where George lies about being a marine biologist and Kramer hits golf balls into the ocean and—you know what? Never mind. Maybe sometime I'll indoctrinate you."

"You know *Jaws* inspired the name of the boat," Wyatt says, and when I look confused, he says, "After Quint. The shark hunter. *QUINTessential.* Get it?"

"Huh. I always thought his name was Quin."

"Nope. Quint."

"Did your uncle name her?" I ask.

"The previous owner. It's bad luck to change a boat's name, but thankfully, my uncle loved *Jaws.*"

Wyatt goes quiet after this, and I get distracted as we head out of the little cove and into Dividing Creek. I only know the name because I have a chartbook I've been studying along with another book I got from Amazon about the Intracoastal Waterway.

We pass docks and see a few other smaller boats tooling around. I'm fully baking in the sun by the time we reach the mouth of Dividing Creek and see the open water of the bay.

Normally, this is where we'd shut off the motor and sail, Wyatt says, but not today.

"Neither of us is wearing sunscreen, and we don't have drinking water."

"Boo," I say, even as I'm wiping sweat from my forehead. He's right. But I already love being on the water.

"If you'd like, we can start going out daily. If not hoisting the sails, I can at least show you some things and teach you to pilot."

"I'll get to drive the boat?" I ask.

Wyatt raises his brows. "Absolutely. There's no way I can do it the whole time. Just . . . don't call it driving again. Piloting, steering, or navigating. Not driving."

Wyatt lets me help tie up as we return to the dock, which I manage, even though it turns out to be a lot more stressful than I thought it would be. I have a feeling I'm quickly going to find that my book and video knowledge barely scratches the surface of preparing me for the trip.

When we get inside, an Amazon truck rumbles down the drive, going a little faster than is necessary. I'm glad Jib isn't out there. Jib barks her little head off from a perch on the back of the couch.

"Did you order more books?" Wyatt asks as I grab the packages and thank the driver.

"Not this time," I say, tearing into the first one and pulling out pink ruffled fabric. "It's clothing."

"A little small, don't you think?" Wyatt asks, frowning as I shake out the dress.

"For me, yes." I take great delight watching his expression shift as I say, "These are for Jib."

18

Fight, Flight, or Kick

Josie

The night before we're set to leave, I have a nightmare.

I thrash awake, a scream caught in my throat, my conscious brain trying to grasp hold of anything to pull me out and tell me where I am while my fight-or-flight instincts are telling me I need to move. Now.

It's dark and I scissor my legs, trying to get free from whatever's holding me—sheets, my brain tries to tell me, though it does little to quell the panic—when there's a sound and then a hand on my shoulder.

"Josie," a voice says.

Wyatt. The knowledge sinks in along with a wave of re-assurance.

But it takes a moment for my body to get the message. As my feet break free from the sheets, still kicking wildly, I make contact with something solid yet soft.

There's a groan, and Wyatt's hand on my shoulder tightens for a moment.

I go still, my brain clearing enough to take in all the data points, flushing out the fear and leaving me panting, heart racing, adrenaline drunk.

I'm with Wyatt at his uncle's cottage. This is his guest room bed. We're leaving in the morning. I had a nightmare.

And I just kicked Wyatt.

Kicked him in the . . . *Oh no.*

"Wyatt?" I whisper, trying to sit up.

His hand releases me and the bed dips as he sits on the edge, facing away from me, bent at the waist.

The room is velvet darkness, the only light a tiny gray glow from the window. It was overcast when I went to bed, and I'm guessing it still is. The night before, the moon shone like a spotlight through the blinds. Jib, who apparently sleeps like the dead, lets out a snore from her dog bed in the corner.

I tuck my legs under me—*Stupid, stupid legs!*—and hesitantly flatten a palm against Wyatt's back. He groans again but leans a little into my touch. I slide my hand over his soft T-shirt, rubbing his back.

"Are you okay? I'm so sorry! I had a nightmare. And I was— Did I . . . kick you?"

"Yep," he grunts, his voice strained.

"In the stomach?" I ask.

"No."

"The knee?"

"Warmer."

"The thigh?" I whisper.

"Hot."

I'm an adult. I know and use the correct names for body parts all the time. But I cannot bring myself to say the word—not the *correct* one, nor any from the robust list of alternate names.

Not when I just kicked Wyatt *there*.

Instead, I say, "I'm so sorry."

He grunts in response. I continue rubbing his back as my own breathing slows and the shakiness starts to settle. I'm a sweaty, nervous wreck who doesn't remember the nightmare that caused this—not a single detail—and now on top of that, I feel terrible.

"Here," I say, scooting over in the totally squeak-free bed he bought. "Lie down."

It's an impulsive request, but before I can take it back, Wyatt folds his big body onto the mattress beside me. He's on his side, curled almost into the fetal position. I hesitate, not sure what to do with him now that he's in my bed. He's *in my bed*.

It should bother me, being this close, sharing this space. I wait for memories to rise up and send me into a panic, but they don't. Instead, I feel comforted by his big, warm presence. Steadied. Safe.

Sucking in a breath, I fluff the pillows behind me and adjust myself into a half-sitting position, with him still in reach. In long, smooth strokes, I rub his back. Even though I was the one needing comfort, it helps to comfort someone else.

"I had a nightmare."

"I know," he says, and I'm glad his voice sounds a little stronger, a little less strained than just a moment ago. "I wanted to make sure you were okay. Guess what they say about not waking a person from a nightmare is true."

"I think that's night terrors," I say. "And I was awake—mostly. Just stuck in the throes of panic. I'm so sorry."

"I know."

"Are you okay?"

"I'll be fine. As to whether or not I can still have children—"

"That's a myth," I point out unhelpfully. Or maybe helpfully. I'm honestly not sure. "Unless I kicked you hard enough to cause torsion and you don't get it treated and—"

"Josie."

"Yes?"

"Please stop."

"Okay. Sorry."

"It's fine. Scratch my back."

His tone is demanding, but in a way that makes me bite back a smile. It's the kind of voice he's used for our sailing practice in the bay, and I like it maybe more than I should. I lift his shirt, tugging it up to his shoulders before dragging my nails over his skin gently.

"What was your dream about?" he asks with a sigh, shifting and settling into the bed more, wiggling a little closer.

He reminds me of my parents' golden retriever, Cloudy. Named to be ironic, since my mom found that Sunny is one of the most popular names for goldens. Anyway, they got Cloudy after I graduated from college, and I've never seen a dog be so shameless about demanding pets. You start scratching Cloudy, and you are not allowed to stop. He will nudge his head under your hand, smack you with his paw, and follow you through the house looking at you with big pleading eyes.

Okay, I guess comparatively, Wyatt isn't as bad as my parents' dog.

I roll over a little, turning so I can use both hands.

"I don't remember the details," I say. "Don't you hate that? Like—your brain is soooo intensely focused on something it wakes you in a panic, but when you try to remember it, all you get are cobwebs and smoke."

"Mmm," Wyatt says, and I'm not sure whether he's agreeing or just responding to my nails on his skin.

"Thank you for coming to check on me. Sorry I showed my thanks by kicking you."

"You're making up for it now," he says. After a pause, he asks, "Are you stressed about the trip?"

As I think about this, I switch up my scratching, moving in small circles rather than long strokes.

"I don't feel stressed, but maybe."

"You seemed stressed yesterday," he says, and there's the smallest hint of amusement in his voice. "About the shoes."

I drop my head back, staring at the sweep of ceiling above us. The *shoes*.

Yesterday, after double-checking Wyatt's list and then my list—because I'm the kind of person who needs her own list—and finding we had everything packed on the boat other than my small bag of toiletries, I had a sudden moment of admittedly overblown panic.

The galley is as stocked as it can be with food. Canned tuna, chicken, beans, and vegetables; boxes of pasta, rice, and couscous—which Wyatt frowned about, but I swore to make him love—spices, cooking oil, and plenty of water. My clothes are in my cabin, along with books I ordered from Amazon since we'll be gone too long for library books. The journal I bought especially for the trip is next to my pillow with fresh pens—my favorite brand that never leave ink blots and also smell amazing. Plus I've got my chartbook and guide to the Intracoastal—a.k.a. the Ditch—which have been my trusty textbooks.

And while I was putting one of those books in a cabinet, I realized one thing I didn't have: boat shoes.

I found Wyatt, who was fiddling with the GPS up on deck.

"I don't have boat shoes," I said. When he didn't immediately look at me, I grabbed him by the chin and turned his face toward mine. His gray eyes were wide with surprise as I repeated more slowly, almost threateningly, "I don't have boat shoes."

Wyatt kept his gaze fixed on mine, his lids lowering slightly and his expression softening. "You don't need a certain kind of shoes, Rookie."

"Yes, I do. Everyone does. You do."

I let go of his chin then, embarrassed at the way I'd grabbed him, and looked pointedly down at his worn, loafery shoes. Boat shoes. "I need those."

"My shoes won't fit you, I'm afraid."

"Not *yours*. But shoes like that. Sailing shoes."

"Your tennis shoes and those sporty sandals are just fine."

"But they're not made for boating. What if I slip? What if they—"

"Josie."

Wyatt shocked me into silence when he took my hand in his. He didn't link our fingers but curled his whole hand around mind, squeezing firmly.

What was I worried about, again?

"I promise you—it's going to be okay. And if you've changed your mind about the trip, we don't have to go."

"What? No! I want to go! This is just about shoes."

"Is it?"

The way he asked was so kind. But also mean. Because I didn't want to examine what he was suggesting. Easier to be worried about shoes than an almost monthlong sailing trip with a man whom, a month ago, I would have said I couldn't stand and vice versa.

His question made me close my mouth, swallowing hard as I focused on the warmth of his palm against mine, the firm clasp of his fingers.

"I want to go," I whispered.

"Good," he said, and then with a final squeeze, he dropped my hand and went back to the GPS. "Then go make sure the life preservers are in place and that we finished stocking the galley."

We'd already done both of those things, but doing them again made me feel better. Somehow, I think he knew it would.

And fine, he was right: The shoes were definitely a physical manifestation of my anxiety. A place to direct all my worries and fears about taking a long boat trip when all my sailing knowledge is stuff I picked up from books, Reddit, and Wyatt over the past few weeks.

Those worries are big. Huge.

Shoes are a small worry. Easy.

The other thing I'm worried about that's much bigger than shoes and even bigger than the boat is Wyatt. More specifically, my feelings for him.

Because a boat trip with a guy you like could feel romantic when it's really not.

It could just as easily be full of unrequited longing and eventual heartbreak. Which I will not think about! I fire my optimism like a cannon at these intrusive thoughts anytime they arise.

But all worries about the trip aside, I *do* wish I had boat shoes.

It takes me a moment, but I manage to dig up words from a not-so-shallow resting place in my mind: "I struggle with change." When Wyatt doesn't say anything, I continue, the words flowing a little more easily as I go, like runoff down a hill. "I mean, I know that's normal. Few people actually like change. But for me it's . . . different. I don't try new things. Or put myself in unfamiliar places."

Wyatt wiggles a little, redirecting my scratching, and it loosens the tight bands around my chest. I smile and think again of my parents' dog.

"You're here," he points out, and I stop smiling. "You came; you stayed. And you're taking this trip with me. Those all seem new. Unfamiliar."

My fingers freeze on his back. Is he . . . challenging me? Saying he doesn't believe me? I start to pull away.

But before I can choke out some kind of defense, Wyatt turns, catching my hands with his and holding my gaze through the darkness.

"Hey," he says quietly. "I'm trying to say you're brave, Rookie. This has been a lot. It's no wonder you're having nightmares."

"Oh." It's all I can think to say. Thoughts are hard to come by when his hands are lightly squeezing mine and his eyes are on me and his words are so . . . understanding. Gentle.

"I would have helped if I'd known. I mean—not that I know how to help. But I would have tried," he says.

"Thank you," I whisper.

"You're so capable and confident." He shakes his head a little, and the compliments burrow deep in the center of my chest. "I'm sorry if I've made things hard. Or worse. I wouldn't have guessed."

"People don't usually. And I don't talk about it much."

Try: *ever.*

I'm startled by this realization. I haven't ever talked openly about this. Not to my brother or parents or Toni. My best friend is around me enough to know my habits and my propensity toward staying in my nice, safe spaces. But she's never asked, and I've never confessed. Heat rises in my cheeks.

"Do you take any anxiety meds?"

"I—no. It's not that bad." When Wyatt narrows his eyes at me, I add, "It's not."

"Did you decide this or did a professional?"

Ouch. Those words hit me like the crack of a whip.

"I don't need a professional to tell me. I can handle it just fine. I don't have anxiety. I just get anxious. There's a difference."

Is there, though? His question has sent my thoughts reeling. I don't need someone else to tell me I'm okay. Definitely not a doctor or psychiatrist. Or a psychologist? I can never remember the difference.

I'm suddenly in need of a subject change.

"Are *you* nervous?" I ask Wyatt, gently tugging my hands from his and pushing on him so I can scratch his back again. He resists at first, but then rolls over with a sigh.

"About sailing? No."

"About something else?"

He's quiet for a long moment. "I have some concerns."

"Like what?"

His silence stretches longer this time, and I'm about to poke him and ask if he's awake when he quietly says, "I want this trip to be good for you."

I smile into the darkness, letting my nails trace a wavy line up his back.

"But this is *your* trip," I say. "The one you were going to take with your uncle and then alone."

"It *was* that," he says. "But now it's ours."

I barely have time to register all the ways his words are sinking deeply under my skin when Wyatt suddenly swings his legs over the side of the bed and walks to the door without looking back.

"Get some sleep, Josie. You have nothing to be nervous about. And you don't need boat shoes."

"Says the man with three pairs."

He chuckles as he goes, and though I fall back asleep, I miss the comforting presence and warmth of Wyatt beside me.

19

Hands on the Wheel

Josie

Our first morning starts as a bit of a bummer. "Holy fog, Bat-man," I say, walking out the back door of Wyatt's house at six o'clock.

I'm talking to myself because Wyatt is already on board. At least I think that's Wyatt and I think that's the boat. The vague shape of a tall person—a hockey player–shaped person— moving around has to be him.

I refuse to see the fog as some kind of omen. But it's wild— other than the one morning I woke to a torrential downpour that lasted less than an hour, every morning since I arrived has been bright. Hot. Sunny.

Then today we get fog. Not pea soup fog either. It's more of a nice, creamy baked potato soup.

"Come on, Jib."

She's off before I finish talking, running ahead and barking out a greeting to Wyatt. She only pauses to lift her leg on a dock piling. Because yes, lifting her leg is Jib's potty preference.

"Really?" Wyatt asks as I reach the boat. He's looking from me to Jib. More specifically, at what Jib's wearing.

"What? Too on the nose for you?"

Today I have her decked out in a little rain outfit: a yellow slicker, matching yellow hat, and black boots that fit over her tiny paws. I've never seen something so cute. Honestly.

Ridiculous and unnecessary? Yes.

But if you have a rain slicker, when better to use it than a foggy morning?

With a sigh, Wyatt scoops up Jib and pulls her onto the boat. She snuggles happily against his chest. I don't blame her—it's a great chest for snuggling into—and though he turns away, I don't miss Wyatt's smile.

I never would have predicted it, but now I see little signs of Wyatt's kindness every day. And it's leaving me with a very nagging sense that I've spent years misunderstanding him.

Such a secret softie.

"Are you coming?" he asks a little abruptly.

A secret softie wrapped in porcupine quills.

I hop onto the boat, saying goodbye to land for the next few weeks.

Okay—that's slightly dramatic. It's not like some ocean passage where we won't actually set foot on solid ground for days or weeks at a time. According to our plan, we'll get off the boat almost every day. We have to, at the very least, for Jib to go to the bathroom. Wyatt swears she'll learn to use the little patch of synthetic grass he bought for her—and he gives *me* a hard time about buying her outfits!—but so far on our test sails out to the Chesapeake Bay, she's proven she won't.

All things considered, the trip down to just south of Savannah and back should take us around three to four weeks. Barring any delays, Wyatt likes to remind me. And we really need to avoid delays. There's still plenty of summer left, but I never intended to be gone more than a week. And if Wyatt's ready, he'll head back to preseason training camp in Boston.

Neither of which are things I want to think about.

When I asked him what kind of delays we could have, Wyatt said, "It's life. There are always unplanned issues, whether you're on a boat or on land."

True. But because I like to be prepared, I googled *What can go wrong on a sailing trip?* and now unfortunately have a whole litany of disasters to worry about. Despite my growing excitement, this trip is so far out of my comfort zone it's not on my comfort *planet*.

Throw in the idea of storms or the boat breaking down and my brain goes to a bad place.

And yes, I know I take the kinds of trips with my brother where he'll text me an address and I'll show up, but that's *Jacob*. We grew up together. Shared life, shared memories, shared DNA. I might not know the details (and honestly, his track record for these trips is horrible), but I know I can count on him. It's not comfortable, but I'm more used to it. To him.

With Wyatt, there are so many unknowns.

We've shared a house, shared a trip to the hospital, and shared some nice moments lately. Like, for example, last night after my nightmare. (And after he recovered from me kicking him in the baby-making parts.) But . . .

But.

But.

But.

I still think this whole thing could blow up in my face.

We'll see, I guess—because after taking a deep breath, I get on the boat.

"What can I do?" I ask Wyatt after stowing my backpack in my cabin.

Jib is at the prow of the boat, lying down on the little grass patch she's supposed to use as her bathroom, while Wyatt frowns at his phone. He glances up and slides it into his pocket.

"Nothing. We're ready. If you're ready."

It's a statement, but there's a question in his voice. I can hear the unspoken offer. *It's not too late to change your mind about this.*

But I smile and tug on the brim of my baseball cap. "Let's hoist the anchor, raise the sails, and bon voyage!"

Wyatt shakes his head. "Please stop with the sailing terms. You sound like someone who spent the last few weeks researching sailing."

"That's exactly what I did."

Lo and behold—Wyatt chuckles. "I know. But technically we'll be motoring a lot of the way, so what you're saying is also wrong. We won't raise the sails until we're in the bay, depending on this fog."

"Sheesh. Batten down your hatches."

He waves a hand toward the front of the boat. "Help me cast off."

"Aye, aye—"

"Don't say it, I beg you."

"*Captain.*"

"Are you going to do this the whole time?" he asks.

"What—be utterly charming and fun? Or pepper every conversation with sailing terms even if I'm using them incorrectly?"

"Both."

"Probably."

"Fine," he says. "Now pull in the bumpers."

And . . . we're off.

⚓

The fog burns off quickly, and things are uneventful for the first hour. And according to Wyatt, uneventful on a boat is good.

We reach the Chesapeake Bay where we'll switch from the engine to sails—just as we've done almost daily for the last ten days. Now, though, adrenaline and anxiety twist in my gut. Because this is it. Not practice. The real thing.

Wyatt and me on the not-so-open seas. I swallow and squeeze my hands into fists.

"Josie?"

I glance over at Wyatt. "Hmm?"

"Are you okay?"

"Totally."

He watches me for a moment like he's waiting for me to confess the truth. Which is that I'm honestly trying not to freak out. I must convince him because Wyatt gives me a brisk nod and moves on.

"Take the wheel," he orders.

Instantly, nerves flutter in my stomach.

But I fight them off by giving them the coldest of cold shoulders. *Nerves? What nerves?* Setting Jib down from her perch on my lap, I stride over to the wheel with all the faux confidence I can muster.

No biggie. I can steer a ship. Boat. Whatever.

I've steered before during our practice sails, but even so, I don't know how many times it would take for me to feel at ease.

How many years of sailing does it take to do all this with Wyatt's confidence?

I watch him move around the deck, tying and untying and fastening and doing all the things needed to switch from motor to sail. Some of the steps I remember; some I don't. Mentally, I go over various boat terms like I'm giving myself a pop quiz. Mainsail, headsail (or jib), cleat, sheet.

And if, while doing so, I happen to admire Wyatt's effortless movements around the boat, not a single person could blame me. I find my brain zipping from sailing parts to muscle groups as Wyatt's strain against his T-shirt: trapezius, deltoids, triceps, latissimus dorsi.

If there were a combo quiz on sailing and men's muscle groups, I'd get an A plus.

It's also great to see him fully mobile with hardly a limp. His progress—once he decided to actually make progress—was impressive. He has an orthotic insert inside his shoe to support the arch, but you'd never know from looking that he's a few months out from a serious injury.

"Watch the markers," Wyatt says sharply, and I realize that while watching the sails and the man raising them, my attention drifted from my one task.

I reorient myself, glancing quickly at the screen a few feet away that shows our speed (four knots) and our direction (southeast). Then I glance out at the water, seeking out channel markers.

"Red, right, returning," I mutter. I remember the phrase, but at the moment, it confuses me.

We're not returning. So red shouldn't be on my right—right? Green. I want green on my right.

"Let me." Wyatt is suddenly beside me, his voice tight as he uses his shoulder to nudge me aside and takes the wheel.

I stand there for a long moment, feeling the sharp sting of embarrassment as Wyatt cuts the boat sharply to the left. A gull glides overhead, laughing.

I know, logically, it's not laughing at me. But I want to throw something at it anyway.

"Hey," Wyatt says, catching my eye. His voice is gentler than before. "It's fine. You were doing fine."

I nod quickly and take a seat, glad when Jib rushes over and plunks down in my lap. She's lost one of her boots. I tug her hat off—after all, the sun is now beating down on us—and stroke her ears.

Wyatt's wrong, of course. I was too far over, past the channel markers. And my brain shorted out and took too long to remember the knowledge I needed immediately. I could have run us aground. The thought of how quickly and easily I messed up has my stomach knotting uncomfortably.

"Josie, I'm serious."

"I wasn't paying enough attention," I say, sounding stubborn. "I lost sight of the channel markers."

"You're still learning. It will take time for this to be second nature. If you beat yourself up every time you make a mistake or forget something, you'll make yourself miserable. Stop."

"Okay," I say, but I can tell by the way his frown deepens he hears the same tremor in my voice that I do.

"Come here," Wyatt says, the command firm but not sharp like when he warned me to watch where I was going.

It's the kind of authority I can't help but respond to.

Nudging Jib off my lap, I walk stiffly over to him, squinting in the sun. Wyatt takes one hand off the wheel and steps back a little.

"Here," he says, but I shake my head.

"I need a minute," I tell him.

Sighing, he pulls the sunglasses from his face and perches them carefully on my nose. All while steering one-handed with an ease and confidence that makes me envious. His fingertips brush my cheek, and though it's heating up out here, a shiver moves through me. He curls his hand around my waist, tugging me in front of him, facing the wheel.

I expect him to step back and bark orders the way he usually does. Instead, he returns his other hand to the wheel so I'm now trapped in front of him.

I guess . . . I don't mind all that much.

"Hands on the wheel, Rookie," he orders.

I place my hands on the curve of metal, and he slides his hands closer until they're bracketing mine.

I expect some kind of sailing lesson to follow or maybe more rebuke telling me to snap out of it. And honestly, he'd be right to do so. I'm violently overreacting.

It's just . . . I want to do well. I tackled sailing knowledge like I did all of my academic classes—*hard*. But also excitedly. I've babbled on to Wyatt about things I've learned, asked him questions, given myself mental gold stars for my efforts.

I've got this, I thought.

But I *don't* got this. Not any of it.

Having my confidence shaken so early in the trip over something so simple as channel markers has rocked me. My insides feel wobbly. My self-doubt is raging, and I'm trying really hard not to cry.

Which only makes me angry at myself for being an overly sensitive baby about this. I don't like to think of myself as a delicate flower, but here I am. Delicate. Flowery.

Wyatt says nothing. He simply shelters me against the firmness of his body, his thumbs brushing over my pinkies as we cut through the open water of the Chesapeake Bay.

Slowly, the tightness in my chest loosens and the threat of impending tears dissipates like the morning fog.

"Thank you," I whisper, not sure if Wyatt can even hear me over the wind and the water.

But he leans forward, cheek brushing mine as he says, "Don't let it happen again."

I laugh because it's so very Wyatt. "I can't promise I won't steer us off course again."

"No—I meant don't doubt yourself again."

I can't promise that either. But his support makes me feel infinitely better.

The rest of the day passes without incident, and by the time we reach our stop for the night, I've fully recovered from my bout of almost paralyzing self-doubt.

I have not, however, recovered from the feeling of Wyatt's strong and steady presence, the warmth of his muscular chest against my back, the occasional puff of breath against my neck. People talk about sea legs, how you have to get used to the water and the rock of the boat. I had zero problem finding my sea legs.

Instead, I'm struggling to find my *Wyatt* legs. I am completely shaken by him.

Even after he backs the boat expertly into the spot the harbormaster gave us over the radio and I hop off the boat, I feel an unsteadiness that's bone deep. Maybe soul deep.

"Come on, Jibby," I say, grateful for the tiny dog who somehow is my only ally, my noncomplicated companion. As long as she's here, I have some kind of protection against the man who is slowly and far too quickly dismantling all of me. A canine chaperone or buffer.

But I can't help wondering: Is Wyatt *trying* to dismantle things? Is he intentionally trying to push past my defenses?

Does he have the same tug of attraction, or am I projecting my own growing feelings?

That I can't answer. And I'm not sure I want to know. How terrible would it be if we had a conversation about feelings and learned that our feelings are not the same?

I try to imagine being on the tiny deck with Wyatt after he's said that he just doesn't see me that way or, like an echo from the past, *Not your* sister.

That was years ago, I tell myself. After all, I'd said I would never be into him, and look where we are now.

In any case, my head is a mess over Wyatt.

Aside from that, I feel really great about our first day sailing. Despite my carelessness, we didn't run aground. We didn't hit anything. We followed sailing protocol when we passed other boats, and I got to chat with a few of them on the VHF radio, which made me feel very official.

A small pod of dolphins—or porpoises? I don't know the difference—swam alongside our boat for almost an hour.

I honestly thought Jib might go overboard to join them. She barked at them for a solid five minutes, running from one side of the boat to the other until she finally fell into an exhausted nap.

I kept watch as the sleek gray heads appeared and then dipped below the surface. A good omen for sailing.

I swear one of them made eye contact with me and we had kind of a moment.

"How many of those did you pack?"

Wyatt is suddenly beside me in the grassy area just outside the marina where Jib has been peeing for probably two minutes straight. She did not learn to use Wyatt's fake grass patch after all.

I glance at the navy-and-white-striped sailor's costume I put her in after the morning fog left.

"Let's just say . . . she has more clothes than I do."

Wyatt watches her for a long moment, his expression un-readable. She's still peeing. Honestly, for a small dog, I don't know how her bladder holds so much.

"Why, though?" he asks finally.

"You said she was ugly. Then I had her shaved and you said she looked like a rat. It's enough to give a girl a complex."

"I did not give our dog a complex."

Our. The word slams into me, and I think it hits him at the same moment because he goes stiff beside me.

Our dog.

Several thoughts compete for dominance in my brain. There's the super hopeful, suddenly romantic part of me that wants to read into this as Wyatt's way of declaring his feelings.

I mean, you don't have a joint dog with a friend, right? That's totally a couple thing.

But a more logical, tragic part of my brain, the part that sometimes rises up to do battle with my optimism, reminds me that at the end of this trip, I'll be going back to Fredericksburg and my normal life.

And Wyatt? He'll go back to Boston where he'll lace up a pair of skates and then resume whatever normal life looks like for a hockey star.

There is no *our* with Jib. What's next will be a custody battle.

Or not, actually. I can't see Wyatt fighting me for her. Not when his job involves so much travel.

Still. He said *our*—that one little word holds way too much possibility.

Jib finishes peeing—finally—and I make the conscious choice to shake off all the giddiness brought on by a single syl-lable. I can't go catching feelings for Wyatt.

"Come on," I say. "Let's walk Jibby before we head inside."

Quietly, Wyatt falls into step beside me.

Tonight we're staying at a yacht club that has reciprocity with Wyatt's yacht club. Reciprocity with a yacht club is a statement that feels silly and pretentious at the same time.

But I won't complain about the fact that there is a locker room with nice showers, or so Wyatt told me, and a great restaurant. We have lots of provisions on the boat, but there will be no fancy meals in the limited kitchen. I anticipate a lot of sandwiches and soups direct from a can. I'm excited for the hot shower and also a few minutes' break from Wyatt to reset my brain.

I expect him to ignore the weirdness of *our* the same as I'm trying to do, but he doesn't. After a few minutes of walking in silence other than to say hello to strangers who stop to admire Jib's outfit, he turns to me.

"At the end of this—"

"Nope," I interrupt, waving the hand not holding Jib's leash as panic shoots through me. "We're not doing this."

"You don't know what I was going to say."

"You're right. But it's day one of the trip. I am in no way prepared to think about the end of it."

"I just think it would be good to have a conversation about expectations," he says.

Somehow, the way he words this and his tone of voice make it sound like he thinks *I* have expectations—and they're not realistic. Or not the same as his. Like he needs to make sure I understand there will not be an *our*, a *we*, or an *us* at the end of the trip.

"You know what this feels like?" I say. "You're trying to force me to read the last chapter of a book I just started so I can be prepared for how it will end. I don't read that way, mister."

He drags a hand through his hair, clearly agitated, leaving the dark blond strands a mess. "That's not what I'm doing."

Maybe not. But that's how it feels. And I'm not sure how I'll make it through the next few weeks if I know every day is taking me closer to certain doom.

Do I really think something could work between Wyatt and me?

No.

Or—I don't know. It's highly unlikely.

Even if I am picking up on signals and there is a real spark here, at the end of the day, Wyatt lives in Boston and has a totally abnormal job. One where the hours and the travel and the intensity make a normal life hard, and where the perks include women waiting in hotels and sliding into DMs. Though I don't think Wyatt even uses social media. Jacob has told me that he hires people to run accounts for his clients who don't want to do it, and I'd place bets Wyatt is one of them.

I also know from Jacob that most of his clients don't *do* normal. They don't date elementary school nurses; they date models and actresses and heiresses. Leggy and booby and on a first-name basis with their eyelash-extension people. Women who are willing and eager to put up with all the downsides of the lifestyle. When it comes to Wyatt, I may have been able to move past my long-held hang-up with athletes, but that doesn't mean I'm eager to be a WAG, the term I learned from Jacob to refer to athletes' wives and girlfriends.

Speaking of Jacob, how would he feel about me and Wyatt?

Any way I try to think about this, about us, about the future, I can't see one ending with us together.

But this—here and now with Wyatt? This, I can see. This feels good—like something real and right.

I'm not ready to look past the present moment, afraid it will pop like a bubble with no warning. There one minute, translucent and delicate and perfect, hanging in the air, and gone the next, like it had never existed at all.

Wyatt is still staring at me, his jaw working like he's trying to come up with the right answer, the arrangement of words that will convince me to have this discussion. And honestly, he just might. I feel my resolve cracking the longer I look at his gray eyes.

Jib provides the perfect distraction by choosing that moment and a flower bed to finish doing her business.

"Can you hold her leash so I can get a poop bag?" I ask Wyatt, handing him the leash.

Because I can think of no better mood killer, no better way to slam and lock the door on an emotional conversation, than talking about poop bags.

20

Definitely Not a Couple

Josie

We leave Jib on the boat while we head back to the yacht club for showers and dinner. The yacht club locker room is gorgeous and mostly empty, despite a group of women in tennis skirts who flounce through, laughing and drinking what I suspect is not water from their monogrammed Stanley cups. I decide while enjoying the luxuriously wide shower that a group of tennis-playing women should be called a twiffle.

Turns out, I didn't do a great job of applying my own sunscreen today after the fog burned off. I've got a few places I missed completely on my neck, the backs of my arms, and my shoulders. They're red and tender. Otherwise, my skin feels fresh after washing off the salt and sweat. There's something about putting on a dress and a little makeup after spending the day on the water that makes me feel like a princess.

It also makes me feel nervous. Like I'm going on a date, not just having dinner with Wyatt the same way I have for the last three weeks.

That thought—plus the fear he might try again to have the conversation I don't want to have—has me mildly panicking when I reach the yacht club dining room before Wyatt. I start to sweat when I see the restaurant's low lighting, with candles and flowers on every table. Not the vibe I want to have tonight.

So when an older couple I met earlier on the docks extends an invitation for us to join them, I'm all too eager to say yes without waiting for Wyatt. And it's a good thing because when Wyatt joins us a moment later, wearing khaki pants stretched tight over his muscular thighs and a polo shirt he's been practically poured into, with shower-damp hair I want to run my fingers through, I know I would have weakened without a buffer. He looks better than any appetizer could, and even Wanda gives an appreciative hum that makes her husband, Greg, chuckle.

There's no way Wyatt can broach any big topics now. And though I'm still not sure what he was going to say, I don't want to know. I can't. Not today.

Whether it's about feelings, which is probably not it, or who will take Jib, or even what the end of this trip will mean for the budding friendship I've grown really used to—I'm just not ready.

I don't want to skip to the end.

I want to exist in the now and only the now for as long as possible—please and thank you very much. Even if this is the exact opposite of how I normally live. It's what I need to survive this boat trip with Wyatt.

"So, where are you two from?" Wanda asks after we've given the waitress our drink orders.

Wanda has the kind of long white hair younger women like me can only aspire to one day. It's tied in a neat braid hanging over one shoulder with a pink ribbon tied around it. Somehow, this feminine touch isn't out of place, though she doesn't have on a stitch of makeup and her clothes almost exactly match her husband's—khaki pants, boat shoes, and a collared polo shirt. Hers is green and his is navy.

"I'm from Fredericksburg," I say, then point to Wyatt. "He's from Boston."

"Oh," she says, sitting back, clearly surprised. "You two aren't a—"

"Nope," I say quickly before she can finish. "We're barely friends."

That is not the best description or even a mildly accurate one, and I don't miss the hurt flashing in Wyatt's eyes. But I can't apologize and make it better. I can't tell him the truth—that he's become much more than even a casual friend.

"Or, rather, we're *new* friends," I amend, wishing I could build a safety barrier that didn't also include hurting Wyatt's feelings. "But definitely not a couple." The chuckle that escapes me sounds less humorous and more like the start of bronchitis.

Any second now, I could stop talking. Probably *should* stop talking if Wyatt's expression is any indication.

"How did you end up sailing together?" Wanda asks. "That must be a story."

Her husband chuckles and reaches over to pat her hand. His cheeks are rosy and his smile wide, giving him the look of a beardless Santa. "Don't be so nosy."

"I'm not being nosy. I'm being polite. It's kind to be curious."

"'Kind to be curious,'" I repeat. "I like that." When Wyatt doesn't seem inclined to speak, I jump in. "The short story is that Wyatt is a friend of my brother's and needed someone to go with him on this trip. I was sort of thrown into it."

So many details are omitted from that explanation. So many gaps and important things glossed over. Hot shame licks at my chest, and I resist the urge to press a hand to my sternum.

"Incorrect," Wyatt says. "She blackmailed me."

Wanda gasps. "Blackmail?"

I gape at Wyatt, whose expression has gone from disappointed to distant and now to what I can only describe as dastardly. There's a spark in his gray eyes. A challenge. And it makes something just as fiery rise in me along with a strange sense of gratitude.

He's saving me from myself and my stupid mouth. And returning us to the plane of existence where we really shine: the one where we're sniping at each other with our words. The pinch in my chest turns into warmth.

I scoff. "I did *not* blackmail you! It was a bargain."

"You say bargain. I say blackmail."

"You're impossible."

"Thank you."

"Wasn't a compliment," I say. "I'll add that you're stubborn and infuriating."

"My, my," Wanda says, and when I glance over at the other two people at the table I'd momentarily forgotten about, she's fanning herself with a menu, a knowing smile on her face. "Barely friends, indeed."

I'm saved by the arrival of the waitress, but I don't miss Wyatt's little smirk before he hides it behind his menu.

After we order, the conversation moves to safer topics: our respective travels, our final destinations, and our boats. I don't try shoving my whole foot in my mouth again, but Wyatt and I can't go more than a few minutes without verbally sparring. We spend a good five minutes arguing about Jib's wardrobe.

The funniest part? Wyatt's argument wasn't about the existence of a full wardrobe but the *kinds* of clothes I packed. I'm not even sure he realized this, but I'm very much looking forward to pointing it out at just the right time.

As the four of us walk to the marina together after dinner, Wanda and I hang back while Greg and Wyatt have a serious discussion about college basketball. I had no idea Wyatt liked sports other than hockey, much less had such strong opinions about them.

"Can I offer up a word of advice?" Wanda asks, and when I nod, she smiles and bumps me with her shoulder. "Better started than perfect. Better tried than unknown."

She looks at me expectantly, then laughs at what I'm sure is a very blank expression. Her words sound like AI's attempt to write a fortune cookie.

"I'm afraid you might need to be more basic," I tell her. "Say it again, but like I'm five years old?"

She laughs, tucking an arm around me. Greg, hearing the sound, glances back, and she waves, but it's more like she's shooing him away. I try to imagine Wanda and Greg around my age. She said they met when they were both nineteen, got married just a week after they met, and have been together ever since. It's kind of adorable.

I lean into her, smelling a soft lemon scent. I'm suddenly very homesick for my mom for the second time this summer. Turns out my parents have been in South Dakota, not South Carolina, and have had spotty reception.

We talked two weeks ago, and I filled them in on what Jacob did—Mom only *tsk*ed—and then somehow didn't tell them that I'd stayed on with Wyatt. I'm not sure why, though I strongly suspect both of my parents would have been delighted by this news.

They've always loved Wyatt—even after the kitchen incident the first time Jacob brought him home. Without ever hearing the full story involving Grocery Store Girl, Mom and Dad thought the whole thing was an indication that Wyatt had a crush on me. They quickly stopped teasing me about it when I threatened to stop coming home, but telling my parents I'm sailing with Wyatt would have been like throwing fresh kindling and some gasoline on the embers of a fire. So I just . . . omitted that part of the story. Easy to do when they wanted to tell me about their trip. I was relieved when they drove into a dead zone and the phone cut out.

Right now, though, with Wanda's arm around my shoulders, I wish for five minutes with my mom. I'd confess everything and maybe even ask for advice.

Wanda squeezes my shoulder. "What I mean is, it's better to try now than to wait until the timing or circumstances feel exactly right. If you wait until things are perfect, you'll be waiting your whole life. And if you never take the risk, you won't ever know."

"Do you mean with Wyatt?"

She laughs again. "Yes, I mean with Wyatt. There's something brewing there."

"Brewing like a storm, maybe," I mutter, kicking at a warped board on the dock. I glance up at the man in question, who towers almost comically over Greg. Not for the first time, I consider how strange it is *not* to be intimidated by a man Wyatt's size.

But then . . . I've been touching him, getting sometimes comically close to him since the day I arrived in Kilmarnock. Not once do I remember feeling nervous or uncomfortable, the way I usually do around men. Especially big men. Most especially athletes.

I swallow, my head swimming a little as I consider this. And Wanda's words. And Wyatt's attempts to talk earlier.

Nope. Still not ready to think about this.

"Brewing like the very *best* kind of storm," Wanda says with a wink.

But I don't believe her. It's brewing like a hurricane, gaining strength off the coast, ready to wash away my safe little town.

Greg and Wyatt stop under a light by the dock to argue, moths circling the flickering bulb overhead. If we don't get inside soon, the mosquitoes, who love me with a very unrequited love, will suck all the blood from my body.

"His coaching style is ruining the players," Greg says loudly.

Wyatt responds, "He's got one of best defensive programs in the country."

"I hate basketball," Wanda says with a sigh, but when I glance at her, she's smiling fondly at her husband. "But a successful marriage isn't about aligning on all points. Just the ones that matter. Which is fewer than you might think," she adds with a wink.

Okay, Wanda. That's quite enough matchmaking from you.

But apparently, it's not.

"A successful marriage takes place in the gaps," she says.

Despite the appeal of diving off the dock instead of finishing this conversation, I find myself asking, "The gaps?"

"People always say opposites attract or like minds find each other. But it doesn't matter whether you're opposites or like two halves of a whole. There will always be gaps where you don't agree or don't understand or don't align. Lots of gaps. A successful marriage is one that works even in those gaps. It's all about navigating and bridging the gaps, even if they never close. Do you see?"

I'm not entirely sure I do, but I know I'll be thinking about her words for a long time to come. Even if they're not exactly relevant right this second.

"I appreciate the advice. And I'll keep it in mind when I find someone I might consider marrying."

"Mm-hmm." Wanda raises her brows. Her upturned mouth calls me a liar as clearly as if she'd said the words aloud.

"He doesn't see me that way," I say, lowering my voice. "He never has."

But I don't think I believe my own words. Maybe they were true once.

Now, though, I think of Wyatt running into my room when I had a nightmare, Wyatt buying new furniture for his cottage because I complained, Wyatt standing behind me at the wheel of the boat until I felt secure piloting alone.

The way he said *our* with Jib earlier, the way he said this is *our* trip. The way my words hurt him earlier, but instead of stewing over them or letting me continue to blunder, he swooped in and saved me.

I realize I'm expecting Wanda to argue with me, to say something like "I see the way he looks at you, and you're wrong," but she doesn't, and my heart shrivels a little in disappointment.

I am fully torn. I want to end this conversation and I also want her to argue with me. To talk again about the storm brewing between me and Wyatt. To provide more outside confirmation that there *is* a storm and I'm not just imagining the way things have shifted between us.

But now she shrugs and gives me a final squeeze before letting go. "Well, then. When you do find that person, remember the gaps. Or, as they'd say in England, mind the gap."

A familiar bark startles me, and I glance back to see Jib running over, tail wagging.

Only she's not coming from the direction of the boat, where I left her in my cabin. She's jogging from the direction of land, and she's not alone. An English bulldog trots along beside her, mouth open and tongue lolling. As Jib nears us, though, the other dog runs off.

I scoop her up. "Jib! You ripped your sailor shirt cavorting with that bulldog!"

The little outfit is hanging off one shoulder, torn along the seam. There's a stick tangled in the fabric and grass stains on the back. Jib looks wholly unrepentant. The other dog turns and heads back where they came from without a backwards look.

Wyatt is suddenly right beside me. He frowns, staring into Jib's eyes, and she wags her whole rear at his attention.

Wyatt plucks Jib from my arms and she nestles into his chest. "Did you figure out how to open the door, smart girl?"

It's funny when Wyatt talks to Jib because he doesn't use a baby voice like most people do when they're talking to dogs. He just speaks to her like an adult human who can understand everything.

His eyes narrow, meeting mine over Jib, though he's still talking to the dog. "Or did *someone* fail her basic door-closing course?"

"Hey!" I step on his foot lightly. His good foot—of course. "I know how to close doors, Wyatt."

"Do you?" he murmurs, but there's a smile in his voice.

"*Yes.*"

"I don't mean to interrupt," Wanda says. I realize how close Wyatt and I are standing and step back. "But is your little dog fixed? Because that guy is definitely not."

I glance at the bulldog, who's making his way up the steps toward the parking lot. She's right. He's definitely *not* fixed.

"Thankfully, yes." And I'm grateful because dog pregnancy is one worry my brain doesn't have room for right now.

⚓

I step out of the bathroom—*head*, I mentally correct—after brushing my teeth and step right into Wyatt. I barely manage not to shriek.

He could step back toward the saloon to give me some space. He doesn't. I shove him in the chest. But the hallway outside the bathroom is tiny and there's nowhere for him to go. We're practically on top of each other.

"You scared me, Wyatt! Why are you lingering outside the bathroom door?" I ask, heart racing. "What if I was pooping?"

"Were you? Because I can wait a few minutes before going in."

"*No.* Not that it's any of your business when I'm doing . . . my business."

"Okay," Wyatt says easily. Then he takes a step forward. I have to tilt my chin to meet his eyes. "Did you mean what you said earlier—that we're barely friends?"

Barely friends would have described us before I arrived in Kilmarnock. But even in the first few days there, things started to shift. Honestly, it might have happened the second day, when I met goofy, fever-fueled Wyatt who stuck his nose in my hair and said I smelled like pie.

Now . . . we're something more. I just don't know what we are. Or what I want us to be.

"No," I whisper.

The answer takes no thought. No debate. It's as simple and uncomplicated as breathing.

Yet the moment I say it, I'm terrified by the enormity of my admission. I freeze, the only movement my erratic heartbeat.

Wyatt reaches out one hand slowly, giving me time to say something or to move. I do neither, and he gently cups my jaw, his thumb brushing over my cheek.

"That's not what I want either," he says.

I close my eyes, allowing myself to feel the sweep of his thumb over my skin, the warmth of his body so close to mine, his breath on my cheek.

"But what *do* you want, Josie?" he asks, his voice a quiet murmur that has the hairs standing up along my arms. "Do you want to be barely friends?"

"No."

"Good friends? *Only* friends?"

I swallow. "I don't know."

I expect his hand to drop. For him to flee or sigh with frustration or press me for a clear answer. To try to force the conversation I avoided earlier about what comes next.

The one I'm still—mostly—wanting to avoid.

Instead, he says, "Okay."

I open my eyes, blinking sleepily at him. "Okay?"

"Okay," he repeats. Then adds, "For now."

"For now?"

He nods once, decisively, and his hand flexes against my jaw, like he's barely restraining himself from sliding his fingers into my hair.

And maybe, from the look in his eyes, pulling my mouth to his.

I suddenly want nothing more than exactly that.

And yet.

And yet.

Something still holds me back. A little pocket of fear, a tiny hiccup of hesitation.

If Wyatt kissed me now, I wouldn't stop him. I wouldn't be sorry.

But I'm also not sure I'd be ready.

With no warning, he wraps me in his arms and tugs me closer until my cheek rests against his chest, feeling the rapid thump of his heart. I stiffen in surprise, not fear, and one of his big hands slides up my back, his palm a comforting sweep of warmth.

"This is called a hug," he says, and I remember saying this same thing to him a few weeks ago.

I snort. "I'm aware. Thank you."

Sighing, I snuggle in, allowing him to pull me closer, hold me tighter. When I breathe in his masculine scent, I feel comfortable. Sheltered. *Safe.*

Yet also like I'm dancing unsteadily on the edge of a blade.

"I'm a patient man. I won't push you," Wyatt says then. "At least, not *too* hard. Hopefully, just hard enough."

"How do you know what's just hard enough?" I ask, my fingers flexing on his lower back.

"You may not realize this," he says, "but I've become an expert in reading you, Josie."

"An expert, huh?"

"Certified."

"Or certifiable?"

He hums, a low, rough sound that's almost a growl. With my face pressed against his chest, I can feel the vibration move through me. I want him to do it again, to feel the rumble on my skin.

"Just know that you're in charge," he says. "If I push too much or if you want me to stop or if you don't feel safe, say the word. Do you understand? It's about when *you're* ready."

"Yes," I whisper, my fingers clutching his shirt, tugging the material into my fists, torn between wanting to be closer and wanting to run away.

"Good."

Pressing a kiss so quickly to the top of my head that I barely register it, Wyatt lets go of me and strides back to his room. Leaving me standing in the cramped hallway, wondering what I just agreed to and if it's too soon to tell him I'm already ready.

Or if I want to run to shore, find Wanda, and hitch a ride up north with her and Greg.

21

Grasping at Tiny Paper Straws

Wyatt

"You only made one real mistake yesterday," I tell Josie the next morning.

At the flash of surprised hurt on her face, I immediately wish for a large cartoon boulder to fall on my head. Or an anvil. Maybe a baby grand piano.

Because I'm running my idiot flag up the pole and flying it high this morning.

Josie hands me a mug of coffee from the counter with a tight smile. "Just the way you enjoy it—black like your heart. And it's a little early in the morning for criticism, isn't it?"

I *meant* to be encouraging. To tell Josie she did a great job on her first day sailing. One tiny mistake when she missed seeing the channel markers. We didn't run aground or hit anything. No biggie—though she beat herself up over it. I meant to reassure her.

But what I just said was the equivalent of a negative performance review. Like some kind of terrible boss. Or a very bad captain.

Per usual, I don't know how to fix my bumbling words.

I take a sip of coffee and study Josie, who is adding cream to her mug. When I got up a few minutes ago, I was surprised to find her already boiling water. The sight of her here—in this familiar, nostalgic, and at times painful place—stole my breath as surely as if I'd been hit right in the diaphragm.

It still is. And, clearly, stealing my ability to speak.

"Come up and sit with me?" I ask, a flare of nerves like I haven't felt for years zipping through me. Somehow, asking Josie to drink coffee with me on deck feels like asking her on a first date.

She hesitates, like she's mentally scanning through a list of excuses.

"Please," I say. "I'll make breakfast in a little while."

She raises an eyebrow at this. And I get it—she's done all the cooking since she arrived. Mostly because I get the sense she likes it. Once I got off my crutches, I could have taken over. I know my way around the kitchen. But I didn't miss the way Josie hums under her breath while chopping and stirring or the pleased look on her face when she finishes a meal.

"You can cook?"

"I make a mean egg sandwich."

"Deal." She nods and starts up the steps with Jib scrambling ahead of her.

I do my best not to stare at Josie's bare legs as I follow her up, but it's hard. I really like the sight of Josie in her pajamas, which are the same blue ones with clouds.

The back of her neck is a little pink from the sun the day before. A piece of hair escapes her bun, curling over her shoulders as she settles on one of the bench seats on deck. Normally, I'd give Josie space and sit across from her.

Today, I press my luck—especially after my stupid comment—and sit next to her. Josie glances at me, blinking in surprise.

Then, as though my earlier words are stamped on my forehead, she angles her face away, looking toward the thin band of gold glowing on the horizon.

She's beautiful in the gray light of predawn. Even when she's upset with me.

There's something so simple about Josie's beauty. Natural, like the sky or the sea. It's in the line of her jaw and the curve of her cheek, the pout in her full lips. The way her brown eyes are lit from within by a brightness that's all her own.

Right now, though, that brightness has dimmed.

Because of me. And my inability to say what I mean to her. Around her. About her.

I reach over, ghosting my fingers along her forearm until they come to rest on her hand. Josie stiffens. Then with a sigh, she surprises me by turning her hand over and linking our fingers.

But she still keeps her gaze averted, watching a few boats already moving this morning.

"I have this problem with you," I say, and when she starts to pull her hand away, I realize how that sounds.

I am zero for two this morning. Keeping her hand clasped in mine, I gently squeeze her fingers, holding her hand hostage. If she tugs away again, I'll let her go.

She doesn't.

"What I meant to say is that I have this problem *around* you. I don't say what I mean. In fact, usually, it's the *opposite* of what I mean. Or, I say the right thing in the wrong tone of voice."

"My mother calls it foot-in-mouth disease," Josie says, finally turning to look at me, her eyes gentle, her smile faint but there.

"I have a wicked case," I confess. "But only around you, Josie."

Those words don't land with the significance I want them to. And they don't convey the full extent of what I mean.

Only around you, Josie. Do you hear me? Only you.

Because only you twist me up like this.

Only you *matter so much I can't think when I'm around you. And I definitely can't be trusted to speak.*

With my track record this morning, if I try to tell her how I feel about her right now, how I've always felt about her, I'll probably end up insulting her again somehow.

But she is still holding my hand. So there's that.

"What I was trying to say earlier is that you did a great job yesterday."

She scoffs, shaking her head. "Yeah, me and my one mistake."

"You'll probably make more today," I say. Once again—a swing and a big miss. I groan. "That was supposed to be encouraging."

Josie laughs. "You really do have foot-in-mouth disease."

"I'm practically touching my tonsils at this point. But in all seriousness, mistakes happen. I meant to reassure you that it's not a big deal."

"Do you make mistakes?" she counters.

I nod. "The first time I went sailing with Tom, he let me take the wheel and I ran us aground." She laughs. "Twice."

"That does make me feel better," she says. "Wait—how old were you?"

"Eight."

She groans. "Okay, now I feel worse. You were doing all this when you were eight?"

"My uncle taught me through the school of *Figure it out or fall off the boat*. He mostly let me do the map reading and GPS, especially after the running aground thing. One night we couldn't get a spot at a marina, so we anchored in what I thought was an approved spot."

"Uh-oh."

"Uh-oh is right. We woke up to the sound of a horn blaring. We were basically anchored in the middle of the Ditch, and a barge couldn't get by. Tom had to get up and find another anchorage. One not in the very center of the ICW. Another time—on the same trip—I had him anchor in a spot that was too shallow. The tide went out and the keel caught on a sandbar. The whole boat was tipping sideways."

Josie's eyes go wide. "That can happen? The boat can capsize?"

"We were never in danger of capsizing. It wasn't that shallow, and the keel is too heavy. The weight prevents it. But the boat stayed at an uncomfortable angle until the tide came in."

Josie doesn't look reassured. Then, her expression brightens. "Wait—is this where the expression 'keeled over' comes from?"

"Yep."

"That's cool." She takes a sip of coffee, then glances over at me with a smile. "Except all your stories of mistakes you made are now making me think of more things that can go wrong. And I already had a long list."

"Great. Maybe I should stop talking."

Her expression turns soft. "Please don't. I like you talking. Even when half the things you say are borderline insulting."

"More like a third."

Josie only hums in response, and when I squeeze her hand again, she laughs.

Jib scampers up the steps, bypassing Josie to hop in my lap. Jib knocks my elbow and a little coffee sloshes onto the back of her outfit. Which is a tutu.

I set down my mug and pull the material away from her

shaved grayish-brownish fur, not wanting her to get burned. Not because I care about her outfit. Thankfully, the coffee has cooled somewhat and Jib seems fine. But now there's a coffee stain on her outfit.

"Wyatt," Josie groans, "that tutu needs to be dry-cleaned."

I glance down at the pink leotard and scratchy skirt. Ridiculous for a dog. Also, surprisingly cute. "You can't be serious."

"I'm not."

"A tutu doesn't seem very practical."

"Don't judge," she says. "Jibby hopes to star in *The Nutcracker* one day."

I snort, and Josie puts a finger to her lips. "Shh! Do you want to be responsible for the death of her dreams?"

She's grinning at me, and though I don't smile back, warmth spreads through me like warm honey. I feel it reach the tips of my fingers, the ones linked with Josie's.

Holding my hand—that's a good sign, right? Telling me she likes when I talk—despite the things that keep coming out of my mouth—is also a good sign.

Or a sign that I'm grasping at the tiniest of paper straws.

"Can you believe Wanda and Greg are sailing to the Virgin Islands?" Josie asks, shaking her head.

I hadn't given one thought to the couple we met last night. I'm pretty sure Josie picked them up to be a buffer at dinner. I didn't mind. Having Wanda and Greg carry the conversation eased the tension between Josie and me, giving me time to regroup and try a different approach before bed.

Maybe standing outside the head in a cramped hallway wasn't the most romantic setting, but Josie didn't seem to mind. She fisted my shirt like she was torn between yanking me closer and pushing me away. Which is an improvement from before— when she would have *only* wanted to push me away.

If she ever got near enough to push me at all.

I didn't make a confession, didn't press her for one of her own. Instead, I opened an already cracked door wide and invited her to enter. And hoped . . . what—she'd come running through, running to me already?

That didn't happen. She doesn't seem ready for any next steps, but she also didn't run away from me.

Progress, I keep telling myself. But the waiting, the tiny steps, the incredible restraint is perhaps the hardest thing I've ever done.

"They'll be out at sea—open sea—for *days*. I looked at our charts." Josie shivers, like the idea is horrifying.

She is obsessive about looking at the charts, maps, and her book on the Intracoastal, as if she feels like this knowledge will make up for her lack of experience. I did the same when I started sailing with Tom. Her excitement refreshes my own. It helps dull the ache of missing my uncle, new experiences with Josie smoothing over years' worth of memories.

"People do it all the time," I tell her. "Tom once sailed to Bermuda."

"No way!" She shakes her head, and coffee spills over the rim of her mug, a single drop traveling down her hand to her wrist. "I couldn't do it. I need to see land."

"You took a cruise with Jacob. Weren't you on the open sea then?"

"Norovirus, remember? I spent five days looking not at the ocean but at the inside of the toilet." She makes a face. "Or at the inside of a trash can. Anyway, it's different. A cruise ship is like . . . well, it's basically like a whole city. You can't capsize those things."

"You can, actually. It doesn't happen often, but it happens."

Based on her horrified expression, I really should have kept my mouth shut—the theme of the morning.

"Don't tell me that," she says. "Now, I'm going to obsess. Actually, I'm going to google it."

"Don't," I tell her. "You don't want to see it."

"There's a video?"

"Videos. Plural."

Shut up, Wyatt. Any old time now.

"And you've seen them?" Her expression is shocked, like the idea of me watching ships sinking online is so outrageous.

I don't know why I did it, honestly. Probably the same weird drive that makes me watch shark attack videos and footage of sports injuries happening in the middle of games. All are things I have no business watching—no one does, really—but somehow, it feels like if I desensitize myself to them, I won't worry as much.

But I know it would be the opposite for Josie. If she watched any of the videos showing cruise ships sinking or capsizing, she'd probably climb off the boat now with Jib and swim to shore.

Something she also might do if she knew I don't actually need her to sail.

At the follow-up appointment just before we left, my doctor— not to be confused with "Dr." Parminder, the PT—cleared me for normal activity. Running. Exercise. Sailing. Hockey.

He didn't seem to understand why I wasn't elated.

All I could think about was telling Josie I didn't need her after all. I worried she might pack her bags, tuck Jib under her arm, and drive back to Fredericksburg. She only agreed to come on the trip because she thought she was needed. And she's only here in the first place because Jacob is paying her.

So . . . I didn't tell her.

In my defense, she didn't ask.

Okay—I realize this is a terrible defense. No defense at all, really.

But I wanted her here. *Needed* her here. This trip feels like *it*—one big chance to finally tell Josie how I feel.

Clearly, broaching the subject on the first night was a mistake. I need to slow down, even if I feel like I've already been waiting forever. Josie has to set the pace. If there will *be* a pace.

Please let there be a pace.

If Josie isn't ready yet, I won't force her. But I won't say goodbye at the end of this without letting her know how I feel. Which starts by making her feel safe.

Josie and I are quiet, sipping coffee as the colors start to wash over the sky, going from pastel to blinding brilliance, our hands still clasped. It's a perfect moment. And while I want so much more, for now this is enough.

"I'm excited about the Great Bridge Lock," Josie says after finishing off her coffee.

"Yeah?"

"It's the only lock on this stretch of the Intracoastal," she says like she's reading straight from the guidebook she's always lugging around. "Did you know that today and tomorrow we'll pass every kind of bridge and have every kind of experience that we'll find on the whole stretch of the ICW? My book calls it an appetizer."

"Sounds delicious," I say, and she elbows me lightly. "Have you memorized that book?"

"I wish. But I have highlighted, underlined, and tabbed it about to death."

"Tabbed?"

Josie proceeds to tell me about tabbing books, a subject she apparently can talk at length on. Normally, I guess, it's something people do for fiction books, but she applied it to her guidebook. While the sun continues its slow ascent, painting Josie's cheeks with a gorgeous glow, I watch her mouth and her eyes and her hair as it steadily escapes from her messy bun with every passionate gesture of her hands.

I want more moments like this. In fact, I want *nothing* but these kinds of moments stretching out ahead of me for as long as possible. Quiet mornings and afternoons and evenings with Josie telling me about things I only care about because they matter to her.

22

Keeping the Professional Nurse Hat On

Josie

A girl could get used to this, I think while brushing my teeth after breakfast.

The kind of deep, satisfying sleep that comes from exhaustion, made sweeter by the gentle rock of a boat. A lazy, early morning on the water, drinking coffee and talking with Wyatt about books.

Holding his hand was a surprise bonus. Also surprising: what he shared this morning.

And last night. Especially last night. The things he said. The way his eyes darkened to slate as he spoke. How good it felt when he pulled me against his chest and held me.

I'm still processing all of it.

Too bad my processing is taking place at the speed of a

ten-year-old PC where someone clicked on every pop-up and sketchy email link.

It's dumb to think about getting used to this, though, considering the fact that after this trip, we'll head back to our respective cities miles and miles and miles apart. Where Wyatt is a famous hockey player and I am me—a woman who spends her days putting My Little Pony Band-Aids on skinned knees and looking at real estate she can't afford.

Correction: *couldn't* afford.

It's weird, though, how I can house hunt for real now . . . but still haven't. Not once since coming to Kilmarnock. Now, the idea of buying a house and settling into my life the way I always planned has started to sound like a consolation prize. A participation trophy.

That is *not* good.

Because if my life plans now seem underwhelming with a side of meh, there is one reason. And that reason is up on deck somewhere, waiting for me. Probably with a scowl on his handsome face.

Somewhere, I can imagine Toni cackling. A very *I told you so* kind of laugh. A *Finally* kind of laugh.

As much as I like to downplay this, my last serious relationship was in high school. How serious can a high school boyfriend be? In my case, not very.

But until now, until spending all this time with Wyatt, I haven't wanted to consider being in another relationship. Even thinking about it now has my stomach cramping with the kind of dread that always accompanies change and new things.

"Josie! Are you ready to cast off?" Wyatt sticks his head down the hatch. He's frowning—of course—but even his downturned lips and flinty eyes feel softer aimed my way. My stomach flips as I stare up at him, the sunlight splashing over his cheeks.

I join Wyatt on the deck, where he's messing with the GPS. Today we'll pass Mile 0 as we head through Norfolk and officially enter the ICW. I know this from *The Intracoastal Waterway, Norfolk to Miami: The Complete Cockpit Cruising Guide*, which Wyatt teased me about earlier. Right before listening to me ramble about books for far too long.

When I finally came up for air and realized I'd been talking for maybe ten minutes straight, I wanted to dive overboard. But Wyatt was watching me with an expression I'd never seen before—one that made heat creep up my neck to my cheeks. Rapt attention mixed with what looked like . . . hunger.

When he glances up from the GPS now, he's wearing the same expression. I don't know what to do with it. With him.

So I blurt out a boat question. "Did you switch our GPS from nautical to statute miles?"

A smile lifts one side of his mouth. "Were you like this in school?"

"Like what—a total nerd and know-it-all?"

"I was going to say someone who loves learning, but okay."

"That does sound better. Jacob preferred to call me a nerd and know-it-all."

"And were his grades always as bad as they were in college?" Wyatt asks with an arched brow.

I laugh. "Yup."

Wyatt nods, and instantly he's back in serious sailor mode. A relief, since I know how to handle this version of him.

"I took Jib for a walk. But maybe today she'll start using the turf," Wyatt says.

We both glance up and laugh at Princess Jib-Jabberwocky, still in her ballerina outfit, lying on the fake grass, back flat on the ground and belly toward the sky.

"I should put her in her bikini for sunbathing," I say.

Wyatt's gaze swings my way. "Tell me you didn't buy the dog a bikini."

"I didn't buy her a bikini."

There's a pause. "You bought two."

Three, actually, but who's counting? I don't answer, only smile. Wyatt shakes his head, taking a long drink from a water bottle. The sun is barely up, but the day's already hot. My skin feels tight and sensitive in the places I couldn't reach with sunscreen yesterday. It's not a full, angry burn, but I definitely don't want it to be worse.

"Before we go, could you put sunscreen on my neck and shoulders? I missed some spots yesterday. I don't want to get more sun and—"

"Come here, Rookie."

This shouldn't make me nervous. It's just rubbing on sunscreen. It could almost be considered a medical thing, considering skin care prevention and all. Basically skin-cancer prevention.

Or so I tell myself as I walk over to Wyatt and hand him the tube of sunscreen. I almost believe it too.

But when I turn my back, anticipation sparks across my skin, like every cell is now a live wire. It's torture facing away and waiting, listening to him open the cap. The noise the bottle makes when he squeezes some sunscreen on his palm should break the tension, but apparently not even sounds that would make my elementary kids giggle can dampen my mood.

I'm about to move my hair—I need to pull it back into a ponytail anyway—but Wyatt's hand gets there first. His fingers gently move up my neck as he takes my hair in his hand.

"Hold your hair back," he commands, voice low and rough.

My eyes flutter closed. Yeah . . . the way I feel about his touch is anything but professional.

His hands are big and lightly calloused, but they're gentle

as they glide over my skin. He smooths the lotion on my neck, then my shoulders, his fingertips just barely slipping underneath the neck of my tank top and the holes of my sleeves.

"I've got to be thorough," he murmurs, and now he's leaning down, his breath a whisper on my skin. "Can't have you getting burned."

"Do you, um, need me to get your neck or anything?"

"Sure," he says, and he says it so easily, like he's unaffected by this.

I guess *his* insides aren't trembling like he's standing on a fault line.

When Wyatt finishes, rubbing the last of the sunscreen down the length of my arms, I have him sit on one of the benches so I can stand next to him.

"Too tall," I tell him. "Or I'm too short."

"You're just right," he says with a small smile.

And then he tugs his shirt right over his head.

Well, then.

I know what I'll be writing about in my journal tonight. And maybe dreaming about for nights to come.

Look—I'm not the kind of woman who's ever been into thirst traps. Especially not after hearing a fifth-grade girl casually drop the term. Why a fifth grader knows about *thirst traps*, I don't know. But I'm guessing it has something to do with her newly divorced mom.

My point being: I'm not someone who considers herself superficial about guys and their looks. I've never had a type and have always placed physical attractiveness somewhere down the list of things that matter to me, way after character traits. In fact, big, muscular guys have long been on my *absolutely not* list.

But maybe I'm shallower than I thought, my absolutes now

more relative. Because I can't stop myself from taking a good long look.

It's impossible to view Wyatt's bare torso with anything but admiration. And a little disbelief, because I really thought maybe the shirtless abs I'd seen in his ads were airbrushed. Like maybe his abs were actually drawn by AI.

Nope. I can now confirm every one of those abs exists in reality.

And they're right here, inches away.

I saw them during physical therapy, but that was mostly while Wyatt was at a safe distance, in a pool.

He clears his throat, startling me into putting way too much sunscreen on my hand, and I swear I catch the edge of a cocky smile as he gives me his back. Which, of course, is as astonishingly muscular. I didn't know backs came like this.

Wyatt has to clear his throat again before I set the sunscreen down and rub my palms together until they're both coated, reminding myself that I have a job to do. A medical job. Totally professional and not involving any feelings or anything personal.

He stiffens as my palms touch his shoulders. "Cold," he says.

"Don't be a baby," I tell him.

He grunts at this, or maybe it's more of a groan as my hands slide over his back and shoulders. His muscles feel even better than they look, and I am struggling to locate my nurse hat. The metaphorical one I pull out when I'm engaging in professional tasks.

It's just a back, I tell myself. *Skin, muscle, bone. Nothing to see here, folks! Just a perfect specimen of a man!*

"I think I'm good," Wyatt says, startling me as I realize the massive amount of sunscreen I used is almost totally rubbed in.

How long have I been touching him?

I give his shoulders a pat with a little too much force. Wyatt flinches.

"Skin cancer sucks. SPF matters," I say, like I've been suddenly turned into a commercial touting the benefits of sunscreen.

"Yes," Wyatt agrees, "it does. Thank you."

When I step away, he grabs his shirt and pulls it back over his head.

"All that and you're wearing a shirt?"

"For now," he says. "But I'll be ready for the sun. Grab the bow line."

"Aye, aye, Captain Bossy," I mutter.

"I heard that."

⚓

"What was the highlight of your day?" Wyatt asks.

Of course, it's right after I've taken a big bite. Coinjock's restaurant, like the marina itself, is packed. I'm grateful Wyatt made the reservations for the marina ahead of time, as there's not much space. Only one long, fixed dock with room for fewer boats than the yacht club in Hampton. The food is far better than the yacht club's last night, with a much more casual feel. I might die from the sheer number of fried things on my plate: onion rings, hush puppies, clam strips. Zero regrets. It's all delicious. Wyatt keeps stealing clams off my plate. Which is only fair, as I grabbed his fork a few minutes ago and ate the bite of steak he had halfway to his mouth.

No regrets about that either.

While I'm still chewing, Wyatt adds, "My mom used to ask my brother and me this question every night at dinner."

I can picture Susan, resting her chin in her hands, listening with interest to a boy version of Wyatt. This is the first time he's willingly brought up his brother, and I resist the urge to ask one hundred follow-up questions.

"Highlight of the day . . . let's see." I take a sip of water as I think back over the day, which was much more eventful than yesterday.

I think I saw just about every kind of ship in the Norfolk Harbor, including an aircraft carrier and a mothballed—Wyatt tells me that's the term for *decommissioned*—submarine. There were so many things to look at, but it was crowded and loud and smelled like exhaust and diesel fuel. I was too stressed to drive when Wyatt asked. No way do I trust myself with so many potential objects to collide with. I'd probably run into a battleship.

I preferred the calm once we got to the Elizabeth River, though the current was swift and the river had more turns and boats than I expected. Wyatt says there are even more during the fall and winter months when snowbirds head south in their sailboats, houseboats, and yachts. I hate winter, so that sounds like a plan to me. I mean, forgetting about my job, that is.

Which is honestly way too easy to do when we're on the water. Or when I'm with Wyatt. He makes me forget a lot of things.

"I think I'd have to say the radio was my highlight." I feel lame as soon as I say it and focus on cutting another piece of steak rather than meeting Wyatt's gaze head-on.

"The radio," he repeats, sounding more curious than judgmental. "What about it?"

"I liked talking to the bridgemasters and other boats. It made me feel like an official sailor."

"You *are* an official sailor."

"More like an official passenger," I say, but Wyatt shakes his head.

"You're an integral part of my crew, and I don't appreciate anyone talking bad about my crew. Stop it."

"Speaking of your uncle," I say, needing a respite from Wyatt's intense, protective gaze. "I couldn't help but notice you brought him along. I found him yesterday." I pause, then look over at him. "Behind a block of Swiss."

Now, it's Wyatt's turn to look away, and I regret bringing it up. Sometimes he speaks so easily about his uncle, and other times he seems to close down.

I'm just about to apologize when Wyatt says, "In his will, Tom asked to be scattered along the Intracoastal at various points."

I let this sink in. Suddenly, I see this trip in a slightly different light. It's not just a trip Wyatt planned to take in memory of his uncle. It's a trip he planned because of his uncle's last wishes as well.

No wonder Wyatt was so frustrated by his injury, by the idea of missing this. His foot wasn't just an obstacle to a fun sailing trip but to something much more meaningful.

People talk about peeling back the layers of someone like an onion, which I have always found to be an off-putting comparison—mostly because it instantly makes me think about the pungent, tear-inducing smell. Like the idea of learning more about a person is smellier the deeper you go. But getting to know Wyatt is different. It's like unwrapping a present only to find a smaller wrapped package inside and another one inside that. I've peeled back the paper a few times now, moved on to the next box and the next, but I have no idea how many are left to open. I'm learning more about him, learning *him*, but there's still so much I don't know. I'm getting impatient, ripping the paper now instead of carefully peeling back the tape.

Maybe that's how it works with people—you never really get

to one central truth of who they are. People aren't static. We're always in motion—growing, changing, shifting.

"Have you, um, done that yet?" I ask.

Wyatt gives a quick nod. "I've started."

I wonder when. We've been together most of the time, and it makes me ache to think of him doing this alone.

I want to reach for him but still don't feel fully comfortable. Holding hands this morning doesn't mean it's now on the table to hold hands any old time. It's much easier when he initiates, which just shows how much I've grown to trust him.

When I find his foot under the table and press mine to the top of it, his gaze snaps back to mine.

"If you want company, let me know," I say. "But no pressure if it's something you'd rather do alone."

"I'd like company," he says. "If it wouldn't be too weird for you."

"Less weird than keeping him in the fridge in a Cool Whip container."

He barks a short laugh, and I grin, delighted.

We're interrupted when the hostess, who definitely recognized Wyatt and fangirled no small amount when we sat down, appears at our table with a package in her hands. I'm instantly annoyed. Partly because she's shaken her blond hair loose around her shoulders and added more eye makeup.

But also because she's bringing a gift for him. I'm tempted to stab her with the tines of my fork.

But how did she get something for Wyatt? Especially since it looks like a FedEx package. I squint, trying to read the address.

"The dockmaster said this arrived for you," she says, holding out the box to Wyatt with a smile.

The package has a stamped label saying it's been rush-shipped. One corner looks a little smushed, so I hope it's not breakable.

Wyatt takes it with a nod, not even glancing up at her. Disappointment makes her wilt, shoulders drooping. I almost feel bad for her.

But not quite.

When she lingers by the table, Wyatt says, "Thank you," in a firm voice that sends her scampering back to the podium.

"You got a package delivered here?" I ask, and Wyatt nods, frowning at the damaged corner of the box. "I didn't know we could do that."

"Don't even think about ordering more clothes for Jib." He gives me a stern look.

"I wasn't." I totally was. "Did we forget something we need for the boat?"

"Yes." Wyatt holds my gaze as he hands me the package.

I stare at it, blinking. "For me?"

Wyatt only nods, and I take the box, hesitating. I want to tear it open, thrilled at the idea of a surprise but also strangely overwhelmed by the gesture. My heart is doing something weird in my chest, and there's a rushing sound in my ears.

I swallow, then grab my unused butter knife and slice through the tape.

When I get the box open and move aside the tissue paper, I can only stare inside. Words fail me.

"They're boat shoes," Wyatt says.

Indeed, they are. I recognized what they were as soon as I opened the box. A light brown leather top with white rubber soles, they're a less broken-in version of Wyatt's. It's not *what* they are that made me freeze.

It's the *why* of it.

"You bought me boat shoes . . . and had them shipped here." It's a question, but it comes out like a statement.

I can't look at him. The intensity of my emotional reaction is too much. I think if I move at all, I might burst into tears.

So, I just sit there, the noise of the restaurant buzzing around me, the smell of salt hanging in the air, and my hands gripping the box of new boat shoes in my exact size that Wyatt had shipped here. For me.

"They're just shoes," he says, but when I look at him, it's clear neither of us believes that.

23

A Three-Letter Word

Josie

"Boat shoes suit you," Wyatt says, nodding down at my feet.

It's been a few days since he gave them to me, and we're having coffee on deck again—our new morning routine and one of my favorite parts of every day. Jib is curled up in his lap in her pirate outfit. She fell asleep a few minutes ago after ripping off her eye patch and chewing it up. I can't even be mad.

Because I actually agree with Wyatt on this point: The eye patch was ridiculous.

"Thanks." A pleased flush rises in my cheeks. I wiggle my feet, showing off the light brown leather shoes with their rubber soles. The ones I've barely taken off for the last few days. I would have slept in them, but they aren't *that* comfortable.

But fit isn't the reason I don't want to take them off. It's the same reason people joke about not washing their hands after touching a celebrity. Or—sort of the same reason. I'm still getting over the fact that Wyatt bought me the shoes I'd been stressing over just before we left.

And then had them mailed ahead to one of our stops.

"I'm not sure I want to know how you knew my shoe size."

Wyatt smirks. "Please. I just picked up one of your shoes and looked."

"Hey! That's an invasion of privacy." I poke him in the arm, tempted to leave my hand there. It's a very nice arm.

But I'm still a little hesitant with my touches. Not because I'm nervous or feel uncomfortable. It's more that I don't know yet where we are. Or where I want us to be.

One minute, I'm totally feeling like I shouldn't worry about the ending. About what comes after this trip. I want to enjoy the moment and whatever is blossoming here.

Carpe diem and all that.

The next minute I'm terrified to let anything blossom here because if something goes wrong, we'll be stuck on a boat together for the next few weeks. Also, he is my brother's best friend and client. Who plays a sport in another city hours away. A professional athlete. One who has never shown any interest until now. In fact, he actively didn't like me until recently.

Maybe most importantly, after not dating for basically my whole adult life, is this where I should start—with *Wyatt*?

So, yeah—I can't decide how much touching is too much. How much to share. How much to allow myself to daydream or flirt without pulling myself back to safety. My question is not the classic *Should I stay or should I go?* It's more *Should I hope or should I nope?*

Only now, each time I pull back, I'm disappointed in myself. I'm the Cowardly Lion personified. And wearing boat shoes.

"Should I send them back then? Since they were gained by invasive methods?" he asks.

"That's okay. I'll keep them. Just don't let it happen again."

"No promises," he says, and the look in his eyes makes my stomach flutter. "But I wasn't talking about the fit. I mean they *suit* you. All of this does, Josie."

He glances around, and I do too. The water is glassy, and other than the occasional bird calling or fish breaking the surface only to disappear faster than we can see it, it's a quiet morning. Cloudy, so even the sun is on mute.

Last night the marina at the River Rat Yacht Club where we planned to stay was crowded and loud, with a large group having some kind of reunion or meetup. I was relieved when Wyatt suggested we press on a little in the fading light and anchor at the mouth of Campbell Creek—after a brief stop at the club for showers, a meal, and laundry. I don't know if the yacht reciprocity thing still works or if Wyatt just flashes his famous face and his wallet around.

Either way, I'm not complaining. I've never appreciated showers so much. Ones where I'm not cramped in a space so small I'm forced to wash my body with T. rex arms in the boat's tiny shower. I don't know how Wyatt fits in there at all.

It's quiet here in a little inlet off the Ditch, and since the other boats pulled away this morning before I was even out of my bed, it feels . . . private. The perfect kind of morning.

I could do this forever, I think, looking back at Wyatt. He wears a soft smile as he looks at Jib. *I could do this with* you *forever.*

The words stay lodged in my throat. For now. Though the idea behind them is starting to expand, growing larger by the day, too big to be held inside my body. Even if there's another part of me—the part that's been playing protector for years—urging me to run. My feelings for Wyatt kick my fight-or-flight instincts into overdrive, which I'm pretty sure is not what's supposed to happen when you like someone.

It shouldn't be terrifying, right?

I realize Wyatt is studying me, his gray eyes soft in the morning light. How much of my inner struggle is written all over my face? I get the sense he knows me maybe better than I know myself. At least some parts of me.

Others I've hidden away, blocked from his view, burying them so deep no one could know. Not without some kind of excavator to unearth them. Or by dosing me with a truth serum.

I could talk to Wyatt. It's strange to realize when I think back to how I've always viewed him, but I may trust Wyatt as much or even more than Toni. And if I decide to ignore my fight-or-flight instincts and consider exploring the feelings I think are mutual, I'll *need* to talk to him.

I'm looking forward to that about as much as I'm looking forward to the stinky task of pumping out the boat's holding tank at the next stop.

"Shall we go over our day?" Wyatt asks.

I nod with a thick swallow. *Our* day. People talk about four letter words, but this three-letter word is the one that does me in. Every time.

Our trip. Our dog. Our day.

Wyatt pulls out his iPad with the Aqua Map, and I grab my guidebook and chartbook—the next part of our morning routine. Wyatt is team tech and I'm old school, using books and binoculars. We bicker about it every time we discuss routes. Honestly, it's probably better that we use both. And I think we both enjoy the back-and-forth about it. Just one more part of our morning routine.

Today's potential issues on the route include rough water in the Pamlico Sound and shallow waters in the Neuse River. My guidebook says we're likely to see porpoises today, which has me kicking my feet. We haven't seen any since the first day, and I'm hopeful.

Wyatt glances at the sky, overcast in towering clouds, muting the sun. "We should keep an eye on the weather. Don't want storms during this stretch—winds could take us off course and leave us stuck in the shoals."

I nod. Off course is the current story of my life.

"But if we avoid trouble, it will be a short day," he says. "And a night in a real bed."

A bed. I'm already grinning at the thought. It's why I've been looking forward to our stop at the Oriental Marina & Inn. Emphasis on the *Inn*.

Not that I mind sleeping on the boat. Actually, I love it. This has honestly been some of the best sleep of my life. I'm not sure if that's due to the gentle rocking at night or simply because traveling by boat in the middle of summer is exhausting. I fall bonelessly into bed every night and pretty much crash the moment my eyes close.

But . . . I can hear a hotel bed calling my name. A *real* mattress, one thicker than a few inches. Sleeping on firm, unmoving land. With really good air-conditioning and maybe even a bathtub.

It's the last one that does it for me.

I hop up from my seat, which wakes Jib. She scurries in circles with a bark, looking for danger or excitement. Finding none, she shoots me a dog version of a glare and stalks off to the fake grass—which she still refuses to use as anything other than her personal sunbathing area.

"Then let's get a move on, slowpoke," I say, holding out my hand to Wyatt. Not that he needs help getting up. I'll never forget the way he smoothly went from the floor to standing on one leg the night he got all the splinters.

Why does that night feel like it was years ago, not weeks?

When Wyatt slips his hand into mine, he doesn't move for a few seconds, his eyes on me and our palms gently pressed together. My heart beats an unsteady rhythm that I feel all the way in my toes. Then, Wyatt stands, gives my hand a quick squeeze, and disappears into the galley with both our empty mugs.

I'm still standing there, palm tingling, when he returns—with the Cool Whip container. His expression is hesitant, and it makes my throat tighten.

"Is this . . . okay?" he asks.

"It's not about me, Wyatt. Is it okay with *you*?"

He glances down at the container cupped in one big hand, then nods. I follow him to the stern, imagining him standing here alone, honoring his uncle's wishes. Saying his goodbyes.

I stand next to him, unsure what I should do, what I should say. I settle on leaning in and wrapping an arm around his waist. I feel him relax against me with a sigh.

He opens the container, hesitates for a moment, then dips his fingers inside. I swallow, pressing even closer, feeling more emotional than I have any right to.

Wyatt opens his fingers, releasing a handful of ashes quickly carried away by the gentle breeze.

We stand there for a few moments, the humid heat pressing in on us both, as a gull circles overhead, for once not laughing. I give myself a silent pep talk until I'm able to ask a question that I've been wanting to voice for days. "Would you like to talk about him?"

When he says nothing, I mentally kick myself. It's such a big, vague question. I should have asked something specific rather than a yes or no question. I already know Wyatt's favorite answer to those.

So I'm shocked when he starts talking. "He was his own man. Not like anyone else and not trying to be anyone else. He laughed often and loudly—he sounded a bit like a honking goose when he did it."

His smile is faint but there, and I find myself smiling back. "Your mom said you spent summers with him? You and your brother or just you?"

"Just me."

I almost ask why but think better of it when I see his jaw clench. I'm not as adept at reading him as he seems to be at reading me, but I don't need a Wyatt Instruction Manual to recognize tension. To feel it where my arm is still curled around his waist.

"And we're sailing the route you took with him each summer?"

Wyatt nods once. "Many people travel this way in fall and winter. The weather's much more pleasant."

"But you had school."

"And hockey."

"Did you start playing hockey when you were really young?"

"My dad wanted me to take over the restaurant group," he says, and I open my mouth to say something because this isn't what I asked, but Wyatt continues. "From the time I was, oh . . . about eight. When other kids were playing tag outside or reading picture books, I was learning how to use spreadsheets, being hammered with information about portfolios and investment capital. He made me sit in on business meetings wearing a little suit. One time someone laughed—chuckled, really—and made a comment about me playing dress-up. It wasn't mean. Just a statement about a kid looking out of place in a board meeting. Which I did." Wyatt pauses. "Dad fired him."

I want to laugh. I want to cry. It's ridiculous and so, *so* sad. My throat feels too tight, not unlike the way it did when I had my poison oak encounter. But this feels worse.

A boat passes by, sail billowing, and a gray-haired woman on deck in aviator sunglasses and a tank top waves. We wave back, Wyatt still clutching the Cool Whip container in one hand, my other arm still locked around his waist.

He waits for the boat to move away before he continues. "Hockey was my way out. I'm not even sure why my father allowed me to play, but I fought for it." He pauses, and I can see how difficult it is for him to swallow. "Mom fought for it too. Fought for me—maybe one of the only times she stood up to him."

It's hard to imagine the vivacious woman I met who tricked me into a shopping spree being cowed by anyone. Then, I think about a man who would fire someone for making an innocent comment about a child being a child.

"And then I was *good* at hockey. I thought it would just be an escape, but my father decided he didn't want a son with a divided focus. He saw it as a character flaw. So, he moved on to Peter."

"What do you mean, *moved on?*"

Wyatt is quiet for a moment. "I mean, it's like I didn't—and don't—exist to him anymore. Peter got all of Dad's attention, focus, and training. At home it was like I wasn't there. At least not to anyone but my mom."

"Wyatt," I whisper. Stunned. Horrified. Aching for the boy he was, the man he is. The surge of protectiveness almost bowls me over.

"And your brother went along with it?"

"Not at first," Wyatt says, and I catch him rubbing his thumb on the edge of the plastic container in his hands. His voice is steady, carefully blank, but this motion continues, almost like a tic. "But Dad didn't want me being a bad influence, so he discouraged our relationship."

Discouraged our relationship.

This is the kind of thing a parent might say when their child is dating someone sketchy or hanging with the wrong crowd. Not something a father should do with his own sons. And most certainly not because of something like Wyatt wanting hockey as a break from the serious business stuff he was too young to be doing anyway.

"So, hockey became who I am," he finishes. "And it was the start of my summers with my uncle."

I want to tell Wyatt it's okay, that *he's* okay. I want to tell him his dad really, really sucks. I want to tell him he's more than hockey.

But Jib runs up, issuing a sharp bark and a little butt wiggle. I drop my arm as Wyatt steps back, the thick emotional tension of the moment lifting like fog.

"If you'd learn to use your fake grass like a good girl, you wouldn't be so desperate for us to get going," he tells her, then bends to scratch her behind the ears.

Then he disappears below deck, leaving me alone with my thoughts and a dog dressed as a pirate.

24

We Can Manage

Josie

It's a bad idea.

I know it's bad, *really* bad, even as I tell Wyatt, "It'll be fine."

He turns his back to the hotel desk and the frazzled woman on the other side of it. The one who had trouble locating our reservation.

Lowering his voice, Wyatt asks, "Are you sure there's nothing else?"

He certainly doesn't look sure. Jaw clenched, shoulders rigid. Gray eyes flintier than usual.

For some reason, his hesitation makes me more determined. Why should this be a big deal? So, they screwed up our reservation and put us in one room, not two. Without a single other vacancy.

One room. Me and Wyatt. My mouth is the Sahara. My heart is a galloping horse. But my face belongs to a high-stakes poker player as I repeat what I said moments ago. "It's fine."

"I'll sleep on the boat," Wyatt says. "You take the room."

There's no way his oversize bulk can be comfortable sleeping in his cabin's tiny twin berth. I've seen him shuffling around after getting up in the morning, stretching his back and rubbing his neck when he doesn't realize I'm looking. This is a man who needs a *bed*.

And I'm not about to give up my chance to sleep in a real bed.

It's stupid to think sharing a room isn't something we, as two mostly functioning adults who've spent weeks now in close proximity, could manage.

I readjust Jib in my arms and snatch the key cards off the hotel desk, handing one to Wyatt. He hesitates, then takes it, his fingers trailing over mine as he does. I pretend not to notice.

Giving him a little grin, I say, "I think we can handle sharing a room for a night, Wyatt."

We can . . . *can't we?*

I mean, we've shared a tiny murder cottage. A boat. Some deep conversations.

What's a hotel room?

But when I walk in, stopping so quickly Wyatt bumps into the back of me, I realize how *not* fine it is, after all.

The door closes behind us with what feels like a very appropriate slam of doom.

There is one king-size bed. No couch. No floor space—not that anyone should *ever* sleep on a hotel floor.

How did I miss this not-at-all-tiny detail when we were at the front desk downstairs?

A single room . . . with a single *bed*.

Wyatt leans close, his lips almost brushing my ear as he parrots back my words from the lobby. "I think we can handle sharing a room for a night, Josie."

And we really do handle it fine. At first.

Before dinner Wyatt takes Jib on a long walk, allowing me time for an almost luxurious bath. The *almost* is no fault of the bathroom but more because of my paranoia that any second, Wyatt will return to the room. A fluffy bath towel might cover more of me than the bathing suit he's seen me in a few times now, but it doesn't feel the same. Not even a little.

Wyatt must have the same kinds of thoughts, because I'm dressed, fully ready, and about to call in a search party when he finally returns with Jib. His shirt is damp with sweat, and his expression is relieved when he sees me sitting in a chair by the window, fully dressed. His gaze moves over the simple sundress I pulled out of my suitcase. It's still wrinkled even after I did the lazy girl's steam by hanging it in the bathroom while I took my bath.

But he doesn't look like he cares about the fabric. His gaze falls to my legs for a long moment until he blinks and looks away.

He clears his throat. "I'll take a quick shower."

I nod like *No biggie*.

It shouldn't be. I mean, the murder cottage was maybe a few times the size of this room. I got used to the weirdness of knowing only a single door separated me from Wyatt when he was showering. It's no longer a big deal on the boat, where the head is right by my cabin.

Whether it's the change in location, the looming reality presented by the one bed, or the tension that's been building between us, I cannot stay in the hotel room while he's showering. Instead, I scurry to the balcony as soon as I hear the sound of the water turning on in the bathroom.

The air outside is still warm, but my skin and cheeks cool when I slump into a chair overlooking the marina. I watch the sun dipping low over the water with Jib asleep in my lap.

Needing a distraction, I decide maybe it's time to stop ignoring my family.

Since Jacob spilled the beans, Mom and Dad have texted
a few times to hear all about my sailing trip. Thankfully, their
interest has mainly centered around sailing, not Wyatt. But
they don't answer now, which probably means they have no
service.

Jacob answers on the first ring. "So, you're not dead or lost
at sea," he says wryly. "Guess I can call off the search party."

"Alive and breathing," I tell him cheerfully. "Not even a little
bit lost." Okay—actually that's not true. I might be more lost
now than I've ever been. But not in a way I'm prepared to talk
to Jacob about. "How are you?"

"Good. Busy. You know—the usual."

"Right."

"Tell me about a sailor's life. I'm trying to picture you and
Wyatt navigating down the East Coast and . . . I just can't."

"I'll send you a picture. Proof of life—and sailing."

And because Jacob is in a rare listening mood, I babble on
about the trip. How stressful it can be at points when we're
navigating around other boats or through a narrow passage
with debris. The different kinds of bridges—swing and bascule
and lift. It's refreshing to talk to my brother without him
pumping me for information about Wyatt's recovery and
whether Wyatt is coming back to Boston soon.

It feels like progress.

"I'm kind of jealous," he says when I'm done.

"Hey—you're the one who skipped out on the Super Summer
Sibling Extravaganza."

"I know, and I'm sorry. And I'm planning to make it up to
you," Jacob says.

"How?" I demand.

He scoffs. "Like I'd just tell you. That's not my style."

Yeah, his style is more in the vein of making plans and coercing everyone else to go along with them. Still, the idea that he has something in mind to make up for ditching our trip makes me happy. And slightly nervous. I think I've dealt with enough surprises lately to last me for a while.

"Before you go, I've got a question for you." One I've been wondering ever since Wyatt told me he's from Richmond. "Do you know much about Wyatt's family?"

The quiet on the line tells me Jacob does. "Enough. He talked to you about them?"

"A bit."

"I used to pay to fly his uncle up to games."

"You did?" Every so often, my brother says something like this, reminding me he's not entirely self-focused. "I'm surprised Wyatt didn't do it."

"I think he thought if he offered, his uncle would feel like he had to go. Wyatt is always concerned with not being burdensome to people. He didn't want his uncle to feel like he *had* to go."

It's hard to see an offer of flying a person to a hockey game for free as anything but a great gift. But then, for someone who grew up with a father like Wyatt's, I can see his understanding of love and family being twisted up and confused with the idea of duty and being a burden.

"That was really nice of you," I say.

My brother chuckles. "Don't sound so surprised. I'm nice."

"I never said you weren't nice. You're just also . . ." I fish for the right word, but there isn't one that's both accurate *and* kind.

"I see how it is. But just remember to thank me when this is all over."

"Thank you for what?"

"I've got to go. Call or text a little more. And send me the photo like you promised. Just so I know you're alive. Unless you want me to fly down and find you."

"Good luck with that."

"I don't need luck. I have your location on my phone, and Wyatt gave me your tentative schedule before you left."

"Wait—then why'd you even ask if I was lost at sea?"

My brother ends the call instead of answering my question, and half a second later, Wyatt opens the sliding glass door, looking like a four-course meal in a button-down shirt and damp hair.

My throat muscles seem to have lost the ability to swallow. Because now, when I look at him, he's not just a grumpy yet secretly soft man but a man who has endured family trauma and come out on the other side of it okay. It's dangerous to have this knowledge that makes me like and respect him more.

Because it only makes him look more delicious to me now than he did before.

"Ready?" Wyatt asks, and my mind goes back to our conversation a few nights ago. The one where he essentially told me that I get to set the pace.

I want to yell, *Yes, I'm ready!*

But he's asking about dinner, so I nod and smile, deposit Jib in the room, and follow Wyatt downstairs.

25

Pity Truth with Zero Qualms

Josie

Per my usual since we started the trip, I eat dinner with the appetite of a teenage boy mid–growth spurt. Though our simple galley breakfasts, lunches, and occasional dinners when we're in an anchorage are fine, restaurant meals feel extravagant to me now. And I'm always starving. Sailing—even if Wyatt does most of the work with the actual sails and lines—is exhausting.

"You decimated your flounder," Wyatt says, a smile in his voice. "It was good?"

I nod, dragging my fork wistfully over my plate, like it can magically produce more. "Seafood always tastes better by the ocean. Even if they're importing it from somewhere else. I don't want to know."

Wyatt points to a chalkboard menu sign that reads *Local fish caught fresh daily* across the top. "I think you're safe there."

He drops a fried shrimp on my plate, and I snatch it so fast he actually chuckles. I grin, mouth closed while I chew.

"Thanks," I tell him when I can. "Everything is just better right now."

My words land with more weight than I intended. I meant everything tastes better, but everything is better. Wyatt's gaze catches mine. And when he casually extends his hand across the table, palm up in a low-pressure invitation, I slide my fingers between his, easy as breathing.

This I can do. Hand-holding. Flirting with Wyatt. Flirting with the *idea* of Wyatt.

Anything more or anything having to do with the future and my frontal lobe shuts down, leaving me with the panicked, cortisol-fueled drama of my lizard brain.

Wyatt said when *I'm* ready.

But what if I never feel ready?

⚓

All of the comfortable ease from dinner vanishes the moment we open the hotel room door and are faced, once again, with the one bed.

At least it's a king?

We pull apart like we're holding hot potatoes instead of hands. I laugh awkwardly, then walk inside the room to Jib, who is completely oblivious to the sudden tension burning up all the oxygen around us. With a little grumble, she rolls over, offering me her belly for scratches.

"You can use the bathroom first if you want," Wyatt offers.

"Sure," I reply, giving Jib a last scratch before ducking into the bathroom, where I give myself a very strong, silent talking to about being a mature adult while toothpaste dribbles down my chin.

While Wyatt's in the bathroom, I switch on HGTV and watch as two people search for the best bargain property on the beach. I never care about which house the couples choose—they never pick the one I think they should—but I make it a game to guess which one they *will* pick. I've gotten good too.

Wyatt settles next to me in bed, still a respectable distance away, but so close it sends a shudder through my limbs. Jib is curled up, separating our legs like the perfect little barrier, but she groans as Wyatt messes with the blankets, then hops down and climbs into one of the armchairs. She's snoring again in seconds.

Traitor! What happened to the ladies sticking together?

"Are you in the market for a beach house?" Wyatt asks.

"On my salary? Please." I almost tell him about my plans to look for a house in Fredericksburg. But since I still haven't done more than think about thinking about it, instead I ask, "Do you have a place in Boston?"

"No. I've moved around so much, I rent wherever I go."

"That makes me feel better. Sometimes it seems like I'm the only adult who doesn't own a house." He's quiet so long, I glance over and see a pinched look. "Wait—you *do* own a house, don't you?"

He blows out a breath. "Two. One in Northern Virginia and one in Cape Cod. Plus, now, the murder cottage." He grins at this last one. "I just don't happen to live in any of them."

I'm most curious about where his house in Northern Virginia is. And why he owns a place there. Now that I know he grew up in Richmond, I guess it makes more sense. Plus Jacob works out of a satellite office in DC for his agency.

I am also not far.

I shelve all those thoughts and the accompanying questions—like *Where do you want to live when your hockey career ends?* and *How long do hockey careers last, anyway?*—and instead go with:

"I'm guessing you didn't buy a bargain beachfront property in Cape Cod?"

His lips twitch. "I don't think it could be technically classified as a bargain, no."

"I've never been up there."

"Neither have I."

"Wyatt!" I smack him in the stomach with one of the small, brick-like pillows, which probably has no effect on his brick-like abs. "How can you own a house you've never even been to?"

"Ow." He grabs the pillow and stuffs it behind his head. "It's an investment property. Didn't need to see it. Jacob saw it. He stayed there with . . ." He pauses and clears his throat. "With *someone* recently."

I roll my eyes. "*Someone*, huh? Ugh. You don't need to downplay my brother's propensity to play the field. Maybe one day he'll bring a nice woman home."

Wyatt glances over, one brow lifted.

I laugh. "Or not."

"You know, he says the same thing about you. Not that you'll bring a nice woman home but that maybe sometime you'll find someone and settle down."

Nerves suddenly zing through me. "Jacob talks to you about my dating life?" Really, it's a lack thereof, but I don't clarify.

"I think he worries about you," Wyatt says slowly, but I get the sudden and distinct impression Wyatt is the one worried. Not my brother.

"He shouldn't," I grumble. "I'm fine. What about you?" I ask the question before I've thought through it and realize I may not want to know.

"Do I talk to Jacob about my dating life, or do I *have* a dating life?" One side of his mouth barely lifts in a smile.

"Both?"

"No."

"That word again," I groan. "I swear, it's the most used one in your vocabulary. Expand past one syllable, please." I'm already this deep in—might as well rip off the bandage and hear all the details of the supermodels Wyatt's probably been dating.

"No, I don't talk to Jacob about my dating life because—also no—there isn't much of one to talk about."

"But you're . . . you," I sputter.

Wyatt angles his body so it's clear he's looking at me, but I can't bring myself to look back. "I'm not interested in games. When I know what I want, I don't settle for less. I don't waver. And I'm really, really good at waiting."

My heart is like the drumline at a college football game. I'm surprised it doesn't beat its way right out of my chest.

Once again, I find myself balancing on a precipice, not sure why I keep holding back the words I want to say or the things I don't want to admit I feel.

But I do force myself finally to look at Wyatt, to meet head-on that intense "grayzel" gaze. "Patience is a really admirable quality," I whisper. "I hope you don't have a limited amount."

"Infinite," he promises, and a tremor ripples through me.

And because I've reached the limit of how far I can go, especially while reclined in a bed next to Wyatt, I shift my attention back to the television. "What's your place in Boston like—the one you rent?"

"Empty," Wyatt says, thankfully not seeming to mind the sudden subject change.

But he doesn't add anything more to the one-word summation of his place in Boston, and I can't help but wonder if the word encompasses something bigger. Not just his apartment but his life.

The Wyatt of a month or so ago when I arrived had an

air of defeat about him. At the time, I saw it as just his usual grumpiness—plus the beard and the boot. But now that I've been with him day in and day out, I understand more in hindsight.

I don't think it's just the loss of his uncle or his injury that sent Wyatt to live in the town of Wallowland, population one. There are still little mysteries about him I need to solve. Like what the deal is with his father and brother. And what the blueprints on his kitchen table are.

I ache to ask nosy questions, to drill down below the surface, but the look on his face makes me feel like this might just be poking a bruise.

Or a bear.

Plus, how fair is it for me to press him with questions when I keep skirting my own vulnerability at every turn?

"Are you a betting man?" I ask.

"No."

"Tonight maybe you'll make an exception." I point to the TV. "In this show, they look at three houses. We each bet on the one we think they'll pick."

"I haven't even been watching," Wyatt says.

"Neither have I. You can pick first. They're about to do a recap of all three. Then there will be a commercial, and then the reveal."

He starts to argue again, and I shush him. He frowns but watches like a good boy as the couple discuss the merits and the downsides of each property over glasses of pinot. When the show cuts to commercial, I turn back to Wyatt.

"Well?" I ask, poking him in the arm. "What's your pick?"

"I still don't have enough data."

"That's all the data we're going to get," I tell him.

"What are the stakes for this bet, Rookie?"

"Not money," I say quickly. "I can't compete there. How about a truth?"

"A truth?" he repeats.

"Whoever wins can ask the other person a question that they have to answer truthfully." His frown deepens, harsh lines bracketing his mouth. I poke him again. It's only partly because I like the way his muscles feel under my fingertip. "Come on. I won't be too invasive with my question when I win."

His eyes narrow, but even so, I can see the spark in them.

I bite back a grin. I *knew* this would get him. Maybe I haven't seen him on the ice, but I've heard enough about his drive.

And I know this much about athletes: Competition is their catnip. So here I am, dangling it right in front of him. *Here, kitty kitty!*

"Fine," Wyatt says. "Winner gets one truth."

"Per episode."

"How many of these can we watch?" He sounds astounded.

I shrug. "We'll see. You bet first. I have the advantage because I watch this show more than you do." I hold up both hands when he assesses me. "I haven't seen this episode though. I'm no cheat."

The show comes back from commercials.

"We've got about ninety seconds," I tell him. "They'll summarize one more time while pretending to debate. In or out, Jacobs."

"In," he says, sitting up a little straighter and giving the television his full attention.

Why is this so attractive?

When they're done summarizing, I turn to Wyatt with my brows raised. "So, which house?"

"If I were choosing for *me*, I'd go with option one," he says. "Good views but far enough off the beach it won't be wiped out by a hurricane. It's fine as is but could use some fixing up. Good bones."

That would be my personal choice too. Not the show winner, but the house I'd pick for *me*. His reasons are almost the exact same as mine, but I don't say it.

"But you don't think they'll pick that one?" I ask. "Ticktock, Wyatt."

He turns to me, and not for the first time, the intensity of him knocks my pulse off course. The dark blond hair. The piercing gray eyes. That sharp jaw—all on top of broad, muscled shoulders straining against the sleeves of his T-shirt.

"They'll choose the new build with no personality."

I can't hold back my grin. Even if his guess is the same one I would have bet on. Which leaves me with option three.

"I'll say . . . the high-rise condo."

A risky choice, since the couple clearly said they wanted a house. But I can just tell they're the impatient types. They don't want to wait on renovations, and they certainly aren't going to do it themselves. Plus, the views from the tenth floor were hard to beat, and there's a doorman.

"Is that really your best guess?" Wyatt asks, studying me.

I grin. "No," I confess. "I would have gone with your pick."

Which is exactly what the couple chooses. I groan, and Wyatt sits up straighter in bed, adjusting the pillows behind his back.

"Double or nothing?" he asks, and I laugh. "Double or nothing."

In the end, we watch three shows and I owe Wyatt three truths. He is *shockingly* good for a man who swears he's never turned on HGTV before.

"No fair," I grumble, turning off the TV before he can suggest we watch another episode.

"Hey," he protests, grabbing for the remote.

I toss it toward the door and it clatters against the baseboards, scaring Jib awake. She makes three turns in her chair before groaning and going back to sleep.

"You're not allowed to be good at everything," I say.

"I'm not good at everything," he grumbles.

"True. You're very bad at some things. But you're good at too many things."

"I'm afraid to ask what I'm bad at," Wyatt says. "You'd tell me, wouldn't you?"

"Yep. But we can save that for another night. You've got three truths. So, go ahead. Ask about my deepest, darkest secrets. I'm an open book."

I settle in, punching down my pillows as I turn fully on my side and prop up my head with my hands. Wyatt mirrors my position, then twists back and clicks off his lamp, which was the only light in the room. Now the glow of the moon seeps like mist through the curtains, blanketing us in soft blue-grays.

My heart immediately picks up the pace. I'd gotten used to being in this room with Wyatt, being in this bed with him. Now, suddenly, things feel more intimate.

"Are you going to sleep?" I ask, a little confused. "What about our truths?"

"Telling the truth is easier in the dark, don't you think?"

I want to hug him. Not at this moment, because that would be the exact thing I don't need right now, but I appreciate the thoughtfulness. Even if I am an open book, there's something about Wyatt having the power of three questions.

"Thank you. Considering you're getting three whole truths out of me."

"I'll let you have one to start with."

"A pity truth?"

"You don't want it?"

"Oh, I'll happily take my pity truth with zero qualms." I jump in before he can change his mind or before I rethink my question. "Do you think you'll go back to playing hockey this fall?"

A simple question. One I feel like I should know the answer to by now. One I'm not sure I *want* the answer to. It's almost like we've been living in a little hockey-proof bubble.

Is it bad if I prefer it that way?

Considering the fact that Wyatt views hockey as a part of his identity . . . probably.

"Yes," Wyatt says finally, and there's no real justification for the swell of emotion this one word produces in me.

It's his career. Something he's good at. Something he loves. Why wouldn't he go back?

And why am I so disappointed?

"My turn," Wyatt says, yanking me out of my thoughts.

I tighten my fingers around the edge of the comforter, wishing I'd suggested we bet for something else. Like . . . bragging rights. Or candy. Even money.

Why did I think truth was a less valuable currency than money?

"How many bathing suits did you really buy for Jib?" Wyatt asks.

The question is as unexpected as the laugh that bursts out of me. "Seriously—that's your first question?"

"Yes. And you have to tell the truth."

"Are you going to judge me?" I ask.

"Definitely."

I pause. "Only three."

"Only?"

"No, wait! Only three *bikinis*. There's also a one-piece. It's a fifties pinup style—"

"Stop," Wyatt says with a groan, dragging a hand over his face.

"—with ruffles and—"

Reaching over, Wyatt covers my mouth with his hand. I laugh behind it, my lips brushing his palm.

"I am sorry I asked," he says. "So very sorry. Can we move on?"

I nod, and slowly he lifts his hand away from my face. I'm tempted to grab it and press it against my cheek. But I let him go.

Wyatt readjusts his pillows. And he scoots just a little closer to me. Not quite touching. But close enough that I can feel—or maybe I'm just imagining I feel—his warmth.

"Why did you stop wearing nail polish?"

Never in a million years would I have expected Wyatt to ask me about this. "You noticed my nail polish?"

He's quiet for a moment. "Yes."

Maybe it shouldn't, but his question throws me. Why did I stop wearing nail polish? And when? There was a time when I used to change bright colors week to week. When I started in nursing, I switched to more muted, standard colors. Then I wore no polish at all.

"I don't think it was a conscious choice. It started to feel like too much."

"Too much work?" Wyatt asks.

"No. Like . . . *I* was too much," I confess. I've never thought about this until now, and I don't like the realization.

"You could never be too much," Wyatt whispers. "And for the record? I always liked the nail polish."

This knowledge makes me unreasonably happy.

"Last question?" I ask, feeling buoyed by Wyatt's words. "Hit me."

Wyatt doesn't make me wait, which means I don't have time to prepare for his question, asked in the softest, haltingest voice possible. The unbearable gentleness has me smiling in the dark, thinking that fans of Oscar the Hockey Grouch will never get to see this part of him.

It also makes me miss his actual question at first. I see his lips moving and hear the words but don't immediately process them.

Until his words start reverberating inside my skull, clanging like a drum. Or an alarm bell. A tornado siren.

Did something happen to make you dislike athletes?

That's Wyatt's third question.

It's like he launched an axe at the center of my chest with deadly perfect aim.

"Wow." It's a strangled syllable. "That's . . . a big one."

I halfway expect or maybe hope that Wyatt will roll it back. Apologize and tell me never mind. Ask for my most embarrassing memory or maybe if I'm really okay with the way Jacob derailed my summer plans.

But he doesn't.

What Wyatt *does* do is reach out and curl his hand around both of mine, which are now white-knuckling the comforter. Closing my eyes, I draw in a shuddery breath and find that I do actually want to talk about this.

I knew I'd need to if anything *more* were to happen.

The truth is easier in the dark.

Wyatt planned this, I realize. Turning off the light wasn't because he planned to give me a pity question, but for this exact moment.

"Okay," I say, my voice breathy but stronger than a moment ago. Building momentum.

I can do this.

It's not such a big deal. That's what I've been telling myself for years, to the point I can almost believe it.

Almost. Wyatt's thumb traces a gentle, soothing rhythm on the back of my hand. His touch eases the tightness in my chest, even as I'm forced to remember the sour-sweet smell of alcohol on a boy's breath.

Hands, everywhere. And his weight on me—so, *so* heavy.

You're not there now, I remind myself.

Letting go of the comforter, I curl my fingers around Wyatt's hands, which were still cupping mine.

"Jacob had some friends stay over the summer before he left for college. One of them"—I pause, swallow, draw in a slow breath, remind myself that it's *not a big deal, not a big deal*—"came into my room while I was sleeping. The bathroom that connects our bedrooms only locks from the inside. Anyway"—I clear my throat—"he . . . climbed in bed with me. *On* me, really."

A sound comes from Wyatt—a low rumble that sounds like it's coming from the back of his throat. Almost a growl.

"When I woke up, I just froze for a few seconds. Probably minutes, I'm not sure." Wyatt's hand moves, and I realize it's shaking. I tighten my grip on him, drawing strength from him or giving it to him. Maybe both. "I really don't remember much. Just the broad strokes. He was on me, and I couldn't move, and then the anger took over. I grabbed the closest thing I could and clocked him with it. Then dragged him back to Jacob's room and put a chair under my doorknob."

Wyatt's breath hisses out of him, and I can feel him tense. I pull one of my hands away from his and slide my fingertips up to his face, brushing them over his jaw.

"You don't need to do that," he says.

"Do what?"

"Try to make *me* feel better. This is about you. And I'm *so* sorry, Josie. I wouldn't have asked if . . . I should have realized—"

"Stop. I was going to tell you anyway. Maybe just not . . . tonight."

"You don't have to—"

"Wyatt, please. It feels good to tell you. It isn't a big deal," I say. Wyatt rears back in the dark, but I keep my hand on his cheek. Steadying him, steadying myself. I'm not sure which. "I was still fully clothed and he didn't—"

"*Josie.*" Wyatt's voice is a harsh whisper, a rusty blade sawing through the darkness.

I blink away the tears gathering. "I mean, comparatively, it was nothing. Legally speaking, it was barely assault. Almost nothing happened. So many women face so much worse."

"It's not a competition," Wyatt says. "You don't need to place what happened to you on some sliding scale and decide how you *should* feel based on what could have happened or what happened to someone else. Trauma is trauma."

I scoff. "It wasn't trauma. Just something that made me skittish around athletes."

And maybe men in general. But I don't say that. This experience isn't why I haven't had a serious relationship. It's unrelated. I just haven't met the right guy.

I can feel Wyatt fighting with himself, tension radiating through him.

"When we met and I tried to shake your hand," he says, and I know where he's going with this. "You flinched. This is why?"

"The guy was a football player. Huge. Maybe it's not fair, but you're a big guy. I just . . . reacted."

"What's his name? The guy who did this."

"Why?"

"No reason."

"Yeah, I don't think I should tell you."

"I think you should. I hope you hurt him."

"Knocked him out." I'm proud of this fact, and I'm sure he can hear it in my voice.

"Good."

"I hit him with a ceramic unicorn I made at camp in middle school. I'm not even sure why I still had that or why it was in reach. The thing was ugly and covered in glitter. Apparently, some got in his eyes. Scratched his cornea."

"I hope he went blind," Wyatt says. I'm used to him sounding gruff but not fierce like this.

I like it a lot.

"He didn't. Went on to play college ball at some D2 school."

Now Wyatt does growl. Not a rumble, but an actual legitimate growl. It makes me grin in the dark.

"Are you going to turn feral?"

"Who says I wasn't feral already?" he asks, and I shiver, then snuggle closer.

"Touché."

Silence descends. A comfortable one. Soft, like the dim light blanketing us. Forgiving. Kind. A sense of relief unfurls in my chest, easing the tightness that wound through me at Wyatt's question.

I want to wiggle even closer. To wrap myself completely in Wyatt's warmth and solid presence.

"Should I sleep on the boat?"

Apparently, I'm the *only* one who wants to be closer.

I sit up, dropping my hand from his face. "What? Why?"

He sits up, too, and scoots back so far I'm concerned he'll topple out of bed. The inches between us feel like miles.

"I don't want you to feel uncomfortable with me. If you need . . . space. Physically or otherwise."

He slides his legs toward the edge of the bed like he's going to climb out, and I fist my hand in the front of his T-shirt, tugging him back toward me.

"Wyatt," I say, a soft admonishment. "Don't you know by now?"

"Know what?"

"I trust you."

They aren't the only three words I could say, but they're the ones that best fit this moment. The other ones, the ones I suspect are also true, stay tightly curled behind my ribs. Where they probably need to stay. Possibly forever.

"I don't know why," I continue, "considering your constant grumbling about everything and the way you answer no to eighty-seven percent of questions you're asked—"

"That's a very specific data point. Josie, are you counting my nos?"

"*No.*"

He chuckles, and I loosen my hand, letting go of his soft T-shirt and smoothing it over his chest. I keep my hand there. Though I can't feel his heart beating, I know it's there, steady and strong below my palm.

"Stay," I whisper. "Please."

"You're sure?"

I am.

After a few minutes, Wyatt and I both settle back down on our respective sides of the bed. He makes a joke about building a pillow wall between us. I kick him in the shin. He traps my feet between his.

I don't think it will be possible to fall asleep, but I must because I wake in the soft hush that exists between midnight and morning. Wyatt's feet still bracket mine and he has one of my hands clasped in his, right up against his mouth where I can feel the steady whisper of his breath on my fingertips.

26

Saved by the Air Horn

Josie

When I wake up the next morning with a mild headache and a medium-to-large vulnerability hangover, I'm alone in bed except for Jib, who's curled up by my feet, snoring softly.

I slide my hand across to Wyatt's side and find the sheets cool. Disappointment curdles in my belly.

It shouldn't matter if he's not here. But after what I told him last night, I'm feeling extra vulnerable. Extra sensitive, too, apparently, because my feelings are hurt.

Did Wyatt freak out because of what I told him? Or because we shared a bed? Did he open his eyes and immediately feel regret? Did I drool on him?

I'm just sitting up when the door opens. Wyatt steps inside, and I suck in a breath at the sight of him, sweat dripping down his bare chest and holding a to-go cup of coffee in each hand.

Sensitivity and hurt feelings and overthinky thoughts evaporate when Wyatt's gaze softens and his mouth curves up in a rare smile. The sight of him smiling and shirtless and with coffee floods me with warmth. I'm sure my cheeks are pink even before I regain my breath.

"You're up," he says.

"And you've been busy." As he approaches the bed, holding out a paper cup, I do my best not to ogle all the shiny, smooth muscle. I take the coffee, then almost drop it. "Wait—were you *running?*"

Wyatt takes a small step back and rubs a hand over his neck. "About that. I need to tell you something," he says.

The phrase that no one *ever* wants to hear. I wait, taking a sip of coffee for fortitude. Only, it's not just coffee. It's a latte with one pump of vanilla—my standard coffee shop order. So much for fortitude.

How did he know? I take another sip. How—

"I was cleared to sail before we left," Wyatt says finally.

"I know. That's why we're here. Sailing."

He shakes his head. "No. I was cleared to resume normal activities. Like: sail *alone.*" When I still don't say anything because he seems more upset about this than I am, he adds, "I lied to you."

"You didn't lie. I mean, I suppose it's *technically* a lie of omission since you didn't tell me," I say slowly. "But it doesn't bother me."

"It doesn't?"

"No. It wouldn't have made a difference to me," I tell him. "I wanted to come."

"Really?" Wyatt smiles again, and it feels too early in the morning for the onslaught of such things.

I take another sip of my latte. "But why *didn't* you tell me?"

He shifts, then fixes his gaze on his feet. "I wasn't sure you'd come if you didn't have to." Now he peeks up at me. "And I didn't want to come without you."

This makes me smile. I put a hand over my heart. "Aw—this coming from the man who wanted to have me arrested."

Wyatt closes his eyes and shakes his head. But I don't miss the smallest twitch of his lips. "You're never going to let it go, are you?"

"I told you—never."

It's only when Wyatt's in the shower and I'm taking Jib for a walk that a realization hits me like the slap of a rogue wave. Wyatt's been cleared for all activity. *All* activity, he said.

Which would include hockey.

I asked him last night if he thought he would go back, and he said yes. Which felt theoretical. But it wasn't theory. Wyatt already knew.

My mind scans back a little earlier in the day yesterday, when I talked with Jacob on the phone. Jacob—who didn't ask about Wyatt's recovery for once.

I thought it meant we were just having a nice conversation. One with zero business mixed in. But no—it meant that Jacob didn't need to ask. He *knew* Wyatt was coming back.

I'm not necessarily *mad* that neither of them told me. I have no right to be. Not when I've told Jacob I don't want to hear about his work. Not when Wyatt and I almost never discuss his hockey career. Except last night. And Wyatt did say he planned to go back. Maybe he honestly thought that *was* telling me.

This knowledge feels like a lead weight settling between my shoulder blades, pressing me down. Boston. Wyatt will go back to Boston in probably a matter of weeks. And I'll go back to my apartment and its fake plants. The physical distance doesn't bother me so much as the figurative distance that will once again be between us. Two very different people living very different lives in very different places.

His return to hockey will be a period at the end of the last sentence of the final chapter—the chapter I didn't want to talk about with Wyatt. And this is exactly the reason.

Then the hockey star went home to play hockey while the school nurse went home to keep living all alone. And they lived unhappily ever after. The end.

No, I tell myself, *this is good to know*. Because I was starting to crumble, starting to think that maybe this could be something. But up until a few weeks ago, Wyatt couldn't stand me.

Did I really think we could move from mutual dislike to—I struggle to even let my brain think the word—love? Or very strong like?

I would do good to remember all this. The reality check—crushing though it may be—will help me keep my head on straight and keep Wyatt firmly at arm's length. At least in the romantic sense. On a boat, arm's length isn't really a thing.

As Jib and I head back, I resolutely toss my still half-full latte in the trash while silently weeping over it. Telling myself it's a symbolic gesture. That I can make it through the rest of this trip remembering the end and staying strong, putting my heart back in its protective glass case where it's safe.

But then I get back to the room and find Wyatt fresh out of the shower in only a towel, his skin a warm olive and glistening, and a giant breakfast tray in the middle of the small room. "I ordered your favorite," the man I need to keep at arm's length says. "Belgian waffles with whipped cream."

⚓

My resolve turns out to be about as firm as a sopping wet roll of paper towels.

Sharing a bed—and sharing my history—apparently threw open a cracked door. Blew the thing right off its hinges.

Because now Wyatt can't seem to stop touching me. Every single chance he gets. Which is a lot, considering our close proximity.

Light, small touches. The kind I'm amazed that someone his size—whose literal job is to pummel other big dudes on the ice—is capable of. A delicate brush of fingertips on my elbow when passing by me to raise the sails. A warm palm barely resting on my lower back as I climb the stair-ladder to the deck. A shoulder nudging mine as we drink coffee and discuss our route for the day.

Butterfly kisses were immortalized in song, but someone should really write a banger about bird-feather touches. Wyatt's contact is hummingbird fast—there and gone. Whispers of warm skin disappearing before I can lean in for more. He leaves goose bumps and shortness of breath in his wake.

I swear, I've never met a man so steeped in patience. So restrained. A study in self-control.

It's driving me crazy.

And maybe that's the point?

Wyatt gives me careful space—but not too much. Always, there are reminders that he left the door open for me to make a choice. To take the next step.

And I know, considering the fact that every day is one day closer to our return to real life, my next steps should be ten big ones—backward.

There's too much of a disconnect between our lives.

Me: humble elementary school nurse. Only in high demand because so few people want to work for so little.

Wyatt: famous hockey player. In multimillion-dollar demand because he can help teams win trophies.

Or do they win cups in hockey? I don't remember. I probably never knew in the first place.

See? More disconnect. I don't even know the basics about Wyatt's career. The one he committed to when he was just a kid and said he made into his identity.

When we finish this trip, I imagine a giant reset button being pressed. Wyatt will go back to Boston and his big, important life and then remember he barely tolerates me. I'll go back to Fredericksburg and buy a house like I've always wanted. And it won't make me feel queasy like it does anytime I think about it now.

Even though I do my best to think about these things, to tell myself I should be moving back not forward, I can't seem to stop drifting into Wyatt's orbit. Not when he's being so sweet and thoughtful and still somehow gruff and serious—a combination that really works for me, by the way—and won't stop touching me.

When I call Toni that night and explain everything in hushed whispers underneath my pillow so Wyatt can't hear, she laughs. Laughs!

"You should just kiss the man," she says.

"What? I— *No*. Absolutely not. That would be the worst thing I could do."

"The worst thing for who?"

"Whom," I absently correct. "And for me. For him. For everyone."

"Josie, can I tell you something?" Toni asks.

"No," I say weakly. "But you're going to anyway."

"You run scared anytime someone gets close. Maybe it's time to stop running."

I disagree. I don't do that. I haven't been running. I just haven't met a great guy. Someone who likes me for me and doesn't think nude body painting is a good idea for a first date. A guy who's thoughtful and trustworthy and fun to be around and attractive . . . like Wyatt.

Maybe a month ago I would have laughed at the idea. But things are so different between us now.

For now, I mentally correct. They're different for now, but they'll snap right back into place just like an elastic band stretched to its limits. We're at the stretching point. It's not sustainable. And I know the snap back is going to hurt.

After getting off the phone with Toni—who is again insisting I kiss him when I hang up on her—I decide to help ground myself by watching clips of Wyatt playing hockey. This will be the reminder I need of our very different lives and how things can never work between us.

But it backfires.

Because Wyatt on the ice is a thing of beauty. Brutal beauty.

I don't understand the game aside from the idea that the puck needs to get into the net, but it doesn't matter. There is no shortage of Wyatt Jacobs highlights on YouTube. Wyatt Jacobs playlists organized by fans. A few full games, but I quickly realize following a game is beyond my pay grade. I can't ever tell where the puck is. Too fast.

But I can't take my eyes off Wyatt.

He's a sight in pads and a jersey and helmet, the smooth line of his jaw—a rarity in a sport that seems to prize beards in equal but opposite proportion to how much it doesn't value teeth.

Wyatt's teeth are perfect, for the record. Either he has an amazing mouth guard or a superexpensive cosmetic dentist. Maybe both.

Secretly watching him slam guys into the boards—fun fact I learned: this is what the rink walls are called in hockey—does nothing at all to quell the rising tide of feelings. It should scare me into remembering how my small life doesn't fit with his big one.

It only leaves me wanting more, acutely aware of all his bird-feather touches.

My self-control is close to snapping when we stop not far from Camp Lejeune the next day. Which, until now, had been a mythic place existing only in commercials about class action lawsuits. Turns out, it's a real base. And when soldiers are doing firing drills, all traffic on the ICW screeches to a halt. Minus the screeching, of course.

We anchor in the Ditch with a whole group of boats, some I'm starting to recognize from other marinas. Since the drills are taking a while, Wyatt and I head down below for an early lunch and to escape the sun.

I make our lunchtime staple, which Wyatt calls Josie's Famous Grilled Cheese. It's honestly just grilled cheese with a unique rotation of ingredients to keep things interesting.

Today it's extra-sharp cheddar with a little goat cheese, fresh spinach, and sliced tomatoes we picked up at a small market in Oriental. I use Himalayan pink salt (something I insisted on bringing), cracked black pepper (something Wyatt insists I use liberally on everything even though it makes me sneeze), and basil, all topped with a fried egg.

Wyatt groans, shoves his empty plate away, and slumps down a little in his seat. "You're in the wrong profession," he says. "You should quit nursing and open a food truck making only this. I hear that chefs rarely have to deal with lice in their profession."

I laugh, head tilted back, hands gripping the table so I don't tumble out of the little banquette. "Noted. And thank you for the compliment, even if it's undeserved. I think being on a boat makes everything taste better. Also? Maybe *don't* bring up the L-word around food."

"Okay, but *I* don't *have* any food." His eyes move from his empty plate to mine, which still has a bite left.

"You're not very subtle."

"Never claimed to be."

I push my plate his way, and he shovels what's left of my sandwich straight into his mouth. "Hey—slow down and enjoy!"

"I *am* enjoying," he says around a mouthful of sandwich. "Trust me. I'm enjoying."

His words and the look in his eyes send a little thrill curling through me. Under the table, his knees touch mine. A little bump, then a brush. My skin hums with awareness and our gazes snag. He licks crumbs from his fingers, still watching me intently as the early notes of "These Arms of Mine" play softly through the Bluetooth speaker on the table. It's almost too apropos.

We've been feasting on a steady diet of sixties music: Otis Redding, Sam Cooke, Creedence Clearwater Revival, Smokey Robinson, Roy Orbison, Woody Guthrie, Joan Baez, and, of course, Elvis. I haven't asked, but I'm pretty sure Wyatt's playlist is made up of songs he grew up listening to with his uncle. It's somehow the exact right soundtrack for sailing. Minus the Beach Boys, who are a little too high energy and feel a little too on the nose.

Wyatt stands abruptly. "Do you dance?"

"Not well."

"Me neither." Wyatt holds out a hand, shaking it a little when I don't immediately take it. "Dance with me."

Bad idea! Bad, bad, bad idea! the self-protective part of my brain shrieks like a banshee.

Definitely dance with him! Then kiss him! the voice of Toni in my brain argues.

I stay seated, gripping the table for dear life. "We both just agreed we don't dance well."

"It's perfect. Let's dance not well together." Wyatt gives me a look. "Josie, it's *Otis*."

I slide my palm into Wyatt's and get to my feet, legs a little shaky. "For Otis."

But it's definitely less for Otis and absolutely more for me as I reach up, running my hands across Wyatt's broad shoulders. I keep one there and let the other move to the back of his neck, playing with the strands of hair just brushing his shirt collar. He wraps his arms around my waist, pulling me close as we start to sway.

He immediately steps on my foot.

I laugh as he grimaces. "Sorry," he says. "You okay?"

Then I step on his foot. His good one, thankfully.

"Sorry!"

"I see how it is."

"That wasn't retribution! I swear. I told you—I don't dance well."

"I think you're doing just fine—*ow*."

I drop my forehead to Wyatt's chest after stepping on him again, hiding the flush in my cheeks as I laugh. "How about this? We don't lift our feet and just sway?"

"You think we'll be able to handle a small shuffle?" he asks.

"Probably not. It's weird you're bad at this when you're so good on the ice." I realize my mistake as soon as the words leave my mouth.

His eyes glitter. "Rookie, have you been watching hockey?"

"No." I'm sure the flush in my cheeks will give me away, so I duck my head. "No more talking. We're ruining Otis."

"Otis cannot be ruined by bad dancing or by talking." With a sigh that sounds more contented than frustrated, Wyatt tugs me a little closer. He dips his chin so his cheek rests near the top of my head. "And I know you're lying to me, Josie. I heard the videos. I know what hockey sounds like."

I pull back. "I was wearing headphones!"

His wicked grin does things to my stomach. I drop my head to his chest again so I don't have to see it. "You are the worst."

"Not at hockey. You said so yourself."

I grumble but don't try to argue. It's futile. So is, it seems, my resistance to Wyatt.

His hands move ever so slightly, tightening on my hips. I'm practically vibrating with tension, suddenly aware of how small the space in the saloon is, the galley on one side and the seating area on the other. How close Wyatt and I are. How firm his hands feel against my back. How good he smells. The heat of his skin. The way his fingertips flex lightly, as though they're itching to move and explore.

But what I'm most aware of is the thrum of my own impatience like a plucked string.

I like Wyatt. I trust Wyatt. He's been nothing but amazing on this trip. The kind of imperfect perfect I didn't know he could be.

So what if this can't be long term? So what if he leaves for Boston once we get back and I head home? Why can't I just enjoy the moment for once?

Maybe Toni was right. Not about the running—she's wrong there. Definitely wrong. But maybe she's right about the kissing. What's the harm in a kiss?

Plenty of harm! So much harm! the same protective part of me screams.

I hit the Mute button.

Tilting my head back, I scan Wyatt's handsome face, his smooth jaw and gray eyes. His full, frowning lips. That's when I notice it.

"You've got egg on your face," I say, brushing it away with a fingertip. "Literal egg. Not figurative egg."

"Can't have that," he murmurs, eyes locked on my mouth.

"Your affliction is catching," I tell him.

He frowns, and the little divot appearing between his eyebrows is adorable. I want to press a kiss there, to smooth it out beneath my lips.

"What affliction?" he asks.

"Foot-in-mouth disease." I pause, tell myself to be brave. Lick my lips. His eyes track the movement. "I'm not very good at saying what I mean."

"What do you want to say, Josie?" The husk in his voice tells me he knows what I meant to say. Or, at least, he suspects. Hopes.

"I don't want to *say* anything."

I also don't know that I'm brave enough to kiss him first. Or that we should be kissing at all. But I've passed the point of no return, of letting logical thought steer the ship. I've stepped over the edge and am in free fall.

Wyatt sways closer, his face dipping down as I lift up on my toes. His nose bumps mine and then—

"Let's goooooo!"

The moment is rudely interrupted by blaring horns and cheers and shouts. There's even an air horn in the mix. Or is that a bullhorn? I think it's actually both.

Bullhorns or matterhorns or whatever, they do the hard work of ruining the moment—or saving it, depending on which part of my brain I'm listening to at the moment.

"Guess we should get moving!" I say, and with what I know is probably a disturbingly wide and completely insincere smile, I scramble up on deck.

27

Permission to Board

Wyatt

By the time we reach Carolina Beach a few days later, where we plan to stop for two nights, my patience is a frayed cord.

A frayed cord with a razor's edge hovering millimeters away from the last intact thread.

Josie is the one holding the handle.

I think, at this point, she's holding everything. The razor to my frayed patience. All the cards. And my heart.

She's also holding back, and I don't know why.

Is it because of what the guy did when she was in high school? Understandable.

Even if it's not, I still want to track that guy down and do things that would probably be career ending and possibly result in jail time.

If I had to guess, there might be some long-standing trauma—no matter what she said about the word—from that event impacting her ability to connect. You can't just go around telling people they need therapy, but I would feel better if Josie did talk to someone. To help her with this and with her anxiety, which she down-played as *anxious thoughts*. One more way she's making herself small.

There could be other reasons, like our rocky shared history, the complication of her brother being my agent and friend, or maybe just my job. Not only does it create distance, but being in a relationship with a professional athlete isn't everyone's cup of tea. Of course, the women who actively seek out professional athletes—the money, the fame, the everything—aren't *my* cup of tea. Never have been.

Most of the happily married guys I've known didn't choose someone who was showing up at a hotel or dropping into DMs. They chose women who were normal, who didn't just like them because they played hockey or even liked them in *spite* of it. And it's not like I'll play forever. So, it doesn't need to be a barrier.

If that's the barrier.

I'm not even sure.

A conversation could clear it up, but the last time I tried talking to Josie—admittedly, too early on the trip—she shut me down and I promised her she could choose the speed. I guess I didn't expect her to keep zipping forward and then jamming her foot on the brakes. I've made myself the passenger, but what I want to do is yank her out of the driver's seat and take the wheel.

The one thing holding me back is my promise not to. "I'm a patient man," I mutter, repeating my own words in a mocking tone. "I won't push you."

"Wyatt?"

My head snaps up as Josie comes up from below. "Hmm?"

"Who are you talking to?"

She's smiling and carrying Jib under one arm. The little dog is dressed today in one of the bikinis Josie bought for her. It's red with ruffles. She looks ridiculous. And adorable. I'm not sure when my position on clothing for dogs changed, but I actually look forward to seeing each day's outfit.

I probably should ask my doctor for a CT scan when I get back. Just to make sure I don't have some weird tumor growing in whatever part of the brain controls liking dogs dressed up in people clothes.

"I was just talking to myself," I tell her.

"Must have been some conversation."

Josie shifts to put Jib down and her white cover-up slips off one shoulder, revealing the strap of her bathing suit. Red. I frown.

"Are you and the dog . . . wearing matching swimsuits?"

"Yep. And I don't want to hear a single comment about it, mister."

I can't make a comment. Because if they're wearing matching swimsuits, it means Josie has on a red bikini.

My thoughts are prevented from wandering too far in a direction they shouldn't go when a shout startles us both from the dock. When I look over, I have to blink a few times to make sure what I'm seeing is not a mirage.

Because it looks a whole lot like Jacob striding toward the *QUINTessntial*, flanked by two of my former teammates.

"Well, well, well," Jacob calls with a grin. "It looks like my two favorite people haven't killed each other after all. Permission to board?"

⚓

"So," Josie says, glancing between Van, Eli, and me, "the three of you are . . . good friends?"

Van, elbows on his table and chin in his hand, flutters his dark lashes at Josie. "Why? Do we not seem like we'd be besties?"

She giggles, and I consider punching him. Even though I know him well enough to know he's just being Van and not actually flirting with her, it's still too much. I settle for kicking him under the table. He shoots me a glare and rubs at his shin.

I'm still in disbelief that Jacob planned this—showing up out of nowhere and bringing two of my closest friends from my old team in North Carolina. Though it's great to see Van and Eli and Jacob, too, I'm feeling a little off just from the surprise of it.

We're at a restaurant right on the beach, the kind with a roll of paper towels on every table and the smell of fried fish lingering in the air. The patio doors are open, letting in the sound of the surf, and there's sand gritting beneath my shoes.

"You just all seem pretty different," Josie says, and it's not hard to know what she means.

Van and Eli talk enough for ten people and have kept Josie laughing with stories and teasing. And because I'm not entirely sure how to act around her in front of other people, I've kept my mouth closed and my hands to myself.

Josie and I are not . . . together. But we're more than just friends. Even friendship is really a change from how we've always been. It's not easy to keep my distance from her. Or to share her attention. Not when I've had her to myself for weeks now. I'd love nothing more than to toss her over my shoulder and carry her back to the boat. Alone.

Glancing at Jacob's arm, casually slung over the back of Josie's chair, I'm reminded I'll have to talk to him about my feelings for his sister. I don't think he'll be mad, exactly, but I'm not sure. The only time we ever talked about me and Josie in any kind of romantic context was the day she and I met. When Jacob told me she didn't like jocks.

Now, knowing what I know from her, this makes so much more sense. It makes me want to go back and wrap her in a hug. Or maybe protective Bubble Wrap.

Her gaze meets mine for a brief second, and the happiness I see there loosens the tight squeeze of anxiety.

"I've still got those friendship bracelets you made us," Eli says, elbowing me. He's got Jib in his lap, and she's staring up at him like he's her new favorite person in the world. "I should have brought them as proof. Since, apparently, it's hard to believe we're your friends."

"I don't make friendship bracelets," I grumble, which makes Josie giggle again.

"He does," Van says, flipping his dark hair out of his eyes. "Though he doesn't call often enough."

I grumble and fidget with a piece of paper towel I've been crumpling in my lap. It's almost as soft as tissue paper now. "I text."

Eli laughs. "I'm not sure the occasional text equivalent of a grunt in the group chat counts."

"Wyatt's in a *group chat?*" Josie sounds like someone just told her bigfoot exists and he's actually the quarterback for the Seattle Seahawks.

"Here." Van unlocks his phone and slides it across to Josie. "See for yourself."

Eli's brows shoot up. "You're letting her read the group text?"

Van takes a sip of his beer and leans back in his chair. "There's nothing too incriminating. And for a bunch of hockey players, we're surprisingly—sometimes annoyingly—appropriate."

Though I really don't contribute much to the group chat that started when I was playing for the Appies, I feel a pinch of nerves at the idea of Josie reading our messages. I try to remember anything I've said recently, but Eli isn't wrong about my contributions. They're minimal. Guilt swirls in my gut, and I take a long drink of water, watching Josie's face.

Other than Jacob, who basically attached himself to me like a barnacle from the time we met, I've never made or kept friends easily. Not even in hockey, where team camaraderie comes pretty easily with all the time spent on and off the ice together.

Except for this team and these two guys—plus a handful more who are in the same group chat. We've kept it up even after many of us scattered to different teams or different lives. I'm not sure if only Van and Eli were available to come, or if Jacob invited only two because he knew the more people he brought, the more overwhelmed I'd be. He winks from across the table. Probably the second option. For all Jacob's self-involvement, he's incredibly insightful and thoughtful—when he's in the mood.

"Wyatt!" Josie says, looking up at me with wide eyes. "This is scandalous."

I frown. "What?"

Chairs scrape the floor as Jacob, Eli, and Van lean across the table to read whatever's on the screen. I reach over and pluck the phone from Josie's fingers, then glare down at the screen. And have no idea why she reacted to the pretty typical back-and-forth. There's nothing remotely scandalous. Still, I click off the phone and slide it into my pocket.

When I look up at her, Josie's smirking. "Did you see it? You actually said *yes* to something."

The whole table erupts into laughter as the waitress brings our orders. And though I'm uncomfortable being the center of attention or the cause for laughter, warmth stretches and expands in my chest. Because I know everyone seated around me is someone safe. They care about me—and not because of anything in particular I've done to earn it—maybe even in spite of me not keeping in touch well. And saying no too often. Josie isn't wrong about that.

As we start to eat and the conversation moves to our plans for tomorrow, a foot finds mine under the table. Immediately, I know it's not one of the guys. They'd probably be kicking me. No, it's Josie, pressing the top of my foot gently, as though reminding me she's here. I glance across the table at her, and when our eyes meet, it's like there's no one in the room but the two of us.

"So, tell us how this came to be," Eli says, pointing between Josie and me.

I choke, glancing quickly at Jacob. "What?"

Van pops a french fry into his mouth. "Jacob said she's your live-in nurse."

Josie chokes. It takes some pounding on her back from Jacob and a few gulps of water before she can speak. I'm just relieved Eli wasn't asking about something else. I didn't think it was obvious that something has been brewing between us. Keeping my distance from her tonight has helped. And nothing sucks any romantic tension out of a room like the arrival of an over-protective sibling and two guys who never shut up.

"Not his nurse. More like his handler," Josie says, her foot pressing down on mine beneath the table.

"An overpaid babysitter," Jacob says. "Emphasis on overpaid."

"Hey—you have no idea what I've endured." Josie's eyes meet mine as she says, "I mean, the first day I got there, he asked if I'd give him a sponge bath."

Jacob drops his fork. Eli's mouth hangs open, and Van looks like he's about to fall out of his chair. I pinch the bridge of my nose.

Only at the sudden silence does Josie realize how that sounded. Her eyes go wide. "Not like that! He didn't really mean it—he was just trying to scare me off."

"He better not have meant it," Jacob says, glaring at me across the table. He's picked up his fork again and looks ready to stab me with it.

Not inspiring confidence in how a conversation with him will go about my actual feelings for Josie.

"And I found out later he had a fever, so nothing he said could be trusted anyway."

Is that what she thinks? Because I know for a fact that I told Josie she was pretty. And I faked being more out of it than I was because I liked her touching me. The fever exposed exactly how I really feel about Josie. How I've felt for years.

"I barely got him into bed," Josie says.

Now Van does fall out of his chair. Eli throws his head back and laughs, and the only thing keeping Jacob from diving across the table at me is Josie's hand on his shoulder.

"He was sick!" she says. "I had to get him into bed because he was *sick*. Calm down!" She glances at me across the table, shaking her head. "I've caught your foot-in-mouth disease. I think I'll spend the rest of the night in silence."

"Please don't," Van says, picking himself up off the floor. "We need more stories just like that."

"I'm going to the bathroom," Josie says, pushing her chair back to stand. "Please be good while I'm gone." She directs this to Jacob, who only rolls his eyes.

The moment she's gone, they pounce.

"When's the wedding?" Van asks with a grin.

Eli leans closer and ruffles my hair. "I always wondered what kind of woman would snag your grinchy little heart. I approve. And I'm not just saying this because her brother's right here."

I don't even bother protesting. Instead, I glance over at the brother in question, expecting him to be glaring. Not stuffing his face with fried catfish like this conversation doesn't involve his sister. And me.

"What?" he asks around a mouthful.

"I just . . ."

Jacob takes a sip of water. "You're just in love with my sister? Yeah. I know. I've known for years. Oh, and you're welcome, by the way." He wipes his mouth with a paper towel while I gape at him. "I wasn't quite sure how I was going to play matchmaker, and your injury made the perfect setup. Though next time, go a little easier. You had me slightly concerned that disc golf would end your career."

"You . . . know? You've *known*?"

He rolls his eyes. "Dude. You've looked at her like a lovesick puppy for years. Hard to miss when I know you as well as I do. The question is—what are you going to do about it?"

That's the question indeed.

"I do know one thing," I tell him. "It's time to implement The Plan."

Jacob beams. "Really? The Plan? I didn't think you were ever going to agree."

"What's 'The Plan'?" Van asks, using finger quotes.

Before either Jacob or I can answer, Josie returns from the bathroom, effectively ending the conversation.

"Wow. This looks like an intense conversation," Josie says, dropping back in her seat. "What'd I miss?"

28

Purely Scientific

Josie

I had no idea going to the beach could be so . . . challenging.

Not discovering sand in unmentionable places or dealing with hair tangled from salt water and humidity or even getting sunburned.

It's the *thighs*.

"That's mine!" Van shouts, leaping across Eli to snag the Frisbee out of the air. When he lands in a crouch, grinning, his quads flex in a way that's hard not to stare at. Especially when his shorts end about six inches above his knees, just like the other guys on the beach.

Including my brother, whose pasty-white legs I could have done without seeing.

"I'm not interested in Van," I tell Jib, who's watching the guys play with similar interest. "Or his thighs. I'm not even into thighs. Or I wasn't? It's just . . ."

I don't bother finishing the thought. Not because I'm talking to a dog but because there's no need to explain. Anyone seeing Van, Eli, and Wyatt running around in their apparently stylish short shorts would understand.

All of them are clearly athletes, though all have different builds. Van is shorter than Eli or Wyatt with a stockier build and a massive dragon tattooed on his chest. Wyatt and Eli both are a little lankier, though with no shortage of impressive muscle groups from their shoulders to their abs. But it's the athletes' quads that set them apart from normal humans.

Massive. Bulky. Flexing with even the smallest movements.

I'm not even sure what game they're playing with the Frisbee. Nor do I care.

"I'm not ogling," I say, and I swear Jib snorts. "I'm observing. Like a scientist."

Okay, there's nothing scientific about the way I stare when Wyatt wrestles with Eli over the next throw. I had no idea legs even had so many muscle groups.

"Enjoying the game?"

Jacob startles me, likely on purpose, as he appears next to me, hands on hips and a little out of breath.

"Or," he adds with a smirk, "just enjoying the view?"

I smack him on the calf, and he grunts. "Shut up."

"Do you see the appeal of athletes now?" he asks, clearly not even close to being done giving me a hard time. "I would have arranged something like this years ago had I known you were so . . . into it."

"Will you stop? Please?"

"Probably not." But he does dash off, snatching a Frisbee from Wyatt's hands.

As the two of them start wrestling, Wyatt dragging my brother toward the surf, Van and Eli plop down on either side of me. I shift a little, making sure to keep my eyeballs away from their legs. Jib wiggles away from me and climbs in Eli's lap, licking the bottom of his chin. He laughs. Everything about him, from his blond hair to his wide smile to his kind eyes, is so *sunny*. I'm not sure I've ever met a person so effervescent. My brother should have sent Eli rather than me to pull Wyatt out of his slump.

"You must love dogs," I say.

"I do. My wife is in vet school, and we keep picking up strays. I'll show you a picture when we get back to the boat."

"Of your wife or the dogs?" Van teases.

Eli reaches around me to smack Van in the back of the head. "Both."

Though the three of them stayed in a hotel last night, the boat has been our home base. It was a pleasant—if somewhat hot—walk down to the beach where we spent the morning. Despite Jacob's job, I haven't spent time with professional athletes before, aside from Wyatt. Who doesn't count since I met him when he was in college, just on the cusp of his career.

They're surprisingly and refreshingly normal. Aside from the thighs.

I've loved watching Wyatt around his former teammates. He's never talked about them to me, but it's clear they have a bond. I swear, Wyatt has smiled more in the last twenty-four hours than he usually does in a week. It's been hours of teasing, smack talk, and easy physical playfulness. Wyatt is still a man who exists with a little storm cloud hanging over his head, but he's lighter with them around. There's an ease to him around Eli and Van. His limbs seem looser, his posture more relaxed, his jaw at least forty percent less clenched.

I'm a tiny bit jealous, wishing he was that way around me too. Or maybe he is and I just haven't noticed because I'm with him day in and day out.

My brother, though I don't think he'd met Eli or Van before, folded into the group like he's known them all forever. It's what my parents and I call the Jacob Effect. My brother makes things louder, livelier. He doesn't need to go to parties; he *is* a party. It's been a while since I've seen him let loose like this, though, and I wonder how often he and Wyatt get to spend time together that's not work related.

"How did you both meet your wives?" I ask, scooping up a little sand and letting it sift through my fingers.

It's polite conversation, but I'm also intensely curious. Last night at the restaurant and today at breakfast and now the beach, women have been watching them, if not directly trying to flirt. Van and Eli, as friendly as they are, shut it down quickly and completely each time. Clearly, they are settled and happy in their relationships. No one has been brave enough to approach Wyatt, whose looks could shrivel the leaves of a healthy plant.

Both Van and Eli are more than happy to answer my question, but while I'm listening to their stories, at least part of my attention is on my brother and Wyatt. They're having what appears to be a serious conversation in the surf. Every so often, one of them glances my way. Despite the temperature, goose bumps stand up on my arms.

Are they talking about me? About me . . . and Wyatt?

I've given almost zero thought to how my brother would feel about me dating Wyatt. *If* it were to happen. And I still feel jittery about that *if* whenever I consider what this would look like outside of our present reality.

Which isn't anywhere close to actual reality. For either of us.

I force my attention back to the two men on either side of me, feeling guilty I was listening distractedly. Though I did hear enough to know that neither one had a typical relationship and they're both stupidly happy in love.

"Is that a hockey thing?" I ask. "I mean, how quickly you both got married. Is that normal?"

Van laughs. "Not particularly. A lot of guys enjoy the single life for a long time."

"Or take things at a more normal pace. But when you know, you know," Eli says, scratching Jib behind the ears.

Something uncomfortable shifts in my stomach. I glance out again to where Wyatt and Jacob are now in the shallows with their backs to us, staring at a shrimp trawler off the coast. Stacks of gray and white clouds form an imposing skyline, taller and more regal than any cityscape. A little ominous too. They're far off but gathering and building quickly.

"And you both just . . . knew?"

"Sounds kind of woo-woo or whatever, but yeah," Van says. "There were a few question marks and some things to work through at the start, but I knew."

"Took me a minute. But only a minute," Eli says with a grin. "It probably took Bailey longer. Being married to a guy in our profession isn't easy."

My stomach does a flip. Not the good kind.

"I can imagine it would be challenging," I say.

Van stretches out on his towel, linking his arms behind his head as he grins. "But worth it. We come with perks. Money, good looks—"

"Humility," Eli adds.

I can't help but laugh at Van's cockiness and the way Eli counterbalances it. I wonder briefly if this camaraderie translates to the ice and how they play.

"It's not a normal life, that's for sure," Eli says. "But what is normal?"

"Overrated," Van says. "Normal is overrated."

I think of my steady job, the only surprise being which kids might pop into my office with real—or fake—afflictions. My apartment. My friendship with Toni. There's always been a comfort in the quietness of my life. It's easy. Safe.

Now it feels like not enough and, at the same time, like a cocoon of protection I can't wait to return to.

"Why all the questions?" Eli asks. "Are you and Wyatt . . . ?" He trails off, the question in his voice echoing in his blue eyes.

"Something," Van finishes. "Are you *something*?" The arch of his dark brow seems to indicate he knows the answer. Or thinks he does.

"I don't know," is the best I can do.

"There's definitely a vibe," Van says.

"Is there?" I ask weakly. I thought Wyatt and I had done a pretty good job pretending to be normal. And not dancing on a cliff's edge the way we have been.

"It's the way he looks at you," Eli says. "Like you're all he sees."

"Or wants to see," Van agrees.

Eli bumps my shoulder lightly with his. I'm surprised to find I'm comfortable enough with him that I don't mind the contact. "You couldn't ask for a better guy."

"Though you could ask for a less grumpy one," Van adds, and he and Eli both laugh at this.

"So . . . yeah?" Van says hopefully. "You and our boy?"

It's a great question. One I can't even answer for myself, much less Wyatt's friends.

I think of our quiet, mundane conversations about our travel plans every morning. Of the bossy yet confident way Wyatt orders me around when things get hairy on the boat. Of our lingering conversations, lingering looks, lingering good nights as we retreat to our own cabins.

I *do* know. But as for Wyatt . . .

Reflecting on all our exchanges over the years, these weeks with him have been an exception. Not the rule. There's no way *he* knew.

When Wyatt goes back to his normal life, he might blink at this little blip of time and wonder what he was thinking. It's almost like I've been with an alternative version of him—the fever version on a grander scale. Injury and vacation Wyatt. Not normal Wyatt.

So even though I can relate to what Van and Eli said about knowing, I don't think this is *that*. Not for Wyatt, anyway.

Or am I doing what Toni accused me of—running when someone gets close?

"Ugh, I'm burning." Jacob's voice yanks me out of my thoughts. He and Wyatt have ambled over, and my brother has his head angled, trying to look at his back. Which is definitely pink.

I jump to my feet, brushing sand off my legs and avoiding Wyatt's laser-like gaze. "I told you to wear sunscreen."

"I did!"

"You used tanning oil with an SPF of eight," I tell him. "That's not sunscreen. You're roasting like a turkey. Should we get out of the sun?"

"We actually need to head back to the hotel so we can shower," Jacob says, glancing at his watch, an expensive one I'm surprised is waterproof. "We've got flights to catch. I promised these guys I wouldn't keep them long from their wives."

"You're leaving today?"

If I sound panicked, it's because I am. The idea of being alone again with Wyatt should in no way freak me out. But spending time with my brother and Wyatt's hockey friends has left me feeling more uncertain. I'm shaken for reasons I can't quite pinpoint.

You're running, Toni's persistent voice accuses.

And I'm starting to believe she's right.

⚓

Jacob gives me an extra-long hug on deck while Wyatt says goodbye to his former teammates.

"This was a really thoughtful surprise for Wyatt. Thank you," I tell my brother. When I try to wiggle away, he holds me tighter.

"I didn't do it just for him," he says. "Are you saying you didn't enjoy seeing your only brother after all the complaining you did about the Super Summer Sibling Extravaganza?"

"Maybe it's time to let the Extravaganza go in favor of something more reasonable. Like dinner once a month. FaceTime. Texting regularly."

Jacob finally lets me go, stepping back with a frown. "Really? No more trips?"

I shrug. "I mean, we gave it a good go. But it's been hard to make it happen. And when we did . . ."

"Norovirus," we say at the same time.

"You might have a point," he says. "But this was nice, wasn't it? And I'm proud of you."

"For what?"

Jacob waves an arm around the boat vaguely. "Look at you, being adventurous!"

"I can be adventurous," I protest, though I'm not sure it's true.

"Learning to sail and doing this whole trip. With a man you thought hated you, I might add." He leans closer. "Emphasis on the *thought*. Seems like maybe it's the opposite of hate, eh?"

Immediately, I throw my hand over Jacob's mouth and glance toward Wyatt. Though his eyes were already on me, he's toward the cockpit with the guys and probably didn't hear. But now he makes his way toward us with a frown.

"Stop talking," I hiss.

I remove my hand from Jacob's mouth, and the stupid man immediately starts talking again, clearly not seeing Wyatt approaching. "Or did you not realize I had a grand master matchmaking plan at work? I'll take my thank-you now."

"I want to throw you overboard," I tell him through gritted teeth. My cheeks are flaming, and I also know Wyatt probably heard most, if not all, of that. From the back of the boat, Van and Eli are watching with interest.

"Too bad you're not strong enough to do it," Jacob says with a smirk.

"Yeah, but I am," Wyatt says.

And almost before I can blink, he's got my brother hoisted up in the air and has tossed him off the boat. It's perhaps one of the most attractive displays I've ever seen.

"Dude!" Jacob yells as he comes sputtering back up to the surface. "You suck!"

"You remember how to swim, right?" Wyatt calls, zero ounces of concern in his tone.

"That's cold, man," Van calls. "I approve."

I pull out my phone to take a picture as Jacob swims toward a ladder at the end of the dock. Wyatt steps closer, curling his arm around my shoulders. I sigh as I lean into him.

I had no idea how much I've missed his touch since my brother arrived—nor did I realize how little Wyatt has touched me—until now. But I'd like him to throw everyone overboard so I can burrow into him shamelessly.

And equally, I also want to jump overboard myself and hitch a ride to the airport.

I choose to stay put, leaning my head against Wyatt's chest.

"You know," he says as Jacob reaches the ladder. "This makes me think about calling Peter."

I'm so shocked it takes me a moment to realize who he's talking about. "Peter—your brother?"

"That's the one."

Wyatt says this so casually, like it's not a massive thing to consider reaching out to his estranged brother.

This is huge. But—

"My shoes are leather!" Jacob shouts, starting to climb.

I can't hold back a laugh. Wyatt glances at me, surprised, then offers me a rare full grin.

"What?" he asks.

"I just think it's funny that this"—I gesture to my drenched brother, nearing the top of the ladder—"is leading you to want to mend family ties."

"I lost my sunglasses!" Jacob shouts, as if to prove my point.

"Oh no! You lost one of your fifty pairs," I tease. "What will the other forty-nine do?"

Jacob glares.

"It's weird that this makes me miss my brother," Wyatt says. "But if you can't throw your family overboard, are you even family?"

Touché.

"I'm serious about my stuff," Jacob says, pulling his shirt away from his body and wringing it out. Already, a puddle surrounds him on the dock.

"I'll write you a check," Wyatt says. "New shoes and sunglasses are on me."

"I regret the present I got you, Josie." Jacob reaches the boat, dripping and still griping.

"What present?" I ask.

"It's in your berth or cabin or whatever you call your bedroom. But I should just return it. You don't deserve it. Neither of you does."

"He said neither of us," Wyatt says as the three guys pile into their rental car after hugs and goodbyes. Jacob was still grumbling as they left. "Guess it's a gift for me too."

So I bring it to the saloon, setting it on the table. Wyatt watches as I tear into the box, which is wrapped in layers of duct tape. Very Jacob.

But the gift isn't for Wyatt and me. It's two matching Appies jerseys—one for me and one for Jib. Wyatt picks mine up and turns it, swallowing hard when he sees his name on the back.

"These are the new style," he says, sounding dazed, still looking at the jersey and not meeting my gaze. "I don't even know how Jacob could have gotten these. Especially since it's not my team anymore."

But I'm not surprised. My brother always finds a way to get what he wants, and I have to wonder if this will come to include setting his best friend up with his sister.

29

A Panic Sinkhole

Josie

"You're very quiet," Wyatt tells me as we start walking back to the boat from dinner at a restaurant not far from the yacht club.

"Maybe it just feels quiet with them gone," I say, even though I know Wyatt's right. I am quiet. Quiet and pensive and, admittedly, a little moody.

Our seafood dinner looked good, but I'm not sure I tasted it. I was glad baseball was playing loudly on several screens in the restaurant to provide a distraction for Wyatt. Though it must not have been distraction enough. Clearly, he noticed my current mood.

I'm not sure what brought it on. Maybe being surrounded by people for a solid twenty-four hours—more noise, more engagement, more being *on*. But I think it has more to do with the conversations I had and the worries that sprouted in their wake.

My brain has devolved into chaos, thoughts ping-ponging from the idea of *knowing* to the concept of a "normal life" to what it would mean to be a hockey girlfriend. Or a hockey *wife*.

"Still with me?" Wyatt asks, his voice a gentle nudge.

I force a small laugh. "Mostly."

Wyatt's hand brushes mine, but rather than linking our fingers easily as he might have done just a day or two ago, he hesitates, then shoves his hands in his pockets. I could really use his steadying touch right now, but I'm not about to reach for him. Not with the unmoored thoughts banging around in my head.

A breeze lifts my hair off the back of my neck, a momentary break from the humidity, which seems to have swelled since the sun went down. Then the night goes still again, and I feel sweat gathering at my lower back. In the distance, there's a quick flash—lightning hidden by the clouds. The tension crackling between Wyatt and me mirrors what's hanging in the air tonight.

"Anything on your mind?" Wyatt asks.

Lots. But nothing I want to say out loud.

"Sorry—I'm kind of rotten company tonight. It was good to see my brother, but I think I've got a Jacob hangover."

My attempt at humor falls flat. Or maybe it's just that Wyatt knows me well enough now to perceive there's more to my mood.

"Do we need to worry about that?" I ask, waving vaguely toward the sky. The moon is visible for a moment, then disappears between wispy, fast-moving clouds. Far off, there's another quick flash.

"This storm should stay to the east," Wyatt says. "Though I think a more serious system is moving in tomorrow."

"What do we do if there's a storm? Like, what's the protocol?"

"It wasn't in your books?" he teases.

I elbow him, and for half a second, the tension eases between us. "Not really."

The guidebook talked about a few spots you wouldn't want to be in during bad weather. Mostly because of shoaling and muddy bottoms making it hard to hold anchor. Before this trip, I thought dropping anchor meant literally just that. But it actually involves dragging the anchor as the boat moves forward, trying to catch it securely along the bottom. Which is only as easy as the conditions of the channel bed. Some areas are too silty or muddy to hold.

I haven't worried about this before now, and maybe it's just the combination of the distant storm and my muddled thoughts, but there's an uneasiness swirling in my gut.

"It shouldn't be too big of a deal," Wyatt says. "I've got us a spot booked at a marina."

"Wouldn't it be better to be at an anchorage? Away from other boats and solid things?" Images flash through my mind of boats splintering against one another or against the docks.

Wyatt shakes his head. "It'll be fine. Just a few bumps."

Somehow, I doubt riding out a storm on a sailboat will be *just a few bumps*, but I guess I'll find out.

⚓

When we set out in the morning, the awkward tension still lingers. Probably because I'm leaking it like oil from a damaged car engine. Even the conversation plotting our route over coffee felt stiff. I considered putting Jib in her new jersey and dressing to match but instead opted to put her in a striped shirt with an anchor on the front.

If Wyatt is disappointed, he doesn't say it. The things unsaid seem to be stacking up like bricks in a wall. Or dominoes, ready to topple.

I'm grateful the passage today doesn't allow us time to relax. There are a lot of boats combined with a narrow stretch of deep water. The current is fast, the wind is wicked, and everyone seems to be hurrying to their next stops ahead of the storms. It's hazy and cloudless now, but by evening that should change.

We pass a number of wrecked boats, which only ramps up my nerves, though Wyatt assures me they washed up in hurricanes. Not normal travel. Still. They seem like some kind of sign.

Way to go, emo, I tell myself, trying to dislodge the negativity clinging to me.

Wyatt is, as always, patient, and I find myself wishing he weren't. Part of me wishes he would take me by the shoulders, stare into my eyes, and demand I talk to him like a mature adult. He doesn't.

Which makes *me* want to grab *him* by the shoulders, glare into his eyes, and demand he tell me that whatever's happening between us is real and will last beyond this trip. I don't.

What I do is call Jacob from my cabin after another awkward meal with Wyatt. The storm system, threatening all day, seems set to miss us completely with distant lightning and thunder lingering but not coming closer.

"Miss me already?" he asks in lieu of hello.

"Debatable," I say, then pause. Because I'm not completely, one hundred percent sure why I called my brother instead of Toni.

"Still there?"

"I'm here."

"And you called me because . . . ?" I can hear him drumming his fingers on something.

"What if this ruins everything?" I blurt. "Or what if it doesn't work? Or what if it doesn't last and then there will always be this awkwardness between you and Wyatt or maybe your friendship will be completely destroyed?"

"Wow, okay. So you're in a panic spiral."

"It's less of a spiral and more like a vortex or a sinkhole. A panic sinkhole."

Jacob chuckles, but it's kind and gentle. Just like his voice when he speaks. "Hey, I know this is probably scary. For a lot of reasons, not the least of which being that you just now figured out what a good guy Wyatt is."

"He really is," I say miserably.

"Why do you sound upset by that?"

I wiggle into my bed, tracing my fingers over the low, curved ceiling above my head. "Because it was easier when Wyatt was a jerk. When he was the guy picking up your sloppy seconds with Grocery Store Girl and—"

"Whoa, whoa, whoa. Hang on. Is that what you think happened?" Jacob sounds incredulous.

"That is what happened. I should know; I literally walked in on them."

"Yeah, but you don't know the whole story. Turns out Grocery Store Girl recognized Wyatt."

"But he wasn't even famous!"

"She was some crazed hockey fan and knew of him. And the contract he'd just gotten. Her endgame was Wyatt, not me. And he was shutting it down when you walked in."

I think back to the night Wyatt and I met, the awkward kitchen incident, trying to reframe it from this perspective. I guess this explanation could make sense.

Unfortunately, if so, it shaped my every interaction afterward with Wyatt.

"That doesn't change what he said."

"What did he say?"

I want to roll my eyes, but of course Wyatt's words wouldn't have haunted Jacob. Just me. "He said, 'Not your *sister*.' Like I was some kind of disgusting virus."

"Uh, that might have actually been my fault, considering I kind of told him to leave you alone before we got there."

"Jacob," I growl.

"Sorry! Don't worry—he knows now that I wholeheartedly give my stamp of approval. In fact, I've already nominated you as couple of the year."

"We're not even a couple yet!"

"Ah-ha! I heard the *yet*."

"You're exasperating."

"And yet lovable," Jacob says. "Also, don't worry about my friendship with Wyatt. You know what they say. Bromance before—"

"Don't say it."

"Romance. What did you think I was going to say?"

"Not that." I pause. "So, you think I could handle dating a professional hockey player? Would I have to quit my job? Move? Would I need to worry about women slipping into his DMs?"

Jacob laughs. "Wyatt hates social media. And so far as I know, he's never hooked up with a fan or had any interest."

"Really?"

"Maybe you should, I don't know—be a grown-up and go talk to the guy."

My brother is right. I should. But after we hang up and I change into the new jersey—hoping it will bring me some kind of luck—and spend a little time overthinking, I instead end up drifting off to sleep.

⚓

I wake up sometime hours later as I'm rolling into the wall. My forehead smacks the edge of the built-in shelves, and pain spears through my skull.

Lightning flashes in the tiny windows, and I realize how loud it is—sheets of rain hit the side of the boat and the wind sounds like an angry banshee. The boat tilts again, this time in the other direction. I barely manage to keep myself from rolling off the bed.

Using the momentum, I get to my feet, steadying myself against the walls as the boat tips and pitches, thunder rolling. How did I manage to sleep through the storm until now? I throw open the door to find Wyatt standing in the hallway just outside, hand raised to knock.

Lightning flashes, revealing the worry etched in his face— and a bump on his forehead. "Are you okay?" he asks.

"Are *you*?" Keeping one hand on the doorframe, I reach up to touch his head just as the boat rocks hard to one side, sending us both practically flying into the saloon.

Wyatt grabs the table with one hand and wraps the other around my waist, keeping us both upright. Barely.

"Where's Jib?" I ask, practically having to shout over the noise of the storm.

"Believe it or not, sleeping. She tucked herself into a little storage nook so she's not rolling around."

As though reacting to his words, the boat tilts again, accompanied by a bellow of thunder. Lightning highlights the gray in Wyatt's eyes, and suddenly I'm aware of how closed off I've been. Wyatt seems to remember at the same time, the expression on his face shifting.

Before either of us can speak, the hatch flies open. Instantly, rain is slanting inside the saloon. Wyatt grabs for the hatch, and I hold on to him when the boat sways again, the wind howling through the opening as water pours in.

"Do we need to check the sails or anything on deck?" I shout over the gale.

Wyatt hesitates. "I prepped things earlier, but sometimes things blow loose."

"Let's double-check. I'll go with you."

He's already starting to climb out. "I've got it. You stay—it's not safe on deck."

But I've already slipped on my boat shoes and am following him up. We're both soaked through by the time we get on deck. I swing the hatch closed behind me to keep more water from going inside.

It's wild up here, and Wyatt steadies me with a strong hand on my arm, tucking me close as the boat dips. All around us, I can see boats being tossed wildly. We aren't the only ones on deck, securing things in the rain, though there are just a handful of people in sight.

A few slips over, a couple is fighting with a sail that's ripped right off and is flying around them.

Thankfully, our sails are in place. Wyatt probably secured everything while I was on the phone with Jacob. Or while I was asleep after.

A few ropes are whipping around, and Wyatt and I each grab one, firmly tying them up again. One of the bumpers has come loose, and Wyatt tucks it back into place, tightening the knot while I stand behind him, one hand on his back.

"I think that's about all we can do," he shouts. "Let's go back down below!"

I nod, but there's a pressure building in my chest. Remnants of my earlier anxieties are shifting, taking a new shape. Expanding until there is no longer any room for them inside me.

Before Wyatt can open the hatch, I grab his arm. "Wait!"

He turns to face me again, a sheet of rain plastering his hair to his face. Wet like this, it almost looks black. So do his eyes.

And still—even like this, he's the handsomest man I've ever seen.

"I'm sorry about how I've been acting!" I shout.

Thunder booms and the boat tips. Wyatt's fingers grasp my hip while another hand grabs a railing, keeping us balanced.

"You really want to talk about this now?!" Wyatt yells, tipping his head my way. Even so, it's hard to hear over the storm's din.

"Is this not a good time for you?"

I'm not sure where the sarcasm comes from or why I'm screaming at the man instead of telling him I think I might be in love him, but here we are—soaking wet, on deck in a storm, and shouting at each other in what has to be the worst relationship talk ever.

But Wyatt laughs, head thrown back until he chokes on rain, spluttering as he tilts his head back down, his eyes meeting mine.

"Let's finish and get back inside." Wyatt leans closer but still needs to shout over the wind. "Then we can talk, Rookie."

I grab his arm as he starts for the bow, tugging him back. "I don't want to wait!"

"What *do* you want, Josie?"

The bravery that fueled me to start shouting at Wyatt in the first place ebbs, and with the next boom of thunder, I jump.

Tucking me closer to his chest, Wyatt holds me steady. I'm no longer sure if the wetness on my cheeks is rain or tears.

Wyatt bends, placing his ear near my lips with a simple command: "Tell me."

"I'm scared, and I don't want to be. I don't want to mess this up. I don't want to keep running. But I don't know how to trust this when . . ." I swallow around a growing lump in my throat, temporarily losing my ability to form words.

"When what?" Wyatt says, and I realize he's not shouting anymore. That the storm, though still raging, has suddenly lightened up a bit.

I rest my cheek on Wyatt's, feeling the slight burn of his closely shaven skin as I force myself to say the words that scare me most.

"It's hard to trust this when you've hated me for so long."

He reacts as though I've struck him, rearing back until those gray eyes—almost black in the darkness—practically burn into me. His hand on my back flattens, pressing me closer, holding me tighter. "I—what?"

"Just because I helped you through a hard time, and you flipped a switch—"

"Flipped a switch?" Wyatt practically bellows.

"You used to hate me; now you like me. A switch flipped."

"That's really what you think?"

"Isn't that what happened?"

Wyatt stares at me for a very long moment. There's a feeling not unlike dread swirling in my gut like water around a slow drain. What I don't understand is why.

Or why he looks like I've just stolen his puppy.

"Am I wrong?" I ask.

I *know* I'm not. I know how things have always been with us. *Don't I?*

I think back to what Jacob said about that night so long ago, how different it seems with a new perspective. I remember Wyatt telling me he has a problem saying the wrong thing to me.

Though it feels like entering an alternate reality, I realize it's entirely possible that I've read things wrong for years.

Droplets of water fall from Wyatt's hair into his eyes, but he doesn't take his hands off me to wipe them clear. It's like he's frozen, staring at me with a look I can't understand. My stomach flips right out of my body and lands with a soft *thud* on the deck.

"You couldn't be more wrong when it comes to how I feel about you," Wyatt says, then leans closer, pressing his wet forehead to mine. "How I've *always* felt about you."

The deck moves underneath me. But this time, it's not the storm. No—it's the world as I know it, tilting sideways. Collapsing.

Sucking me through a black hole and shooting me out the other side into a whole new galaxy.

Wyatt has feelings for me—has *always* had feelings for me?

I—

He—

We—

"I don't understand."

"Yes, you do," he insists. "It just doesn't fit with the narrative you've apparently had in your head where I hate rather than love you."

My world isn't tilting anymore. It's a globe that's been knocked off a table and is being kicked like a soccer ball around the room.

"Did you say—"

Wyatt suddenly surrounds me, his chest pressed to mine, his arms around my lower back. When he slides his arms up and over my shoulders, sparks cascade over me like I'm a malfunctioning socket.

"*Love.* Yes, I said it." He sighs, thumbs stroking my cheeks. "I didn't mean to tell you like this. So soon. Or when we're soaking wet in the middle of a storm. But this is still my curse with you—I can't ever say the right thing."

"Oh, it's a curse now? I thought it was foot-in-mouth *disease.*"

His eyes snap to mine, like he can't believe I'm teasing him right now. It was a risk, and for a moment I think a bad bet. I hold my breath, hoping I haven't offended Wyatt by making light of things right after he confessed that he *loves* me.

"Maybe it's both," he says, the smallest of smiles lifting one side of his mouth. "Should I try to say it again—say it better?"

"Not yet," I tell him. "I need a minute."

The truth is, I may . . . need a lot of them.

My brain needs to play catch-up. I need to spend some good long hours reframing all my memories. Examining all the little clues that told me Wyatt felt one way about me—clues I read wrong this entire time.

I lean closer, trailing my hands up Wyatt's chest to his shoulders. When I touch his neck, my fingers slip over his wet skin.

"You know what they say is the best way to break curses?"

Wyatt's brows pulse together. A look of confusion. "No."

Of course he doesn't. His dad made him watch documentaries on the stock market rather than watching classic cartoons or reading children's stories.

"The way to break a curse is with a kiss," I tell him, lifting up on my toes as he sways forward to meet me.

And then we're kissing. Or curse breaking.

The kiss is messy—we're soaked and slippery and moving like we're in some kind of desperate panic. Maybe we are.

Wyatt's fingers tangle in my hair and mine tug him closer

by his shirt. When he chuckles, I feel the rumble of it through his mouth.

A mouth I want to spend a lot more time with.

Any fears or hesitations or worries I had evaporate. Because there is none of that coming from him. Only a pure male confidence and surety that reminds me of all those videos of him on the ice.

Wyatt kisses like he skates.

Not with brutal force, but with power and the delicate precision that allows a man who must weigh more than two hundred pounds to balance on tiny blades, changing directions on a dime.

He kisses me like a hero returning from war. One who has been dreaming about this exact moment for days or weeks or months. Maybe years. Like the meeting of our lips is the culmination of so many long-held hopes and dreams.

With gentle fingers, Wyatt tilts my head, deepening the kiss until my legs aren't just boneless. I'm not sure they exist at all.

Wyatt drops his hands, wrapping them around my waist as though he sensed my impending fall to the floor.

It's hard to stand up when a kiss has stolen your legs.

I want to commit to memory the gentle command of his mouth, the way his neatly shaved jaw still manages a pleasant burn where it drags against my skin. Wyatt isn't always a man of words, but his kiss speaks promises. Softly, sweetly—and, okay, yes—with a little dash of roguishness.

I didn't know that was a thing I'd recognize or even like so much, but it's the only word flashing through my brain as Wyatt pulls me closer, a small sound at the back of his throat making me suddenly desperate to catch it.

"We should probably get below deck," he says, lips brushing mine with every word.

"We're already drenched," I say. "What's the point?"

"The point," Wyatt says between kisses, "is that I'd like to kiss you without fear of either one of us falling overboard or being struck by lightning."

"Reasonable," I say, while pressing a kiss to his jaw.

"Also—I don't want this jersey to get ruined," Wyatt says, pulling back to look me up and down.

I'd forgotten I was wearing it.

"How does it look?" I ask. "It's way too big."

"It's perfect," Wyatt says, bending forward to kiss me again before gently turning me around and brushing my hair away from my neck. "My last name looks good on you, Rookie. Maybe we can find a way to keep it there."

30

WAG Pants

Josie

We definitely should have started kissing earlier. I'm amazed by how it makes everything instantly more enjoyable. Like magic.

Planning our day's route over coffee? Better with kissing. (After we've both brushed our teeth, of course.)

Piloting the boat? Better with kissing.

Calling another boat to let them know we're passing? Better with Wyatt's lips grazing my neck.

Even waiting for an hourly bridge to open while fighting a wicked current is better with kissing.

Releasing more of Uncle Tom's ashes? Okay—we didn't kiss while doing *that*. But we did hug, which led to kissing later.

When we reach Savannah, our turnaround point for the trip, it starts to sink in that we'll be heading home. But I stomp out that thought like it's a little fire and choose to focus on my excitement about visiting the historic, romantic city I've heard so much about.

Doing a little touristy shopping sounds great too.

We check Jib into a doggy day care so she can spend a few hours running freely while we head to the waterfront. Thankfully, Wyatt had the foresight to bring paperwork we got from the vet.

Tugboats and a large steamboat motor past as we stroll hand in hand. Wyatt doesn't complain once when I drag him into shops that line the cobbled street along the river. Even though it's clear from his ever-present scowl he is not a shopping kind of man. No surprise there.

"Wyatt, you've got to look at this."

"Another kind of fudge?" he asks from the doorway of the candy shop, where he's been hovering, waiting to leave. "I think you already sampled them all. And bought several."

"Not fudge." I wave him over. "Come here!"

He sighs heavily but crosses the low-ceilinged shop with its wooden barrels of candy, eyes burning into me as he does. The moment he's close enough, he reaches for me, wrapping an arm around my waist. His fingertips lightly dance along my side. With a sigh, I lean into his chest and he drops his chin to the top of my head.

His touch has become comfort to me. Safety. Something I can trust. And yet I'm not sure if it will ever stop making my heart race. Wyatt is the best kind of addiction.

"Now what am I supposed to be looking at?" he asks.

"This arch!" I point up toward the doorway connecting the candy shop's two rooms.

"You called me over to look at the architecture?"

"It's amazing, right?" I run my fingers along the brick arch, surrounded by walls made of chunky black stone with thick grout that looks like nothing used by builders today. "How old do you think this building is?"

"Vintage," he says.

I can't help grinning, remembering the first time he said this to me on the way to the hospital. Why does it seem like a lifetime ago?

"So it's about your age, then?"

His light finger movements turn to tickling, and I have to dart away, almost knocking over a stand of gummy alligators in the process.

We step back out into the sunshine, me carrying a bag of fudge and a few other candies in one hand. Wyatt insisted on buying it for me but keeps glaring at the bag. Apparently, the man sees sugar as a mortal enemy. While I, on the other hand, tried a sample of every kind of fudge and feel slightly ill. I showed *some* restraint, at least, and chose only three kinds to purchase.

I bet I can fix his vendetta against desserts. Over time.

Assuming I *have* time. Hopefully, lots of it, which is my current working assumption. A shaky, unsure one. Though Wyatt did use the word *love* the night we kissed in the storm, it wasn't in the form of *I love you*. And he hasn't said it again.

Are we in a relationship? It feels that way. And though I'm anxious to have a firm understanding of what we're doing, I am equally anxious about knowing. Every time I think about bringing it up, about dipping my toe into the water of that conversation, my stomach clenches with nerves and my tongue acts like it's been frozen by a paralytic agent.

For now, I'm buoyant, existing in a very pleasant kissing limbo with worry banished to the edges. Mostly.

I might have a Google Doc of questions and topics to cover. But when we *do* talk, I'll try to pose them naturally. Just in case creating a Google Doc of questions is the kind of thing that would scare Wyatt off.

"We've established that you don't like candy," I say as we pass a set of stairs so old and far from modern safety codes that it actually has a warning sign. "You don't like looking at historic architecture. What *do* you like?"

Turning my way and capturing my gaze, he says, "The view."

If someone had told me before this summer that Wyatt the Grouch could say sweet things, I'd never have believed it. I couldn't even sell this story to a tabloid—not that I would, of course.

I steer us toward the shell shop, where I find about a dozen things I don't need but really want, and he pets the owner's dog. Wyatt thinks he's been sneaky, but I've caught him checking the doggy daycare's webcam feed multiple times, glaring at his screen. His features only soften when he catches sight of Jib.

"Stop putting things back," Wyatt grumbles, appearing right next to me.

I startle and drop the shell I was holding back into the bin. "What?"

Wyatt picks it up and returns it to the basket I'm carrying. "I've been watching you put back all the things you've been carrying around. Stop it. Put them at the register."

He's using his bossy sailing voice, but I hesitate. "But I don't need any of it. It's just random stuff."

His eyes are piercing. "Spoiling you isn't about just taking care of what you *need*. It's about taking care of what you need and *then* buying you everything you want. Because I can. And I want to. Get the shells, Josie."

He crosses his arms, looking more fearsome than any man should while saying something so ridiculously sappy.

I could float right out of the store, but the part of me not used to this treatment still grapples with the idea of being spoiled, being taken care of.

"Are you sure that—"

His low rumble of protest has the store dog running over. She butts her head into Wyatt's thigh, whining. I laugh, grabbing a few things I'd put back and scurrying over to the register. If the man insists . . .

After we drive away from the waterfront in our rented car, we stop to walk through one of the historic squares that Savannah is known for. We eat fudge—yes, even Wyatt, begrudgingly—from the paper bag while sitting on a bench under a live oak draped with Spanish moss. It's wonderful, despite me sweating through my clothes. I know my hair has taken on a life if its own in the humidity. I miss the constant feel of wind in my hair while on the boat.

While a piece of dark chocolate mint fudge melts in my mouth, I briefly consider broaching the subject of the future. But I don't want to ruin this lovely moment. Especially when Wyatt spends more time than he needs to kissing fudge from the corner of my lips.

"Maybe I don't dislike *all* sweets," he murmurs against my mouth.

I should definitely have bought more fudge.

Wyatt surprises me by taking us to Grayson Stadium, the home of the Savannah Bananas baseball organization. I follow the team on Instagram, but Wyatt doesn't use social media. And other than his brief argument over basketball with Greg that one time, he hasn't talked about sports other than hockey.

"How do you know about the Bananas?" I ask. "Are you even a baseball fan?"

"I don't live in a cave, Rookie."

"Debatable."

"The social media manager for the Appies used them as

inspiration." He pauses. "I might have watched some of their videos on YouTube."

When I gasp dramatically, Wyatt kisses me until I forget why I was teasing him in the first place.

Though the teams are out of town today, I'm giddy when a staff member with a bright smile is waiting to give us a private tour. This has my brother written all over it. Wyatt probably called him to call in a favor.

We get to sign the fan wall on the outfield and even go inside the locker rooms, where I sneak a picture of the caddy of toiletries next to the sinks.

Wyatt shakes his head at me. "Of all the things to take pictures of, why?"

"Because when will I ever have a chance to know what kind of deodorant the Savannah Bananas use," I whisper.

"Are you going to take pictures of *my* deodorant?"

"No."

"Why not?" he asks, sounding offended.

"Who's to say I haven't already done it?"

After he buys me half the gift shop and picks out a jersey for himself, Wyatt drives us to Tybee Island, where we eat delicious seafood on the upstairs deck of a crowded restaurant.

Ask him about it now, I tell myself as Wyatt cracks a crab leg, butter dripping down the back of his hand. *Just ask how soon he'll go back to Boston. And what he's thinking about this. About us. Maybe he has a plan.*

But maybe he doesn't. Or maybe I won't like the plan.

I don't know what it looks like to be the girlfriend of a famous hockey player. Or how to do an adult relationship of any kind. A long-distance one, no less. So instead of asking questions, I eat hush puppies like they're about to be discontinued.

Stuffed with amazing food, Wyatt and I walk hand in hand

along the ocean, leaving our shoes by the beach access. I squeeze his fingers and lean a little closer with a sigh. We didn't get to do this at Carolina Beach because we were busy pretending we weren't together in front of Jacob, Eli, and Van.

But as we walk, the questions and worries I've been stuffing down grow larger, gathering like storm clouds. How does a long-distance relationship work? I barely have actual relationship experience. Will I travel to see him? Does Wyatt have time to see anyone during the season? Is he into phone calls or FaceTime? What about texting? How will he respond if I send a string of GIFs?

Do I need to learn hockey things—like, more than the puck goes in the net? Probably. The idea gets me a little excited. I could do what I did with sailing just with hockey. A total deep-dive immersion. I wonder if hockey has terms as ridiculous as *baggywrinkle*.

But perhaps the most important question of all: Do I need new clothes? Are there specific items I'll have to buy—like WAG pants? Is there some kind of hockey girlfriend supply store, or can I just use Amazon? Or maybe hockey WAGs don't wear pants. Maybe they wear short skirts and dresses.

Will this require me to consistently shave above the knee? Am I going to—

"You look like you're constipated," Wyatt says, and it shocks a laugh out of me.

The ugly kind you wish you could suck back in. I'm embarrassed until I look at Wyatt and see the warm amusement in his eyes.

"Not that I would know," he adds quickly.

I almost say, *But maybe if we stay together, you will.* Then I remember we're talking about constipation, so I snap my mouth closed.

"What were you thinking about?" he asks.

"Pants."

"Pants?"

I give him a tight nod. "Pants."

He looks like he's about to add a follow-up question or ten, but then he pulls his buzzing phone out of his pocket. I see Jacob's name across the screen and suppress a groan.

"I've got to take this," Wyatt says in the kind of serious voice that makes me immediately think something terrible is happening. Like Wyatt is being traded to a team in Europe.

Could that happen? I add it to my mental list of things to research.

Wyatt stops walking but keeps holding my hand as he answers. "Hello?"

I can hear the familiar tones of my brother's voice but not what he's saying. I resist the urge—barely—to snatch the phone and put it on speaker. It's hard to remain calm when Wyatt's frown deepens and he doesn't give me any clues as to what my brother is prattling on about.

From what I can hear, Jacob sounds excited. Which, when it involves his clients, usually means money and deals.

The dread simmering in my stomach dials up to a full boil.

Is Wyatt signing a longer contract in Boston? How long is his current contract?

Do I want to live in Boston someday? Is that where Wyatt wants to be long term? Does he want to be with *me* long term?

Wyatt must notice my mounting panic because his frown deepens when he glances at me. Letting go of my hand, he tugs me to his chest. Gladly, I wrap my arms around him. Breathing with my nose pressed to his T-shirt is much better than breathing into a paper bag.

"Thanks," he says finally, slipping the phone into his pocket and then resting his other hand between my shoulder blades.

"What is it?" he asks. "You're shaking."

"Oh, you know. Just a little bit of panic. What was that phone call about?"

"Work stuff," he says, and I'd like to take Wyatt's phone and throw it into the ocean.

Maybe along with Wyatt. And my brother. Definitely my brother.

"Come on." Wyatt turns me so I'm tucked against him with his arm curled around my shoulders.

I let him lead me down the beach to a more secluded area. We're at the tip of the island, I think, with a channel of water barely wide enough for a few ships to pass separating us from another point of land. There are signs about dangerous currents, warning against swimming.

Wyatt walks us toward the water until the waves are lapping at our feet. Stopping, he pulls a plastic bag out of his pocket.

"Is that . . . Uncle Tom?"

"It is."

"I'm not sure if this is an upgrade or downgrade from the Cool Whip container," I say, and Wyatt smiles.

His smile fades as he stares down at the bag. "This is it," he says. "The last stop he requested."

The mood shifts instantly, all my worries and questions shoved out of the way in favor of compassion. I hook my arm around Wyatt's waist. "How do you feel?" I ask.

Wyatt doesn't move for a moment. "Sad. But also . . . okay." He looks at me as he says this, a soft but genuine smile on his face. "Now, I'm okay."

Because of me? I am seriously not used to feeling this needy or desperate for validation. And I'm not about to demand Wyatt tell me what his intentions are when he's holding his uncle in a plastic bag.

It's windy, so Wyatt kneels and I drop down with him as he gently opens the bag and empties it into the next wave. There's something oddly anticlimactic about the moment, which should feel huge, but it only takes a second for the last bits of Tom's ashes to disappear. A few tiny fish streak through the shallow water and vanish from sight.

Wyatt stands and pulls me to my feet. "Now we can head home," he says, tucking the plastic bag into his pocket again.

My chest grows so tight I can hardly draw in a breath. "Wyatt?" I whisper. "What happens when we get home? Where even is home?"

He turns and blinks in surprise at me. I'm sure my face is broadcasting every fear and worry I have about whatever comes next. Two big hands cup my cheeks, and I'm horribly embarrassed when a tear runs onto his finger. Leaning forward, he presses his lips to my forehead in a gentle kiss. He lingers there, thumbs stroking my face as his lips brush my hair.

"I wasn't trying *not* to talk about it," he says. "I wanted to go slow and let you set the pace for everything. Including talking about the future. I didn't want to scare you."

"I'm already scared. Why would you talking about this scare me?"

He's quiet for a moment. "Because what I want—what I've *always* wanted with you—is everything."

The words settle lightly on my shoulders, a soft shawl of re-assurance. *Everything.* Wyatt wants everything. The idea thrills me. It also terrifies me, but it thrills me more.

"You didn't think I was ready for everything?" I pull back until our eyes meet.

Wyatt drops his hands from my face to my shoulders, lightly kneading muscles I didn't know were sore. "Are you?" he asks. "Ready for everything with me, Rookie?"

I'm set to say yes, but there's a mild catch in my throat. "I think I'm ready for everything . . . slowly. But I need some reassurance. I need some concrete ideas of what this will look like. How to be a girlfriend—your girlfriend—and what long distance looks like and—"

"I don't want you to be my girlfriend for long," he says.

"Oh." My stomach drops. "Well, I guess that answers that."

His eyes widen and his fingers squeeze my shoulders. "No! Foot-in-mouth disease again. What I *mean* is, I don't want you to be my girlfriend for long because I want more. I want you to be my fiancée, then my wife." At the look on my face, he laughs softly. "See? I'm scaring you with my everything."

"You already know you want that with me?"

"I've been wanting that for years. I'm just waiting for you to catch up. And if that's slowly, it's slowly. If it's next month, it's next month."

"Next month?" I practically shriek the words.

"Just as a hypothetical," he assures me, but I get the impression he also means it. "And as for the distance, it may not be that long if your brother works his magic. That's why he called."

"What's why he called?"

And then my eyes glaze over just a little as Wyatt talks animatedly about a trade deadline and contracts and throws out names of other players who made big moves like Eichel and Tkachuk.

Feeling almost dizzy from all the information, I ask, "Are they friends with Liz Frank?"

He grins. "Probably not. The point, though, is that I might

not be in Boston next season. If your brother is as good as he says he is, I'll be in DC."

Wyatt will be in DC. For a moment, a bubble of happiness eases the tightness in my chest. An hour away—or four, depending on the nightmare Northern Virginia traffic.

Then I groan and drop my forehead to Wyatt's chest. "You mean the fate of whether or not we'll be hundreds of miles from each other depends on my brother?"

"Yep."

"Please tell me he's as good at his job as he always says he is."

"We'll see. But it might take a few days."

Once again, I lean back to meet Wyatt's gaze. "You're really thinking about moving cities and teams? For me?" I suddenly feel totally embarrassed. "Oh—right. It's closer to your mom."

"I'm moving for you. With the added bonus of being closer to my family. Especially if I want to repair things with Peter."

Wyatt doesn't mention his dad, and I wonder if it's too late there, or if maybe that's a longer-term plan. I'm not about to push now. Especially when I'd rather think about Wyatt being closer to *me*. Having Wyatt just up the road from Fredericksburg is better than all the way in Boston. I could even catch a train. I've done it before to see Jacob.

"Wait—so did you already have this plan in place?" I ask.

"It's something I've considered for a long time, but there wasn't any urgency." He pauses. "Not until now."

Wyatt's eyes darken, revealing a different kind of urgency. One echoed in the searing kiss he gives me while waves still lap at our feet. And then they cascade over our ankles and calves as the tide rolls in. When we finally pull back, breathless, we're the only ones on the beach, and the sky has darkened to a soft, velvety purple.

"I don't want to overwhelm you," Wyatt says, trailing a finger along my jaw. "And I think I very easily could."

"Maybe I want to be overwhelmed," I whisper.

His eyes meet mine. "Then know that I love you, Josie. And I don't expect you to say—"

"I can't promise to overwhelm you back. I don't think I'm the overwhelming type." He frowns and starts to argue. I shake my head and smooth my thumb over the furrow in his brow. "But I think I can shake you up. Make you smile every so often."

I drop my thumb to tug at the corner of his mouth, which lifts and then drops into a playful frown.

"I'm happy to be shaken up. And to sometimes smile. For you."

This all feels so right. And maybe this is what love is. Not trying to be everything for someone or to complete them, like a person could somehow be incomplete without another person. But perhaps love is being the exact right size of drill bit to tighten the other person's very specific loose screws.

Okay, this analogy may not fully work since I don't use tools and it sounds unnecessarily dirty. What I mean is that maybe love is giving the other person the something they may not have on their own.

It doesn't sound scary to me. It sounds wonderfully terrifying. Like the floor is opening beneath me, but it's not the real floor; it's a ride. And I'm dropping, but with a safety harness that allows me to enjoy the fall.

"I love you, too, Wyatt Jacobs."

His smile is a thing of beauty. There's more kissing, and I think we might have gone on until we were waist-deep in high tide if an alarm didn't go off on Wyatt's phone. He pulls it out despite my grumble of protest and glances at the screen.

"The doggy day care is closing soon. Time to get the rest of our family," Wyatt says, and it makes me unreasonably happy to think about him and about Jib as *family*.

But these thoughts screech to a halt when we stop to pick up Jib and an employee who looks no older than seventeen mentions that our dog is pregnant.

"Oh, she's not . . ." I start to say, then trail off, remembering a certain incident our very first night on the boat.

"The bulldog," Wyatt and I say, looking at each other wide-eyed.

Is it even possible? Would they be able to tell so fast? How long is a dog's gestation period? Could Jib already have been pregnant when I found her? And if she wasn't spayed like the vet thought, what was the scarring on her belly from?

A million new questions flood my mind, and I find myself laughing as we walk out, carrying Jib. Who, apparently, is *not* fixed.

Wyatt takes Jib from me, and she stretches up in his arms to lick his chin. I want to take a picture, but I just commit the image to memory instead.

"The look on your face is scaring me," Wyatt says with a frown. "What are you thinking about?"

I give him my very best smile, and though he's still frowning, I don't miss the tiny twitch of his lips.

"I'm just wondering if they make maternity clothes for dogs."

EPILOGUE

Can't Quit the Murder Cottage

Wyatt

Two years later

There is what looks like an entire welcoming party waiting for us on the dock as Josie steers us into the cove, grinning.

I don't like it. The welcoming party. Not Josie's smile.

I always love her smile.

Josie waves so hard her hand goes blurry and she gets a little too close to the shoals.

"Watch it," I grumble, trying to nudge her away from the wheel. She refuses to move, though, so I sigh and stand behind her, bending a little to rest my chin on top of her head. My hands come around hers on the wheel. "Was this really necessary?"

"It's our homecoming," she insists. "Don't be such a party pooper."

"Did you plan this?" I ask.

"Nope. I'm just going along with it. My money is on *the mothers.*"

"Who even are all those people?" I squint as Josie cuts the engine and steers us toward the dock like she's done it a hundred times before. In truth, it's only been half a dozen. "Is that my brother?"

"Stop being so shocked every time he shows up. We've been over this. Peter loves you. After two years of being back in touch, you need to realize he's not going anywhere."

Easy for her to say. She has Jacob. Who, despite his penchant for dating the kind of women he won't bring home and planning terrible trips, has always been there for Josie.

It's hard to believe it's been two years since I reached out to Peter, only to discover he was never mad at me for leaving him as the restaurant group heir. But he *did* feel abandoned after I shut him out. Dad apparently told him all kinds of lies about me, mostly centered around me thinking I was better than Peter. Nothing at all has been resolved with Dad, but I didn't really expect anything to be. Mom says to give it time, and I smile and nod like I believe time is all it will take.

With Peter, it took a phone call to set things right. One. Reconnecting was so easy that I hate thinking of all the time wasted, years we could have spent being actual brothers and friends.

But we're working on making up for it now. Even if it still feels new.

I dip my head to bury my nose in Josie's hair. This *also* feels new. Though she still smells like coconut pie, she now smells like coconut pie while wearing my rings on her finger. I like seeing them there, just as much as I like seeing my own wedding band. A reminder that we're a matching set now.

Or, a little bit of a mismatched set, but a set all the same.

Josie giggles. "Did you just smell me?"

"Yes. And I'll do it again."

When I bury my nose in her neck, Josie's giggle turns into a laugh. "Maybe you should stop now that we can see the whites of their eyes. Why don't you worry about tying up the boat?"

"Aye, aye, Captain," I mutter, hiding my smile when Josie laughs again.

Unfortunately, she throws her head back this time, and for just a few seconds too long, takes her eyes off where she's going.

"The dock!" I shout, just as Jib lets loose a stream of barks while Josie fights with the wheel.

Someone screams shrilly. I'd place bets on it being my mother. Actually, by the looks of it, both of our mothers screamed. They're clutching each other, dressed completely differently, with Josie's mom in Birkenstock sandals and mine in some kind of flats she probably bought at Saks. The two of them have become a little *too* close despite their differences in shoes.

Don't get me wrong—I'll take all the family harmony I can get. It's just that Josie's mom and my mom together . . . get *ideas*. Like the smaller yellow sailboat tied up on the other side of the dock. They have yet to take the sailing excursion they keep talking about, which is probably why they're both still alive.

"Whoops," Josie mutters, correcting, then overcorrecting, then managing to straighten up and avoid plowing right into our dock. "I've got it!" she calls loudly, definitely more for the people waiting than for me.

There's a cheer, and I want to roll my eyes because I've never had—nor wanted—anyone cheering for me when I didn't crash into the dock. Then again, this is Josie's first trip with her certification, where she was officially the captain and I was the first mate.

It also happened to be our honeymoon.

Or—the first one, anyway. The one Josie knows about.

While all the people waiting here for us were a surprise, I have my own surprise waiting for Josie. I know she meant it when she said this was where she wanted to spend our honeymoon, on the boat where we erased the lines we'd kept drawn between us for years. The place where we started to draw new ones and have built so many new memories.

But what I want is to have a honeymoon where we aren't crammed into a small bed with an uncomfortable mattress. One where we don't need to plot our daily course and watch out for shoals and weather or anything else.

I'm talking all-inclusive. Luxury. The kind of vacation I've never taken the time for and Josie's never had the money for. We leave tomorrow, and the wink Toni gives me as we disembark tells me she's got all of Josie's things packed and ready to fly out to St. Thomas in the morning.

It takes five minutes to get off the dock through all the hugs and pats on the back, Jib running between everyone's ankles and miraculously managing not to knock anyone into the water. She reunites with Jab, the only one of Jib's litter still in the family. My mother fell in love with the runt, who looked just like Jib. And now dresses like her too. Mom and Josie shop online for their outfits together.

It's oddly endearing.

Someone—or more likely, considering the way our moms are flitting around, *someones*—have decorated the house. White and pink balloons arch across the lofty living room alongside flowers and a three-tiered cake.

"We already had a wedding," I grumble to Josie.

A bigger one than I wanted. Though we kept it private, our friends and family plus various teammates past and present ended up making it much larger than I hoped. The idea of saying our vows in front of so many people made me twitchy, but

Josie being Josie, she surprised me the morning of our wedding by bringing the officiant to a private room in the church. Our actual, official wedding took place with just him and the two of us in that room.

Most people wouldn't think it would matter. But Josie knows me, and she knew it would. To me.

Reciting our vows together, privately, took all the pressure off the ceremony with the audience. I was able to relax and actually enjoy. To look at the woman who was secretly already my wife.

Watching her across the room now, I wish I could chase everyone out with my hockey stick and have her alone again. But she's laughing with Toni, Peter listening in with a big smile as Jacob tells a story. I'm not going to drag her away.

But that doesn't mean I have to stay. Taking one last look at my wife's wide smile, I slip outside.

⚓

Josie finds me half an hour later in Uncle Tom's old bedroom. She flops down on the bed beside me, grinning before she tucks her hands behind her head. "You just can't quit the murder cottage, can you?"

"It makes a good hideout."

"Agreed. Aren't you glad I convinced you to build next to it rather than tearing it down?"

"I am. And I think I've told you that at least a dozen times."

"What's a few dozen more?"

I roll over until I've got her mostly pinned beneath me. "Think they'll miss us if we take a nap?"

We started out this morning with the sun barely peeking over the horizon.

Her fingers drag through my hair, lightly massaging my scalp, and I sigh, nuzzling closer.

"I think they'll assume we're doing more than napping," she says, sounding amused.

I drag my lips across her neck, smiling when I hear her sharp intake of breath. "I'm not opposed to that either."

"But it's a party for us," she protests, even as she tilts her head to give me better access to her neck, which I make good use of.

"We already had a wedding," I say against her throat. "And a reception. Two showers. Isn't that enough?"

"Tell our mothers that."

With a groan, I fall back to my side of the bed and throw a hand over my eyes.

"What?" she asks.

"You mentioned our mothers while I was kissing your neck. Kind of kills the mood."

"Probably better that way," Josie says, but she doesn't sound like she thinks it's better.

"Maybe we could—"

"Hey, honeymooners!" Jacob's voice is the only one I want to hear less than either of our mothers' right now.

"Stay very still," Josie says. "If he doesn't know we're here, he'll go away and bug someone else."

Jacob calls, "I can hear you. And we need you out here. It's your party."

"And we'll hide if we want to!" Josie calls.

"Can't you just entertain them?" I ask Jacob. "That's your specialty."

"I could. I have been. But this is a problem I can't handle." He sounds out of breath, I realize, and since he is Mr. Cool and Collected, this might mean a legitimate problem.

"Fine." I sit up, swinging my legs over the side of the bed. I turn to look at Josie. My heart gives a resounding thump in my chest at her soft smile, the way her wavy hair spreads over the pillow.

I really, *really* wish Jacob would find someone else to handle whatever it is.

"What kind of problem?" I ask, even as Josie reaches for me, wrapping her arms around my waist and trying to tug me back into bed. I wiggle out of her grasp and swing her over my shoulder.

"The thing is," Jacob says, "someone left the back door open, and a few guests crashed the party."

I stride out of the bedroom, and Jacob grins at the sight of Josie hanging like dead weight over my shoulder. "Kick them out," I say, even as I wonder who would come all the way out here to crash a party.

Jacob scratches the back of his neck. "I would, but the party crashers aren't people. They're pigs."

I drop my head to my chest, muttering something that shouldn't be repeated about my neighbor, who clearly needs better fences. But Josie laughs brightly, gives my backside a light smack, and says, "I'll take care of this. Where's your hockey stick?"

Author's Note

Dearest Readers,

I wish you could see me smiling as I write this. I'm totally picturing you smiling as you read. Honestly? That is one of my main goals in writing the books I write: to package joy into words and hand it off like a happy little baton to you.

Except . . . without any running, please.

If this is the very first book of mine you've picked up, I am SO glad you're here. Welcome! If you have been with me from my early days or my independently published books, I'm so happy to have you with me. I hope all y'all stick around for more stories.

The setting and premise of this book really has a special personal meaning, which made the writing so much more fun. When I was in middle school, my aunt Jo and Uncle Tom announced they bought a little cottage in a town called Kilmarnock, Virginia. They lived in Atlanta full-time, so for many years, my family would drive from Richmond to gather at what they called the Oyster House just for holidays.

We had Christmases, Easters, birthdays, and even a dog funeral, which my not-yet-husband was roped into presiding over with no warning. (Welcome to the family, Rob.) I even got to sail a little on my uncle's sailboat, which is similar to the boat Wyatt has in the book.

By the time Jo and Tom fully retired, the Oyster House had been replaced with a beautiful home Uncle Tom built himself. They made plans to sail their way down the Intracoastal Waterway through winter. I bought Aunt Jo a journal for their first trip, and she faithfully wrote in it almost daily, recounting the fun times as well as the frequent misadventures. I used her journal as I planned out the trip for Wyatt and Josie, though honestly, the things that happened to Jo and Tom would be almost unbelievable if I wrote them into a book.

For the record—the pigs are very real and definitely terrifying.

Writing this was bittersweet because we lost Aunt Jo a few years ago. I know she would have celebrated this book not only because it took inspiration from her life but because she was always so supportive of my writing—right along with the rest of my family. I felt a very special connection to her while writing, which made this book much more meaningful, if a little bittersweet. I channeled memories of Aunt Jo as well as her adventurous spirit. This book made me think so often about the St. Clair family and happy (and ridiculous) childhood memories.

I hope one day to take the trip down the ICW myself, though after spending some time on sailboats while writing, I think a houseboat is more my speed.

If you'd like to read more on the behind-the-scenes of this book, see some real-life photos, and learn more true things from the fictional pages (like Josie's poison oak, based on my husband's reaction to it), you can get a companion guide when you subscribe to my newsletter at emmastclair.com/sailingbonus. (I send emails once a week, but you can unsubscribe anytime, even right after grabbing the companion guide.)

Every book I've written is filled with so much joy and also so many struggles to get words on the page. I'm grateful to you, dear reader, for helping make this childhood dream a reality. I hope you stick with me—I have a lot of stories left to tell.

Yours,
Emma

Acknowledgments

Books don't happen in a vacuum or with the author typing away in some writing cave. I had so much help at every step and am so grateful! In no particular order, I'd like to pass out some figurative participation trophies to those who helped with the book!

A big thanks to Michelle, the agent who started this journey with me, and to Kim, the agent who helped finish it. I'm also grateful to the team at Thomas Nelson—especially Becky for all the emails in the world, but also to Savannah, Lizzie, Laura, and Kerri. I feel so grateful to have a home with you!

I couldn't have written this without the support of my family and the often-ridiculous memories I share with Tom and Jo, Mom and Dad, Geoff, and Rich. Thanks to Tom and Dorothy for the lovely afternoon and for getting me on the dry-docked boat—even though it was a harrowing experience.

The biggest thanks to my husband, Rob, for putting up with the person I become on a deadline and to my kids for understanding my weird job.

Thank you, Charlie and Amy, for answering my Lisfranc (and other rehab) questions and to Sarah for answering my nursing questions. Thanks to Captain Tom, not to be confused with Uncle Tom, for answering questions and taking us sailing!

Finally, to my readers and those who would call themselves Sheeters. I write my books with you in mind.

While I did my best research through interviews, actual experiences, and good old-fashioned googling and reading, some choices were made to fictionalize things to better serve the story.

Discussion Questions

1. Family dynamics can be really complicated and hard to change—even if you want to. Why do you think those relationships can be so difficult to change?

2. Wyatt and Josie got off to an epically wrong foot. Have you ever had a first impression of someone you later realized was not accurate? What helped you to see the person in a different light? Has someone ever had a wrong first impression of you?

3. What do you think the most challenging part of a sailing trip would be? What would be the most enjoyable?

4. If Josie and Wyatt had met without Jacob being involved, do you think they would have fallen for each other sooner? Or did his involvement ultimately help them connect?

5. Josie tells herself she wants to buy a house but then finds herself hesitant to look when she actually has the means. Have you ever experienced a time when you thought you wanted something only to discover your actions showed something else?

6. Wyatt and Josie both become stuck in holding patterns—Josie after the assault and Wyatt after his injury. If you or a loved one ever experienced this kind of overwhelming paralysis, what helped end the cycle?

7. Josie diminishes her feelings after the attempted assault because she feels like, relatively speaking, she got off easy. When do you think this kind of comparative perspective can be helpful? When might it cause us to be too dismissive of our struggles or situations?

8. Wyatt's mother immediately takes Josie under her wing like she's part of the family. Why are these kinds of non-family relationships so special?

9. Jib helps to soften Wyatt and deepen the connection between him and Josie. What is it about animals that enables them to have such an impact on our lives? Do you currently have or have you had a pet with this kind of significant influence on you?

10. Both Wyatt and Josie have conversations with friends that help them process emotions and make decisions. Why are these trusted, outside opinions so important? Who in your life do you go to when you need guidance, and what makes you trust those people?

About the Author

Emma St. Clair is a *USA TODAY* bestselling author who loves sassy heroines, witty banter, and love stories with heart and humor. Her books have sizzling chemistry while keeping the bedroom door closed. She has an MFA in Fiction and lives in Katy, Texas (go Tigers!), with her hubby, five children, and Great Dane. Her favorite place to write is tapping on her phone while on the elliptical machine. No Emmas have been hurt in the writing of these novels (yet).

⚓

Visit her online at emmastclair.com
Instagram: @kikimojo
Facebook: @thesaintemma